SWEET MYSTERY

"Simon, about us . . ." Rae tried to shout down the half of her that said *give in.*

"You feel it, too. There is something about you that makes me . . ." Simon curled a tendril of her hair around his forefinger. His lips brushed hers . . .

"We should both have our heads examined." Rae placed both hands on his face and kissed him.

For a long time they stood wrapped tight, exploring the sensations of touch and taste. Rae wanted to devour his sweetness.

Hunger, a deep sexual hunger, shot through her, and the force of her desire shook her down to her toes.

Rae pulled back on the verge of guiding his hands to her pelvis. *She had indeed lost her mind!*

BOOK YOUR PLACE ON OUR WEBSITE AND MAKE THE ARABESQUE ROMANCE CONNECTION!

We've created a customized website just for our very special Arabesque readers, where you can get the inside scoop on everything that's going on with Arabesque romance novels.

When you come online, you'll have the exciting opportunity to:

- View covers of upcoming books
- Read sample chapters
- Learn about our future publishing schedule (listed by publication month *and author*)
- Find out when your favorite authors will be visiting a city near you
- Search for and order backlist books from our online catalog
- Check out author bios and background information
- Send e-mail to your favorite authors
- Meet the Kensington staff online
- Join us in weekly chats with authors, readers and other guests
- Get writing guidelines
- AND MUCH MORE!

Visit our website at
http://www.arabesquebooks.com

SWEET MYSTERY

Lynn Emery

Pinnacle Books
Kensington Publishing Corp.
http://www.arabesquebooks.com

PINNACLE BOOKS are published by

Kensington Publishing Corp.
850 Third Avenue
New York, NY 10022

Pinnacle, the P logo and Arabesque, the Arabesque logo are Reg. U.S. Pat. & TM Off.

First Printing: October, 1998
10 9 8 7 6 5 4 3 2 1

Printed in the United States of America

One

Rae stared ahead without really seeing the faded blue paint on the wall of the dressing room. One hand was still on the phone, which sat on the table with her combs and hot curler. Her brother's voice, far away, had delivered the news that had not surprised her. Lucien was dead.

"Look here, if you want I'll let Buddy know you've got to cancel." Jamal, her drummer and best road partner, spoke in a voice filled with compassion.

"We just got one more song, man. It'll take no time and Kevin can start packing the bus while we're still on stage." Wesley, one of the guitarists, rubbed his top lip.

Jamal turned on him with a scowl. "You're one cold-blooded—"

"All I'm saying is we been on the road for four years with finally a solid rep. You know how this business goes, man. We can't get no name for not sticking through a job." Wesley did not back down from his position. He considered himself the only true businessman among them, though Rae's astute management had brought them this far.

"One song, Wes. Buddy isn't going to object under the circumstances." Jamal gave a grunt. *"He's* got a heart."

"Hey, I didn't say Rae shouldn't leave. Give me some credit. But—"

Rae held up a hand to cut off the argument. "I'm okay. And Wes is right, we got one more song, and I'm going to do it." She took a deep breath before picking up a brush. She pulled it through her shoulder-length hair then pulled her hair all back into a long braid down her back.

"Rae, baby, you sure about this?" Jamal gazed at her with concern in his eyes.

"Yeah, I'm sure. Now go on, both of you. I'm fine." Rae met his gaze and nodded. With one touch to her shoulder, Jamal followed Wesley out.

Rae looked down at the phone again. Strange, this numb feeling. "I can do this."

She said the words to test her voice again, to make sure it was steady. But she also wanted to reassure herself that she had the strength to go on stage after that phone call. Singing a few notes, she cleared her throat. As she walked to the stage of the combination dance hall and supper club called Buddy's Blues Shack, Rae tried to conjure an image. None came until in a flash she realized she was humming a tune Lucien had taught her. Beautiful summer mornings while she trailed after him down at the river dock, he'd sing songs in a rich baritone. Songs about life, funny songs that made her laugh with delight. Lucien Dalcour was a mixed bag kind of man, with good memories jumbled with the bad. For too many years, the bad memories had ruled in Rae's mind. Now she would not have another chance to talk with him about the good times.

"I know y'all done had a rockin' good time tonight. We have been fortunate to have these fine performers with us, ain't that right?" Buddy Rolston, a short round man the color of ebony, shouted to the crowded nightclub audience. They clapped and yelled their agreement. "Just wanna tell Rae and the guys, you know you're always welcome back to Oakland, California. Now give up some love for the Bon Temps Band!"

The crowd erupted into a welcoming clamor as the band took the stage. Rae went to the microphone, her guitar hung around her shoulders. Rae saw a sea of faces watching her. She felt a wave of emotion. This was her life, one she'd carved out with sometimes ruthless determination. There were days when her music pulled her back from the deep valley of despair. How many times had she sworn to never leave the road until she was too old to move? Hundreds? Thousands? Yet in a split second of looking out, she was tired of it all.

"This last song is about hard times. Something we all been through, I guess." Rae's voice was soft, pulling everyone into the mood with her. She could see heads nodding in affirmation. "But it's also about having the guts to make it when everybody says you can't. When folks say you're no good."

"That's all right now!" Buddy called from his favorite spot in the wings.

"Go on, babe," Jamal said from his place at the drums.

"It was written by somebody who knew a lot about hard times. Bear with me 'cause I haven't sung it for a long time."

Rae felt a rush of love for the band as they hit the beginning notes of the blues tune. Wes blinked at her with eyes shining, his hard businessman shell gone. He gave a slow bow of his head, a gesture of empathy and affection.

"So this is 'Can't Let It Get You Down' by my father, Lucien Dalcour." Rae closed her eyes. Lucien's smiling face was there, a color snapshot.

"My baby," Aletha murmured. She gathered Rae into her plump arms. "You had something to eat?"

Rae stroked her mother's cocoa brown face. Her skin was still supple despite her fifty years. Trust Mama Letha to think of comfort food. "I'm not hungry right now, Mama. Thank you."

"Come over here and give your tante some sugar." Tante Ina, round and the color of caramel, did not wait for an answer before gathering her up in a tight hug. Her father's sister was her favorite aunt. And the quintessential mother hen. "Get you a plate, cher?"

"No, really, just give me a cola." Rae felt soothed at being fussed over by the two women.

They greeted relatives and friends paying their respects in the run-down Acadian style house where Lucien and Aletha had raised their three children. Aletha filled the house with delicious food she'd prepared at her home in New Iberia. Her second husband, George, had even accompanied her.

"Hey, baby girl. Don't complain when there's nothing left." Andrew, with a lopsided grin so like their father's, stuffed another mound of jambalaya into his mouth.

"Stop making a pig of yourself." Neville, the eldest of them, frowned at his younger brother in distaste. "Sheila, stop hitting your brother." He switched his attention to making one of his four children behave. Mumbling, he wandered off to separate the squabbling youngsters.

"Don't mind him, Andrew. He's just upset." Neville's wife, Trisha, tried to prevent hurt feelings.

Andrew gave a shrug. "I don't mind Neville, Trish. Don't know why he's so down. He . . ."

Aletha placed a hand on her son's shoulder. "Don't start nothing, Andrew."

"Now, y'all be nice." Tante Ina shook a finger at them.

Neville had gone out of the back door and come back to the living room through the front door. "No, let him say what he was going to say."

"It's not like you gotta get all respectful now Daddy is dead. All but denied the man, the past ten years." Andrew pushed away the plate of food as though full. "Living in your big fine house on four acres with a stocked pond."

"I work hard and I'm proud of it," Neville shot back. "I want something better for my family."

They all fell silent, including a host of cousins nearby. After whispered comments, they withdrew from the gathering conflict and went out to the front porch.

What Neville left unspoken was how they had suffered because of Lucien's drinking and wild money schemes. The family never had enough. Lucien was a big handsome man the color of brown sugar. He never could really settle down to be a family man. For twenty years, Aletha stayed with him. But Lucien's wild rages finally drove her away. At the same time Rae left home to live on campus at college in Lafayette, Aletha left her first love.

Now with all these old wounds being opened, Rae wanted to run again. The way she had eight years ago. Once they were all so clear on how they felt about Lucien. Rae had seemed to side with Neville, yet deep down she felt gut-twisting turmoil about their father. Leaving Belle Rose to pursue a singing career had been her solution. Andrew's response was to endlessly make excuses for Lucien, while Neville soundly condemned all he represented.

"Oh, right. That big fine house we keep hearing about." Andrew waved a hand in the air. "So what?"

"Don't knock it. I mean, look at this place. And that tin box you live in isn't much better." Neville jerked a thumb in the direction down the road where Andrew lived in a small mobile home.

"Me and Daddy wasn't owned by nobody though. When we got tired of work, we'd take off for fishing. I'll never forget wasn't but a few months ago we was down at Mulatto Bend—"

"Did more drinking than fishing, I'll bet," Neville cut him off.

"Shut up, Neville!" Rae stunned them all by shouting. "And Andrew, Daddy wasn't perfect so quit making him sound like some lovable father from television." She rubbed a hand over her face. "I gotta get out of here."

"Now look what y'all done!" Tante Ina boxed Andrew's ears. "Shame, Neville." She glared at the tall man as though he were ten years old.

"Hey! That hurt, tante." Andrew wore a pout.

"He didn't have no business saying . . ." Neville's voice went weak at the look of disapproval from both his aunt and his wife. "Sorry."

Rae crossed the porch in a long stride and jumped down to the ground. The sunlight of early spring splashed the leaves and road. She started off toward the worn footpath down to Grande River. Usually the splendor of a sunny day with blue skies in south Louisiana would comfort her. But not today.

"Raenette, wait for me," her mother called out. Aletha caught up with her. She squinted up at the cloudless blue sky. "Wanted me some fresh air, too."

"Sure you did." Rae glanced at her sideways.

They were so different. Rae had been her father's daughter

from the moment she'd been born. Where Aletha was quiet and unassuming, Rae was brash. Rae resisted efforts to be babied, pushing out on her own. Aletha had many scares when she turned to find her little girl out in the bayous or on the river with children older than her or alone. Adolescence had been a especially turbulent time for mother and daughter. Rae was in constant rebellion, seemingly intent on establishing a reputation as "That wild Dalcour girl." They clashed frequently over Rae's behavior, the drinking and sneaking to bars. Yet somehow the rift had not been with her mother. Aletha understood her daughter better than anyone knew. Now Rae sensed her mother needed to nurture her.

"All them Dalcours, Cavaliers, and Ricards coming out the woodwork." Aletha laughed. "Can't turn around without stepping on one of them."

"Un-huh." Rae tried to smile, but could not summon up the energy. Her brothers' angry words kept buzzing in her head. They walked on until they reached a curve in the river. It went through the small town of Belle Rose. They stood on a grassy bank staring at bateaux bobbing on gentle waves. Aletha looped her arm around Rae.

"Your brothers still got to work out what they feel for their daddy. Takes boys longer, just like we fought more. Remember?" Aletha gave her a tug.

"Thank goodness you never gave up. No telling where I'd be if you had. Daddy sure was no role model." Rae was not bitter, just able to see Lucien clearly. "You did good with all of us, Mama. Andrew could have slipped down further if you hadn't been there."

"He still might, Raenette." Aletha bit her bottom lip. "I'm scared he's gonna decide to take up where his daddy left off. And he's still drinking too much. Old man Ventre loves Andrew like he was his own boy, otherwise he would have fired him long ago."

"He's got to do it himself, Mama."

"Andrew ain't strong like Neville. Or you. He's beginning to talk just like Lucien about the old days." Aletha let go of Rae to cross her arms. She seemed to feel a chill in spite of the warm weather.

"Daddy never gave up on that, did he?" Rae looked at her mother. "He might have stopped talking about it so much, but Pawpaw Vince—was never far from his thoughts."

"You know better than me." Aletha raised an eyebrow at her. "When you came to visit two years ago when he had that mild heart attack, what did he tell you?"

"You know about that?" Rae was shocked. She had not mentioned their conversation to anyone, not even her close girlfriend Marcelle.

"Lucien told me." Aletha nodded at her. "Last few years, he kept in touch. Him and George even got on kinda good." She laughed when Rae's mouth fell open. "No reason why they shouldn't."

"Guess you're right." Rae shrugged.

In fact, George was like Lucien in some ways. Both men were quick to smile and forgive. George had the easygoing temperament of a man who was happy with himself. Maybe if life had been different for her father . . . Rae thought of her last talk with Lucien.

"But you got your own life. Don't rake up the past. Nothing you can do about it after all this time anyway. It's fifty years since what happened with your pawpaw." Aletha looked out at the river then down where it wound toward downtown Belle Rose.

"Maybe not."

"He's gone, baby. Ain't one thing gonna make it right now."

Rae did not know if her mother was talking about Lucien or Pawpaw Vincent. It did not matter. "I can't turn my back on him this time, Mama."

"You listen to me. Folks still get plenty nasty just at the mention of your pawpaw's name. Especially them Joves. Toya is big in town, like her mama was."

"Really? Toya always did like being a big fish in a little pond." Rae felt a flash of rancor at the mention of Toya's name.

"Take care of your daddy's business and get on with your life. Neville won't care if you sell the dance hall, and Andrew won't fuss when he sees he might get some money out of it." Aletha's voice took on an intense tone.

Rae looked at the rich green vegetation swaying in the river breeze. Yellow, red, and blue wildflowers bloomed. Even on a weekday afternoon, people fished from the banks or in small boats. There was a rhythm to life in this rural parish that had never left her. She could not stand the thought of leaving it again.

"Mama, I've been wandering all around trying to find myself. This is where I've been all along." Rae waved to several folks in a passing boat. "I'm home now."

"Cher! Come here and give me some sugar." Marcelle stretched out her free arm. Her new baby girl was perched in the other as she sat in the rocking chair on her veranda.

"Hey, now, you still producing little Browns I see." Rae laughed out loud for sheer joy to see her oldest and dearest friend.

Kissing and hugging went on for several minutes. They shared remembrances and news in a rush, chattering at breakneck speed as though to make up for the years they'd been apart. Soon Marcelle's other four children poured out of the house to see the newcomer. Four boys, all rough and tumble, competed to show off in front of Rae.

"Lord, Marcelle. These boys have grown." Rae beamed at the smooth faces of cinnamon, all looking like their father.

"Now don't pretend you remember these rascals. Truth is, I get confused they all look so much like Freddie. This is Freddie Jr. He's my big boy just turned eleven. That's Tremaine. He's nine. Eric Paul quit that! Eric Paul, is eight. And my sweet boy Torrence is five."

"Come here, sweet things." Rae gathered them to her. The boys were a squirming, dusty little crew, suddenly acting shy. "You're right, girl. They all look like Freddie just spit out." She pinched Torrence's plump cheek.

"Un-huh, got his mischief in them, too. Now y'all go play. And you better stay out Miss Pearl's fig trees," Marcelle yelled at the disappearing shirttails. "Lotta good that's gonna do." She lifted a shoulder. "Here now. Hold your godchild."

"Now this one here is going to be beautiful like her mama. Hello, Felicia Lynette," Rae said.

She settled onto the swing with the infant cradled in her arms. Rae stared down at the little brown face, smooth with sleep. Looking at the baby tugged at Rae's heart in an unexpected way. Tiny Felicia Lynette smelled of baby lotion and formula. Rae gazed at the wood frame house. Brightly decorated, Marcelle managed to keep it neat after a fashion. But the toys of four active boys were scattered around the front yard. What did she have to show for her life? A modestly successful band, a couple of recordings on compact disc that sold fairly well, and not much else. Rae kissed the baby's head. Had she been wrong to choose the path she'd taken?

"Girl, you doing so good. I've got both of your CDs. I envy you." Marcelle sighed. She smoothed down the cotton dress over her still plump tummy.

"What?" Rae was startled out of her reverie.

"Mais yeah. Living a carefree life. Traveling all over, even to foreign countries. I spent my twenties either being pregnant or wiping baby butts." Marcelle sighed again. "Sometimes I wonder, what if I had gone to New Orleans to study accounting, instead of getting married?"

"I was just sitting here thinking . . ." Rae touched one of Felicia's hands. "You've made such a good life for yourself."

"I love my babies. But I just wonder what if, you know?"

"Yeah." Rae stared off across the blacktop road. But she did not see the trees swaying in the spring breeze. Being back in Belle Rose was like a time machine. She went back fifteen years to when she and Marcelle were teenagers.

"Things haven't changed around here too much. I mean downtown is a little more spruced up in the last four years. We got that new crawfish processing plant. Them Joves—" Marcelle broke off with a sharp glance at Rae.

"Since when you walked on egg shells around me?" Rae did not look at her.

"Listen, cher, talk is all ready started about you and Darcy. You'd think it happened yesterday."

"You know since I got home, sometimes it does feel like it's fifteen years ago. Sorta like being in two time dimensions." Rae shook her head. Strange how this town was affecting her.

"Oui. Coming home can be like that, I guess. Especially after so long." Marcelle was in tune with Rae, as usual. The two had always been like sisters.

"So Darcy is doing well for himself. Well, I'm not surprised." Marcelle studied Rae's expression for several moments before speaking. "Yeah. He's got several businesses going. The canning plant, crawfish ponds, and real estate. At least his businesses are doing well."

"What do you mean?" Rae looked at her with interest.

"Darcy just got divorced from his second wife. She left him. Said he's crazy. Said his sister's crazy, too."

Rae laughed. Darcy and Toya Jove had grown up in an old Creole family with an inflated value of their social status. Their mother, Lorise, was fond of reminding everyone of her proud French heritage. Two years older than Rae, Darcy was handsome and self-possessed. After seeing him from a distance throughout their childhood, Rae fell in love with him the summer she turned fourteen. To her amazed delight, he turned his attention to her. They would sneak off together, both knowing his parents would never approve, to stroll through the fields. Toya followed them one day and told her parents.

"Toya Jove. She always took it on herself to protect her brother from females." Rae remembered how Toya warned her to stay away from Darcy.

"Pooh. With his track record, he don't seem to need much help running off women these days." Marcelle sniggered.

"How does he look?" Rae could not resist wondering about the boy she'd wanted so much. For two years they defied all efforts to keep them apart. Until Darcy succeeded where his sister and parents had not. One day with blinding pain, Rae discovered the real Darcy Jove.

Marcelle pursed her lips. "The same."

Rae knew what that meant. He was still almost too pretty to be a man. Dark curling hair, full lips, and large eyes like Louisiana dark roast coffee. Yet the thrill was long gone.

"Well, I'm through with that," Rae said. "Guess what?"

"What?" Marcelle followed her swift direction change with

ease like always, ready to play the question game from their childhood.

"I'm thinking about staying in Belle Rose." Rae was as surprised as Marcelle to hear the words from her mouth.

"Quit lying! You're gonna give up being a singing star to live in Belle Rose? Pooh-ya!" Marcelle stared at her with big round eyes.

"I'm not a singing star." Rae laughed "We did okay, but I'm not famous or rich."

"Still, why would you wanna get stuck in Podunk Belle Rose? Especially with . . . you know."

"That's the main reason why, Marcelle. Daddy lived here all his life under a cloud. I'm not going to accept that the Dalcour legacy is going to be shame."

"And what about Toya and Darcy? Not to mention old man Jove. I just don't wanna see you get hurt. They own land around your daddy's dance hall you know."

"Nobody told me that." Rae went rigid.

"Bought it up and was trying to force him off, too. Mr. Lucien was talking a lot about his daddy and all that stuff that happened back in the forties. Mr. Henry was hot about it."

Rae glanced at her. "He's been bad-mouthing my grandfather for years. But I won't let him or any of the Joves rule my life."

"What you gonna do?" Marcelle's eyes gleamed with excitement. "Better watch out for Toya."

"I'm going to do exactly what they don't expect, that's what."

"Things about to get interesting in this town for the first time in ten years. Welcome back, sister." Marcelle sat next to her on the swing and put an arm around Rae. "I can't wait to see what you're up to this time."

Rae gazed around at the willow trees dancing in the wind. Yellow wildflowers covered the ground in a field down the road. This was the warm, vibrant land of her family. No other place spoke to her like the lush vegetation and hot sunshine of south Louisiana. Kudzu vines, bushes, and trees crowded every space of earth, encouraged by the hot, moist climate—all a tangle of greens in various shades. Life in Belle Rose was like that, she mused, a tangle of relationships that stretched back years. Her father, her grandfather, and the Jove family were connected for better or worse. Maybe it was time to stop trying to run from it. Yet doubt tickled through her. Sometimes tangles should not be disturbed. But she did not feel as though leaving was a choice anymore.

"Marcelle, do you think I still belong here? Like you said, I've been traveling so long . . ." Rae turned to Marcelle.

"Some folks come back, you can tell this isn't their home anymore. They've got roots in California or Chicago now." Marcelle took a deep breath. "Not you. You're right to wanna be home, Rae."

"I sure hope so, Marcelle. I sure hope so."

"Okay, quit joking around. It's been three weeks and I can't put JoJo Lawson off again. When are you coming back?" Wesley stood with one hand on his hip.

Wesley and Jamal had stayed with her for the weekend. They enjoyed fishing and small town life in small doses. Now they were ready to leave. Jamal helped Rae load groceries into Wesley's Chevy Blazer.

"I'm not. I keep telling you, I'm going to stay here and run the dance hall." Rae yanked on a sack of potatoes with Jamal's help.

"No." Wesley dropped a bag of groceries onto the gray seat of his vehicle. "No, no, no." He waved his head back and forth. "You can't just quit the band." His voice was positive, as though his saying it would make it so.

"Yes, I can." Rae gazed up at the tall, lanky man with a look of resolution.

Jamal slapped him on the shoulder. "Told you she wasn't kidding."

"Just like that. Walk away." Wesley wore a look that was a mixture of disbelief and betrayal. "Well if that's all we mean to you, fine."

"Get real, Wes." Jamal barked out a harsh laugh. "You of all people trying to lay an emotional guilt trip on somebody."

"We've been like family and you know it." Wesley turned to Rae. "Baby, we've been through the fire together."

Rae thought of the tough times when they only had each other. Nights of rowdy crowds and surly club owners. One record producer even told them they had no chance to make it. Yet they pushed on.

"You're right, Wes. Like family, we've had hard times and stuck together. So now I need you to understand that I've got to do this. For Lucien, and for me." Rae put a hand on Wesley's arm.

"He was a sweet dude, your daddy. I don't care what anybody says." Wesley, for all his gruff exterior, had a sentimental core. "Sure gonna miss you. Come here, girl." He gave her a quick hug.

Jamal joined in for a group hug. "Aw, man, leaving you behind is going to be tough."

Rae blinked back tears. "It's going to be hard watching you leave. But, hey, you're coming back." She thumped Wesley's chest firmly. "I expect you guys to play for me at least twice a year."

"You got it, little sister." Wesley winked at her.

They went back to loading the last few bags. Jamal and Wesley teased Rae about the joys of living in a small town as they rode down into the old part of Belle Rose. Antique shops and boutiques lined the main street.

"Let's stop here. I want to get my mom a souvenir." Jamal's mother lived in Detroit but collected southern figurines. They stopped at a shop with small statues made from pecan shells.

"Whoa, who is that?" Wesley did not follow Jamal into the shop. He lingered on the brick sidewalk staring down the street.

Rae followed his gaze. An unpleasant tingle went through her at the sight of the curvy figure in a white pant set. "Toya Jove," she murmured more to herself than to answer Wesley's question.

Toya straightened the stylish white short-sleeved shirt, with flowers in an applique pattern across the front. A wide white woven belt with a gold buckle was wrapped around her waist. The pants were loose fitting, but still showed her figure to advantage. She touched the designer sunglasses on her face as she looked at Rae. Her lips lifted at one corner, a perfect expression of disdain, then she turned and walked away. A tall man emerged from a store front. After a brief exchange, Toya went past him to another store.

"Some lady. Maybe I could arrange to hang with you a while longer." Wesley seemed in a daze. "You know, help out with the hall."

"How thoughtful," Rae said. Toya still had that effect on men it seemed. "Wouldn't have anything to do with Spider Woman would it?"

"She's something else." Wesley still stared in the direction Toya had gone.

"Save your libido, Wes. Toya has an income requirement for her men. Besides, she was just with some other poor sucker. Guess he's in her web." Rae examined the tall man who had spoken to Toya. To her surprise, he came toward them.

Rae watched him approach wondering why he seemed so familiar. He was at least six foot four with skin like burnished bronze in the bright sunshine. His hair was a cap of tight black curls, a short afro. Muscular arms came out from the light green cotton knit shirt neatly tucked into chino slacks. Graceful like a trained athlete, his stride was smooth. Rae felt a prick of disappointment that he wore dark sunglasses. She wanted to see this stunning man's eyes. *What the heck is wrong with you?* Rae wondered at her reaction to this stranger. Though she'd had at least two serious relationships in the past six years, Rae had never been one to fall for a handsome face on sight. Life had made her wary of good-looking men. Still, she was quite content to watch this man walk by. He smiled, revealing even white teeth. Rae nodded a greeting, expecting him to continue on his way.

"Hello, Ms. Dalcour," he said in a voice that hinted he sang bass.

"Hello." Rae took his out-stretched hand. The flesh was smooth and cool.

She tried to recall his face and voice. Strange, but she liked the solid feel of his hand in hers. It seemed to steady her, giving a hint of how good the rest of him would feel. His broad chest seemed perfect for touching. Rae wondered if he were single. *Being home might be even better than I thought.*

"You probably don't remember me. We met only a few times years ago. I'm Simon St. Cyr." He smiled at her.

So that was it. The St. Cyr clan. Now she recognized him. His grandfather was the third partner in the ill-fated venture that had left a stain on the Dalcour name all these years. Joseph St. Cyr, Henry Jove, and Pawpaw Vincent had been best friends. As young men they'd decided to go into business together. Things had gone terribly wrong, all of it blamed on Vincent Dalcour. Yet the St. Cyrs and the Joves not only survived, they prospered. Rae gazed at the strong profile. Cold dislike crept through her. This well-dressed pretty boy could not help but strut in front of her.

"Oh, yeah," Rae said in a short tone. All amorous thoughts of snuggling up to him vanished. "Sure you want to be seen talking to me in public?"

Simon stopped smiling. "Ms. Dalcour, what's past is past. I don't have any interest in a fifty-year-old feud. When you get situated, give me a call." He took a business card from his shirt pocket.

Rae did not take it. "Why?"

"You might be interested in the discussions I had with your father several months ago. He was planning to work with me on developing your family's property."

"I have a hard time believing my father would give you the time of day." Rae was intrigued despite her words. Lucien had spoken to a St. Cyr? More to the point, why would a St. Cyr talk to a Dalcour?

"Meet with me and I'll explain it all to you." Simon nodded. He still held out his card, his expression behind the sunglasses hinted at a challenge to her.

After a few seconds, Rae took the card. HERITAGE CONTRACTORS AND DIRT SERVICE.

"Thursday morning at ten okay?" Simon pointed to a building. "My office is down on Front Street, just a short distance from here."

"Okay."

Rae watched him walk away. She definitely liked the way the man moved. While her body reacted to the sensuous presence of Simon St. Cyr, her mind issued a strong warning. What could it hurt to listen for a few minutes? What she remembered of him was neutral. Since he was four years older, she'd not been in school with him. Simon was away in college during her high school years. Besides, she'd been too infatuated with Darcy to notice other boys. Darcy. That experience alone should have taught her that men from those two families were trouble. A stab of regret and pain made her wince at the memories. Maybe she should not go. Keeping her distance could be the best way if she was to remain in Belle Rose. Rae ground her teeth in frustration. Within ten minutes of seeing Simon, she was torn with confusion. Trouble from the St. Cyrs and Joves already!

She sat on a bench waiting for Wes and Jamal to finish shopping. The small business district was quiet with only a few tourists wandering from shop to shop. Rae was still lost in thought when a shadow fell across her.

"Look who's back in town." Toya stood over her, a tight smile on her face. "Hello, Raenette."

"Hello, Toya." Rae gazed up at her. She resisted the urge to stand up. Toya always had a way of making her feel outnumbered, somehow at a disadvantage.

"Sorry to hear about your daddy. Mr. Lucien was a real character. Amusing in his way." Toya wore an indulgent smile. She sat down on the opposite end of the bench from Rae. "So you've been busy becoming a star I hear."

"Hardly, but we did okay."

"You're being modest. You always could play a mean blues guitar."

Rae wondered where this conversation was going. Toya hardly cared about her or her music career. She settled back against the bench and waited. "Thanks."

"I'm sure you have lots of engagements. Before you leave, tell me when your band will play around here again. I'd like to see you perform." Toya started to rise. Her tone made it clear she expected Rae to waste no time leaving Belle Rose.

"No problem. Since I'm staying, you'll get to see me as often as you like." Rae grinned at the effect of her words on Toya.

"Staying?" Toya echoed.

"Sure, Daddy's business is still here. I think it could be successful."

Toya's expression was taut. "Dalcour business deals have a way of going up in flames. I shouldn't have to remind you of that."

"Yeah, well Simon St. Cyr doesn't think so. He practically offered me an engraved invitation to do business with him."

"Simon did what?" Toya snapped through clenched teeth.

Rae laughed. So mentioning him had touched a sore spot. "Made it a point to find me. Seems a real nice man." She made the simple words sound suggestive. "I *really* look forward to meeting with him."

"You stay away from . . ." Toya's voice trailed off when she realized Rae was enjoying her irritation. "You never could recognize when you were out of your league." She flounced off.

"See you around, Toya," Rae called out in a false friendly tone.

Jamal and Wes came down the sidewalk carrying several bags of purchases. Wes tried to get Toya's attention but she never looked his way.

"Let me guess, she wasn't exactly a pal of yours back in the old days," Jamal said.

"My, oh, my. Some fine-looking woman." Wes gave a low grunt of approval.

"Wes, the woman is a chainsaw in expensive leather pumps," Rae said. "Toya is ten times more deadly than both your ex-wives."

"Ouch!" Wes wore a pained expression at the mention of the two women who'd pursued him relentlessly for alimony.

"Listen, Rae, seems there are a lot of bad memories here for you. Not to mention bad feelings." Jamal jerked a thumb in the direction Toya had gone. "Sure you wanna hang around here?"

Toya threw one last glare at them before getting into her white Mazda 929 and slamming the door.

Rae smiled "Oh, yes, I'm looking forward to it more and more."

Two

"Look at this place. I don't know how you expect to make anything out of this," Neville said.

Her older brother had taken several days off from his job at the Bryer Chemical Plant. He'd insisted on helping Rae. What he really meant to do was convince her not to operate the dance hall.

Rae gazed around at the dilapidated juke joint her father had operated for over twenty-five years. She had to admit it looked pretty bad in the light of day. The weather-beaten cypress wood planks that made up the outer walls were broken in several places. One end of the roof sagged, where a corner post leaned crookedly.

"It's not so bad. We had some good times in here." Andrew put up a weak defense. Even he grimaced when they walked inside.

"How long since it was open for business?" Rae pushed a broken chair from her path. The only light was from the two windows since the electricity was turned off.

"At least three years." Andrew ran a hand along one wall. "Poor Daddy."

"Even when he had it open, Daddy had to work to support himself." Neville was not feeling sentimental about the dance hall. "Then he had to stop just about everything when he went on disability. Not a thriving business."

"When we was kids, this place would jump. Remember how

we'd sneak over here and listen to the music?" Andrew ignored Neville's attempts to push reality into the room.

"Yeah, Robert Cheval's band would come in on Saturday afternoons. Some of the best blues in south Louisiana was right here." Rae looked at the rickety tables with fondness. She still played songs that were old when she was a child.

"I can't believe this." Neville threw up both hands. "This place kept Daddy away from home. Mama struggled by herself with bills and three children. I would just as soon see this place bulldozed."

"What's wrong with making it work, Neville?" Rae went to him and touched his arm. "The Dalcour family deserves some kind of legacy."

"Not this, Raenette. This is not the legacy I want my children to have. And you shouldn't want to have any business where liquor is served after what it did to Daddy." Neville spoke with bitterness.

Rae could not answer him. That was one aspect of having the dance hall that bothered her. Rae had used music as her escape and Neville pursued middle-class respectability with a vengeance. Andrew alone seemed to be tracking their father's path to dependence without any realization of it. But how could she operate the dance hall without liquor and hope to make it work? Giving up on Lucien's pride and joy seemed a dishonor to his memory. Rae shook her head slowly.

"I've got to do this. I don't know how but I'm going to bring the dance hall back," Rae said.

"Go on, little sister. In between working down at the crawfish plant, I'll help. Speaking of which, I got to go. See y'all later." Andrew slapped his hands together. He went outside whistling.

"Sure, he's looking forward to another place he can sit around drinking all the time. Let it go, Rae."

"Most people around here still think of us as trash. Daddy hated the thought that his grandchildren would think of the Dalcour name like it was something to run away from." Rae spoke with a fierceness.

"You left a long time ago for that same reason. So did I." Neville stuck his hands in his pockets. "I hated having folks whisper behind my back. Now it's going to start up again. I don't want my children to hear the old stories."

"Daddy always swore Pawpaw Vincent was no thief." Rae sat down hard in one of the old chairs.

"He was just six years old and he never knew for sure. I don't care what he said." Neville took a deep breath. "Pawpaw disappeared, they never found the money and Estelle Jove went with him."

Rae closed her eyes at his succinct summary of a generation of misery. The shameful family secret that was still whispered about when Rae and her brothers were children. Vincent Dalcour, thief and adulterer. Lucien had never accepted this as truth, though his mother cursed her missing husband's name until she died. The money that would have made Belle Rose a prosperous community was gone. Instead of investment from the large machine parts plant that would bring jobs, the company had gone elsewhere. So Vincent Dalcour had not only robbed his business partners, he'd robbed his community.

Neville made valid points. In the face of a no-nonsense presentation of the facts, her plans seemed a misplaced attempt to make up for all the hurt Lucien had suffered. Then there was the deep guilt that she had betrayed Lucien by leaving all those years ago. The ugly words she'd spoken that day were still with her.

"Daddy wanted me to change things." Rae leaned against the old bar.

"But you can't. Not anymore than he could. That's why he was so miserable most times. Don't let it drag you down." Neville put an arm around her shoulder and led her out of the dance hall.

"Well, after we get the succession in motion we can decide." Rae felt a tension headache coming on from the effort to sort out her feelings.

"Daddy didn't have much. This land and his little house. I say we sell." Neville looked around.

"We'll see."

"Jarvis says he left most of it to you, which is fine with me." Neville wore a sad smile. "I'm surprised Daddy even made a will. He wasn't one to think about dying."

"Lucien really did love you. He bragged about you behind your back." Rae hugged her older brother's meaty arm. " 'My son is a big time supervisor running an entire chemical lab,' he used to say."

"Yeah, well . . ." Neville turned away from her. He rubbed his eyes. "I just wish we hadn't spent so many years mad at each other."

Rae and Neville stood quiet, wrapped in memories of their father. Tomorrow they would sit with Jarvis Eames, a childhood playmate and now a lawyer, and go over Lucien's will. Then maybe Rae would have a better idea of which direction she would take.

"What do you think they're going to do about his land?" Ellis Mouton dabbed at his lips with a delicate motion. He watched Darcy's expression.

"Sell it if they have any business sense." Darcy sipped from the china cup filled with strong Louisiana coffee.

Darcy, the color of café au lait, was dressed in an impeccable custom-tailored suit. He sat in the plush office of Mouton Enterprises. Ellis Mouton was one of the wealthiest white men in Acadia Parish, as had been his father and grandfather. In fact, the Mouton family had been prominent in Louisiana for almost two hundred years.

"To you?" Ellis raised a dark eyebrow at him.

"Not even Neville Dalcour would stomach that," Darcy said. "No, Simon will make them an offer." He wore a sly smile.

"We need that property for a new plant. Pantheon won't wait forever. Bob Caskill is coming down next week to meet with us." Ellis put down his cup. "I want this to happen before there can be a lot of screaming from those folks who live around there."

Darcy laughed. "So what if they do? Promise them jobs and build a few prefab houses to replace their swamp shacks, and they'll quiet down."

"What about their property? They won't want to give up the land so easily."

"Give them money to buy beer and they won't care," Darcy retorted.

"You don't think much of your people do you?" Ellis wore a superior look. His lip twitched at the effect his words had on Darcy.

"My people don't live in shacks," Darcy snapped. He pulled back his shoulders. "Creoles with intelligence would never squat in the bayou the way those people do. Fact is, we'd be doing them a favor clearing the way for a plant to be built."

Ellis gave a soft chuckle. "Now if we could just convince them of that." He frowned after a few seconds. "What about the environmentalists?"

"Busy fighting Langston Industries over in Beaufort. That should keep them well occupied for months. The timing is perfect." Darcy nodded with satisfaction.

"And the report from the civil engineer?" Ellis rubbed his chin. "The flooding problem—"

"Bailey wrote his report so that we can argue flooding is not appreciably increased by the construction on that land." Darcy waved a hand as though making his point disappear.

"But it interrupts the flow from that small creek, which means water will back up into Bayou Latte. Those houses back on Decuir Road could be under water with one hard rain."

"Bailey said it would have to rain buckets for several days. Even so, we can work with the Corps of Engineers to dredge Bayou Latte and part of the lake."

"That could take a long time. The Corps has all its projects scheduled as much as three years in advance." Ellis examined his silk tie. He was not the least bit concerned, only making a point.

"They could move it up based on the damage potential to the wetlands. If need be, we'll enlist the aid of the environmentalists to make it happen." Darcy shrugged. "You know how those people go into spasms at the thought of wetlands being destroyed."

"Clever, clever man."

Darcy got up and poured more coffee into his cup. "All in all, I think things will fall into place quickly."

Ellis gazed at Darcy's slim build. "You've orchestrated everything down to the last detail. Except . . ."

"Yes?" Darcy turned to him.

"Simon St. Cyr doesn't impress me as being an easy dupe. When he realizes you used him to get the plant built there could be big trouble. Then what will you do?"

Darcy wore a hard expression. "Explain the facts of life to him."

"You'll use Simon St. Cyr to get Dalcour land and environmentalists to take heat off the Pantheon project." Ellis stood facing Darcy, gazing into the younger man's hazel-green eyes. He moved closer to him. "How are you using me, Darcy?"

"You already know the answer to that, Ellis." Darcy returned his gaze steadily for several moments before moving back to the leather chair facing the large mahogany desk. "Now lets talk about Pantheon's last offer."

"Why were you talking to her?" Toya sat glaring at Simon. "Eames is their attorney, you just have to deal with him."

Simon heaved a sigh. "For the tenth time, don't tell me how to conduct business. Whoever heard of trying to do business with someone that you never meet? Don't be ridiculous."

Simon gazed at his ex-wife and wondered once again about the wisdom of having his office in Belle Rose. Toya seemed to think she had a right to pop in at will. Of course, he had to take part of the blame. Setting up offices in New Orleans or Baton Rouge made more sense. But sentimentalism had tugged at him. His great-great-grandfather operated a carpentry and blacksmith shop on this same spot for fifty years. Gilbert Williams had been one of the few blacks operating a business in reconstruction rural Louisiana. But now seeing the angry woman across from him, Simon wished he'd been less nostalgic.

"Rae Dalcour is trouble. Something you should know well enough."

"I know what you've told me, Toya. All I remember hearing is that she was a teenager who liked to party."

Simon stared out the window next to his desk. A wash of

sunshine painted the small downtown scene visible from his
corner building. Rae Dalcour. She was not what he'd expected.
Growing up in the community six miles down the highway from
Belle Rose and being four years older, he'd only heard talk of
the Dalcour children. Rae Dalcour's exploits had become legend
even with the older kids around the bayou community. Simon
found it hard to believe the wary young woman who had stood
studying him was the same person. Her voice was smooth with
just a hint of huskiness to it. That almond brown skin had looked
soft and inviting. *She must be about five foot six. Nice curves,
too.* He had to admit he was intrigued by the woman he'd met.
Simon wanted to know more about her. Toya's sharp voice
snapped him back from his musings.

"So you're going to get into her underwear as soon as possible." Toya stared at him through narrowed eyes.

Simon cleared his throat. He had to be nuts daydreaming
about any woman, much less Rae Dalcour, with Toya sitting six
feet away. What was wrong with him? Toya was right about one
thing, Rae Dalcour was trouble if she could send him off on
such a tangent after only seeing her once.

"My dating habits are none of your business." Simon did not
need another scene with Toya today.

"When we separated, I told you we should try again," Toya
said in a quiet voice.

"We did try. It didn't work. You talk like we just split up."
Simon picked up a stack of papers. "It's been six years. We got
married for the wrong reasons."

Simon did not want to cover this old ground again. With their
families so closely bound by ties that stretched back to the infamous scandal fifty years ago, the Jove and St. Cyr children
socialized together. His grandfather and Toya's were delighted
when the young couple became engaged. Toya was twenty-one
and Simon twenty-five. But Simon realized within the first year
of their marriage that they were not in the least suited for each
other. Toya was possessive and willful. There were numerous
screaming matches until, after only two years, they had separated. For years Toya held onto him, refusing to settle their

divorce. She'd used every legal excuse to delay until finally her own attorney told her it was no use.

"You came back to me once." Toya leaned forward. "I remember that night."

Simon winced. Driven by guilt and misdirected compassion, he'd made the mistake of staying with her after the annual Mardi Gras party. And he'd regretted it immediately. "It's no good between us, Toya."

She stood up abruptly. "Sorry to bring up such a painful memory . . . Try not to get sick," she hissed. "You go on sniffing around Rae Dalcour. I'll be there to gloat when she drags you down into her own filth."

"Toya, stop it. This is what pushed me away from you." Simon tried to hold onto his temper. "Now I have work to do. Goodbye."

As usual they could not part on cordial terms. He watched her stomp out. The door to his office banged shut behind her. Simon let out a groan. His office door opened again.

"Well what's up with Queen Toya now?" Baylor Hill, Simon's friend and sometime business partner, strolled in. "She snapped my head off just for saying hello."

"Same old, same old." Simon waved him in.

"Ah." Baylor grinned. No further explanation was needed. "Man, you've got more patience than any ten saints. I would have cut the woman off completely years ago."

"In a way I can't help but feel sorry for her. Ms. Lorise died when she was only twelve and her father was killed ten years later in a boating accident."

"Yeah, well that doesn't give her the right to treat people like dirt." Baylor was not in a forgiving mood when it came to Toya. "Of course, having Rae back in town is probably not helping." He leaned forward with interest.

"Baylor, you're a worse gossip than my elderly aunts." Simon shook a finger at him.

"So what was she like when you talked to her the other day? They say she is one wild woman. Been playing blues in tough nightclubs all over the country." Baylor ignored the jibe.

Simon once again thought of the lovely face that had turned

up to look at him that day. Yes, she had an air of suppressed energy. Rae had stood straight and looked at him without a hint of shyness. She was strong, but there was something else in those big brown eyes. A prick of heat touched his spine.

"I expected her to look . . . different," Simon murmured.

Baylor nodded. "From the way folks talk about her you'd think she look all used up and rough." He stared at his friend with speculation. "But I hear she's good-looking."

"Yeah," was all Simon said. He saw the thick black hair pulled back in an effort to tame its coarse curls, one large braid down to her shoulders. What would it look like loose, framing her face?

"And you're meeting with her tomorrow." Baylor was silent for several minutes. "Uh-oh, I see flashing yellow lights signaling caution."

"What?" Simon blinked at him.

"Don't get pulled in. Everybody knows the Dalcours are trouble. Besides, there are loads of women you can choose from that don't carry that baggage. You've still got to do business in this parish." Baylor goaded Simon, and was rewarded with the expected reaction.

"You should know better than to quote one of those 'everybody knows' kind of generalizations." Simon crossed his arms.

"Lucien Dalcour was always picking fights with Mr. Henry. Proof he wasn't screwed too tight." Baylor said. "Toya's grandfather is the meanest old dude around."

"Darcy and his grandfather think that property could be a prime campground area. And so do I." Simon got up to point at the large map on the wall behind his desk. "It's already popular. You know the old beach area. Kids especially like to go tubing down the river from there."

"All three of you are hallucinating if you think Rae Dalcour is going to sell any part of her family's land to you guys." Baylor crossed his legs.

"Why not? She's got a career to pursue. I don't think either of her brothers will refuse the price we'll offer." Simon lifted both hands.

"Why is Darcy pushing you out front? That dude has something up his sleeve, man. Watch him."

"We both decided to handle it this way. I don't have the history with them that Darcy and Toya have."

"Your grandfather was one of the partners." Baylor lifted an eyebrow at him.

"Papa Joe didn't go on the crusade Mr. Henry did when Vincent Dalcour split." Simon shook his head. "No, the only thing to do is make sure Rae Dalcour understands the potential for profit. I'm going to take my time on this deal."

Baylor grinned at him. "That won't be such a bad job after all. She's got it all the way. Smart move, my brother."

"Like I said, this is business." Simon affected what he hoped was a convincing matter-of-fact tone.

"Uh-huh. Sure it is. A sexy woman with a wild reputation blows into town after a lot of years. She's got a walk that makes you wanna holler, and it's just business." Baylor stood. "Peddle it to some other sucker 'cause I ain't buying." He strolled to the door.

"Hey, my mind isn't always in the same direction when it comes to a fine woman," Simon shot back.

Baylor whirled to point at him. "So you think she's fine? That's how it starts. Like I said, danger ahead."

"Get a grip. This isn't 1988 or 1948. We're not locked in the past, Baylor." Simon looked out the window at the restored store fronts. Some dated back to the 1880s. "I think we all know it's time to move on."

"You could be right. All I know is, people are talking about it again like it happened yesterday. Be careful of Ms. Dalcour." Baylor paused before leaving. "And Darcy, too. Like I said, something is up with him."

"Lighten up. This is a simple transaction. She'll leave town and life will go on."

"I hope you're right." Baylor said with a look that was not convinced in the least. "See you later."

Simon stared after him for a few minutes. He'd tried to convince Baylor that Rae Dalcour meant only business, now what about convincing himself? He tried to think of the shapely woman, a look of world-wise wariness in those big brown eyes, without feeling she was a mystery he wanted to solve. Simon shook his head as though to clear it. *Man, you gotta be out of your ever lovin' mind.* A booming male voice came from the outer office. Another excellent reason to curb this train of thought, Simon mused. A loud knock sounded only to be followed by the door swinging open immediately.

"Hey, son. How's my boy?" Tall and lightly tanned, Joseph St. Cyr was still a commanding figure at seventy-five.

"Hi, Papa Joe." Simon got up to hug his grandfather. "Come on in here. This is a rare visit. Since you retired, you avoid anyplace that reminds you of work." He grinned at Papa Joe.

"Working your butt off for forty years will do that to you, Simon. Of course, you're working for yourself, which is different." Papa Joe looked around the office. "This is why I laid bricks for Acme all those years. To see my sons and grandsons have their own businesses." He lost his smile at the reference to Simon's father. "How is your daddy."

"You could pick up the phone once in awhile and ask him."

Papa Joe sat down with a grunt. "Well, he could do the same," he retorted. "Phillip threw away a chance to build something for you. I handed him the future and he spit in my face."

"Daddy didn't want to be in the bricklaying business. And Uncle James did." Simon had heard this all his life. He'd been close to Papa Joe in a way his father had never been.

"James would have an easier time of it if Phil helped him. I love my boys, but James doesn't have as much smarts as Phil."

Simon sighed. The two men had been at war with each other for years. Papa Joe was a take charge-man with strong opinions and so was his son Phillip. Phillip had chosen to be a college professor, something Papa Joe still did not understand or accept. The result was the two men rarely spoke. Both were too stiff-necked to bend. Simon feared they would realize too late the price of estrangement.

"Which is why he loves being a political science professor, Papa Joe. Daddy would be real happy if you took pride in his accomplishments. He's been a consultant to several governors and a senator." Simon knew that his father would never admit to wanting his father's approval.

"Lying politicians. And that's another thing, helping Taylor Caldwell get elected." Papa Joe looked to the ceiling as though seeking divine forgiveness. "My kin working for that rhetoric-spouting bag of wind."

"Caldwell may be too liberal for your taste—"

"That's an understatement. The man wants to keep our people in a perpetual welfare state." Papa Joe wagged a finger in the air in preparation of launching into a debate of government policy.

"But Daddy believes he's a good, honest man." Simon pressed on.

"Oh, give me strength! He's an idiot you mean." Papa Joe leaned forward. "You agree with me and don't bother to deny it."

"The point is, you and Daddy should find a way to stop fighting each other. It makes no sense whatsoever," Simon said.

"It's his fault." Papa Joe's mouth turned down in a stubborn pout.

"I give up . . . for now." Simon squinted at his grandfather. "But you two are going to see reason if I have to knock your heads together. This bickering is stupid."

"Let's not argue, Simon. Maybe I'll give Phil a call later today." Papa Joe tried to appease his grandson. "Guess I oughta be old enough to know better. Don't be mad at me."

Simon gazed at him with affection. Strangely, the bond that had never been between Papa Joe and his son had skipped a generation. Simon's earliest memory was of following Papa Joe around brickyards when he was only four years old. His mother and grandmother had objected on grounds of safety. Yet Simon had howled with such force at being left behind, they relented.

"You know I can't be angry with you more than a minute. Now what brings you to town?" Simon fixed him a mug of coffee.

"Oh, just came in to pick up a few things at Lawson's Hardware. Thought I'd say hello." Papa Joe accepted the mug and took a sip.

"I see. What things?"

"Some nails. A handle on the dresser in our bedroom broke. You know, odds and ends."

Simon eyed him for a few seconds. "You fixed the handle last week. I was by the house. Another one broke?"

"Oh, I, uh, got an extra just in case. And your grandmother wanted me to get some of those headache pills from the drugstore." Papa Joe did not look at him.

"I see." Simon waited for the real reason Papa Joe had left his beloved sanctuary six miles out of town. Several moments passed as Papa Joe sipped from the mug.

"I hear Raenette Dalcour is staying around to settle up her daddy's affairs." Papa Joe affected a matter-of-fact tone.

"Yes."

"I suppose she'll be here a few more days then leave."

"Maybe." Simon lifted a shoulder.

"I mean, no reason for her to stay around here. Is there?" Papa Joe looked at him intently.

"I guess not. Don't really know."

Papa Joe put the mug down. "Damn it, this is like pulling teeth. You talked to the girl. What did she say?" He puffed with frustration.

"I spoke to her a total of maybe five minutes. She's meeting with me tomorrow. That's all I know. It is," he said when Papa Joe looked at him with a doubtful expression.

"About that property, I know Darcy and Henry want to buy it. Lucien spit in Henry's eye when he tried to talk to him about it four years ago. Think she'll sell it?"

"She didn't spit in my eye. Could be a good sign," Simon said with amusement. "But I don't know. She could decide to stay, at least that's one rumor I've heard."

"Why would she want to do that? She's a singer making money recording records and such."

"From what I hear, Rae Dalcour is not an easy woman to figure out. Could liven up this town, eh?" Simon wore a slight smile.

"Humph."

When Papa Joe's worried expression remained, Simon became serious. "Why does this bother you so?"

"Lord, we don't need all that stirred up again." Papa Joe raked fingers through his iron gray hair.

"Papa Joe, this has nothing to do with what happened all those years ago. It's a simple business proposition. She'll either say yes or no." Simon tried to reassure him.

"Just like young folks. I was the same at your age. All that old-timey stuff didn't have nothing to do with me." Papa Joe, with his head tilted, looked back to previous decades. "But it does, Simon. Somehow it just won't go away."

"I don't understand. How can what Vincent Dalcour did fifty years ago have anything to do with his granddaughter?" Simon shook his head slowly. "I know it's hard for you to forget what happened. But . . ."

"Seems like yesterday Vince was standing right there on that corner. Laughing and joking with us. We used to come to Mr. Peter's store, one of only three black drugstores in this part of the state back then."

Papa Joe was too caught up in memories to hear him when Simon crossed to him. He placed a hand on his shoulder. "What Mr. Vincent did is in the past, Papa Joe. It was bad, but it's over. Rae Dalcour will most probably sell and that will be that."

Papa Joe blinked his eyes at him. He sighed. "Maybe you're right, son."

"Of course, I am. And even if she doesn't, it won't matter. Sure folks will talk, but they'll soon get bored and move on to more recent gossip. You'll see." Simon gave his shoulder a pat.

"Hope she sells and just leaves," Papa Joe said with a fierce gleam in his eyes. "Talk to her, Simon. Offer her a good price she can't refuse. All the Dalcours love somebody else's money. She's probably no different. Just make her think she's taking money out your pocket for free."

"I've never heard you talk like this about anybody, Papa Joe." Simon was disturbed by the hostility toward a young woman Papa Joe had probably never even met.

"She's a Dalcour, that's all I need to know. You'll see." Papa Joe looked at him. "Don't get too close, son. They're trouble."

"So everyone keeps telling me."

"Listen to them, Simon." Papa Joe nodded soberly.

"Oh, come on. Stop getting yourself all worked up over nothing. I'm a big boy. I think I can handle Rae Dalcour, even if she is a package of firecrackers ready to go off." Simon chuckled. He tried to joke his grandfather out of his somber mood.

Papa Joe studied his grandson. "I know she's attractive, boy. That spark in your eyes tells me you know it, too. Just remember what damage firecrackers can do if you get too close." He patted Simon's hand. "Well, enough of this serious talk. I'm getting too grim in my old age. Let's go over to LeBeau's for some lunch."

To avoid upsetting Papa Joe, Simon did not pursue the subject. Yet he could not help but be intrigued that Raenette Dalcour could inspire such concern by simply coming back to her hometown. In spite of Papa Joe's warning and Baylor's remarks, Simon found himself anticipating a chance to spend time with her. He'd seen her from a distance only once more, laughing at something one of her band members had said. The sound was musical and rich, her dark brown hair shone in the sun when her head went back. Yes, tomorrow would be an interesting day indeed.

Three

"Well, what are you going to do, boy?" Henry Jove stood holding a coffee cup made of fine china, red roses painted on its sides. An antique mirror behind him reflected the image of a man used to being in control. He could easily pass for ten years younger than his seventy-seven years.

"I'll handle it." Darcy wore an irritated expression. He hated being called "boy" by his grandfather in that tone of voice. "I've got a plan."

"You've got a plan," Henry mimicked. "I damn well hope so." He swallowed some of the contents of his cup.

"Simon is meeting with her today. I have a feeling she's going to sell."

Henry gave a snort. "Feeling, hell. Take action and make sure she sells."

"I have," Darcy snapped. He drew up short at the dark glance Henry gave him. He softened his tone and expression. "The offer Simon is going to make will be more money than her family has ever seen. She'll take it."

"You'd better hope she's not as mule-headed as that father of hers was." Henry wore an angry scowl. "Drunken fool could have been sitting pretty years ago if he'd taken my offer. That land has got to be in our hands."

"It will be. I'll see to that." Darcy sat down across from his grandfather. "Just as I've made our investments grow twelve percent in the last two years alone."

"Well, at least you're no dummy." Henry appeared to give the compliment grudgingly. "Whatever else your faults."

"Nobody's perfect." Darcy spoke in a mild voice without looking at him.

Henry looked at him sharply, then exhaled a puff of air. "What does Simon say to this oil field waste facility? He must think it's a good idea."

"We haven't discussed it yet."

"Oh? Tell me, boy. Tell me all of it." Henry leaned forward and tapped his knee.

"I'm not ready to tell him my plans for the land have changed. Besides, I'm still discussing it with Mouton and Pantheon. It's not a certainty just yet."

"Don't give me that bull! I'm old, not senile. I talked to Preston Cazes at the chamber meeting Tuesday. He's excited about the possibility that Pantheon will locate nearby. He's not sure just where, but feels it's going to be close. Preston knows what's going to happen in the state before the governor."

"They haven't decided between three possible sites. But . . ." Darcy wore a sly smile.

Henry smiled back at him. "But you have inside information they'll favor our land. Good for you, boy."

Darcy nodded. "All we need is that extra one hundred acres. Twenty of which is still in the Dalcour family. Strange how Mr. Lucien never failed to pay the taxes even with all his other weaknesses."

"His uncles helped him," Henry said. "Stubborn bunch of no-goods." His voice was bitter.

"Well, Rae won't cling to that worthless property. After all, renting out to hunting clubs doesn't make much profit."

"Lucien let a lumber company cut, too."

"Yes, but it takes fifteen to twenty years for the trees to come back enough to make it profitable." Darcy lifted a shoulder. "I know Rae. She won't want to be bothered with it."

Henry gazed at his grandson for a time. "Yes, you do know her. And I hope she's out of your system."

"It was a long time ago and we were kids." Darcy stared down. "She probably wouldn't even speak to me these days."

"She's not for you, boy."

"So you impressed upon me back then, Grandfather," Darcy said in a quiet voice. "It worked. We broke up." He looked out the window at the expanse of green lawn in front of the house. "End of story."

"Good." Henry gave a curt nod. "What about Mouton?"

"What about him?" Darcy went very still.

"Can he be trusted? The Moutons have been cheating our people for over one hundred years. Seems strange he wants to hook up with the Joves in a deal."

Darcy relaxed. "He has little choice since our property lines intersect. If he wants to negotiate with Pantheon, he has to work with me."

"Keep your eyes on him. You can bet he wants more than he's telling. And he's just as devious as his grandfather and father." Henry stood up. "He won't stop until he's got what he wants."

"Mouton and I understand each other." Darcy brushed the front of his crisp cotton shirt. "I know exactly how to handle him." He smiled up at Henry.

"Humph" was Henry's only reply. He walked out of the room. "I'm going to a meeting. Hello, cher." Henry pecked Toya on the cheek before continuing out the door.

"Morning, Darcy." Toya strolled in. She dropped down in the chair her grandfather had just vacated. "I was driving by and saw your car."

"I see." Darcy poured himself more coffee from the pot set on a large tray on a table nearby. "How are you this fine morning?"

"Okay. Have you talked to Simon?" Toya asked in a rush. "He's meeting with Rae. I don't like it."

"You don't like Simon talking to any female, Toya. No wonder the man headed for the nearest exit not long after you two were married." Darcy did not mince words.

Toya turned on him. "Let's not get into failed marriages, shall we? You haven't done very well in that area. Simon and I had differences but that doesn't mean we won't resolve them. You on the other hand . . ." She waved a hand in the air.

"It takes a special woman to hold my interest." Darcy smiled.

"I suppose you're referring to Rae Dalcour. You enjoyed humping her in cemeteries for the thrill." Toya smirked at him.

"Not our rendezvous of choice. I seem to remember *you* were caught in St. Anthony Cemetery at the tender age of fifteen with Roy Ballantine huffing away. Ring a bell?" Darcy lifted an eyebrow at her.

"Oh, shut up." Toya wore a tight expression. She fixed herself a cup of coffee. "The point is I don't want that woman anywhere near Simon. For some reason I'll never understand, she draws men to her like flies to a cow patty."

"Rae has a quick wit and she's pretty. A nice package." Darcy looked thoughtful. "I'm not sure how she'd react to me or I'd . . ."

"You'd what? Don't tell me you find her attractive! Oh, please." Toya got up to pace.

"We clicked like crazy. I still don't understand it."

"You're not by yourself, believe me." Toya stood over him. "Don't forget what Grandfather thinks about you and her."

Darcy grinned. "I don't give a rat's butt what Grandfather thinks these days."

"Brave words now that he's long gone, Darcy." Toya sneered at him. "You just remember to stay away from her. You're not even divorced from that last moron."

"Katherine and I will be divorced by October. I'll be free." Darcy frowned. "As for Simon, he's strictly interested in business. But maybe I'll test the waters. It would be nice to see her again."

"And what will your latest friend think of all this? I mean, you finally got Katherine out of the way." Toya sat down again, a wicked gleam in her eye.

"I don't know what you mean." Darcy gave her a cold look.

"Don't you?"

"Careful, sister. I'll only take so much." Darcy's jaw muscle jumped.

"Darcy, your sex life, interesting as it is in its variety, is your affair." Toya stared back at him without flinching. "But we could get very rich with this Pantheon deal. Don't get so devious that you outsmart yourself. Ellis Mouton is nobody's fool."

"I know exactly what I'm doing. Haven't Grandfather and I

always taken care of you?" Darcy gestured to her three hundred dollar Coach purse. "You've had the best of everything all your life. I won't do anything to jeopardize the family's financial health."

"See that you don't. As you say, I'm used to the finer things. Which includes Simon. Keep him away from Rae, Darcy." Toya reached out to clutch his wrist.

Darcy patted her hand. "I intend to get that property. As for Simon, he's not going to be interested in her. You know how he is. Conventional."

Henry's wife, seven years his junior, looked older than her seventy years. Her light skin, the color of country creme, was lined with care. She sat across from Henry at the large dining-room table. Pauline, the lady who cleaned and cooked for them three times a week, stuck her head though the door leading down a short hall to the kitchen.

"Y'all need anything else, Miss Cecile?" Pauline looked at the brooding couple.

"No, Pauline. We're fine." Cecile nodded her head in a regal manner. "You can go now."

"Okay. I left some tuna salad in the ice box and French bread is on the counter." Pauline withdrew.

Cecile waited until she heard the sound of the back door slam. "The Dalcour girl is in town."

"Yes." Henry continued to spoon the hot corn and shrimp soup into his mouth. He paused to pat his lips.

"They seem to sprout back like weeds, those people," Cecile said with distaste.

"Hmm, Darcy knows what do to." Henry did not look at her.

"The stories are already being raked up again. As though I haven't heard enough about Estelle—" She stopped at the steely look he gave her.

"It doesn't matter. Simon will buy the land, she'll go back to the wasteful life she was leading, and that will be the end of it." Henry spoke in a measured tone. "Darcy has it all worked out."

"Why can't Marius be in charge for once?" Cecile put her spoon down.

"Darcy has more skill in business," Henry said. "We've been through this before." He went back to his meal.

"Marius is just as smart as Darcy, Henry. You know that very well. You should not show such favoritism just because—"

"Woman, don't start nagging me again. Can't get peace in my own house." Henry threw his napkin on the table.

"You're hardly here. If I'd known when we got married—"

"Cecile, you've been whining for forty years. Give it a rest." Henry stood and walked from the room with Cecile right behind him.

"I've given you everything and how do you repay me?"

Henry spun to face her once they were in the living room. "You never complained about the jewelry, cars, and trips."

"Things. All you ever gave back was things." Cecile swallowed hard.

"Be satisfied. You've got what you wanted and more." Henry lit a cigar.

"Did I?" Cecile spoke with bitterness. "You still hold onto that woman's memory, hugging it you at night. She was between us every time you touched me."

"Don't talk foolishness."

"You favored Estelle's son over my children. Now you're favoring Darcy over my grandchildren. I won't have it." Cecile grabbed his arm.

"You don't have a damn thing to do with my business decisions." Henry jerked free of her hold.

"No, I've kept quiet all these years. But the whole town will be interested to know where you got a sudden windfall of cash back in 1948 to expand the business." Cecile gave him a nasty smile.

"Shut up!" Henry snapped. "I'm sick of listening to you. I've put the most expensive clothes on your back. Sent you on trips all over this country, to Europe even."

"So you could shack up with your sluts! I know about every one of them. They were glad to rub my face in it," she shouted back.

"If you'd done your job as a wife, I wouldn't have needed other women," he spat at her.

Cecile collapsed onto the sofa with a moan of anguish. "How can you be so cruel?"

"You clawed for years to get me. So congratulations."

"I loved you, Henry. Even after you humiliated me in front of the whole town by marrying Estelle. Everyone knew we were engaged." Cecile spoke as though these were events that had only happened in the past few weeks.

"How long will you try to milk that for sympathy." Henry gave a snort of derision. "Silly woman."

"You never stopped loving Estelle. Even after—"

"Enough!" Henry roared. He stood over her with a look of dark fury, both fists raised. "This family has prospered because of my hard work. No one, Estelle, no one will threaten everything I've built."

Cecile looked defeated, tears rolled down her cheeks. "You called me by her name again."

Henry looked shaken and pale. He pulled a hand over his face. "You're mistaken."

"You did." Cecile stared ahead bleakly.

Henry poured himself a generous serving of Crown Royal. "Will you get off my back?" His hand trembled when he lifted the glass. "Just leave me alone."

"Yes, I'll keep quiet as I've done all these years." She heaved a sigh. "Habit is hard to break."

"Your taste for the good life is the only habit you haven't wanted to break," Henry shot back.

Cecile wiped her eyes with a tissue. She watched him take a sip from the glass. "You'll kill yourself drinking and smoking, Henry. The doctor has warned you."

"Don't get your hopes up, woman. I'll live a few years longer. And make the Dalcours pay, too." Henry wore a stony look of determination.

Simon straightened the items on his desk for the third time. He smoothed down his hair. Nine forty-five. She would be there any minute. *What is up with you?* Simon forced his hand down from tugging at his shirt collar. He tried to tell himself that like any other business meeting, he wanted to make the right impression.

"Here are the beignets." Nola, his secretary, came in with a small tray. "Mr. Auzenne just dropped these off from the bakery. Must be a real special client." She pointed to the fresh flowers in a vase on the credenza.

"Every potential customer is special, Nola." Simon took the tray from her and set it down next to the coffee pot.

"Uh-huh," Nola said. "And this office hasn't been so clean in a lo-ong time."

"You know I clean this place up at least—"

"Once a year, I know." Nola laughed. "The janitorial crew just sorta dust any tiny space not covered with paper."

"You know I don't like anybody moving my things but me." Simon faced her with his arms crossed.

Nola held up a palm. "Hey, fine by me. I'm here to type, do data entry, and organize project schedules. If you don't mind operating in a landfill, who am I to argue?"

"Nola, you have the most irritating habit of—"

"Telling it like it 'tis." Nola let out another laugh in her deep contralto. "I know, bossman." She gave him an affectionate pat on the arm then left.

"And not letting me finish a sentence," Simon called after her in a peevish tone. "Mouthy woman." He looked at the digital clock on the credenza. His hand was still brushing his hair back when Nola came in again.

"Now I get it," Nola said with a wink. "Yep, you look just fine."

"What are you talking about?"

"Miss Raenette Dalcour is here to see you." Nola wore a mischievous half smile.

"Fine." Simon forced a neutral tone to his voice. He went past Nola in the open door to the outer office. "Good morning, Ms. Dalcour. How are you?"

Rae took his hand with a cautious expression on her face. She wore only a little lipstick. Her hair, worn loose, had thick waves from the braids she'd worn before. Two small silver combs pinned it from her face. The sleeveless denim shirt and white jeans fit without being tight. Simon held his breath a moment when her soft skin brushed his.

"Morning." Rae followed him into his office. She waved away his offer of the fluffy donuts. "Just coffee."

"I was sorry to hear about your father, Ms. Dalcour."

"Thanks." Rae took off her sunglasses. "So what is this proposition you mentioned the other day?" She got right to the point.

"Well your father's land along Bayou Latte is a prime location for development." Simon sat next to her rather than behind his desk.

"Don't believe in it," Rae said shortly. She drank from the cup.

"Care to expand on that?" Simon raised an eyebrow.

"Listen, I know what happened on Bayou Verret and on Grande River when they jumped on the development bandwagon. A bunch of fancy houses went up right on the water and so did the pollution levels." Rae stared at him as though to dare a contradiction.

"Yes, but—"

"The natural beauty is history. Now what you mostly hear is the sound of jet skis and speedboats. Especially in the summer when the new-money folks from Baton Rouge and New Orleans come to their summer homes."

"Well the economy—"

"Sure the tax base expanded. So did sales tax collections. But do we really need it? Belle Rose is making a solid comeback with tourism for one thing." Rae raised a finger.

"We—"

"Not to mention being a popular sports destination. We've already got enough fishing and hunting camps that fill up almost all year round."

"Can I say something please," Simon burst out in a fit of exasperation. First Nola and now this one.

"Sure." Rae appeared to say he could have spoken at any

time. "Go ahead." The corners of her mouth twitched as she drank from her cup.

"I agree with you about Bayou Verret and Grande River. The local aldermen didn't do a very good job of planning. And you're right, we are doing very well in town what with tourist excursions. We even have an annual antique festival every May that is steadily growing." Simon took her empty cup and refilled it without asking. He sat down again.

"Okay, so tell me what you're talking about."

"More tourist development really. A sort of modified beach front." Simon held up a hand to forestall another objection. "But with full-time monitoring. Almost like a national park."

"You mean a ranger wearing a cute little hat?" Rae wore a teasing expression.

"Sort of." Simon smiled. He got up and pulled out a set of plans. "Look here. This is where it's proposed. Part of this is land I own. My father sold it to me."

"I see." Rae looked at the map showing Bayou Latte. A large area was outlined in blue. "And this?"

"Part of it might be used for industrial development."

"Now wait a minute—"

"Nothing heavy. Pantheon Corporation might locate one of their divisions on that spot. A plant making underwear. Cotton-wear is the brand I think."

"Oh, yeah, I own some of those." Rae grinned at him.

Simon gazed at her figure. A mental picture of her full hips covered only by a soft cotton panty winked on before he knew what was happening. Warmth crept through him. He blinked in embarrassment when he realized she was looking at him looking at her. He averted his eyes fast.

"Ye-es, well it means at least seventy construction jobs and sixty or so permanent jobs," Simon managed to stammer out.

"That doesn't sound too bad," Rae said. "I mean, we've gotta have drawers and bras, right?"

Simon resisted an urge to look at her again. "Uh, right. Anyway, this would be the beach area here. We'd build a visitors guide center with restrooms. The state might even hire a part-time employee to give out tourist brochures about the area."

"You've done your homework, Mr. St. Cyr." Rae leaned closer to get a better view of the plans.

Her scent, light and floral, floated to him. "Er, I knew you'd have questions." Simon pointed to another spot close to where her family home was located. "Of course, you'll want to keep a few acres around here." That was obvious, but it made her move just a bit more toward him.

"For sure." Rae looked into his eyes. For a moment neither spoke. "So how bad do you want it?"

Her face was so close, he could count the thick lashes framing those clear brown eyes. "I, uh . . ." He tried to focus.

"The price, Mr. St. Cyr. What are you offering me?"

Simon steadied his breathing. "The property, yes, the land." He cleared his throat. "Five thousand an acre."

Rae gave a low whistle. "Not bad. Not bad at all."

"This is waterfront property near a historic town. After all, Belle Rose is about to celebrate one hundred sixty-seven years since its founding."

"I'll need to discuss this with my brothers, of course. By the way, I want to keep five acres at least. My dad's old dance hall is located a ways down the road from the house." Rae stood up. "If I sell at all."

"No problem. That leaves us with twenty acres. Exactly what we need." Simon rose, too.

"You said 'we.' You have a partner?"

Simon thought for a split second before deciding to lay his cards on the table. "There is my grandfather. He's a silent partner in my business. And Darcy Jove and I are working together to bring Pantheon in. His property is adjacent to yours."

Rae's eyes narrowed. "I don't need to discuss this with my brothers. Forget it," she said in a voice taut with anger.

"Ms. Dalcour, we've formed a corporation. Darcy won't own the land." Simon was afraid this would be her reaction.

"You must think I'm seven different kinds of fool. The Joves have been trying to take our property for over fifty years." Rae turned to go.

"We're offering to buy it at a fair price. And you'll still own five acres." Simon blocked her exit. "Darcy only owns fifteen percent of the company. If anyone ends up with the land, it would be me. And we can draw up an agreement that I have to give you first shot at buying it back if ever I want to sell it."

"Oh, great. The St. Cyrs, another family that trashed my grandfather's name, would own it. That makes a big difference." Rae gave a grunt.

"Listen, if it means anything to you, I never heard Papa Joe say one bad thing about Mr. Vincent in all the years I was growing up." Simon was sincere. In fact, Papa Joe had been careful to point out that there was no proof of Vincent Dalcour's guilt in the theft.

"Yeah, well . . ." Rae looked at him, the scowl on her face softening a bit.

"You know Papa Joe even tried to help your dad. Of course, Mr. Lucien told him no." Simon took one step toward her.

Rae chuckled. "Very diplomatic. Daddy told him to kiss his you-know-what." She lifted a shoulder. "Okay, so the St. Cyrs didn't exactly spit on us."

Simon took this as an encouraging sign. "Look, I realize your family was put through a lot. But unless you have plans to use all that land, why not hold onto a sizable amount and still make a profit?"

Rae studied him for a moment. "Let me get back to you." The corner of her full mouth lifted. "You're not a bad pitch man at that."

"I want you to feel like I'm dealing with you honestly. That's all." Simon felt a tingle at the small compliment.

"I appreciate it. I know I'm a bit prickly about all this, but . . ."

"Sure, I understand."

"See ya 'round." Rae put on her sunglasses.

Simon's heart sped up at the sight of her about to leave. "Ms. Dalcour, maybe if we walked over the property together you'd get an even better picture. To explain to your family, I mean." He could not see her eyes behind the dark lenses. "We could have lunch afterward." There, he'd said it. Seconds beat out like hours while she stood considering his invitation.

"Friday good?"

"Yes, sure. I'll pick you up around ten thirty."

"Okay." Rae nodded and sauntered out closing the door behind her.

Simon exhaled. Now all he had to do was check his calendar to make sure he was free Friday morning. Her floral scent came back to him. If not, Nola would just have to reschedule everything else.

Four

A breeze stirred the swamp oak leaves. Bright sparkles of sunshine bounced off the ripples on Bayou Latte. Rae stood on the bank in a clearing where small boats were turned upside down waiting for their owners to come back. This was one of the many places where fishermen launched to head off deeper into the swamps and bayous in search of speckled trout, choupic, or catfish. Rae savored the feel of warm air brushing across her skin. It brought relief from the hot sun. Yet she did not mind the heat. She enjoyed the smell of fish and wet earth and the sound of birds calling to each other. Nowhere else was she as much at peace. Even when she was a child, she never felt rejected on the bayou. Memories of crawfishing with Lucien came back as vividly as a technicolor movie. They would follow the waterway into Bayou Choctaw, then on to Houmas Swamp. All bitterness could be forgotten back in the bayous.

Rae gasped at the sight of a man standing about sixty yards away on the bank. He was dressed in a red shirt and blue jeans. His brown skin glistened. For a moment, he bore a striking resemblance to Lucien. Rae blinked away tears. If only it were him. There had been so much left unsaid between them. Unfinished business. That's what made death so painful for survivors, the unfinished business of life.

"Hey, trying to catch some dinner!" Andrew called in a voice full of cheer.

Rae turned away as he approached, hastily wiping her face dry with a bandanna taken from a back pocket.

"You skipping another day of work? A wonder you have a job, Andy," Rae said when he got about fifty yards away. She used his old childhood nickname.

"Contrary to popular rumor, I work hard. I got off at two, but I went to work at six this morning." Andrew yelled back. He closed the distance between them in no time with his long-legged stride. "Say, you all right?"

"Sure. Nothing wrong with me." Rae wiped her face with a hand.

Andrew peered at her. "You've been crying. Come here, cher." He wrapped her in a sweaty embrace.

"Go on now, I said I'm okay." Despite her words, Rae leaned against his chest. She pushed away from him after a few seconds. "Whew! You smell like crawfish."

"You ain't exactly smelling like a rose yourself," Andrew teased. He pinched her chin with affection then looked out over the water. "Yep, Daddy is all over this place. I feel him myself when I'm out here." He did not have to ask what prompted her tears.

"Daddy was always a contradiction, Andy. Somehow he held onto this land. But he'd stay drunk for days, yelling and playing that accordion." Rae sat down Indian style on a grassy mound. Andrew plopped beside her.

"One thing he wouldn't do was lose Pawpaw's land. Been in the family for almost a hundred years. Our great-grandfather had to fight to hold onto it," Andrew said.

Raimond Dalcour's white grandfather had left no legitimate direct heirs. Yet his nieces and nephews had filed a lawsuit that went on for seven years trying to take it from him. Amazingly, the courts upheld Raimond's claim since whites and blacks wrote letters attesting to it.

"You know he paid the taxes on time. Even paid back his Uncle Jules the times he had to borrow from him to do it," Rae said.

"He had his faults, our papa, but he wouldn't let go of his heritage." Andrew spoke with fierce pride in his voice. "Always said we'd get rich one day because of it."

"Andy, I met with Simon St. Cyr yesterday. He wants to buy part of the land." Rae looked at him.

Andrew grinned at her. "Wish I coulda been there when you told him to go to hell and take his no-good grandfather right along with him."

"That's not what I told him." Rae shifted under his gaze.

"Then what exactly did you say?"

"I told him I'd get back to him after talking it over with you and Neville and . . ."

Andrew lifted a shoulder. "Okay, so you were polite. Now you can tell him no."

"Andy, I . . . think we ought to consider it. Neville wants to sell." Rae thought of her older brother. Neville wanted to move on in a different way, to wipe the past clean.

"You don't have to tell me that," Andrew shot back. "Our older brother has about as much sense of family tradition as that driftwood over there. He's ashamed of Pawpaw Vincent. And Daddy."

"That's not true. Neville stuck by us and you know it. He just didn't want to spend the rest of his life being looked down on in Belle Rose." Rae looked down at her hands folded in her lap. "Neither did I."

"Sure, leavin' was the easy way out." Andrew tossed a rock across the water causing a splash. "There are still older folks around who turn up their noses when I pass them on the street downtown. But I don't give a damn. This is as much my home as theirs."

"Andy, Neville and me wanted more of a life than we could have here. I didn't want to work at the processing plant, be a waitress, or end up driving thirty miles to some boring job." Rae skipped a small shell across the water's surface.

"So you made your choices. Mine is to stay right here like Daddy wanted and pay the taxes. This is our land." Andrew had a stubborn set to his jaw.

"Remember two years ago when Daddy got real sick and I came home?" Rae rested her chin on his shoulder as she had when they were children.

"Yeah."

"We had a long talk. He just knew he was about to die." Rae paused remembering his drawn face. "Daddy told me he was sorry for nursing his anger all those years and not doing more with his life. He made me promise to somehow find out the truth about Pawpaw Vincent."

"How in the world you gonna do that? The man's been gone over fifty years. He's likely dead by now." Andrew shook his head.

"Hire a private detective, I guess."

Andrew sighed. "Let's face it, he left and so did Estelle Jove. Now in my experience when it comes to men and women, those kinda coincidences mean one thing."

"You mean you believe what they say?" Rae was stunned. Andrew had always been as vehement in his defense of Papaw Vincent as Lucien.

"No . . . I'm not sure. Look, a black man with that kinda money would have been noticed back then."

"That's what Daddy used to say." Rae had only in recent months begun to seriously think about the grandfather she'd never known. All Lucien's accounts of the old scandal came back to her now. "It makes a lot of sense, too."

"But I do think he and Estelle went off someplace together. They could easily lose themselves in a big city like Detroit or Chicago. Hell, I don't know. Maybe they went to one of them Caribbean Islands."

"Oh, come on." Rae raised an eyebrow at him.

"We've got roots out that way. Let me see, was it Barbados or St. Lucia? Daddy said our great-great-great-grandmother came over as a servant first to New Orleans."

"She did?"

"Yeah, Pawpaw Vincent even had old pictures. Daddy kept them in a metal box up in the attic. Anyway, I think the old man lived out his life with a whole new family someplace far away."

Rae stared at him wide-eyed. "I never thought of it like that. We could have uncles and cousins somewhere."

"I'd like to prove Pawpaw Vincent didn't take that money, too. But that ain't gonna happen."

"Maybe not, but I've got to try. It's the one thing I can do for Daddy. But it's going to take money. A good bit."

Andrew threw another rock. "So you want to sell out." It was a statement that sounded more like an accusation.

"Don't put it like that, for goodness sake." Rae did indeed feel like a sell out, a traitor to the Dalcours.

"Darcy Jove is in on this," Andrew spat out as though it were a nasty taste in his mouth. "You know that?"

Rae did not answer him for a moment. "Yeah, St. Cyr told me. He's a minor partner. But Simon will own the land."

"What do you think of him?" Andrew glanced at her.

"He seems . . . sincere." Rae tried to identify the feeling his name brought on. "He could have lied about Darcy."

Simon St. Cyr was the kind of man that definitely made an impression on women. Rae thought of the shape of his lips, smooth like dark taffy. He had a way of crossing his arms when considering something, which accentuated that broad chest. And those big hands. The skin was dry with a few rough spots on the palm. He was a man who worked with his hands. What would it feel like to have him touch her skin.

"Oh no! Don't tell me you got the hots for Simon St. Cyr!" Andrew slapped his forehead.

"Don't be crude." Rae punched his arm.

"Of course, the fact that Toya is his ex-wife and still dyin' to get him back in her bed don't have a thing to do with it." Andrew gave her a pointed look. "Right?"

"They were married? Well, well." Rae smiled as she gazed at the scenery without seeing it. "Isn't that fascinating."

Andrew's brows came together. "Now, look here, don't go startin' nothin' with Toya."

"Why whatever do you mean?" Rae put on an innocent face.

"I should have kept my big mouth shut about Toya wantin' him bad. Now you're gonna go after the guy just to drive her up the wall."

"Gee, I hadn't thought of that. That would be a nice bit of lagniappe." She grinned. "Seriously, Andy, I don't think selling even most of the land would have bothered Daddy if it meant we could keep the dance hall open and clear Pawpaw Vincent's name."

"What if Pawpaw Vincent stole the money?" Andrew said in a quiet voice.

"A few minutes ago you said he didn't do it."

"No, I said it was strange he got away with havin' that kind of money to spread around. They might have been able to hide out all these years." Andrew tugged out clumps of grass. He would not meet her gaze.

"No, it doesn't make sense." Rae stood up. "I'm going to look into finding the truth. You think about this land deal. I'm meeting St. Cyr again Friday."

Andrew stood to face her. "Raenette Marie Dalcour . . ." He wore a fatherly frown of censure.

"Hey, it was his idea, not mine. He wants to give me a better idea of his plans." Rae lifted a shoulder. "Can I help it if the man also wants to treat me to lunch?"

"Make sure that's the only treat you get." Andy shook a forefinger under her nose.

"I'm grown, so I'll thank you to keep your fat nose outta my business." Rae brushed his finger aside. "Just think about the deal, okay?"

"Sure. Be careful." Andrew gazed out over the water with a troubled expression. "Maybe Mama's right, we oughta let this alone."

"What are you talking about, Andy?" Rae put a hand on his arm. His tone sent a small twist of anxiety through her.

Andrew opened his mouth as if to speak then stopped. He put a weak smile on his face. "Nothing. It's nothing. Well, guess I better get goin'. Bring you some of my fish after I clean 'em."

"Okay," Rae called after him. Andrew walked away with his familiar loping gait.

Rae wondered at Andrew's strange mood when they were discussing Pawpaw Vincent. The old scandal seemed to reach back across the years and give them all the jitters. For the rest of the day, she thought about her grandfather and Estelle Jove.

* * *

"Here's what Kelsey has so far. The first section is on Raenette Dalcour, the rest on the others."

Henry Jove opened the brown folder and scanned the first page. "I must say, he's done quite a lot in a short period." He sat at the desk in his combination office and library at home.

"He's come through for me before."

Henry flipped through the pages. "So he has. Careful we don't get too cute for our own good, Marius."

Marius Jove wore a confident half smile. "I'm more than careful."

"See that you are, young man." Henry eyed him for a few moments then went back to reading the file.

Marius, two years older than Darcy at thirty-four, was determined to have things his way. Henry was well aware that the cousins were fiercely competitive. He approved up to a point, since he believed competition between him and his brothers had made them tough. Henry's father had encouraged it, and now so did Henry.

"Not much here except she's something of a free spirit. Of course, we could use our connections to make things happen for her band." Marius sat down across from his uncle. "You know, an offer she can't refuse."

"Hmm." Henry kept reading.

"Maybe the chance to be an opening act for a big artist or a lucrative recording contract." Marius rubbed his chin in reflection. "Yes, that would be hard for her to let go based on her file. She's really into the music thing."

"That along with selling the property just might do it." Henry tapped a finger on the desk.

Marius looked at his grandfather. "Of course, if she sells, then you'll have most of what you want." He paused to see Henry's reaction before going on. "Shouldn't matter if she stays in Belle Rose."

Henry returned his gaze with a look of intensity. "Yes, it does. I don't want any of them taking what's mine. Lucien was pushing to have Bayou Latte dredged. I won't have it!"

"I know. It will affect the water level on your property farther down stream. You've told me that." Marius shifted in his chair. "Of course you could take measures—"

"Listen, son, don't tell me how to handle my business. This family has made a tidy sum from fishing. Dredging will affect the water quality."

"But the environmental studies say it probably won't if handled correctly." Marius drew back even though he sat a few feet from Henry. The older man glared at him.

"No Dalcour is going to get in my way ever again. See to it that she gets out of town." Henry closed the file. "I don't care how."

"What about her brothers?"

Henry waved a hand. "Andrew is harmless. All he cares about is fishing and drinking. The older boy would just as soon never come back here again." His eyes narrowed. "But Raenette is different. I want her gone."

"Darcy might not like that." Marius raised an eyebrow at him. "They were close at one time. Maybe he'd like to renew his acquaintance."

"What do you mean?" Henry said.

"Yes, Marius. Why don't you explain."

Darcy stood in the door with one hand in his pants pocket. The expensive suit had a casual style to it, his shirt open at the collar. Though his posture indicated a relaxed attitude, the glitter of animosity was in his light brown eyes.

"You two had a bad case of love." Marius did not seem in the least intimidated by his formidable cousin. "And she's still quite attractive."

"So?" Darcy did not move.

"So, maybe you figure to catch more flies with honey, as the old saying goes." Marius examined his maroon Edmonds shoes. "And you do have a way of using your charm to entice." He put emphasis on his last words, which made them sound decadent.

Fury flashed across Darcy's face for an instant before he recovered. He replaced it with indifference. "At least you understand the value of charm, though you've never quite been able to use it. Of course, there is value in being behind the scenes. Someone has to arrange for coffee and donuts."

"I helped engineer higher profits. Charm and coasting on the accomplishments of others are your best skills," Marius said with a sneer.

"That's enough." Henry sat back in his chair.

"Forget it, errand boy." Darcy abandoned his control. "You'll only get to be third banana, if you're lucky."

"You wish. I've proven my worth ten times over. What have you done lately, sweet boy?" Marius spoke in a taunting voice.

"Why you—"

Darcy crossed the room with two long steps and would have slapped Marius had not Henry been faster.

"I said that's enough!" Henry shoved Darcy back.

"I'm sick of his insults!" Darcy pointed a finger at his cousin.

Henry knocked his hand down. "The Joves have always stood together to benefit this family. Bickering will only bring you down. Remember that!"

"Yes, Darcy. Try to control yourself." Marius straightened his silk tie. He wore a smirk.

"Wipe that arrogant grin off your face, boy!" Henry snapped at Marius.

"But I—"

"Shut up!" Henry cut him off. "I spent years creating profitable businesses despite what Vincent Dalcour did to me." He wore a bitter expression. "I lost more than money to that man. Your childish fighting makes me sick."

"You're right of course, Grandfather. Sorry, Marius." Darcy nodded to his cousin. Marius gazed at him with a look of suspicion.

"I expect who ever takes over as CEO to have guts and brains. And to be able to keep this family together, Marius. Not tear it apart by being arrogant and unbending." Henry stared at Marius hard.

Marius blinked as though his grandfather had hit him with an admonishing blow. "Sorry," he mumbled to no one in particular. If the apology was meant for Darcy, it was hard to tell, since Marius did not look at him.

"Well, on to business." Darcy seemed undisturbed by his attitude. "Simon seems to at least have Rae listening to his proposal. Of course, she'd be more open to recreational use with careful planning."

"Good. I feel confident in Simon's ability to handle such a delicate negotiation." Henry nodded.

"I could have done just as well. Rae doesn't even know me." Marius sounded a touch petulant that he had been vetoed as the one to approach Rae.

"Marius, this required careful handling." Darcy smiled at him.

"You have a way of irritating people, Marius." Henry was blunt. "You're too impatient to have your own way. You can't skip right into bullying people to get what you want. A good businessman understands hardball is a last resort."

"Yes, sir." Marius bristled but said no more.

"And be sure you have leverage to force them into a corner," Darcy added.

"Exactly," Henry said. "Which we don't have with Dalcour. She has nothing to lose by holding onto that land. She could sell it later to someone else. Or directly to Pantheon."

"But we have the advantage of being able to get tax breaks for them from the parish and state government. I've let them know that," Darcy bragged.

"So? We'd still need to offer that, even if they dealt directly with her." Henry's words deflated his grandson's puffed up posture. "No, we must rely on Simon to reason with her."

"And when Simon finds out Pantheon plans to build a waste treatment plant not make underwear?" Marius glanced from Darcy to Henry.

"Won't matter. He'll have the recreation center." Henry stood up.

"What?" Darcy yelped. "Grandfather, I told Ellis we'd have all that land!"

"Simon will never stand for it. Besides, if he pulls off a sale with the Dalcours, he deserves to be dealt with fairly. Your plan requires diggin up my woods north of Glaises Creek. I won't have it." Henry stood up.

"But, Grandfather, be reasonable. Simon won't have much choice. Who would want to camp so close to a treatment plant with the truck traffic and odors?" Darcy faced Henry.

"You'll get assurances from Pantheon that won't happen." Henry said. "Simon is a smart young man who's done right by me numerous times. This is my chance to pay him back. I've closed on the Aucoin property, which means the plant can be far away from there."

Darcy's jaw muscles worked. "The best thing to do is go on with our original plans. That's what I sold to Ellis Mouton and the Pantheon people. It's close enough to the Grande River junction to make barge traffic shorter from the Mississippi."

"I don't want dredging done. It will affect our property." Henry patted his pockets then drew out his car keys. "Now, I've got a meeting."

"Grandfather, be reasonable." Darcy had finally lost patience. "I had surveys done, consulted with the Corps of Engineers—"

Henry drew himself to his full height and scowled at him. "The subject is closed, boy. We'll do things my way until I retire . . ."

"But, Ellis—"

"I don't give a damn what you told Ellis Mouton. No Mouton is going to push me into a deal I don't want." Henry stabbed a finger in the air. "You kissing his butt?"

"Of course not!" Darcy blurted out in a shocked voice. When Marius cleared his throat loudly, he shot him a threatening glance.

"Good. You've got no business making promises to Mouton, I don't care what he dangles in front of you." Henry marched out without saying goodbye.

"Grandfather knows you very well." Marius wore a sly grin.

"And knows you well enough to know you're incompetent to run Jove Enterprises," Darcy snapped.

Marius lost the grin. "He hasn't made that decision yet."

"Who did he have handle Pantheon?" Darcy lifted a shoulder.

"You're too cocky for your own good. He also said Simon

has done a lot for him." Marius looked smug as his insinuation hit home. "Oh, yes, it could be Simon."

"No, Grandfather wants a Jove to run the business." Darcy did not seem confident of his argument.

"You sure of that?" Marius goaded him.

Darcy thought for a while. "Your paranoid delusions are getting the best of you." He dismissed the notion. "Grandfather will reward Simon, but not that way. If you're really nice to me, I just might let you keep your job."

"Don't start planning on all the changes you'll make as the new boss just yet," Marius snarled. His balled up his fists.

"Goodbye, Marius. By the way, we're low on coffee down at the office." Darcy strolled out with a chuckle.

"You'll get yours, cuz," Marius mumbled. "I'll see to it."

Marcelle wiped her mouth and sighed. "It's so nice to eat somebody else's cooking for a change. I don't get out much, you know."

"Gee, I never would have guessed." Rae laughed, remembering the way Marcelle arranged for her mother-in-law to care for the baby in record time.

"It's a blessing to have two grandmothers, both of them housewives, living within fifteen miles."

Rae and Marcelle sat in Nadine's, a small po-boy shop on the highway just of out town. Marcelle was taking her time over a ham and cheese po'boy while Rae ate a fried oyster sandwich.

"Hmm-mmm, good. I missed Louisiana home cooking more than I realized." Rae had her eyes closed. She chewed the oyster with Louisiana hot sauce slowly, relishing it.

"Girl, you were lucky to be traveling all over. Going to Sweden and everything. I'd give up a little fresh seafood for a while just for that."

"It was great. You know, my band is better known in Sweden and Great Britain than in the United States. Those folks go crazy for blues. Zydeco, too." Rae thought of the enthusiastic crowds shouting for more into the early morning hours. "I did love that part."

Marcelle finished the last piece of her po-boy. "You sure you want to give that up. Hey, you said your CD is selling pretty good."

"Yeah, well." Rae fiddled, then took a deep swallow of strawberry soda. "I don't expect we'll be super stars, not playing zydeco or blues. But we made a living at it. I even managed to put away some money."

"Hey, you're spoiling my image of the party-hard blues woman living for today. Come on now, cher. I was having fun living vicariously." Marcelle grinned at her impishly.

"Oh, I partied. For a long time, I was young and stupid. I'd have a lot more money, if I hadn't been."

Rae thought of the first three years after leaving home when she concentrated on forgetting Belle Rose and Darcy. She'd come close to losing herself in drugs. A succession of men did little to ease the loneliness.

"Rae, about Darcy . . ." Marcelle glanced around to make sure no one was sitting close by. "Are you—"

"Over him? Oh, yeah." Rae gazed out of the window at cars passing. "It took me a while to figure out why he got to me."

"And?"

"He treated me special. Darcy had a way of making me feel like I was the center of his universe. I needed to feel that way, Marcelle." Rae thought of the ache being treated as an outcast caused during her childhood.

"I know. But you hid it well."

Rae reached out and squeezed Marcelle's hand. "You stuck by me when the other kids were treating me like dirt, even in high school. You're the best, girlfriend." Her voice broke. Outside her family, Marcelle had been one of the few people she could count on to stand with her.

"So are you." Marcelle squeezed her hand back. "And I'm glad you didn't let that slimy nightcrawler ruin your life."

"Teenage intensity. I thought I'd die when he cut me off cold." Rae shook her head slowly. "I wanted to be loved so badly, the oily charming surface seemed like genuine caring."

"Little weasel." Marcelle took a sip of her soft drink. "You know what? He's been sorry ever since. Had the nerve to tell me you were the most exciting woman he'd ever been with."

"Now that's pitiful," Rae said with a sharp laugh. "No wonder he's got so many ex-wives." She sighed. "Lord, I'm glad adolescence is behind me. Isn't it something how it takes all your twenties to get over it though?"

"Who's over it? I still think my nose is too big. And Carmela Tate is not forgiven," Marcelle said.

"Oh please, girl. We were fifteen. So Carmela told everyone your bra size." Rae looked at her with astonishment.

"And she waved around my little double A cup she'd sneaked from my gym locker." Marcelle was just as angry now.

"Everyone knew Carmela was a jealous big mouth. I warned you not to tell her your business. But you wouldn't listen."

"She's still like that. I saw her at mass the other day. Had the nerve to say Freddie Jr. made an eighty-nine on a quiz while her Darvin made a ninety-four. Pooh-ya!"

"Get over it, Marcelle." Rae laughed out loud. "What do you care what she says? Gee, small town life."

"That's right, Rae. Can you take it after being in big cities all this time?" Marcelle studied her.

"I've thought about that." Rae looked around her at the modest diner. "But I'm not that rebel trying desperately to make everybody sit up and take notice."

"Hey, lots of our old classmates been asking about you. Now that you're a recording star up for a Grammy, they wanna be your pal," Marcelle said.

"I'm not up for a Grammy. Where in the world did they . . . Marcelle! You didn't!" Rae's mouth hung open.

"Well . . . I might have mentioned something to Carmela. You should have seen her face." Marcelle cackled.

"Shame on you, telling tales in church."

"We were in the parking lot. Besides, I said you *might* be up for a Grammy." Marcelle put her hands on her hips. "Well, you've got as much chance as any other musician."

Rae could not refute her logic. "You're priceless." They both laughed until tears flowed. After several minutes they sat still weak, drinking soda refills.

"Seriously, Rae. Being back home means you'll run into Toya and Darcy on a regular basis."

"I've already seen Toya." Rae felt a tightening in her stomach.

"And?"

"She said hello, I said hello. That was about it." Rae shrugged.

"For now. You keep meeting with her ex and the claws will come out." Marcelle nodded with vigor.

"What do you think of Simon St. Cyr?" Rae tried to make the question sound casual. She remembered the warm, tangy smell of his cologne. It pulled her to him, making it hard to keep her mind on his talk of wetlands and tourism.

"The man is fine. He's got a body that won't quit. Girl, that chest, those arms, thighs like steel, and a cute—"

"Marcelle, you're a married woman." Rae cut her off.

"I'm married, not dead. I can enjoy the view." Marcelle gave her a sassy wink.

"I meant what kind of person is he? A great body and handsome face isn't everything."

"So you agree he's superfine, eh?" Marcelle leaned forward to peer into Rae's eyes.

"He looks okay. But I'm more interested in how to deal with him. Can he be trusted?" Rae fiddled with the straw in her glass without looking at Marcelle.

"You think he's hot, admit it." Marcelle poked her with a finger.

"Will you grow up? This isn't junior high, for goodness sakes."

"Rae, don't try to fool me."

"I ask you a simple question and you gotta get all into this stuff." Rae huffed.

"Well, that answered my question. And I hear he gave you the look, too." Marcelle wiggled her eyebrows. "Miss Jarreau says that day he came up to you downtown he was really smiling and Toya was furious. She said—"

"Give me a break! I just met the man. He seems like a nice person." Rae thought of the handsome profile. A finger of heat traced a line up her back. "With a great smile and sexy voice. So what?" She stared out the window toward town as though trying to see him.

"Beep-beep-beep, danger ahead!" Marcelle said in a sing-song voice. "You're gonna have a serious Jones for that man, if you don't watch yourself."

"Get real. Simon St. Cyr is not going to use any fake charm on me. Bet he's got as much moral fibre as Darcy. The St. Cyrs and the Joves hung together dumping on my family." Rae tried to conjure up the old bitter feelings to counteract her reaction to the sensuous man.

"The Joves more than the St. Cyrs. Simon wasn't even part of that since he was older than us and went to a prep school in New Orleans." Marcelle eyed her. "And he's nothing like Darcy, or most of the young men around here. Except for my Freddie, of course."

"Oh, really?" Rae affected a nonchalant attitude. She sat back in her chair in a casual pose.

"He's got a reputation for being honest in business." Marcelle's lips twitched with mirth at the studied indifference Rae tried to convey. "As for women, the talk is he's a real gentleman."

Rae considered this statement. In Louisiana being called a real gentleman meant he treated women with respect without lying or sleeping around. Very interesting. So Simon St. Cyr was an upstanding citizen, as far as anyone knew. That did not mean she should trust him.

"All the same, I'm going to check out his proposal seven different ways from Sunday, as the old folks say." Rae lifted her chin. "He's not going to fool me with superficial charm."

"Right. Judging from the look on your face when his name came up, I'd say you don't think his charm is all that phony." Marcelle leaned forward and tapped her arm.

"It's business."

Rae thought of her promise to Lucien. It was all so complicated. To find out what happened to Pawpaw Vincent, she needed money. Getting the dance hall in shape the way she wanted would take a sizable amount of cash. But what would

Lucien really think of selling even a small portion of their land to a St. Cyr, much less almost two thirds. *Coming home has opened up old wounds and a new can of worms.* Rae wondered how she could stay true to herself and her father.

"Your daddy would understand if you can't handle all this on your own, Rae." Marcelle seemed to read her thoughts as usual.

"There's got to be another way. I can't let St. Cyr and Darcy think they're my only chance." Rae tapped out a beat on the tabletop.

"If I could, I'd float you a loan. Of course, pennies won't help," Marcelle chuckled.

"That's it!" Rae hugged Marcelle. "Sugar, why didn't you slap some sense into my head before now."

"What?" Marcelle wore a baffled expression

"I'll apply for a loan from the bank. Of course I'll need a business plan. Only part of the property could be used as collateral." Rae looked pleased with herself.

"If you say so. But . . ." Marcelle looked doubtful.

"Then I can let Simon St. Cyr know he's not the only game in town."

"Henry Jove sits on First Federal's board of directors. You think he's going to let you get a loan?" Marcelle shook her head.

"Damn, it was nice while it lasted." Rae slumped back in her chair. She sat forward again with a determined expression. "If push comes to shove, I'll put it on my MasterCard."

"Sure you will," Marcelle said with a wave of her hand. Her eyes went wide at the look on Rae's face. "You're not joking!"

"Nope. I'll listen to Simon St. Cyr. But he won't pull the wool over my eyes with his smiling face." Rae wore a smug smile.

"You sure are hot to deny Simon St. Cyr had an effect on you." Marcelle gazed at her. "Doesn't sound like just business to me."

"Well, it is," Rae said. She lifted a shoulder in a careless gesture. "If I let him get close, it would only be to drive Toya crazy. Which doesn't seem like a bad thing at all, the more I think of it."

"Just be careful. You might start off pretending and find the only person you've trapped is yourself." Marcelle said.

"Hey, I've got it under control."

Rae felt a tickle of uneasiness despite her words. The smell and feel of Simon standing close rushed back with a vengeance. Why did he have to look at her with those soulful brown eyes? Why did he have to look so . . . delectable? She pushed away beginning speculation of how his arms would feel around her. *Stop that! Simon St. Cyr is just another man, period.* Rae steeled herself against any more stupid fantasies about a man who could very well be in a conspiracy to trick her. Now all she had to do was figure out a way keep him out of her head for good.

Five

High thin clouds, like cotton balls, drifted across the blue sky. An occasional breeze rustled the green leaves of trees bordering the bayou. Rae stood next to Simon trying hard to keep her mind on business. The lovely weather made it hard to concentrate on such dry matters as surveys, water quality studies, and profit margins. Simon, dressed in a tan cotton sport shirt and jeans, made it even more difficult. Rae kept mentally nudging herself to remember he was a St. Cyr. Yet every time he walked away, her mind flipped the page back to very unbusinesslike activities they could engage in on such a day. He was no muscle-bound type, but his broad chest and shoulders were built well all the same.

"Or do you think this would be too close?" Simon was pointing to something with his back to Rae.

"Hmm?" Rae watched the movement of his shoulders as his arms moved.

"Yeah, maybe the visitors center should be farther down from your property." Simon looked back toward Lucien's house, though it was not visible at this distance. "Don't want too much traffic near your home, right?"

"Uh-huh." Rae followed him, noticing how small beads of sweat stood out on his brown skin. Especially on his top lip. She imagined the taste, a mixture of salty and sweet.

"Of course, it probably won't be a mob of folks. More like a steady trickle most days. But, of course, summers when kids are out of school or on holiday, it could get crowded."

"You bet," Rae said right over his shoulder. She did not move when he turned suddenly to find them almost nose to nose.

"What do you think so far?" Simon spoke in a quiet voice. He looked into her eyes steadily.

"So far, so good." Rae smiled at him. "Show me more," she murmured. She wondered for only a split second if this was wise. But Rae had never been the shy retiring type.

Simon swallowed. "Right. Well, here we have . . ." He tried to open out the rolled up plans but dropped them instead. He bent over to retrieve them.

"Nice view," Rae said.

He straightened up and turned sharply to face her. She was gazing out over the water.

"Yes. It is." Simon's full mouth lifted at one corner. "Ms. Dalcour . . ."

"Call me Rae." She smiled at him sweetly.

"And you can call me Simon."

Rae's heart thumped at the sound of his deep voice inviting her to become more intimate. Was there more? She brushed a stray tendril of hair from her eyes. Simon watched the movement of her hands. Rae could feel a pull between them. Suddenly, she was anxious and unsure whether she was as much in control as she thought.

"Well, Simon, you haven't mentioned environmental impact studies." Rae moved away from him, off balance for the first time with a man this close.

"They've been done. We're just waiting for the written report. Preliminary findings are that our plans for park management would mean little if any negative effect." Simon studied her for a moment.

"Yes, the plans for waste disposal and park rangers." Rae knew all this. She'd read the bound report.

"Of course, I can't guarantee no pollution. But it will at least be kept natural."

"With folks trampling all over the place, I doubt it." Rae crossed her arms and stared at him in challenge.

Simon did not flinch. "True, but—"

"And you don't really know how much pollution there would be."

"We can keep it clean. According to the plans, the state will help," Simon said.

Rae snorted. "Please! You can't count on them. This is a backwater town with a population that's forty-nine percent black. Daddy always said it's why this parish had to fight for everything."

"True. Since the 1930s, we've been scuffling to get our share of public works for the taxes we pay. But things began to change in the fifties."

"You think so, huh? Well, I'd have to see it to believe it." Rae was more skeptical of the system since she had experience being outside it.

Simon looked confident. He had the experience of a man who'd been on the inside forcing things to work. "I'm not saying it's perfect. But we've got the Legislative Black Caucus and several white politicians working for us."

Rae strolled toward the edge of the muddy water. "Sounds good. But I don't know."

"Listen, people have been coming on your property for years fishing, tubing, and having picnics. Mr. Lucien once complained to me that he was constantly running off kids who'd trashed up the place." Simon walked to stand next to her.

"Daddy talked to you?" Rae's eyebrows went up with surprise.

"I'd see him around town sometimes. At first he just gave me the eye when I spoke to him." Simon grinned.

"Yeah, Daddy could give you a look that made you back up quick." Rae grinned back.

"Then one day I was fishing down at Old River. He was there. After a while, we were talking about bait, which fish were running, and stuff like that." Simon shrugged. "I think he was curious about me more than anything. But he never asked about Papa Joe," he finished in a quiet voice.

The mention of his grandfather brought in the past that had separated their families. Both were silent for a time.

"You're right. Andrew and Daddy couldn't keep all this property clean. Though they tried." Rae took a deep breath. "Like I said, I'll talk to my brothers."

"I know Andrew will be a hard sell. I've only said hello to him over the years." Simon smiled. "He seems like a nice guy."

"Yeah, he's easygoing. He tries to be mean about what happened between our grandfathers, but it's hard for Andrew to hold a grudge against anybody really." Rae smiled with affection, thinking of her brother. "It's just not in his nature to carry on feuds."

"And Neville?" Simon stood totally at ease talking to her about her family.

"He's the serious type. Hard-working, nose to the grindstone. Temperament like my Mama's brothers." Rae had never thought of it before but it was true. Neville was like Uncle Ted and Uncle Johnny. "But he thinks we should sell at least some of the land."

"Sounds like a nice guy, too."

"Yeah, they're my darling big brothers," Rae said. She thought of how they had taught her to fish, hunt, and swim in this bayou. Rae adored them with the intensity she'd felt for Lucien. Emotion clogged her throat.

"Rae, I wouldn't do anything to ruin Bayou Latte or Creole Bend," Simon said.

The sound of his voice saying her name sent a shiver up Rae's spine. Down deep in her core, she believed him. Rae felt as though the ground beneath her feet was undulating, moving her closer to him. A shout from a passing fisherman in a bateau broke the spell. *What in the world is wrong with you, girl?* No man had pushed her buttons like this. Not even Darcy at the height of her raging hormonal teen years. This was more dangerous. She was a woman now capable of making a much bigger mistake falling for the wrong man. Rae shook herself. Simon was not going to sucker her. She would command whatever happened between them.

"You said something about a free meal, if I recall." She resumed her brass and sass attitude in defense against the strong signals Simon was sending out.

"Uh, sure. Arnaud's okay?" Simon wiped his forehead. He

let her follow him to his Ford Explorer and opened the passenger door for her.

Rae got in. "Fine with me."

Arnaud's was a restaurant near downtown Belle Rose that looked out over the Grande River. Paintings of swamp scenes and Acadian houses hung on the walls. There was one large window facing the water. Double doors led to a patio. The waiter pointed to a table right near the window.

"Afternoon, I'm Walter." The waiter spoke in his musical Cajun accent. "Is this okay? You want, you could have an outside table."

"It's so nice. Let's sit outside." Simon turned to Rae who nodded.

Rae spoke to several people as they followed the waiter to their table. Since they were earlier than the usual lunchtime crowd, there were several empty tables. Both ordered iced tea.

"Everything looks good." Simon glanced over the menu. "But I'll have my usual, a fried catfish platter."

"Oh, come on," Rae teased. "Live a little, be adventurous."

Simon wore a shy smile. "Afraid I'm not the adventurous type."

"You walked right up to me that day." Rae leaned forward. "Tell the truth, how many people warned you I was a woman likely to take a chunk out of a St. Cyr?"

"Well . . ." Simon was flustered.

"How many?"

"A few. I didn't believe them though." Simon looked at her, a gleam in his eyes. "You didn't look like you'd bite."

Rae lowered her voice. "I thought about it."

Simon looked down at their hands resting against each other on the red checkered cloth. "Wh—?"

"Y'all ready to order?" Walter beamed at them, pen ready. He flipped to a new page on his order pad.

Rae went on right into light banter with the waiter without missing a beat. Simon stared at her. The woman kept lighting his fire! That voice, husky and velvet smooth at the same time, almost had him in knots. Not to mention she could make the most ordinary sentences sound seductive. Or was she flirting with him? Maybe his fevered reaction to her added sensuous overtones that were only in his mind. Simon tried not to stare as she questioned the waiter about several entrées. He guessed she was at least five foot seven. Her full curves were a feast for the eyes, causing several men to look up in appreciation as they walked through the restaurant. She wore stone-washed denim pants and a white knit sleeveless blouse with red stripes along the V-neck. Papa Joe and the others were right. Rae Dalcour definitely had bite. Trouble was, he liked it.

"I'll have the charbroiled shrimp." Rae handed the menu to Walter, who bustled off. "Now you were saying?"

"Would you like to have dinner?" Simon glanced at her then away. Rae Dalcour made him feel like he was an awkward teenager again.

"We haven't had lunch yet, cher," Rae quipped. "My head is spinning." She chuckled.

"Guess I assumed too much." Simon was surprised at the sharp sense of disappointment he felt.

"That wasn't a no, Simon," Rae said.

Simon looked up to find her brown eyes held no hint of rejection. His heart turned over. She was smiling. Simon liked the way she said his name with that voice of hers. He wanted to make her smile for him again and again.

"Tonight?" Simon said.

"You don't waste time, do you?"

"Not when I'm this sure."

Simon shocked himself with this admission. But it was true. He wanted to get closer to her. Simon pushed down his grandfather's warning voice and gave in to the feeling. This was no ordinary attraction. He wanted to know her in every way.

Rae raised her eyebrows at him. "We're straying onto dangerous ground here. What will your family say? And the Joves won't be thrilled either."

"I'm grown. But if you're worried your family won't approve . . ." Simon lifted a shoulder. He wore a slight smile with a teasing glint in his eyes.

"My family doesn't tell me what to do with my personal

life." Rae laughed and leaned forward. "Tonight is fine. Besides, it's just a date. Right?"

"Right," Simon said. He knew better deep down. But he tried to put a light tone to his voice.

They enjoyed the rest of lunch without mentioning the possible complications of seeing each other. Simon enjoyed the easy flow of conversation between them. It was as though they'd sat together like this many times. They would sometimes fall silent, but it was not the awkward kind of silence so common between a man and woman just meeting. Without remembering just how they got there, Simon was telling her about his dreams for the business. He talked about his family and was lost in her account about the Dalcours. They talked on until the lunch crowd was sparse again.

"I never realized how hard it was on you all after your grandfather left," Simon said.

"Humph, folks in Belle Rose got a long memory. They blame us because the money that would have brought a major business into the black community disappeared. The Moutons and other white families still control most of the wealth in this parish." Rae wore a bitter expression. "We were treated like dirt."

"Amazing that you would be harassed for what your grandfather did."

"What folks *say* he did. They didn't prove it," Rae said in a clipped tone.

"Of course. I'm sorry." Simon covered her hand with his. "There is no proof even after all these years." They both stared at their hands, his large fingers entwined around her slender ones. *A nice fit.*

"Y'all want some more tea?" Walter stood holding a pitcher.

"No. I'm sloshing every time I move as it is." Rae shook her head.

"Me neither." Simon waited for Walter to leave. "I'm really looking forward to tonight, Rae." He gazed at her eyes, her lips.

"So am I. Let's go to Pas Patout afterward. Or don't you dance?" The teasing came back to Rae's voice.

"I can hang. Two step, swing out, all the old standards." Simon smiled.

"Then it's going to be some night." Rae's voice dropped an octave.

Simon decided to join the game. "Hope I can live up to your expectations."

Rae gave him an appraising glance from head to toe. "Oh, I'd say you can hang."

Walter brought the check, which forced Simon to let go of her hand. On the short drive down the highway to her house, the silence between them was heavy. Both were wrapped in thought. Simon wondered if Rae was experiencing the same rush as he.

"Well, thanks for an interesting day. And lunch." Rae said. She smiled at him. "See you tonight."

"Say around six?"

"Perfect." She winked at him and hopped down from the Explorer. "Don't forget your dancing shoes." With a wave, she walked away.

Simon blinked, feeling as though he was coming out of a daydream. Had it really happened so easily as that? In a heartbeat he was going out with the infamous Rae Dalcour. She was right, Papa Joe would ask if he'd lost his sanity. And Toya . . . Simon did not even want to think about it. But they would not be the only people in town questioning his judgment. He turned up the radio and swayed to the beat of a pop tune. They'd all have to adjust.

Six

"Girl, you gotta a lot of work on your hands." Marcelle stepped over a broken piece of chair. She looked around Lucien's old dance hall.

"Hey, I've been cleaning up some. You should have seen it four days ago." Rae stood in the middle of the large room with both hands on her hips.

The old juke joint had definitely seen better days. The sign with ROCKIN' GOOD TIMES in red letters was propped against one of the walls. Rae had brought it inside after finding it hanging lop-sided over the front door. The bar was along one wall of the main room. Tables were within a few feet of it. Then the dance floor took up a good part of the space with a raised bandstand opposite the bar. Windows let in light from the bright morning sun. Through a door just past the end of the bar was a hall that led to restrooms. Another short hall led to a kitchen. The equipment looked to be in need of repair or replacement. There were two other rooms, one for storage and the other used as an office.

"This place is bigger than I thought." Marcelle flipped a light switch. "Hey, you got lights."

"Guess who paid for it?" Rae took out her notepad and reviewed everything she'd need to have done.

"Your Mama," Marcelle said promptly.

"Yeah. Mama thinks this is a real bad idea but said she didn't want me to break my neck stumbling in the dark. Mr. George says he wants him a good party spot." Rae gave a short laugh. "He's something."

"Mr. George is a sweet man. And he's crazy about Miss Aletha, too." Marcelle stacked up glasses in a box to be washed. "I mean, no disrespect to your daddy."

"Don't be silly. I love him for making Mama happy." Rae paused in writing down items. "Daddy pushed Mama away. Seems like he poured all his energy into this place and the past."

"What does Neville think?" Marcelle took a large bottle of liquid cleaner and sprayed the tile bar top.

"Well, I talked to him on the phone about possibly selling the land. He's coming over this weekend." Rae glanced at Marcelle. "I was surprised. He wasn't too keen on selling to a St. Cyr."

"Um-humm. Even Neville, who's been preaching you should unload all this, has doubts." Marcelle eyed her old pal. "You got that old look about you these days."

"What are you talking about?" Rae put down the pad. She began to remove the tattered remains of curtains from the windows.

"The time you stalked Celeste Gravier for calling you trash, you had that same look."

Rae finished one window and started another. "I did not stalk Celeste. And what look? This is my normal look."

"That 'I'm up to something that's gonna blow your mind' look. Just like with Celeste."

"No way." Rae smiled despite her protest. "Wonder how old Celeste is?"

"You made that girl's life hell for a week at school. First a dead rat in her gym bag, then dirty pictures in her desk for the teacher to find. She'd jump every time you walked by." Marcelle giggled. "You were terrible. Didn't we have some times?"

"Yeah, until the priest made you reform. Then all you did was preach to me how I was going straight to hell." Rae shook her head. "How did we stay friends when we were so different?"

"You were my adopted sister." Marcelle packed the last glasses away. "I couldn't give up on you."

"I almost gave up on myself." Rae thought of those fast-lane days with the wisdom of maturity. "With all those folks telling me I was no good, I believed it. I was living up to the Dalcour legend."

"Bon Dieu! Remember when you and Charles Malveaux almost got arrested racing his car on top the levee. Honey, I had my hands full tryin' to set you straight."

"I must have been out of my mind. It's a wonder I'm not in prison or dead, some of the stuff I did." Rae shook her head slowly.

"So what are you up to now?" Marcelle walked up to her.

"Marcelle, I'm not that fifteen-year-old girl anymore. I'm here trying to start a business. That's all." Rae lifted her chin.

"There, you see. That's part of the truth, but not all of it. What did you promise Mr. Lucien?" Marcelle plopped down in a chair. She fanned herself with an old piece of cardboard. "Give it up."

Rae turned and started pulling down another rotting curtain. "Just that I wouldn't let the house or this place fall down."

"And?" Marcelle's sharp question jabbed through the air.

Rae could hold it in no longer. She never kept secrets from her best friend. "And I'm going to try to get at the truth about Pawpaw Vincent. I'm hiring LaMar Zeno." She sat down in the chair across the table from Marcelle.

Marcelle stared with her mouth hanging open. "Quit lying, girl!"

"If I'm lying, I'm flying, as we used to say. I got him coming over tomorrow." Rae tapped the tabletop before she jumped up. She spoke over her shoulder as she moved to the next window. "He's going to find out the truth, Marcelle. I can just feel it."

"Well if anybody can, it's LaMar Zeno. He's the best black private detective around, they say. He even helps some major corporations with industrial spying. Freddie told me that."

"Just hope he won't refuse when I tell him he's looking for two people who vanished fifty years ago." Rae frowned. "I'll convince him though. I hear he loves solving a good puzzle."

"Then he'll jump at the chance to take this case." Marcelle was silent for a while. "And then there's you and Simon St. Cyr. Heard y'all was mighty cozy at lunch."

"Man, I'd forgotten how fast news travels in this place." Rae dodged the implied question.

"Keeping in other folks' business is a major sport around here." Marcelle fixed her with a steady gaze. "But the point is, you were getting along very well with Simon."

"He's a nice person. Why shouldn't we get along?"

"Raenette Marie Dalcour, don't play with me." Marcelle got up and yanked on her blouse. "Tell me this instant." With a firm hand, she led Rae back to the chair. "Sit your butt down and don't move until I know everything."

"Nothing much to tell. We had lunch, talked and . . . we're going out tonight for dinner." Rae laughed at the effect of her words on Marcelle.

"Quit lying!" Marcelle's eyes were round and her mouth fell open this time.

Rae winked at Marcelle. "He's picking me up in a few short hours. So let's get to work. I'll need time to look my best by six."

Marcelle became serious. "Rae, I know we've been joking around about the old days and stuff, but . . ."

"But what?"

"Messing with them Joves is like teasing a yard full of pit bulls."

"They don't run this town and they sure as hell don't run me." Rae ripped a curtain in half then stuffed it into a garbage bag with force.

"Just reminding you how Toya can be, cher. Now when she finds out about you and Simon, pooh-ya!" Marcelle said.

"You know me, sugar. I don't take crap." Rae faced her with a daring grin.

"Simon is a sexy guy. Nice, too." Marcelle went back to work cleaning the bar. "You'll make a good pair."

"Wait a minute. Simon St. Cyr hasn't bowled me over with his charm. I don't dance to anybody's tune but my own," Rae said with heat.

"Like you said, I know you. Simon has made more of an impression on you than you think, or maybe wanna admit." Marcelle gazed at her across the space between them.

"No way. Look, so he's nice. But he's not exactly my speed." Rae affected an offhanded tone.

Rae turned her back to avoid Marcelle's probing look. She did not want to feel this racing in her veins when she thought of seeing him tonight. Or the tingle on her skin where he touched her.

"I hope you know what you're doing. With the investigation *and* Simon St. Cyr." Marcelle scrubbed at the tiles. "Remember what my grandmama says, 'Keep it up, missy, an' you gonna get more than you bargained for.' "

"Don't go getting all spooky on me, girl. Whew, we've done enough for today. It's time for you to go get little Felicia anyway," Rae said.

Rae and Marcelle chatted about other things as they packed up to leave. Rae wanted to distract her friend from any more talk of Simon especially. Yet a cloud now hung over the bright afternoon that was not in the sky overhead. Marcelle's grandmother had a reputation for having the gift. More than seeing the future, Monmon Perrine could look below the surface of present events and human behavior, advising others of what they should do. Rae tried to tame the creeping anxiety that Marcelle's words brought on. She would not let old superstitions rule her.

Everything had been going just fine, until they played that song. The sound of the guitar wrapped around the room in the slow, bluesy strain. Now Rae found herself fighting a feeling she'd sworn would not overtake her. Simon's cheek resting against hers made it so hard though.

From the moment he'd picked her up, Rae was comfortable. She resumed her confident demeanor, determined that she would set the pace for whatever developed between them. Dinner went well. They went to Pat's, a large seafood restaurant right on the water near Henderson Swamp. The Creole dishes were spicy, and Rae added her cocky humor to the flavor of tabasco. Simon contrasted his conventional childhood to hers. He even seemed to enjoy her gentle teasing about his staid lifestyle, what's more he made a few jokes about himself. Yes, Rae was on firm ground. Now this pounding in her heart that reached down to her hips, making her want to press closer to him, would not be reasoned away. The singer stretched out the words to the old blues melody "I Need Your Love" as though he was alone with his lover. His voice had clear, slinky smoothness perfect for singing the blues.

After a time, Rae forgot to fight the feeling. The words to the song echoed a poignant note that found a responsive chord in her. For too long she'd been without a special someone. She not only thought this someone was not a necessity in her life, but was something she did not want. In fact, Rae distrusted the head-over-heels kind of love. In her experience, this kind of love led to misery and betrayal. Now the blues singer was making her believe she'd been the one kidding herself.

"Rae, maybe we better sit down," Simon murmured in her ear. He made no move to take his arms from around her. His body still swayed.

"Humm?" Rae's eyes were closed, her face resting against his shoulder. "Why?" She enjoyed the weightless feeling of serenity.

Simon chuckled. "Because the band is taking a break."

"Oh." With great effort, Rae shook herself free of the spell. She looked around to find the other dancers going back to their seats. "Yeah, I knew that."

"Sure." Simon looked down at her with amusement. "Some song, eh?"

Rae was annoyed by the smug look on his face. "It was okay." Her attempt at nonchalance missed the mark even to her ears. Still she put on a strong front.

Simon ordered them two more drinks and waited until the waiter was gone before speaking. "So, tell me about your band. You haven't talked about your career much."

"Let's see, three of us met in school. Jamal and Wes were in the music department with me at Southern University. We were all on scholarship."

"Really? I thought . . ." Simon faltered. "I didn't mean—"

"You thought I barely got out of high school from the stories about what a crazy teenager I was, right?"

"Gossip does get exaggerated." Simon looked abashed. "I should have known better."

"It's okay. In this case, most of the stories you probably heard had a lot of truth to them." Rae wiggled her eyebrows at him comically.

Simon laughed. "Stop that. Now tell me about the band."

"Not much to tell. Me and the guys hooked up about a year after graduation. We worked the club circuit and college concerts hard. It paid off."

"You've got two great recordings and made a couple of national charts. I'd say you have reason to be proud." Simon looked at her with genuine admiration in his sepia eyes.

Rae returned his gaze. "Thanks." She looked away after a while, feeling awkward for the first time.

"And you're going to give up the excitement of a successful career to settle back in Belle Rose?"

"Weird, huh? Like I missed the place." Rae shook her head.

"Not at all. It just means you loved your father deeply. You have a sense of family." Simon nodded when she looked at him. "So you're going to open the dance hall."

"Hey, before you nominate me for sainthood you need to know something." Rae smiled at him. "I'm going to play my guitar every chance I get. So I'm not giving up my career."

"Sounds great."

"Yeah, Wes and I even talked about setting up a recording studio of our own." Rae sat forward.

"Even better."

"Sure. We've got friends who would love to have a good place to make their own recordings. Wes even has some investors interested."

"That would be good for the local economy. You could bring in jobs. But just as important, more sales tax if visitors spend money while in town." Simon rubbed his jaw in thought.

"Yeah, I hate that all the new jobs come from the petrochemical plants. We're too dependent on them. Besides, most of the real poor folks don't benefit. The way drugs have gotten to the kids even around the bayou just breaks my heart." Rae lifted a shoulder. "We need something better in our community."

"Careful now. You'll spoil that bad girl image you enjoy so much." Simon wore a grin.

"Nah, not me." Rae giggled.

"But won't you miss the thrill of traveling?"

"Truth is, being on the road all the time was getting old. When Daddy asked me to consider coming home four years ago, I thought he was nuts. But now I want more than moving from one booking to the next, you know?"

"I see. You'd like to build something," Simon said.

"Yeah, I guess so. I hadn't thought of it like that. But not just for me."

"For your father."

"Daddy wanted me to make some kind of good legacy for his grandchildren. Better than he'd done, he said." Rae's throat tightened. She wondered how long before the lump of grief would dissolve.

Simon put a hand on her arm. "He was a good person in his heart. That's where it counts, Rae."

"It took me a long time to appreciate it though. Too long. I mean, he had lots of faults. But he tried his best."

"And that's all that anybody can do. I wish my father understood that. He's always arguing with Papa Joe." Simon pressed his lips together in an expression of disapproval.

"Really? I didn't think you rich folks had any troubles," Rae quipped. "To hear some talk, the Joves and St. Cyrs have it made."

"Not by a long shot. Money doesn't protect you from everything," Simon said quickly.

"It sure helps a helluva lot." Rae raised an eyebrow at him.

"Listen, I'm not going to say having money isn't important. It's just not the answer to all of life's problems."

"Better not let Henry Jove hear you talking like that." Rae decided to take a chance. "Or Toya."

"Too late, we've already had our battles about what's real," Simon said with a grimace. He glanced at her. "Which brings us to a touchy subject. I'm sure you know by now that Toya and I were married."

"I'd heard." Rae did not say more, preferring to let him talk.

"Let's just say we had different ideas about how we wanted to live." Simon stared down into his glass. "And that was that."

"It happens." Rae doubted very much that Toya would agree that Simon was in her past. She wondered just how much feeling Simon still had for Toya. They sat silent for a while. The band was back playing a quiet instrumental selection.

"Rae, I've really enjoyed being with you tonight. More than just another date." Simon took a deep breath. "I know there's some bad history between our families, but . . ."

"That's an understatement. My father didn't have one good word to say about Joves or St. Cyrs all the time I was growing up. And I can guess what you've heard about the Dalcours."

"The thing is I want to see more of you. I'm prepared for the flak." Simon gazed at her. "I don't care what anybody says."

"Including your grandfather and Mr. Henry?" Rae felt a flutter in her chest.

"Yes. This isn't some passing fancy either. I don't just want to date, I want to be with you," Simon said in a soft voice. He held her hands in his. "You understand what I'm saying?"

Rae could only nod. She understood only too well. Simon was pulling her headlong into a place that scared her. He was promising her heaven with those liquid brown eyes, making her want to lose herself in them. Then a tiny voice reminded her of the way she'd fallen for the sweet lies of another man with inviting eyes, Darcy. Not only that, but all the other men she had met who were experts at deception. Discovering the ugly truth beneath the attractive surface of a lover was a pain she did not need. Still, Simon was not like any other man. There weren't any suave lines or moves to impress her. He was straightforward, down to earth. A refreshing change. Maybe her older brother was right. Maybe she should forget the past. Rae leaned closer to him.

"Simon, I—"

"Well." Toya stood over them, her lips twisted to give her a sour grimace. A handsome man was right behind her looking dismayed.

"Hello to you, too, Toya," Rae said. "Yes, it is a lovely evening." She flashed a toothy smile.

Toya shot her a look full of poison. "Discussing business no doubt." She stared hard at Simon who squirmed.

"Hello, Toya. How's it going, Adrian." Simon pretended not to notice her displeasure. "Adrian Wilson, this is Rae Dalcour." He introduced him to Rae, since obviously Toya would not. Adrian was from a prominent family that lived in Petite Couteau, a small community twenty-five miles southeast of Belle Rose.

"It's going," Adrian replied in a tone full of meaning.

Toya either ignored or did not recognize the criticism of her manners. "With all this meeting, the negotiations must be going well." Toya turned to Rae. "You'll be back on the road soon, I'm sure."

"Oh I really like what I've heard so far." Rae gazed at Simon for a moment before looking back at Toya. "Even more reason to stay."

"You didn't fit in even when you lived here," Toya said. "Belle Rose was always too boring for you. I can't imagine you'll be satisfied in this country town."

"Oh, I can." Rae inched toward Simon. "I can imagine being very satisfied," she purred.

"Rae agrees to our plans for Bayou Latte. We went over the whole layout this morning." Simon spoke to her in an even tone. "Remember how much you liked it?"

"You came up with a great idea, Simon. If only you can carry it out. Most of that property has not been available." Toya's tone implied that the Dalcours had blocked progress for years.

"I think we can retain a good portion for private owners and even preserve it. Toya, came up with a few of the ideas, Rae." Simon wore a placating smile for his ex-wife. "Didn't you?"

"The visitors center for one." Toya loosened up a bit at the recognition of her contribution.

Rae felt her stomach tighten. She wanted to throw her now watered down drink in Simon's face. What a sickening sight.

Simon went on to deflect Toya's wrath with more chitchat that played to her ego. *Look at them. The bourgeosie mutual admiration society.* Watching Simon, Toya, and Adrian brought back the wide gulf between the Dalcours and them. Simon would forever be part of their world. The world of fancy cars, private schools, and all the little luxuries money could buy. She'd been a fool to think Simon was different. Rae made a rude noise when they started talking about the latest news of their social set.

"Well, guess we should be moving on." Simon wore a weak smile for Rae. It faded at the scowl she gave him.

Toya appeared satisfied to be the source of Rae's bad temper. "No, no. Don't let us spoil your night. Bye, Simon." She brushed her fingertips against his face in a gesture of intimacy then flounced off. Adrian followed in her wake.

"Why hasn't anyone declawed that woman before now?" Rae said. She hated how Toya wore the expensive cotton dress, a simple red shift, with such style. Rae looked down at her floral wrap skirt with discontent.

"Toya can be hard to take, but she's had a lot of rough times," Simon said.

"Yeah, getting your way all the time can be really taxing on the spirit."

"Mr. Henry does indulge her a lot. But Toya has an insecurity that makes her so demanding."

"Poor misunderstood Toya. My heart bleeds." Rae sipped her drink then grimaced.

"Let me get you another one." Simon waved for a waiter.

"Don't bother. Look, it's late. I've got things to do tomorrow, so let's go." Rae did not wait for him to reply. She stood up and headed for the nearest exit. In minutes they were sitting in his Explorer outside her house.

Simon cut the engine. "Did I do or say something wrong?"

"Everything's cool." Rae looked straight ahead.

"Downright freezing is more accurate." Simon waited for a few moments. "Just because Toya and I are divorced doesn't mean I hate her. Actually, I understand her better than I did ten years ago."

"Isn't that so nineties. Congratulations, I now pronounce you man and witch." Rae sat stiff, still not looking at him.

Simon reached out to touch her but pulled back when Rae moved away. "I wasn't putting on some act before Toya showed, if that's what you're thinking. I don't operate like that."

"Oh, yeah? Just how do you operate?" Rae wisecracked.

She did not want to feel so much anger. It meant she cared too much. Simon had almost succeeded in making her forget the old rules. Those rules said she was not part of the "right" family. Damn him for touching a secret place she thought was well protected.

"Don't do this. Please." Simon rested a hand on her upper arm, his skin pressed against hers. "I never took you for the jealous type."

"Jealous?" Rae sputtered. Now she was truly outraged. "I barely know you and you think I'm jealous. What an ego."

"Stop it!" Simon's usually mild voice rang with annoyance. "What you think matters to me." He ran a hand through his dark, short hair. "It matters to me very much."

Rae fought an internal war. Half of her wanted to relent. The other half did not trust him at all. Rae came to a quick compromise.

"Sorry for acting so silly," she mumbled in a muted apology. "Guess I let Toya get to me. She's been able to grate on my nerves in a special way since we were six years old."

"It's time to let go of all that history." Simon leaned toward her. "Can we call a truce?"

After a few seconds, Rae smiled at him. "Sure. As a gesture of peace, I'll offer you the hospitality of my humble home. It's not like the big fine houses you're used to . . ."

"The family estate is much smaller than you think." Simon chuckled. He followed her to the door.

"Voilà." Rae swept a hand around the living room.

"This I like," Simon said. He gazed around.

"Thanks." Rae could hear the openness in his voice.

She'd never thought of the house as capable of impressing anyone. It was a simple, modified Acadian style home. But there was a touch of African hut to the way their grandfather had made the sloping roof. The house was constructed of cypress wood with four large bedrooms in addition to a kitchen, dining room, and living room. One bathroom was added when Lucien was a boy. Inside, decorations consisted mostly of simple carvings and mud paintings done by local craftsmen. These were mostly by Lucien's friends who created them as hobbies.

"This one is my favorite." Simon picked up a small figurine of a brown pelican.

"You should have seen this place before I cleaned up. Daddy was no housekeeper," Rae said. "Luckily cypress lasts forever. He didn't spend much time on repairs either. The plumbing is a mess."

"He was kind of sick toward the end." Simon gazed at the scattering of family pictures on a table.

"That didn't help. But trust me, Lucien was not into cleaning up even when he was in good health." Rae chuckled with affection for her father.

"You were a cute kid." Simon held up a picture of Rae standing between her brothers. "What were you? About ten?"

Rae peered at the photo. "Yeah. Man, look at those knobby knees. Wait, don't look at that one." She reached for a gold framed picture too late. Simon snatched it out of reach.

"Oh this is lovely." Simon grinned at her. He gazed at a picture of Rae at four in a bathing suit.

"That is so embarrassing."

"You look quite fetching. Is that a little yellow rubber duckie you're holding? The infamous Rae Dalcour had a yellow duckie?" Simon threw back his head and laughed.

"Give me that." Rae took the picture from him. She gave him a light swat on the shoulder. "Go on. Have fun."

"Goodness, there is so much about you I have to learn. Now tell me, where are your bunny slippers." He followed her into the kitchen.

"Keep talking and you'll be wearing one up your nose." Rae pulled out a can of dark roast coffee. "I don't have instant. So it's going to take a few minutes. Sure you want to wait?"

"Sure you want me to?" Simon walked up to her, his face inches from hers.

"Simon, about us . . ." Rae tried to shout down the half of her that said *Give in*.

"You feel it, too. There is something about you that makes me . . ." Simon curled a tendril of her hair around his forefinger. "Your smile, the way your hair moves in a breeze, even the sparks you throw off when you get angry," he said in a soft voice. His lips brushed hers in a tentative, almost cautious way.

"We should both have our heads examined." In contradiction to her words, Rae placed both hands on his face and kissed him. Her tongue touched the tip of his.

For a long time they stood wrapped tight, exploring the sensations of touch and taste. Rae wanted to devour his sweetness. His lips were warm and full. A hunger, a deep sexual hunger, shot through her, and the force of her desire shook her down to her toes. Rae pulled back on the verge of guiding his hands to her pelvis. She had indeed lost her mind!

"Good gracious," Rae gasped. She leaned against the kitchen counter.

Simon was breathing hard. "Wow," was all he could manage.

They stood apart for a few minutes reeling from the power of their attraction. Neither spoke for a time. Rae needed to gather her strength. She steeled herself not to let go of her heart.

"Things are moving fast." Simon faced her.

"At the speed of light." Rae blinked at him.

"Too fast?" Simon stood very still.

"Maybe we should take a few steps at a time." Rae avoided mentioning straight out how close they'd come to surrendering to the hot flash of passion.

"Sure. That would be a good idea." Simon cleared his throat. "Think I better call it a night or . . ."

"Right." Rae understood without his having to complete the sentence. They both knew that the resolve to take more time was on shaky ground tonight. "We'll take it slow."

"Right. Slow." Simon turned to walk out then turned back. "Pick you up tomorrow?"

"Yes." Rae was back in his arms kissing him deeply within seconds. His hands gripped her shoulders.

"Goodbye," he whispered. "See you about three. We'll go for a ride in my boat, then have an early supper. I have to work."

"On a Saturday?" Rae nuzzled his neck. "What a workaholic."

"I promised to get some figures together for Darcy. But it won't take long." Simon gave her a peck on the forehead.

The mention of Darcy was like a small cold shower. A sharp hard intention formed in her chest. She was such a fool to forget who he was simply because of a kiss. Rae pretended her mood had not changed.

"Then I'll see you at three." She smiled at him.

When he was gone, Rae made herself a cup of strong tea. She sat at the kitchen table rubbing the old wounds raw. Simon St. Cyr was an attractive package to be sure. He was good, no doubt about that. Did he really think she was so gullible that his kiss would be enough to fool her? For all she knew he was with Toya now laughing at her. Well, Rae would show him she was no weak female to be seduced and trampled. Let him think he was in control.

She would enjoy him, no need to deny it. Yet she would also exact some kind of revenge on them all.

Seven

"They disappeared in nineteen forty-eight?" LaMar let out a long, low whistle. "Talk about a cold trail."

LaMar Zeno, private investigator, was dressed more like an accountant on his day off. He wore a light blue short-sleeved shirt with button-down collars tucked into cotton chino pants the color of cement. His sunglasses had a square metal frame. Rae had a very different picture of him based on his outrageous reputation. Maybe this was his identical twin?

"Everybody assumed Pawpaw Vincent did it. But Daddy never believed what they said," Rae put in quickly. She was afraid this conservative-looking young man would refuse such an unusual case. "It's really just a missing persons kind of investigation."

"Yeah, but the persons ran off over fifty years ago and maybe don't want to be found," LaMar replied.

"So it's hopeless?" Rae's spirits sank.

"Depends." LaMar rubbed his chin. He got up to pace the length of Rae's front porch. "Like how well they covered their tracks. Or where they went. In the forties, a lot of black folks headed to California, Chicago, and Detroit."

"I don't know about that." Rae could not see a Dalcour choosing a big city. Lucien had always talked about how Pawpaw Vincent loved bayou country. "A Creole from south Louisiana living in a cold place like Chicago or Detroit? Sounds iffy to me."

"Good point. But on the other hand, he might sacrifice to keep from being found. Nah, you're probably right."

Rae looked up in surprise. "You think?"

"People are creatures of habit. He was a fisherman and worked outdoors you said. At shipyards."

"And anything else he could find. He loved working with his hands Tante Ina says."

"So, I have a few places to start." LaMar came back and sat down in the cane rocker next to her. "You should know that finding folks doesn't always lead to a happy reunion. He could be dead or not be happy at being found. Or he—"

"Might have done exactly what they say he did and be shacked up with another man's wife. I know."

Rae also knew that it would hurt her much less than it would have hurt Lucien. But what about Tante Ina and Daddy's two surviving brothers? Right now the Joves and all the rest of Belle Rose had only accusations. It would be ironic if she helped to confirm that her own grandfather had cheated his friends and the entire town. LaMar read the concern in her silence.

"It's your call, ma'am." He spoke in a quiet voice.

Rae thought of Lucien, his nut brown face twisted in pain the day he made her promise. Find the truth, he'd said. No matter what that truth turned out to be. If he could face Belle Rose all these years, then so could she. Rae made her decision.

"Where do we start?"

LaMar questioned her for another thirty minutes. Since Rae did not know much about her grandfather except old stories from Lucien, he spent two hours in the attic poring over old photos and papers. When he came down, he had an old accordion folder.

"Is it okay if I take these with me?" LaMar opened it to show her old bills and other papers.

"Sure. Don't know why Daddy held onto all that old stuff." Rae shrugged.

"Good thing he did. I'll get a good picture of Mr. Vincent from this. But I would like to interview some other relatives. You say his older sister lives around here?"

"Tante Ina. A feisty sixty-four-year-old. Lives over on Chauvin Road. Let me talk to her, then I'll give you a call." Rae wondered how she would react.

"It would help to find out about Estelle Jove, too. Do you know any of her family?" LaMar opened his notepad.

"I hadn't thought of that," Rae said. She shook her head. "Her husband would freak if you approached him. He's still bitter. But Tante Ina might be able to help you track down other relatives. They may be willing to talk to you."

"Okay. In the meantime, I can check out a few things." LaMar gazed at her. "You're sure about this?"

"Positive. I just hope you can find out what happened."

"I'll check in with you at least once a week whether there's progress or not." LaMar left.

Rae glanced down at the old pictures spread on the coffee table. Pawpaw Vincent smiled in most of them, a good-looking man. But what was behind the smile? The pictures did not show the true man, much as the conflicting stories left a confused account of who he had been. She picked up a black and white photo with the date August 1945 written on it in faded ink. Pawpaw Vincent stood with his two best friends, Henry Jove and Joseph St. Cyr. The men looked barely out of their teens. They stared into the camera looking young, strong, and hopeful. It was like staring into a time machine. Rae separated this picture from the others. Somehow she sensed the key was in what happened between those three men.

"I vote no." Andrew took a gulp from his bottle of creme soda. "Of course, with that kinda money, we could live high. Yeah." He grinned.

"Big surprise." Neville gave a grunt of disgust at his younger brother's attitude. "You might think of saving something for the first time in your life, man."

"For what? So you can have a real nice funeral? Un-uh, I wanna have some fun while I'm alive and young enough to enjoy it." Andrew squinted at him.

"You can enjoy life without throwing all your money down

the drain." Neville opened his mouth to launch another lecture on thrift.

"Will you two stop," Rae cut in. "You've been fussing like this for as long as I can remember. We're talking about this deal we've been offered." She steered them back to the issue at hand.

They sat around the kitchen table over coffee Saturday morning. Rae studied her brothers. Two different sides of the same Dalcour coin. Neville and Andrew shared their father's rugged good looks and dark nut brown skin. Yet though they looked alike, their outlooks were in sharp contrast.

"I don't know." Neville combed his fingers through thick black hair. "Somehow it don't seem right. A St. Cyr having this land."

Rae threw up her hands. "Neville, you were ready to ditch the whole thing no matter who got it. Now what's up with you?"

"I wasn't crazy about the idea when you first brought it up to me," Andrew threw in.

"Look, we'll be keeping at least five, maybe as much as seven acres. And the house." Rae tapped the table with her finger. "Simon says we could even add in that we'll be given first shot at buying the land back if he ever wants to sell."

"She been running around with this St. Cyr guy." Andrew turned to his big brother.

"Say what? Just got home and all ready jumping into trouble with both feet, girl." Neville gave her a look of reproach.

"I'm grown. I do what I please, with whomever I please, thank you." Rae glared at Neville then Andrew. "And that doesn't have anything to do with this deal, which he made before we started 'running around' as you put it, Andrew."

"Yeah, so he can get his hands on our property," Andrew muttered. "Now you all hot to get cozy with them."

"Andy, don't make me say something nasty," Rae warned. She took a deep breath. "Listen, Simon approached Daddy before he died."

"And Daddy said 'Hell no,' " Andrew said.

"He did." Rae put in. "But I talked to him about six months later when he was really sick. He said I should do what I had to do. Daddy knew it would take money to fix up the dance hall and find Pawpaw Vincent."

"And that's another thing, digging up more trouble by looking into what is best left alone." Neville shook his head. "I know you wanna keep your promise to Daddy. But this ain't the way, cher."

"Then what do you suggest, Neville? I'm doing the best I can right now." Rae's voice shook. She was tired of thinking about all the things she'd have to juggle. The dance hall, tying up her business with the band, finding enough money to live on. She blinked back tears.

"Now look what you done, Neville. There now, don't worry." Andrew put an arm around her shoulder.

"Me?" Neville's mouth dropped open. "You were the one that—"

"Will you two stop." Rae shook Andrew's arm off. "I'm fine. Now let's cut through all the crap and think like business people. I want to stay in Belle Rose and run the dance hall not just because of Daddy. I can make a go of it and showcase Creole music, blues, and zydeco. That's something I've always wanted."

"Actually, with tourists coming in you could do it," Neville said.

"Right. But I need cash. I could go into debt, take out a big loan. That's one alternative. Then I'd hold onto the land." Rae looked at them.

"How much money we talking?" Andrew frowned.

"At least forty thousand to fix the place up and hire staff for the first year. I could use part of my savings for operating expenses."

"I got some money. Well a little." Andrew lifted a shoulder with a shame-faced smile. "Guess a few hundred won't go far. But you can have it,"

"Wait a minute." Neville got up and poured more coffee in his cup. "Me and Trisha have some money put by. We could help."

"Thanks so much." Rae got up to hug him. "You're sweet but—"

"About seventy thousand oughta pull you through fine. Then you won't have to sell, for now at least." Neville sipped his coffee.

"Seventy thou . . ." Andrew fell back in his chair.

"Neville, I can't take all your savings. You've got kids to send to college," Rae said.

"Oh, that's not the college fund. Trisha is still getting some royalties from the family's oil well in Port Hudson. It's not much, but we're secure." Neville looked at them. "What?"

"Neville, you own an oil well," Andrew whispered in an awe struck voice.

"No. Trisha's parents own an oil well." Neville spoke in his usual serious, methodical tone. "They share royalties with her and her sisters and brothers. Between six kids now that the price of oil has gone so low, we get a few hundred these days."

"Neville, we're family. You know we won't tell. Just how much are y'all worth." Andrew sat at the end of his chair.

"Andrew!" Rae said. She slapped his arm.

"Owwee! Neville knows I don't mean no harm." Andrew rubbed his arm. "Anyway, you dyin' to know yourself."

"I am not." Rae lifted her nose in the air. "Neville, it's none of our business. Besides, Trisha might not want her business put out in the street." She eyed Andrew. "We all know you'd be slurping beer and bragging on your big brother tonight at Sonny Sonnier's juke joint."

"Ah, Rae." Andrew stuck his mouth out.

"Neville, I'm not at all sure about taking your money." Rae did not like the idea of taking his assets. It could be several years before she could repay even a fraction of it.

"And you wanna throw in with Darcy Jove and Simon?" Andrew wore a bitter frown. "They been dumping on us for years."

"You know I was always mad at Daddy for holding onto the past. Didn't like a lot of what he did," Neville said in a quiet voice.

"I know, Neville." Rae gazed at him. As the eldest, Neville had confronted Lucien about his behavior at the age of fourteen.

They clashed many times after until Neville left home at eighteen.

"But these last few years, we kinda made our peace. I've been thinking we should try to hold onto the land as part of the Dalcour heritage." Neville looked at Rae and Andrew.

"You right, big brother." Andrew nodded, "I stuck up for Daddy. But I didn't always approve of what he did. Told him so a few times."

"You did?" Neville looked at him in surprise.

"Yep. Anyway, he had it hard after Pawpaw Vincent left. I just feel we gotta keep this land for him. To make all that pain count for something." Andrew was serious for once.

"That's what I've been thinking about the last few days. Daddy was a strong man in a lot of ways. He deserved better." Neville stared out the kitchen window that faced him.

"I loved that stubborn rascal." Andrew's voice was thick with emotion.

"Me, too," Neville said.

"Oh, Neville . . ." Rae felt a tear slip down her cheek. At that moment, Neville looked and sounded so much like Lucien it brought back the pain of losing him.

"I'm not criticizing you, cher." Neville misunderstood her reaction. He put a large arm around her shoulder. "We know you're just trying to find the best way to build something, too."

"Yeah, now stop that." Andrew rubbed his eyes. "Women always got to turn on the faucet." He got up and turned his back to them. After a few moments, he sat down again.

Rae wiped her eyes. "I love you both like crazy. Guess I'll break the news to Simon today. We're going out for a ride."

"Humph, let's see how friendly he is after that," Andrew retorted.

"He might just find me attractive you know!" Rae pinched his arm hard.

"Cut it out, girl." Andrew jumped back from her. "Don't know what's gotten into you."

"We keep talking about starting new. Keeping up an old feud isn't the way to do that, Andy." Rae shook a finger at him.

"Bet you wouldn't say that if we were talking about me and Toya." Andrew squinted at her.

"That's different and you know it. She took every chance to make my life hell in this town when we were kids." Rae still felt the sting of scorn heaped on by Toya up until the day of high school graduation. "She hasn't changed one bit."

"Besides, you're broke. Toya Jove wouldn't give you the time of day," Neville added with a trace of humor.

"Well I'll stand on the bayou with a wooden board saying WELCOME and pick up litter myself rather than throw in with them." Andrew crossed his arms in a stubborn expression exactly like the one Lucien used to wear.

"We know how long that would last." Neville gave a snort of cynicism.

"Andy, that's a brilliant idea." Rae beamed at him.

"Let's dress him up in a big crawfish costume while we're at it." Neville gave a short laugh.

"Hey, I ain't wearin' no costume." Andrew looked alarmed at the gleam in Rae's eyes.

"What I mean is we could still make the bayou a recreational site just like Simon proposed. But *we* could keep the land." Rae watched their faces carefully. They were silent for a few moments.

"We don't have the money." Neville shook his head.

"No, not the way he planned. But we could keep it simple." Rae liked the idea the more she thought about it. "We could repair that old dock and let somebody pay us rent to use it. Like Kenny Laronde over on False River. He rents out boats, sells fishing bait."

"We could use the money to keep the land clean," Neville said.

"Right. Of course, that would have to wait. My first priority is getting the dance hall going," Rae put in quickly. "There's just so much we should try to do at once."

"I have to admit, you surprised me." Neville gazed at Rae with respect. "This isn't some wild scheme for you to have a good time on the bayou. You've got a sound business approach to making it happen."

"I surprised myself, Neville." Rae glowed with pleasure at her older brother's praise. "Guess living by the seat of my pants doesn't appeal to me anymore."

"Wish I could see Darcy's face when Simon tells him the deal is off. Oo-wee, he's not gonna be pleased." Andrew cackled with delight.

Rae wondered if Andrew was right. Would Simon drift away? Was his interest only to obtain the property? At the thought an unpleasant pang went through her. She tried to tell herself it was nothing.

"Cher, it's for the best." Neville touched her arm. He seemed to read her thoughts. "If he doesn't stay with you, then you're better off."

"That's up to him." Rae tried to make her voice light. "We're just having fun anyway. I do enjoy dating Toya's ex-husband. She's fit to be tied." She gave him a wicked wink.

Neville gave her a wise look. "If you say so." His tone said he was not fooled by her act.

"I say so," Rae shot back. "Now I made some tea cakes from Monmon's old recipe."

Rae steered them on to other subjects. Even while she chatted with her brothers about family and town happenings, Simon was on her mind. For the hours before he arrived, Rae worked hard to convince herself she would not care if he did pull away. When he stepped up on her porch that afternoon, all those efforts were for nothing. Simon exuded sensuality with every graceful move. Dressed in a slate blue crew neck T-shirt and blue jeans, he was fabulous. The brown skin of his muscular arms begged to be touched. He was tall, dark, and handsome. Just the way she liked them. Even more, he was thoughtful, had a sense of humor and was smart. When he smiled at her, Rae's pulse increased. All this just made her feel irritated with him for having this effect on her.

"Hello. Ready to see the sights?" Simon took off his sunglasses.

"Sure." Rae was short with him. She wanted this feeling to go away.

"I've been looking forward to this all morning. Thinking

about you made it hard to focus, but I finally finished." Simon moved close to her without touching.

"Oh?" Rae gazed up at him. Her mind told her to move away, but her body stayed put. The nearness of him was so good. He had not touched her, yet she could feel him.

"Yes, doing business with you will be very different." Simon grinned at her. "I'll have to work on my concentration from now on."

His reference to buying the property stirred her to action. "Let's sit down a minute, Simon. You may not want to go riding after all." Rae figured she might as well get it over with now.

"I doubt that." Simon's smile faded at the sober expression she wore. "What's happened?"

"I talked to my brothers this morning. We don't want to sell." Rae spoke in almost a defiant manner.

"I see."

"We've never had much, but at least we had our land. Daddy's pride and joy, that and the dance hall." Rae did not look at him. "So that's it."

Simon was silent for a few moments. "Well, I knew giving up ownership to any of the land would be difficult. But I understand." He stood up. "Let's get going. There's a spot on Grande River waiting for us." He held out his hand.

"I didn't spoil your mood for an outing?" Rae eyed him warily.

"The ideas I had for your property weren't a make or break proposition. I could still do a modified version of it on my grandfather's property off Bayou Pigeon," Simon said with a shrug.

"Really?"

"Yes. In fact, I was going to tell you I really only needed about five acres from you. Of course, Papa Joe's land isn't as pretty and doesn't have easy access to Grande River like yours. But it's still a good idea."

"You had a lot of work into that plan. I spoiled it. Just like a Dalcour," Rae needled him for a reaction.

Simon raised at eyebrow. "So you figured I was only trying to soften you up to get my hands on Dalcour land."

"Well I . . ." Rae examined her fingernails.

"That I was pretending to be attracted to you." Simon took her hand. "Come here." He pulled her from the chair and over to the cypress swing at the other end of the porch. They sat close together.

"Our families have been fighting for a long time. Admit it, Mr. Joe thinks Pawpaw stole from him." Rae could feel the heat from his body.

"There was tension between both generations. But that was years ago. My father doesn't care about all that now." Simon put an arm along the back of the swing.

"His brothers and sisters still hate us." Rae knew from Lucien that the St. Cyrs still living in the parish were belligerent.

"And I've told them how silly it is, too. It's time we put this whole family feud thing to rest, don't you think?" Simon put his face within inches of hers. "It's so ridiculous to hold his family responsible for what your grandfather did. They suffered just as much as anyone, more from what I understand."

"Monmon Marie never got over it. She struggled to feed six kids." Rae remembered the grim set to her grandmother's face. She did not smile often. "Daddy used to joke they were too poor to pay attention."

"So it's only natural that Mr. Lucien would want to hold onto the only thing his father left them. With what he went through, no wonder parting with even an acre was unthinkable." Simon gazed out at the scenery before them.

Rae looked at him. The sincerity in his voice was strong. Something deep within told her this was no act. She followed the line of his jaw up to the tight curls like soft wool cut short. Before she knew it, her lips were pressed against his face.

"What's that for? Not that I'm complaining," Simon murmured. He wrapped arm around her.

"For being you." Rae rested her head against his shoulder.

"Now that's good news. All I have to do to get a sweet kiss from a beautiful lady is be myself," Simon quipped. He brushed his lips against her forehead.

They sat quiet, the gentle swaying of the cypress swing lulled them both into a shared contentment. For the first time in her

life, Rae was completely at ease in a man's arms. She wanted
to forget the past. What mattered most was that she hold onto
this wonderful sensation of floating on air. Rae felt ashamed
now that she had thoughts of using Simon to get back at Toya
or anyone.

"It's almost four o'clock. Shouldn't we get moving?" Rae
said.

"If we don't, you may have to slap my face," Simon replied
with a soft chuckle.

"We're taking it slow." Rae said this to tame her hunger for
him more than for his benefit.

He stood up. "I agree. Besides, I have a surprise for you.
Come on."

For the entire ride they played a game of tease. Rae tried to
trick him into revealing his secret. Simon only laughed at her
attempts. Both enjoyed the lovely ride that took them through
the countryside to a portion of Grande River at Ventre's Landing. Next to the wooden dock, a large building housed a grocery
store, cafe, and bait shop.

"Here we are." Simon got out of the Explorer. "We're going
for a boat ride. Courtesy of my pal, Ike." Simon waved to a tall
man the color of milk chocolate who waved back with a wide
smile. "And forty bucks to rent it."

Rae broke into a delighted giggle. "It's been years since I've
been for a boat ride. Oh, Simon. It's a real beauty." She walked
to the bass boat.

"I've got refreshing drinks in my trusty cooler, life jackets,
and a pretty woman. I'm ready." Simon helped her into the boat
tied up to the wooden dock.

Simon steered to the center of the river and gradually increased their speed. Rae reveled in the smell of the river. The
sun sparkled on its surface like liquid diamonds. For the next
two hours they rode at a moderate cruising speed, Simon testing
Rae's memory about favorite landmarks along the river. Luxu-
riant growth of swamp oak, red maple, sweet gum trees, grass
and shrubs of a hundred varieties spread out around them.
Egrets spread white fluffy wings as they lazily took flight. Time

slipped by in a most delightful fashion for them both. After drifting lazily for a while longer, they went back to the landing.

"I'm starving." Simon wiped his hands after removing large rubber boots worn to wade into the water. "What say we head for Savoie's?"

"Perfect," Rae said, happy at his choice of the nearby restaurant with its savory seafood.

Sitting on the patio of the restaurant, they watched boats go by on the bayou. Rae had to admit she enjoyed watching the way Simon's full mouth curved up when she told a funny story. This was not at all what she'd planned. Her feelings for him were the real deal.

"Whoa, I'm stuffed. Two soft shell crabs might have been overdoing it." Simon sat back in his chair.

"Humm, maybe it was all those hush puppies you wolfed down before they brought our order," Rae said.

"Me? You helped if I recall."

"Guilty as charged." Rae wiped her mouth with a paper napkin. "My crawfish bisque was delicious. I'm feeling a bit full myself."

"Then I take it no dancing tonight?" Simon leaned forward to gaze at her.

"No way. A quiet evening with a cup of good old-fashion Louisiana dark roast coffee is all I can stand." Rae propped her chin on one hand.

"Done. I make a mean cup if I do say so myself." Simon handed his credit card to the waiter.

"What?" Rae had an uneasy feeling.

"My town house is in that new complex on Picou Lane. You know the one. It's not far from downtown. We can be there in twenty minutes, if I obey the speed limit." He winked at her.

"Your place. Coffee at your town house." Rae blinked at him.

"You don't trust me on my home turf?" Simon smothered a smile. He tried to look serious at the cutting look she gave him.

Rae hoped her embarrassment did not show. Her doubts were not about his behavior but her own. "Of course not. Let's go." *I can do this, no problem.*

Her fragile confidence wilted the moment the door closed

behind them and they were seated in his living room. The room opened onto a dining area to the right. A breakfast bar separated it from the small kitchen. The carpet was the color of dark clay, the furniture in a striped pattern of clay, brown, and forest green. A combination of African and Creole art made a nice blend. Five small figures were scattered around, the smallest three across the top of the mantel above a brick fireplace. Soft jazz flowed from a compact disc player. All the time, Simon kept up easy chatter from the kitchen. Rae divided her attention between answering him and bolstering her resolve to be cautious with her heart.

"Here we go." Simon handed her a mug and sat next to her. "The Simon St. Cyr special."

"Thank you, sir. So far the service is excellent." Rae took a sip. "Not bad."

"I know my way around the kitchen thank you very much. I cook a mean jambalaya, too."

Rae waved a hand around the room. "Nice place. You decorated it?"

"It wasn't hard. I got some furniture from the house after the divorce. But a lot of this is new," he added quickly.

"Bet you've had a lot of women willing to help you with cooking and housework." Rae kept her tone casual.

"I got more casseroles pushed on me than Father Boudreaux when he organized the church potluck dinner," Simon said with a chuckle. "But there is no one special tucked away. I've dated but that's about it."

"I wasn't trying to get in your business." Rae groaned inwardly. She was being so obvious!

"Yes you were, and it's okay. I've been trying to get around to asking you if there is someone in your life right now." Simon turned to her, one arm across the back of the sofa.

Tension eased from her body. "No. I was dating someone, but we're kinda drifting apart. I wasn't home much. I think he's found someone else and just hasn't told me yet."

"You had an apartment in Houston right?"

"Yeah, but it definitely wasn't home. Oh, I enjoyed being there after traveling for weeks on end. But until I got back to our house here, I didn't realize that I was just sorta camping out in Houston. It had a real temporary feel to it. Everything about my life did. Even my relationship with Kaleb, the guy I was dating." Rae stopped abruptly. She had never told these things to anyone. *Why are you spilling your guts to this man?*

Simon took her hand in a gesture to make her feel at ease. "After my divorce, I felt this kind of emptiness. The divorce was the right thing, don't get me wrong. But I guess I was mourning the fact that my marriage hadn't been the lifetime love affair I'd hoped for. I wanted to be like my parents and grandparents."

"Mr. Level-Headed Business Man. You're a romantic underneath," Rae teased gently.

"Ms. Well-Known Rebel, so are you," he said in a low voice. "And we both feel this thing growing between us."

"Sounds like a wart or something . . ." Rae tried to make a joke. Her voice was weak, mainly because she was having trouble breathing. The lights were low, he was so close and so tantalizing.

"You know exactly what I mean, Raenette Marie Dalcour," Simon whispered.

With the careful, deliberation of an artist, Simon traced a line with his forefinger along her jaw until he touched her bottom lip. Rae watched his face move closer with no thought of resisting. His mouth tasted of love and desire. Under the coaxing of his big but gentle hands moving over her body, Rae shed her hard shell of cynicism about picture perfect romance. She wanted him in every way.

"I know we've only known each other a few weeks and . . ." Simon murmured between delicate kisses to her neck and down her chest. He paused in the act of going farther down the V-neckline of her deep red T-shirt.

"Technically, we've known each other for years," Rae mumbled. She did not want him to stop. "Well, we met at least once when I was a teenager," she added when he looked up at her in amusement. "My point is we're not strangers."

"True. We know all about our families, where we went to school, and lots of other details." Simon resumed his task of kissing every inch of exposed flesh.

Rae sighed. with contentment. "Yes, right there." She shivered as he nuzzled her breast through the fabric.

"So technically we're much farther along than just a second date." Simon nibbled at the cotton harder.

"Fourth. There was lunch, and I'm willing to count that first meeting in your office," Rae put in quickly. "We did share coffee and talk about nonbusiness topics. Don't forget the phone conversations." She guided his hand beneath her shirt. He reached under the lace cup of her bra. The touch of his warm palm covering her right breast made her moan.

"Works for me," he mumbled.

There was no need for more discussion. In a daze of passion, they undressed in slow motion, savoring each delicious stage. Rae lay back against the cushions and watched him push down the blue jeans over his hips to reveal white cotton briefs against his brown skin. Simon stood over her for a few seconds gazing at the her body still clothed in the matching bikini and bra the color of dark wine. Rae stood up and removed them both as she gazed back at him. With one quick motion, he removed his briefs. They stood together kissing and touching for one long luscious game of foreplay. Soon their slow tantalizing caresses gave way to urgent need. They eased down onto the sofa, their bodies molded in a neat fit. Simon drew back to look into her eyes. He entered her, pushing his hips to hers in slow motion until they were locked in a heated embrace that made them one. More than sexual pleasure, she rode a tidal wave of joy at having this wonderful man inside her. She wanted all of him. In a blinding flash, she knew what it meant to be consumed with passion. Simon was moaning her name, whispering endearments in a string of words that meant nothing in particular and everything. The orgasm began like a flower opening, each glorious second taking her higher. Feeling her contract around him pushed Simon over the edge. His thrusts were sharp and deep. He came shouting out a guttural moan, every muscle rigid, his fingers digging into the flesh of her thighs. They lay wrapped together for a long time, unwilling to break contact.

Rae combed his dark hair with her fingers. Strange how each strand seemed to stand out all shiny and beautiful. She glanced around the room to check. Yes, colors were brighter. The feel of everything was somehow better.

"Now what?" she asked in soft voice of awe. So this was love.

Simon eased from her. He retrieved a pair of light gray pajamas from his bedroom. "Now we take a nice warm shower together, put on these and drift off to sleep in each other's arms." He smiled. "I'll get the shower started."

"You know what I mean, Simon." Rae grabbed his wrist.

He sat next to her. "Now we decide that no one, and I mean no one, will come between us. If this doesn't work, it should be because we say it won't. Not your brothers, not my grandfather, or anybody else."

"Sounds simple enough. We just have to ignore ninety percent of the population of Belle Rose and hope Toya doesn't hire a hit man to take us both out." Rae wondered if Simon could take being an outcast.

"Piece of cake." Simon tucked her against him. "Seriously, what I feel for you is like nothing else I've ever felt. I'm willing to fight for it."

Rae looked up at him. He was serious. Not a trace of hesitance or doubt was evident in his handsome face. She was ready to take on everyone to hold on to the joy of being with him.

"You know I'm not exactly a slave to public opinion. So, let the games begin." She giggled.

"There's a shower and soft jumbo bath towel with our name on it, lady." Simon led her to the master bath in his bedroom.

A light-headed, relaxing feeling took control of them both. Warm soapy water rinsed away all cares. Worries about the rest of the world did not belong here tonight.

Eight

The next four days were a busy time for Rae. She spent all her waking hours talking to carpenters, electricians, and beer wholesalers trying to get the best prices. She met with resistance. One liquor salesman finally admitted that the word was out not to do business with her. Henry Jove had lots of powerful friends. Still, greed eventually won out. She had to accept higher prices, but she was determined not to let the Joves win.

No matter how tired she was, the prospect of being with Simon revitalized her. To her delighted surprise, there was no apocalyptic reaction the morning after their exquisite night spent together. No earthquakes or destructive hurricane-force winds swept them away for daring to defy fifty years of history. Rae could not help but hum as she worked, even though she'd despised others for doing it when infatuated with a new lover. It was a hot, humid late May morning. She stood back to survey the dance hall. A new cypress sign was being hung. The sound of hammers and workmen shouting to each other made her feel like it was all coming together.

"This place brings back memories. The first time I caught myself sneaking in, Mr. Lucien walked up on me. Let me know he'd seen me the whole time."

Rae froze at the voice just over her shoulder. She turned to face its owner. Darcy stood not five feet away. He was six feet of classy, upper-class Crèole conceit. His black hair was combed straight back and curled over the collar of his white shirt with blue pinstripes. The expensive navy blue slacks fit his slender frame with the exactness expected of a tailor-made garment. Looking at him brought back a flood of memories. That casual stance, the smile, and the way his light brown eyes traveled her body had been an invitation she'd accepted eagerly at fifteen.

"Hello, Darcy. Fancy meeting you here," Rae said, her tone flip. "They blocked off Highway One or something? Gotta be the only way you found your way to Back of the Bayou."

She referred to the name locals used to designate the area where poor blacks and a few whites lived. For ninety years or more, this part of the parish was where those low on the social and economic scales had lived.

"We're pushing improvements all over the parish these days. The leadership has changed now. Black folks have a real say so."

"Guess I know which black folks you're talking about. The same ones that have always looked out for themselves." Rae renewed an argument they'd had fifteen years ago. "Things haven't changed that much." She stared at him.

"You have." Darcy walked around her. "You've gotten more beautiful, cher. A kind of sophisticated sexiness."

"Your line of bull has improved a little," Rae shot back. "What do you want, Darcy?"

A slow smile curved his lips. He walked up to her. "That's a loaded question, woman. Sure you can handle the answer?" he asked in low voice meant to be provocative.

"There was never anything you dished out I couldn't handle." Rae did not move.

"I remember the days when we couldn't get enough of each other."

"Yeah, well I finally did get my fill of you. That long night in the emergency room where you left me to face the doctor alone. Remember?"

Darcy lost the cocky smile he wore. "You never knew for sure you were pregnant. Far as I knew, you were just having female problems."

"You didn't care to stick around and find out! At least you left me money to get home."

Rae felt nausea rise in her throat at the sight of him making despicable excuses for his behavior. That horrible night rushed back with a vengeance. They were out on the town when the pains started. Darcy stayed with her for the first fifteen minutes, then said he had to make a phone call. Instead he took off for home.

She had been torn for weeks between terror at what her parents would say and joy at the new life she thought was growing inside her. In her young mind, her baby was the promise of a life filled with love. All the sadness meant nothing. Rae had been so blind, she'd been foolish enough to think Darcy would welcome the news. The look of alarm on his face when she told him of her suspicion should have warned her. But she'd been too busy planning a rosy future for them all, her new family. Rae had mourned as though she'd lost a child when the doctor told her she was not pregnant.

"It was only severe cramps. You were fine after they treated you." Darcy lowered his voice and looked around.

"Something you found out when you finally called three days later," she snapped. What was the use? He was a selfish bastard. There was no point opening up that particular old wound.

"I was fifteen and scared. We'd crossed the line from just doing little things to piss off our parents into some serious stuff." Darcy stopped her from walking away. "For a month I begged you to forgive me. I caught hell from my family. Mama, Daddy, and Granddaddy were on my butt night and day. But I still came to you."

"Three days too late, Darcy!" Rae shouted at him.

Several workmen looked up sharply. Rae stomped off away from the dance hall and toward the forest nearby to a well worn path. Darcy followed her.

"You want me on my knees? I crawled to you then, I'll do it now. Please forgive me." His voice choked. "My first wife lost two of my babies. Believe me, I've been punished." Darcy hung his head.

Rae stopped. The despair in his voice was real. "I'm sorry. I didn't know . . ." She was tired of holding onto bitterness. It was time to purge all the old hurts, if she was to start fresh. "You're right. We were both too young and trying to grow up too fast." She did not turn to face him but spoke as though she were addressing the woods around her.

"Say you forgive me," Darcy said softly. "I need to hear you say it."

"I forgive you." Rae felt a weight lift from her chest. She'd thrown off one big chunk of a painful past.

Darcy put a hand on her arm. "Nobody has made me feel like you did back then."

The only thing she felt was annoyance. There was no anger, but no trace of the old attraction either. "Like you said, that was when we were just kids. We're grown-up now." Rae turned to face him and stepped back, breaking his hold. They gazed at each other for several moments.

"Sure." Darcy forced a smile. He fell in step beside her back toward the dance hall. "Now you're a recording star with a plan to start your own business."

"I'm not a 'star,' Darcy."

"But you are going to run the dance hall yourself." Darcy glanced at her.

"Yeah, I'm staying in Belle Rose if that's what you're getting at. And by the way, we won't be selling any land to Simon." Rae stopped walking several yards from the dance hall entrance.

"What did you say?" Darcy frowned.

"My brothers and I are not going to sell off any Dalcour land. Simon is okay with it." Rae looked at him.

"Is he?" Darcy scrutinized her.

"Yeah, he is." Rae returned his gaze with a placid expression.

Several seconds of silence passed between them as the question hung in the air between them, and Rae's silence answered it.

Darcy lifted both hands. "Then that's that. Guess Simon doesn't plan to do anything more about the tourism."

"You'll have to ask him about that. And tell Mr. Henry it didn't work, I've got my suppliers lined up just fine. We'll open for business right on time."

Darcy assumed a blank face. "I don't know what you mean."

"Liar," Rae said in a flat voice. They studied each other in silence until one of the workmen called her to come over. "I gotta go."

"Rae, wait." Darcy placed a hand on her arm. "Belle Rose has changed in some ways. But not that much. Be careful what you open up here."

"Are you talking about the business or the past?" Rae said.

"Both." Darcy took his hand away and smiled. "It was nice seeing you again, Rae. I guess you don't want to get together for drinks, maybe dinner?"

"You guess right."

"Simon works fast. Gotta admire that," Darcy quipped. Yet his tight smile held more suppressed anger than amusement. He spun around and walked off. The wheels of his two-seat red Mercedes squealed on the highway pavement as he raced off.

Rae let out a long breath when he was gone. She may not have seen him for a long time, but she recognized that look on Darcy's face. He would press to have his way if only out of spite. First Toya, now her brother. Rae knew both could be real trouble. *Wait a minute, we're not kids anymore.* Simon had his own thriving business that did not depend on the Joves. What did they care what a lot of small town small minds thought? They would all just have to get over it. Yet even as she decided on wood for the floors, decorations for the interior, and other details, a small kernel of anxiety stayed with her.

"So, your boyish charm didn't work its usual magic." Toya snickered.

"Shut up," Darcy snapped.

"Brother, I do believe you still have a thing for that little swamp trash." Toya's eyes were wide. "I would have thought your more exotic tastes would preclude her now."

"What would you know about taste? I've seen some of your male companions." Darcy sat down hard.

They were in Darcy's home only a mile down the road from his grandfather's house. Toya lived about five miles away.

"Now that wasn't nice. But since you're under stress I won't take offense." Toya brushed back her hair with long fingers.

"So, Rae isn't going into business with Simon and you won't have a chance to get your hands on her land. Pity." She looked quite content.

Darcy faced her with a nasty grin. "No, Rae isn't going to sell the land to Simon. Apparently their all night negotiations still didn't bring them to an agreement on the sale."

"What are you talking about?"

"She was at his apartment until the sun came up." Darcy was pleased that the satisfied expression was wiped from her face.

"That's a lie. You can't believe stupid gossip around this town," Toya bleated in distress.

"It's true, big sister. Simon and Rae were together. And frankly, I doubt they were discussing land prices." Darcy put his glass down. His pleasure at upsetting Toya was short-lived. "Simon has made a big mistake getting in my way."

"Then what are you going to do about it? We can't just sit by while Rae Dalcour ruins everything." Toya started to say more when the doorbell rang. She left and returned with Marius.

"Man, you two look very grim this evening." Marius fixed himself a drink without asking. "Darcy, Grandfather wants to meet with you tomorrow morning about the Pantheon deal."

"How did you know I was here?" Darcy wore a sour expression when he looked at his handsome cousin.

"I was on my way home and saw your car." Marius was not the least disturbed by his mood. He sat down and crossed his legs. "Trouble in paradise?"

"Rae won't sell," Toya hissed.

"I can see where that would have Darcy upset, but you should be happy. Right?" Marius affected a look of ignorance.

"She's seeing Simon. The slut!" Toya set her glass down hard on the table at her elbow.

Marius took a sip of his drink. "Can't say I'm surprised. She's one fine woman. She can really swing those hips, too."

"Don't be disgusting!" Toya shot from her seat.

"Of course, Darcy could answer that question. Couldn't you, cuz?" Marius lifted his eyebrows.

"Rae will toss him aside after awhile." Darcy spoke in a coarse voice. "I know she will."

"Isn't this interesting. Toya is mad because Simon has a new honey. Darcy wants Rae Dalcour for fun and games." Marius chuckled softly.

"If she doesn't sell the land, we might not have a deal with Pantheon." Darcy said. "She found suppliers."

"More bad news. So Darcy's grand plan that so impressed Grandfather is about to crash." Marius shook his head. "Tsk, tsk."

Darcy wore a feral look as he leaned forward. "If that deal falls through, we could lose millions. Without that big expansion, there will be no vice president's position for you. Think of that, cuz."

Marius looked as though he'd been slapped hard. The smug smile disappeared. "Damnit, then let's do something."

The three of them forgot their rivalry and sat quiet for several moments.

"How badly do we need those acres for Pantheon?" Marius spoke first.

"We could go ahead, but it won't be nearly as attractive. And we'll have to dredge for sure, because the new barge route will have to be through Bayou Pigeon instead. Which, of course, means more money." Darcy replied.

"And they'll get antsy with these changes since we assured them construction could start in August at the latest." Marius frowned.

"We don't have a choice now that Rae isn't going to sell." Darcy stared into his glass. "She doesn't need the money as much as I thought. That dance hall will be a gold mine with the popularity of zydeco and blues. Plus the draw of being able to see bayou country."

"She's resourceful. Too bad she won't just leave." Marius rubbed his jaw.

"Men are such dogs." Toya gulped down the rest of the whiskey in her glass.

"Between the dance hall and Simon, Rae will be in Belle Rose. You can count on that." Darcy wore a thoughtful expression. "But when she tires of him, things could work out."

"What if it's true love? They could get married." Marius said. "Then you can kiss that land goodbye."

"Simon wouldn't . . . This is just a fling!" Toya spluttered. She wore a look of shock. "He wouldn't marry a Dalcour."

"I know Rae. It won't last." Darcy did not seem as sure as his words.

"You used to know her, cuz. There is a big difference between a fifteen-year-old girl and a thirty-year-old woman. No, we need to approach this problem logically."

"He's right. We all want the same thing. Now how do we get it?" Toya said in a hard voice. She glanced at Darcy then Marius.

"What's up, brother?" Baylor clasped Simon's hand in a firm grip. "Been a while. Man, this Kinchen job has been whipping my butt."

They sat in Simon's office. Baylor had not been in town for several weeks, as the civil engineering firm that employed him was constructing a cement plant near Lafayette.

"Rough eh?" Simon poured him a cup of black coffee.

"Yeah, but I won't complain. When I make sure the plant is not only efficient but saves money, I'll get a fat bonus, as usual." Baylor winked at him before tasting from his mug.

"Talented and humble, what a guy," Simon said.

"What can I say, I'm good." Baylor grinned at him. "So what's up with you?"

"Nothing much." Simon cleared his throat. "Working hard like you. I've got a new job to put up duplex apartments over in Rougon."

"Nice. Things been the same old, same old, huh?" Baylor propped an ankle across his knee. "No new developments with Ms. Dalcour?"

"Developments?" Simon cleared his throat again. He shuffled stacks of paper on his desk.

"Yeah, you two got together to take care of business?"

"Business? Oh, the property sale. They decided not to sell." Simon avoided his gaze.

"You don't seem upset about your plans hitting a major snag." Baylor looked at his friend with his head to one side.

"It's no big deal. I can understand Rae wanting to hold onto her only family legacy."

Baylor put his mug down on Simon's desk. "Oh, man, tell me you didn't."

"Watch it! You almost spilled coffee on these blueprints." Simon lifted the plans gingerly and moved them.

"Don't even try it, Simon." Baylor pointed a finger at him. "If you've done what I think you've done—"

"Man, you've been working in that hot sun without a hat. You're not making a bit of sense." Simon scowled but still did not look at Baylor.

"Okay, play me for stupid. You go from 'Miss Dalcour should sell her land' to '*Rae* should keep her family legacy' in less than a month. You and her . . ." Baylor clasped his hands together holding them high.

"We're seeing each other." Simon's jaw jutted out in a stubborn expression. "And it's nobody's business."

Baylor's eyes were wide. "That serious. Man, oh, man. And I'm out of town for at least another two weeks."

"What's that got to do with anything?"

"Brother, you are gonna need me at your back when this hits the fan." Baylor nodded to himself as though thinking aloud. "Now if you could just keep it on the down low a little longer we can deal."

"Will you cut it out." Simon drummed his fingers on the desktop. "I don't care about a bunch of stupid gossip or popular opinion."

"She's a special lady, eh?" Baylor lost the teasing tone. "Sounds serious."

Simon could not stop the smile that came with the thought of the last three weeks with Rae. Serious? He could not sleep at night without calling one last time to hear her voice. Resisting the urge to leave his office and go out to the dance hall to be with Rae was a daily struggle. The mere memory of the taste, scent, and feel of her brown satin skin sent his temperature up by ten degrees. Serious was an understatement.

"Yeah, man. You could say that," was all Simon could manage to murmur. Even now, he felt his hunger for her growing.

"I gotta meet the lady. Can't remember this reaction over any woman you been with, including your lovely ex-wife."

Simon came back down to earth with a thump. "Toya will be a little upset. But then, she's always throwing a tantrum about something."

"A little upset? That's like saying a hurricane is a little bit of wind." Baylor looked alarmed at the prospect of being faced with a wrathful Toya Jove.

"I've dated a few times and Toya had to get used to it." Simon shrugged.

"Nah, man. She has never gotten used to it. Besides, this is something entirely different. And if I can see it, so will she," Baylor said.

Simon sighed. Living in a small town meant you were likely to see those you'd prefer to avoid frequently in the grocery store, at church, or downtown. But there was nothing left in his heart for Toya. It had been over long before Rae came along.

"I can't help that. I want someone to spend my life with." Simon stared out window. "I want children, a dog, the whole bit."

"Me, too." Baylor rubbed his face.

"I'll even drive a station wagon for the right woman." Simon grinned at him. He knew how Baylor felt about his white Corvette.

"Let's not get totally crazy, brother." Baylor gave a shudder. "Don't take this wrong, but the quiet family scene doesn't sound like something Rae Dalcour is into. Folks say she likes the free life of a blues musician."

"Stupid gossip," Simon said with force. "Rae is strong-willed and not afraid to speak her mind. But she's got a soft, sweet core. Family is important to her, too. But she doesn't have to give up being a musician. She's opening the dance hall, you know."

"Sounds like you're thinking long term. I'm glad for you, man, straight up. But . . . Fasten your seat, life is about to get real bumpy." Baylor nodded slowly.

Simon wished he could make a convincing protest, but Baylor was right. "I know, my brother, I know."

"Ooo, Raenette!" Marcelle cradled baby Felicia in one arm while holding a tumbler of iced tea in the other. "No you didn't!"

"I did." Rae shot her a look that was a cross between defiance and annoyance. "What's the big deal? We hit it off."

"He is too fine. Can't say I blame you for falling hard." Marcelle made soothing sounds at the fussing baby until she settled back into slumber. "He's got a body that begs for attention, child."

"I did not 'fall hard'. Like I said—"

"Rae, this is me you're talking to." Marcelle gave her a knowing look.

"I . . . He . . . Damn! Why didn't I just pack up and leave after the funeral?" Rae got up to pace Marcelle's front porch.

"Because you made a promise to your daddy, that's why. Wait a minute." Marcelle eased out of the rocker. She took the baby into the house. "She's all settled in the crib. Now, about you and Simon."

"I know, I know. It's stupid and I should back away." Rae twisted a thick tendril of hair through her fingers.

"I didn't say that."

"A minute ago you acted like I'd lost my mind." Rae realized her hair was all knotted and set about untangling it.

"You just caught me off guard. I mean, things kinda developed fast." Marcelle wiggled her eyebrows. "Go, girl."

"Yeah, right. What started out as a way to piss Toya off has gotten me in trouble."

Rae gazed out at the trees swaying in a slight breeze that brought little relief from the heat. What she really saw was the trouble ahead for her. Her mind tried to make her heart believe that being with Simon was something she did not truly want as a woman. So far the heart was winning the argument hands down.

Marcelle folded her hands in her lap and rocked. "Uh-huh, coulda told you so."

"Then why didn't you stop me, Miss Know-It-All? I could have avoided this mess," Rae said.

"Hey, don't try to blame this on me, cher."

Rae sat down next to her. "Marcelle, everything tells me this is crazy. I'm wild with a smart mouth, he's quiet and sensitive. I'm a blues guitarist used to traveling, he's lived in this parish all his life."

"He's a St. Cyr and you're a Dalcour." Marcelle added the obvious.

"Right." Rae pulled her hair back from her face.

"Not to mention he was married to Toya the Terrible. Come here."

Marcelle fished a hair brush from the pocket of her sleeveless jumper. Rae slipped down to sit on the floor in front of her. Marcelle brushed Rae's dark hair back.

"What to do, Marcelle?"

Rae leaned back between her friend's knees. The sensation of soft bristles whisking through her dark, coarse hair was helping her relax much as when her mother would tame her unruly mane when she was a little girl.

"Seems to me you oughta forget what happened fifty years ago. Love is too hard to find, cher." Marcelle wrapped a rubber band around Rae's hair making a thick ponytail. She rested her hands on Rae's shoulders.

"I can't forget my promise to clear Pawpaw Vincent's name," Rae said.

"Then go ahead with that. I mean don't let what happened come between you and Simon. Either your pawpaw did it or he didn't. Got nothing to do with y'all today."

"I don't know. We still have to face folks in this town. I'm not sure Simon realizes how deep feelings run against the Dalcours." Rae got up and sat in the rocker next to Marcelle again.

"He's not dumb, girl. Anybody who grew up around here knows about all that stuff. You worried he don't care enough to put up with it." Marcelle nodded at her with the look of a wise woman. "Which means you're in love, deep love."

Rae jumped up from the rocker. That word scared her. "All I wanted was to show this town what Dalcours are made of. I didn't wanna leave after awhile just because they wanted me to leave, ya know?"

"Uh-huh. Been like that as long as I've known you. Nobody's gonna tell you what to do."

"Then Toya got in my face and I wanted to show her. That and my promise to Daddy, to do what he'd wanted so bad all his life, made me know I couldn't leave . . ." Rae took a deep breath.

"Now you're in love with him," Marcelle said in a quiet voice.

"I don't know if it's love." Rae stared ahead. "Maybe it's just that I need someone, dealing with Daddy's death and all. I've been on the road a lot, doing without the kind of warmth Simon gives."

"And you thought you didn't need it." Marcelle sighed. "Cher, you're only tough on the outside. You've got a whole lot of love bottled up waiting for the right man to unstop the cork. Looks like you found him."

"But a St. Cyr, Marcelle! Why did it have to be him? Daddy is probably setting speed records spinning in his grave." Rae grabbed her head with both hands.

"Come on and have some more iced tea." Marcelle poured a glass from the large pitcher. "Sit down now. Let me tell you how it's gonna be."

"Marcelle, you starting to sound just like your monmon. Next thing you gonna pull out some gris-gris and start predicting the future." Rae sat down as though easing a heavy burden.

"Lord, wouldn't Mama have a fit. She still fusses at her mama about all that old superstition. But you don't need no bones or conjure to see you and Simon are in love."

"I don't know—"

"L-o-v-e, cher. Don't interrupt me again." Marcelle folded her hands in her lap again. "You gonna have rough times, that's a given. But you can make it."

"And my promise to Lucien to find the truth?"

"Simon will understand that, Rae. Tell him about it. He'll support you." Marcelle rocked looking satisfied.

Rae felt a sinking feeling. "Marcelle, we forgot something."

"What's that?" Marcelle sipped her tea.

"If Pawpaw Vincent didn't steal the money, then there are only two other people who could have taken it."

Marcelle lowered her glass slowly. "Henry Jove or . . ." Her voice trailed off.

"Joe St. Cyr," Rae murmured.

Nine

Two days later, Rae sat in Tante Ina's kitchen eating apple pie. Bright yellow checked curtains made the white kitchen even brighter. Sun streamed in through the windows reminding her of those times she'd sat there with her cousins when they were children. There was always laughter and singing at Tante Ina's, in sharp contrast to her house. For two days she'd put off coming here. Not because she did not want to see her aunt. Rae feared asking her the questions that could lead LaMar to unlocking the past. A past that seemed like Pandora's box no matter what answers came popping out.

"My Michael tells me the dance hall is looking good, yeah." Tante Ina eased down into the chair across from her at the breakfast table. "Say it's gonna be the biggest thing to hit this town since the seafood plant opened eight years ago."

"Yes, ma'am." Rae picked at the flaky crust.

"Says you gonna have the best zydeco and blues folk around. People will be coming from all around here, even New Orleans." Tante Ina sipped her strong coffee. *"Mon Dieu,* Lucien would be so happy."

"Yes, ma'am."

"Sa va bien, oui?"

"Oui. Things are going well. The dance hall should be open in another week or so," Rae said.

Tante Ina raised both eyebrows at the morose expression on Rae's face. "You're looking mighy pitiful to say life is going so good."

"I didn't say that, tante. I said the dance hall is coming along okay." Rae put down her fork.

"I knew it. Don't nobody neglect my pie without a good reason," Tante Ina said with a chuckle. "Specially not my *Tite mouche a miel.*" (Little honey bee.)

"Why did you always call me that, tante?"

"Because you can make sweet music, like the bee make honey. But you got a bad sting when you get mad." Tante Ina pinched her chin.

"I never thanked you." Rae caught her soft, plump hand.

"Thank me for what?"

"All those days you let me sit in this kitchen with Elise, Michael, and the rest without asking why I would show up." Rae kissed her skin, rough from hard work. "You don't know how much it meant to me."

"Oh, pooh," Tante Ina said in a gruff voice. Her eyes were glassy. "Stop your nonsense. You're one of my children. I tell everybody I borne six, but I got about twenty altogether." She got up to put her cup in the sink. Before turning back to sit down, she dabbed at her eyes.

Rae laughed. Tante Ina was right. Uncle David would just shake his head when he would come home from work to find a house full of children. Nieces and nephews crowded into Tante Ina's living room and kitchen and spilled out into the yard. Tante Ina was the quintessential mother hen.

"Now don't try to change the subject on me. What's got you frowning like this, cher?" Tante Ina would not be put off.

"Back about two years ago when Daddy was so sick that time and I came home, we had a long talk. We worked out a lot of things. Daddy said he was sorry for making Mama so sad." Rae could see Lucien with the vividness of a color photograph. He sat in his favorite easy chair, a cotton afghan covering him from waist down.

"Broke my heart to see it. Letha was good for Lucien but he hurt her bad. There was women, too, you know." Tante Ina nodded.

"I heard the talk but . . . So it was true?" Rae had already guessed as much, though her mother never said a word against him. Lucien had alluded to being no good as a husband.

"Not so many as some tried to put out, but yeah. I told Lucien one was too many. But it wasn't just that."

"I know. Anyway, Daddy said he wished the dance hall could be open again to give us something of our own along with the land."

"And you're doing that, cher A good job of it, too, to hear your cousins bragging on you." Tante Ina patted her hand. "So why the long face? You made peace with your papa."

"He begged me to prove Pawpaw Vincent wasn't a thief." Rae gazed into Tante Ina's eyes, the color of pecan shells. "I've hired a private investigator to try and track down what happened to him."

"Mais, jamais de la vie," Tante Ina said in a soft voice. (Well, for goodness sakes.)

"He wants to talk to you so he can get more information to go on." Rae watched her with growing concern. Tante Ina sat staring out the window at the landscape. "To find out the truth."

"The truth could snap us up like a big alligator, cher. I ain't talked about that in years." Tante Ina blinked as though trying to regain her bearings. She looked at Rae. "We was all tore up, you know. Us children crying for Papa, Mama half out her mind for days. My, Lord. Then she got quiet. That scared us even more."

"So much pain. Maybe he left and that was wrong. But Daddy was so sure." Rae had been moved by Lucien's faith in the father he had not seen since he was six years old.

"Lucien thought Papa hung the moon. He was still crying for him long after us older children had stopped. But your daddy was just a baby, cher. He couldn't know."

"Maybe, but nobody knows for sure. There could be another explanation." Rae did not add that even she could not think of one.

"I'm gonna tell you something I never breathed to another living soul before now, not even David." Tante Ina leaned forward. "I was there the night Mama caught Papa with Miss Estelle. Couldn't sleep. She followed him one Friday night.

When he got home about three in the morning, Mama let him have it. I was hiding under that old sofa with the claw legs. He finally owned up to it and swore to break it off."

"Then that proves —

"Don't prove nothing. A week later they was back at it, honey. Old Miss Dixie, with her gossiping self, told it. Not that she was much different from the other folks in town. Say Miss Estelle was out with a man and Henry Jove was boiling mad."

"But that was just gossip, like you said." Rae tried to find some hope.

"I put two and two together and came up with four." Tante Ina got up and poured more coffee in her cup. "Tell me you think different."

"That does look bad," Rae admitted. They sat quiet for a time. "But they said some man, not Pawpaw Vincent."

"Yeah, say she was riding in the car toward Lake Charles and couldn't see who was driving. In that Ford Mr. Henry bought for her, too."

"Then it might not have been Papaw Vincent." Rae lifted a shoulder at Tante Ina's look of skepticism. "Yeah, pretty flimsy."

"Child, we're both grabbing at straws. We never wanted to believe the talk but . . . I remember that day."

"Tante Ina, Daddy never told me much besides saying Pawpaw didn't do it." Rae wanted a firsthand account as much for herself as for LaMar.

"It was September, round Labor Day. We was all getting ready for a parade down at Chauvin's field." Tante Ina's voice took on the smooth tone of a storyteller. She smiled at the memory.

Rae did not want her to stop. "Mr. Chauvin's field was where black folks had picnics," she said in a soft voice to prompt her for more.

"Yeah, nice man. I dated one of his boys for a while. Mr. Chauvin had some picnic table he built and would rent out his park, or so he called it. We called it a field." She chuckled. "Use to make him so mad."

"It's a nice park now with swings and such for the kids. A building for receptions, too. Pawpaw Vincent took y'all there?"

"Usually on holidays. But this time, no. He didn't come home that night. Mama got up and packed a basket. I heard her tell Tante Marguerite she wasn't gonna let Papa spoil our fun. She sat off talking with her sisters. Like kids, we knew something was wrong, but soon got caught up in playing and firecrackers.

"Long about two o'clock, Henry Jove come barreling up in that big Chrysler of his and jumps out. He starts yellin' how Papa was a thief. Mr. Joe tried to get him to lower his voice so us children wouldn't hear, but he was too out of his mind. Mr. Henry was yelling about his Estelle. And I'll never forget this, he cried. That man just sat down and bawled. Before long we heard there was money missing, too."

"They searched for them, right? I don't understand why they didn't find them." Rae thought even in 1948 they must have been able to trace people.

"The law didn't much care about black folk's business back then. Old Sheriff Leblanc flat out said he wasn't gonna waste his resources running up and down the countryside. The sheriff in New Orleans found Miss Estelle's car. That fine car would have give them up for sure, the color of a sable coat. Guess that's why they ditched it." Tante Ina seemed all talked out, her face was tired and sad.

"I didn't mean to get you upset, Tante." Rae held her hand.

"I'm okay, baby." Tante Ina wore a slight smile. "Fifty years helped me get used to it. But the talk after Papa left, the way we got treated, was awful."

"You'd think Monmon Marie would have gotten sympathy. She was a victim, too."

"Folks couldn't take it out on Papa, so . . . Besides, Mama had a bad temper even back in those days. She told them just what was on her mind. Said Papa shoulda took their money cause they was all fools to trust Henry Jove. They said Papa must left her some before he took off. Mama kept us going on hard work. If there was extra money, I couldn't tell." Tante Ina closed her eyes.

"Will you talk to LaMar?" Rae had to ask. All she'd heard

left her wanting to follow any thread, no matter how weak. There were too many unanswered questions.

"LaMar Zeno? That boy what helped out Savannah and Paul?"

"Yeah, that's him. Savannah gave me his name." Rae had called her cousin when she remembered how a black private detective had helped her out three years before.

Tante Ina patted Rae's head. "I'll tell him much as I can remember, cher. Just hope you don't get your heart broke fishin' for the truth." She started washing dishes.

A sense of foreboding went through Rae again at her aunt's words. Rae began to wonder if there could be an answer to this mystery that would not hurt someone.

The next day Rae sat on her back porch strumming her fingers across the strings of her old acoustic guitar. She played at least an hour every day. Not so much for practice, though that helped, but as a kind of extension of herself. It was part of her daily routine much as others had a second cup of coffee or read the morning paper. She strummed out a Creole tune Monmon Marie had taught her when she was four years old. The summer evening with still bright sunshine brought a faintly cooling breeze that rustled the leaves of the trees. Rae changed to a blues song that told a sensuous tale of true love finally found. The last notes faded away, a deep thrumming that implied passionate lovemaking without one word of lyric needed. Hand-clapping came from her left. Simon stood there wearing a light green knit polo shirt and cotton pants the color of wet sand. His muscular body outlined against the splash of light took her breath away.

"This is the first time I've heard you play alone. That was beautiful, Rae." Simon sat down next to her. He kissed her forehead. "I've missed you."

"We saw each other night before last." Rae's skin tingled from the touch of his lips.

"You didn't call me at the office yesterday morning. My day got off to a bad start without the sound of your voice. And last

night, you seemed unwilling to talk." Simon watched her for
several seconds.

Rae's heart pounded. "Simon, you think maybe we're moving
too fast after all? The history between our families can't be just
brushed off." She wanted to say more.

"No, but it shouldn't keep us from being happy." Simon
cupped her chin with one strong hand and turned her face to
his. "You make me happier than anyone or anything else. I can't
let you go now, Rae."

His words hit her with such force, her resistance sagged. Rae
welcomed his arms around her. She held on tight, afraid it was
only a lovely dream that this wonderful man wanted her so
much.

"Simon, there are some things you should know about me."

"I don't want to hear confessions, Rae."

"Just listen." Rae pulled back from him. "Please?"

"Okay," Simon said softly. He wrapped his arms around her
again. "If you need to tell me, go on."

"When I was just a teenager, Darcy and I dated."

"Any feelings left for him?" Simon didn't take his arms away,
but he tensed.

"No, none at all. But—"

"Then it doesn't matter. No more than all those girls I swore
to love forever when I was fifteen."

Rae could feel him relax against her. "I felt you should know.
Someone might take great pleasure in telling you about it." She
knew Toya would paint a graphic picture worthy of a tabloid
newspaper.

"Then they'll be disappointed when I don't faint from the
shock." Simon chuckled.

"I've also hired a private detective to find out what really
happened to Pawpaw Vince." Rae looked at him. "LaMar Zeno
has already begun investigating."

"Good," Simon said in a firm voice.

"What?" Rae had not expected this reaction at all. "Everyone
else I've told, even Andrew, said maybe I should leave it alone."

"Strange how even the folks you think would welcome it get

cold feet." Simon held her tighter. "The truth might settle all the bad feelings once and for all."

"Or prove Pawpaw Vince was exactly what folks said he was—a thief. Then they could spit on us for good reason." Rae could see the self-righteous expressions.

"How is that different from the way some of them act now?" Simon asked.

"Good point."

"Actually, most of the people who felt the most bitterness have died since then. Old man Pitre and his son. Mr. Wilson and Mr. Leland, all gone home to rest, as my grandmother says." Simon gently rocked them both back and forth.

"Except your grandfather and Mr. Henry are still here." Rae did not add they were the two most aggrieved by Pawpaw Vincent's alleged betrayal. "Mr. Henry lost more than money."

"Rae, do what you have to and don't worry about it. Papa Joe and Mr. Henry survived their loss fifty years ago. I doubt it will devastate them now. Either your grandfather did it or he didn't."

Rae's anxiety spiked. "But what happened to the money if Pawpaw Vincent didn't take it?"

"There was another thief. Maybe Miss Estelle left with some other man nobody knew about." Simon offered the explanation in a casual way, but jumped at Rae's strong reaction.

"Cher! You're brilliant," Rae kissed him hard on the lips.

She was relieved beyond belief. Why hadn't she thought of that? It did not have to be Mr. Henry or, thank goodness, Mr. Joe. Maybe the truth did not have to destroy her new found happiness.

"Thanks. Uh, what in particular helped you see this profound truth?" Simon grinned at her. "Not that I'm arguing with the results."

"You helped me see the obvious." Rae could not tell him she had suspected his grandfather of not only stealing the money, but framing her grandfather "I was just so worried that since evidence pointed to Pawpaw Vince, it might be true."

"Baby, that old saying about the sins of the father has to be put aside by you and the rest of this town." Simon brushed her hair with one hand. "Even if you find proof he did it, it's his sin. Not yours"

"I know. It's just that it meant so much to Lucien to prove the father he loved wasn't a bum." Rae leaned against him. "Maybe it's just as well Daddy won't be here. In case we do find Pawpaw Vincent stole the money and left his family behind for Estelle."

"From what I hear, Estelle was friendly with more than a couple of men in this parish."

"Simon St. Cyr, you've been listening to nasty old gossip." Rae feigned a look of shocked disapproval then winked at him with a wicked smile. "Tell me more."

"Just that she wasn't exactly Saint Estelle when it came to men. My grandmother, great-aunts, and aunts used to talk while they were cooking or sitting in the yard after supper. They said Mr. Henry shouldn't have been surprised she took off."

"So Estelle was generous with her affection."

"Very generous from what I overheard."

Rae shook a finger under his nose. "Shame on you for eaves-dropping, you little rascal."

"Hey, can I help it if the tree I sat under to rest was near them?" Simon tried to look innocent.

"Don't try that boyish charm on me."

Simon traced the neckline of her shirt to the top button. "I thought you liked my boyish charm, Ms. Dalcour."

"Well, maybe just a little." Rae watched his finger with fascination as it touched the curve of her breast. She felt icy hot inside. "Okay, a lot," she said, her breath short.

"Tell you what, you give me another tune and I'll treat you to dinner." Simon spoke with his lips pressed against her cheek.

"Dinner? Is that all?" Rae murmured.

"Not even." Simon grinned. "Come on now, play for me."

"You don't want to hear . . ." She melted at the sensation of his finger on her lips cutting her off gently.

"Your music is an important part of you. I want to share everything. Please. Just you and me." Simon handed her the guitar.

"You got it, babe," she said.

For two hours all the music inside her welled up and out through her fingers. They sat side by side making love without touching. Simon joined in on some of the old Creole songs he knew, his voice a deep baritone. She watched him laugh at the funny songs and grow quiet at the sad ones. As the sun went down, they became one in spirit. Rae marveled that there could be this kind of heaven on earth.

"Now what are you going to do, Mr. Genius?" Marius sneered at Darcy. He spoke up as soon as the door closed behind the Pantheon project director's representative. "Latham was not happy with the news that you messed up our plans."

Darcy sat in the dark green leather chair behind his massive desk. The office was a study in elegance. Prints of New Orleans jazz bands were on the walls. The polished oak furniture was impeccable. Darcy's spacious office was in a modern building that was part of a new development. Mr. Henry rented these spaces at cost from the owner as he had helped him make quite a few profitable real estate deals.

"I didn't mess up anything." Darcy spoke in a deadly calm voice that should have warned his cousin.

"Really? You got a little too clever. You did exactly what grandfather predicted: outsmarted yourself."

"No one can ever accuse you of that, can they?" Darcy leaned back in his chair.

"What, screwing up a major business transaction?" Marius said. His sneer twisted what should have been attractive features made ugly by his personality.

"No, of being too clever," Darcy retorted. "Don't get any ideas that you can use this against me."

"Who me?" Marius spread his arms wide. "I wouldn't dream of doing anything like that."

"Good. Otherwise I might be forced to tell Grandfather and the U.S. attorney about that deal you cut." Darcy's voice was cold.

Marius blinked at him. "Wha—"

"You got a contract with DHH to sell them office supplies.

But your buddy made sure you got it even though you weren't the lowest bidder and he got a kickback. Using the mail to defraud is a federal offense." Darcy raised his eyebrows. "And Graydon Bell is a very tenacious U.S. attorney."

"I didn't . . . You can't prove . . ." Marius balled up his hands into a fist. He swore under his breath.

"Don't mess with me. Do we understand each other?" Darcy's stare was hard as steel.

"You wouldn't dare risk dragging the family name through the mud."

"Wanna bet? No one will head this corporation but me. No one," Darcy said.

"Grandfather would stand by me." Marius tried to recover some advantage. "It wouldn't even get to trial. Grandfather knows how smart business is done."

"No doubt you'd have the best attorney possible. But do you think Grandfather would let you near a responsible position in any of the family businesses after that?" Darcy shook his head slowly. Both of them knew the answer.

"You bastard." Marius pounded the arm of his chair in frustration.

"I'm sure you'd do the same for me, Cousin," Darcy shot back.

Marius sat fuming for several minutes before the sneer returned. "What about your secret meetings with the police jury president? Grandfather would not be happy."

"How did you find out . . ." Darcy dipped his head in a slight bow. "Seems we have a stand off."

"Let's be honest, Grandfather is not going to cut you out and promote me. But he will make sure we're rewarded equally. So let's protect each other, since we both could lose big time." Marius adopted a practical tone.

"Agreed. Now do you have any suggestions regarding Pantheon?" Darcy waited patiently.

After a few moments, Marius brightened. "We could get the feds to declare part of Dalcour property as wetlands, then they would lose it."

Darcy gave him a look of contempt. "So would we, Marius.

That would take the land off the market for any kind of development. What a stupid idea."

"Well what do you suggest?" Marius glared at him.

"Pantheon wants, no they *need* this plant. The state and the feds are on their backs about the waste they produce at other sites. Part of an agreement they made to avoid hefty fines was to safely dispose of hazardous by-products." Darcy was back in control. He leaned back against the rich leather of his chair.

"Really? Hmm, I didn't know that." Marius rubbed his chin.

"Of course, you didn't. But I did. They won't squawk if we use a different tract adjacent to our land." Darcy brushed the sleeve of his cotton shirt.

"But what will Grandfather say? He really wants to get his hands on Dalcour property." Marius seemed to hesitate in the face of Henry's displeasure.

"He'll get over it. It's time he let us handle the day-to-day affairs anyway." Darcy looked at his cousin. "He deserves a rest after all these years."

"Wait a minute, this means you'll have to have Bayou Latte dredged and a road built. You know how he'll react." Marius went from hesitation to obvious fear. Henry Jove was a force of destruction when angry.

"You want a multimillion dollar deal to take wings and fly away? We either decide to ride out Grandfather's displeasure or kiss that plant goodbye." Darcy did not seem the least bit concerned about Henry's reaction. "Besides, when I show him all those lovely zeros in the profit column, he'll be quite happy."

Marius brightened again at the mention of money. "You're right. So when do we start?"

"I'm meeting with Latham and his bosses in New Orleans in a week. You get started with the process to have dredging done."

"Right. What about Rae Dalcour? Are we just going to let her stay? Toya won't be happy." Marius stood.

"I don't care if she throws one of her temper tantrums. Ignore her."

"Of course, your weak spot for Rae Dalcour doesn't have anything to do with it, right?" Marius scrutinized Darcy.

"I don't have a weak spot for anyone," Darcy snapped. He caught himself when he saw Marius smile with satisfaction.

"I would have thought exactly that. Until now." Marius leaned on the desk. "Keep your priorities straight."

"All she wants is to open some juke joint on the bayou. So what if Dalcours still own property?"

"I don't care about some old family feud." Marius dismissed fifty years of animosity with a wave of his hand. "We can make big money developing that land. Millions."

Darcy gazed at him. "What are you thinking, Marius?"

"That Toya is right about one thing, we need to take care of Rae Dalcour."

"Leave Rae alone," Darcy said. "I'll see she comes around in my own way."

"You've two weeks, Cousin. Then I'll take over."

"Darn, Andy. Looks like a tornado touched down in here." Rae made a full turn to look around the living room.

Andrew lived four miles down the road from their family home in a double-wide trailer he'd bought at a government auction. Despite its clutter, the three-bedroom home did not look too bad. Andrew took her comment with his usual easy going outlook.

"Serena helps me out once a week cleaning up." Andrew shoved a stack of magazines on fishing and cars out her way so she could sit on the sofa.

"You've got some charm. Your ex-wife helps you clean up and your girlfriend comes over to cook. Don't you get a little confused sometimes?"

Andrew grunted. "Serena comes by for her child support check and to beg for money as much as anything. And Marilyn is a nag."

Rae smiled. "Those kids of yours are cute as can be. Little Aletha Ann has the prettiest fat brown cheeks."

"Yeah, they're good looking little rascals. Hey, Robert is on the honor roll at school, too." Andrew went to the refrigerator and came back with two bottles of Barq's creme soda.

"That's wonderful. See what good genes us Dalcours have to pass on?" Rae took a long drink. "Um, I sure missed this stuff. It's good to be home."

Andrew plopped down in the chair next to the sofa. "No place like home." He put his feet on the coffee table with a satisfied sigh. "How is work at the dance hall coming?"

"Almost through. I'm having flyers for the grand opening printed up. Gonna have ads in the Baton Rouge newspaper. Got a listing in four small papers that are mostly about local interests. Those are free."

"You've really got this all planned out. Sounds good."

"We're going to have our grand opening Memorial Day weekend." Rae was pleased with the progress she'd made.

"Three weeks away. You'll be ready by then? I know how much needed to be done on that place." Andrew shook his head. "It was in a mess."

"I lit a fire under those guys. We'll be ready in another week or so. Jamal and Wes are bringing the band and guess who's coming in to sing Monday at the big outdoor barbecue?"

"Who?"

"Kenny Neal." Rae beamed at him.

"Get outta here, girl! You gonna make Neville's investment back in three days." Andrew looked impressed.

"I'll settle for a modest profit to start. But I think this thing is going to take off." Rae heaved a sigh. "I've kept one of my promises to Daddy. By the way, LaMar called the other day. He thinks he's got a lead."

Andrew's good humor evaporated. "Oh?"

"I tell you, Savannah was right about him. He's good. He found out the sheriff in Orleans Parish had witnesses that saw a couple leave the car. One lady is still living in Kenner. Anyway, LaMar thinks he can trace them at least to where they stayed after leaving the car."

"I've been thinking it might be best to just forget about it. What difference could it make after all these years?" Andrew twisted his hands together.

"It will make a difference to our family," Rae said.

"I don't think anybody cares about it these days. Nobody

treats my kids bad cause their name is Dalcour," Andrew said. "Tell that detective to quit looking."

"Since I hired LaMar, you've been acting real funny. What's up?" Rae leaned forward to stare at him hard.

"It's just we don't need no more trouble." Andrew did not look at her. "Once the dance hall starts going, you'll get respect from everybody for bringing business to town."

"I'm not buying that line, Andy. You never cared what folks in Belle Rose thought. What's the real reason?" Rae persisted.

Andrew sat back against the cushion and looked at her. "Remember I told you I went up in Daddy's attic?"

"Yeah, to look for his burial policy and stuff."

"I found some papers." Andrew got up and walked to the open screen door of the trailer.

"What kind of papers?" Rae got up to stand behind him. She tugged on his arm. "Andrew, tell me what this is about."

Andrew turned around. His eyes were sad. "I found some old letters that Pawpaw Vincent wrote. Love letters. To Estelle Jove."

Rae sighed with relief. "I knew he'd been having an affair with her. But that doesn't make him a—"

"And there was some papers where he wrote off for information on living in South America. He said in one letter that money wouldn't be a problem." Andrew shook his head then went back to drop into the chair again.

"But Daddy was so sure . . ." Rae felt a pounding in her head at his words. Could it be that their grandfather had been so selfish that he'd left his family to face poverty and persecution? All this time they had defended him when he'd cared nothing for the pain he left behind.

Andrew looked at her with eyes clouded with pain and anger caused by a man neither of them had ever known. "I think maybe he did exactly what they say he did, Rae. Our grandfather was a lying, wife-stealing thief."

Ten

"Maybe you misunderstood." Rae sat down hard after hearing this news. "Maybe he just . . ."

"See for yourself." Andrew went into a small bedroom he used as a combination den and office. He came back with a big metal box.

Rae read through letters that left no doubt their grandfather and Estelle were lovers for almost a year. Finally, she came to one cryptic note. Pawpaw Vincent wrote that he would meet Estelle to talk one evening. Rae was puzzled.

"Why would Daddy keep these and not tell us? He was defending the man right up until he died." Rae stared at the faded ink on yellowing paper.

"I'm pretty sure he didn't know. They were sewn in the lining of an old trunk from Monmon Marie's house. I wouldn't have found them except I tore the lining when I reached down to take out a bunch of old clothes."

"She knew and never said anything," Rae said in a soft voice.

"Looks like. Why you think she never told?"

Rae grunted. "And make things worse on herself? Bad enough he'd left her with seven children. Remember Monmon Marie was a proud person. She probably didn't want to admit to the world another woman took her husband."

"You right, cher. She was that, maybe too proud. No wonder she was always in a sour mood."

"I just wonder how she got hold of letters Pawpaw wrote to Estelle." Rae saw one mystery being replaced by another.

"I don't know. Maybe Mr. Henry gave them to her for spite when she kept defending Pawpaw." Andrew shrugged.

"Why didn't he show them to the world as proof? Henry Jove hated Pawpaw. I can't see him missing a chance to show the world that Pawpaw's own words made him out a thief."

"Like you said about Monmon Marie, maybe he didn't want everybody to know she was making a fool outta him." Andrew's eyebrows went up. "Some of them letters are pretty hot."

"You know what this means, Andy?" Rae waved a couple of the letters in the air.

Andrew squinted at her. "What?"

"That it's even more important we find out the whole story. I'm gonna call LaMar. He needs to see these." Rae sorted the letters in her lap.

"You done lost your mind. We don't need to pay him to tell us even worse garbage!" Andrew looked disgusted. "Bad enough knowing what we do."

"Too many questions are left unanswered." Rae sat deep in thought for several seconds. "For instance, why didn't they track Pawpaw down? With this information, Henry Jove could have maybe helped the authorities find them."

"Hmm. Maybe he did tell them and like Tante Ina said, the sheriff didn't care enough to follow the man to another country." Andrew took a deep drink of his creme soda. "Maybe they tried and lost their trail."

"Maybe, maybe, maybe. Don't you think something's strange? Like it's a puzzle with a lot of missing pieces?"

Andrew put the now empty soda bottle down. "Now that you mention it, seems awful peculiar that none of this has ever been mentioned. I mean, there's always been a lot of talk about how Pawpaw and Estelle ran off. I've never heard anybody say just what the sheriff did to find them."

"Right!" Rae was getting really fascinated with all the loose ends. "Even racism doesn't explain such a weak attempt to search."

"Of course, he could have just been stupid or incompetent. Sheriff Leblanc was a bigot and dim as an old lightbulb from what folks say." Andrew chuckled.

"Either way, I want to keep looking. And I can tell you do, too." Rae poked her brother on the arm. "It's written all over your face."

"Okay, so maybe I do. Just be prepared. Simon might not be so lovey-dovey when you get the whole story." Andrew gazed at her. "Yeah, you never thought about that."

"Simon isn't a snob, Andy." Rae knew she sounded defensive.

"The St. Cyrs and the Joves have always been stuckup. What with being descendants of French governors sent to Louisiana. He might say all that don't matter to him now, but . . ."

"He cares about me and don't you forget it. When you get to know him, you'll see that you're wrong." Rae put as much conviction in her voice as she could. After the hours spent with him, she could not imagine such a reaction from Simon.

Andrew did appear to be reassured. "I hope you're right, little sister. I really do."

"I am. Now help me put these letters in some kind of order." Rae pushed any budding doubts from her mind.

"Okay, but I got a lot more still in the box." Andrew dug out another stack of papers tied together with twine.

"Good gracious. Well let's get started. I want to call LaMar today."

Rae and Andrew got down to the task of separating the letters from other documents. After an hour of coming up with a system by date and content, they had three neat bundles. Rae took the papers home with her. She was still reading when Simon knocked on her door.

"Hello, beautiful." Simon kissed her. "Looks like you've got a term paper due." He pointed to the papers stacked up on the sofa.

"More like a research project." Rae had letters and old receipts in her lap.

"What exactly are you doing?" Simon sat down in a chair opposite the sofa so as not to disturb her work.

"Digging myself into a hole," Rae said. She fell back against the sofa back.

"You don't look the least bit dirty to me," Simon teased. "Come on now, tell me about it." He touched her knee.

"The way things look right now, my grandfather probably stole the money and took Estelle Jove with him." Rae threw down one of the love letters. She was angry at Pawpaw Vincent for betraying her father. Lucien and the rest of the family had deserved better than what he'd done to them.

"You've found proof after all this time?"

"He was having an affair with her. Add that to his telling her that he would have the money to take care of them both . . ." Rae sat up. "You figure it out."

"It's still only circumstantial." Simon tried to sound encouraging.

"Nice try." Rae brought his hand to her face.

"Maybe this is a good reason to let go of it." Simon carefully moved the stacks of old papers to the coffee table. "We've got each other now, baby. I don't care about the past." He pulled her into his strong arms.

"Your family cares, Simon. When they find out about us—"

"My parents aren't that narrow-minded. Dad never bought into the old family feud. My mother is from Lafayette. I doubt she'd care."

Rae looked at him. "What about my reputation? I haven't exactly been the sweet debutante type." For the first time in her life, Rae worried about what someone thought of her youthful antics.

"I can't believe this! Show me that old Rae Dalcour rebel spirit," Simon said. He pinched her chin.

"I've never cared much what anybody in this town thought, at least that's what I tried to tell myself. But some of the things people said did hurt." Rae rested her head against his chest. It felt wonderful to feel so at ease, so secure. "Guess my reaction when I got to be a teenager was to just break out. A lot of what I did was out of anger."

"I never realized how tough it was for you." Simon cuddled her close.

"Lucien was in a lot of pain, I realize that now. But at the time, all I knew was that nobody seemed to understand. So when Mama, Daddy, and teachers tried to give me rules, I broke them." Rae could see herself fighting for a place in the world, trying to make sense of who she should be. "This sounds so cliche, but I was trying to find myself."

Simon did not answer except to rock her gently in his embrace. Rae wondered at how instinctive it had been to tell him what she'd shared with no one else before. She had poured it into her music. Yet she'd never admitted that the slights and snubs she suffered during childhood had stayed with her. The biggest wonder of all was that far from feeling exposed, she felt comforted.

"Thanks, baby," Simon whispered. "Thanks for sharing a special part of you with me."

Rae looked into his dark brown eyes. He understood. She could see it in his face. A yearning for him flared up like a wild fire in her body. They kissed long and deep, trying to satisfy a hunger but only making it grow.

"I want you so much," Simon murmured, his lips against hers.

"Yes," was all Rae answered.

Without another word, she led him to her bedroom. She'd had it redone with the furniture from her apartment. There was only the soft light of an antique lamp that played across the soft creme, blue, and lavender that were the colors in the room. The curtains and bedspread were in an abstract floral pattern.

Simon kissed her again once they stood next to the bed. "It's lovely, Rae. I wouldn't have expected . . ."

"You thought I'd have music posters on the walls and a bare mattress," she whispered while taking off his shirt. "I like to surround myself with beauty. Like right now."

With one quick motion, she removed her blouse. Simon brushed her fingers away, insisting that he complete the process. He slowly removed her bra. Throwing it aside, he buried his face in the soft flesh with a small moan of satisfaction. His hands tugged at her pants and panties. Soon both were breathless and naked. They savored the sensation of pressing their bodies together while kissing. Rae guided them to the bed then pulled him down with her. She was instantly lost in a world of delight as they explored each other with their hands and lips. Both reveled in raising the anticipation to a fever pitch. Rae could not stand to be separate from him any longer. After a time, the caresses were not enough. She needed to be a part of him.

"Now, Simon. Now."

Rae watched him put on the condom. She touched it with the tips of her fingers. Simon gazed into her eyes as he slowly entered her. Their hips pressed together for a brief, sweet moment before they started to move in long strokes. All the desires to love and be love exploded within her. Sex with him was a magnificent combination of physical and emotional ecstasy. He alternated between taking his time and going fast. His tongue brushed her face, neck, and breasts. Rae cried out over and over until Simon joined her in a frantic need to calm the raging lust that welled up. The short tiny stabs of joy became a blinding light flooding her mind. The orgasm that shook her brought Simon over the edge. He clutched her hips while thrusting hard again and again until they both lay shuddering, clinging to each other.

"I love you so much," Simon said in a hoarse whisper. He was still in her, still holding her. "I love you."

"I love you, too," Rae whispered back.

They lay together, arms around each other, talking for hours. The night sounds of crickets and frogs lulled them to sleep sometime in the early hours of the next day.

"This is crazy!" Papa Joe stared at his grandson as though he'd just announced he was going to the moon. "You've lost your mind."

"We love each other." Simon sat in his grandfather's living room. He hated sounding like a little boy caught stealing cookies from the cookie jar.

"Olivia, will you say something to this boy?" Papa Joe turned to his wife for help.

"Cher, are you certain about how you feel? I know she's attractive and exciting now. But . . ." Olivia let her voice trail off. One dark eyebrow came up. Her head inclined to one side, silver hair swept up in a soft French twist gave her a regal look.

"Grandmother, I'm no ten-year-old with a crush." Simon was frustrated. "Don't tell me you're willing to judge Rae based on hearsay. You taught me better than that."

"Don't get smart with us young man. Telling me what I taught you," Papa Joe muttered.

"Joe, calm down. You were nice to Lucien more than once. Not that he appreciated it, but still you were." Olivia turned to Simon. "Of course, we're not passing judgment."

"Humph." Papa Joe's expression told a different story.

"Hush, Joe." Olivia gave him a warning glance. "But let's be realistic. What have you got in common? You're from very different backgrounds."

"Papa Joe went into business with Mr. Vincent. The Dalcours were good enough back then," Simon put in.

"Yeah, and look how *that* turned out," Papa Joe retorted.

"Joe," Olivia said in a sharp voice.

"If he did take the money, that has nothing to do with Rae." Simon wore a look of justification at his own argument.

"She's pulled some crazy stunts herself." Papa Joe shook his head. "I tell you—"

"I can't believe my own grandparents are snobs." Simon folded his arms. "That sure isn't what you taught me."

"We're talking about facts here, Simon. Hard facts!" Papa Joe shot back. "Fact, Vincent disappeared with ten thousand dollars and another man's wife."

"Never proven." Simon waved a hand as though brushing his words aside. "And again, Rae can't be held responsible for what he might have done twenty years before she was born."

Papa Joe huffed in silence for a few minutes. "Well she was a rowdy teenager. No telling what kind of life she's been leading since. Roaming all over creation with a group of musicians. Men blues musicians at that."

"So what?" Simon scowled at him.

"Everybody knows how those people live. Drugs, staying up all night. Smokin' Dan was a pal of mine back in my days."

"Joe, you can't compare Smokin' Dan to Rae. Besides, don't forget some of the things you did right along with him." Olivia patted his shoulder. "Now be quiet."

"I'm telling you, Olivia—"

"Hush, dear. I'm talking." Olivia was one of two people who could say such things to Joe St. Cyr. His mother had been the other. "So you're that serious about Rae Dalcour?"

"She's a wonderful, kind person. Yes, I'm that serious about her." Simon squinted at Papa Joe. "And she's not the female version of Smokin' Dan."

"I don't want you getting mixed up in anything that might hurt you, son." Papa Joe leaned forward.

"I appreciate your concern, but—"

Papa Joe held up a palm. "I know, I know. Stay out of your business."

"I hear Rae is looking into her grandfather's disappearance. She could find out some unpleasant truths about Vincent after all." Olivia stared at her grandson.

"We'll deal with that when and if it happens," Simon said. "Actually I have this strange feeling that maybe there could be another explanation."

"What? She's really got you brainwashed!" Papa Joe threw up both hands.

Simon did not want to reveal that Rae was having her own doubts about Vincent's innocence. He could not explain why he had begun to think the popular explanation for those long-ago events did not add up. But as he talked to Rae about the contents of the letters and papers, there were gaps that puzzled him.

"Papa Joe, would you tell me everything you remember about back then. You know, how y'all got into business together. Stuff like that. Right up until Mr. Vincent and Miss Estelle left."

Papa Joe crossed his arms. "First you say the past doesn't matter, now you want story hour. Uh-uh, I know what you're up to, Simon Joseph."

"Haven't you always been curious about how Vincent and Estelle pulled it off? You told me once Vincent was fun-loving, but you would not have thought he'd do something like steal." Simon prodded at his grandfather's love for solving puzzles.

"Yeah, well, that Estelle was one good-looking gal." Papa Joe cleared his throat and squirmed at the look Olivia gave him. "Not near as pretty as my Livvy, naturally."

"Humph!" was Olivia's eloquent reply.

"There now, sweetness." Papa Joe winked at her. "Anyways, losing his head over a woman can make a man do strange things. You oughta know." He shot a meaningful glance at his grandson.

"Just tell me the story."

"No." Papa Joe looked stubborn.

"Come on, please." Simon tapped his knee. "A wonderful woman can also make life sweet. That's something you always told me about being married to Grandmother."

"Well I . . ." Papa Joe wavered.

Olivia seemed mollified by Simon's testimony on Papa Joe's behalf. Her look of annoyance melted away. "Go on, honey. Besides, you always loved telling Simon about the old days."

"You'd want to help Grandmother if she were in Rae's position. Please?" Simon placed his ace. Papa Joe's weakness for Olivia was legendary.

Papa Joe was hooked. "Well, all right."

For the next hour, Papa Joe told him how he, Henry Jove, and Vincent had grown up together. Despite the differences in social status, the three boys became fast friends from an early age. Add to that, the Great Depression had left even the old Creole families in dire financial straits. The old class boundaries relaxed as a result.

"We were part of modern times," Olivia put in. "We made fun of our parents' haughty attitudes." She smiled in fond memory of her youth.

"Anyway we were going to go in on a canning outfit. Our plan to get rich." Papa Joe chuckled. "Wasn't a bad idea either. Old Mr. Isidore, Henry's daddy, had a nice farm. We were going to can tomatoes, okra, and such. Later we planned to expand to maybe seafood. But our parents said we had to come up with the money ourselves. They didn't believe in handing you everything on a silver platter."

"Mr. Isidore and your father would have given you the help and you know it." Olivia added.

"After we proved we were serious, yeah. We worked like crazy all through high school, summers and after school even.

Time passed, all three of us got married. Henry traveled back and forth to Southern in Baton Rouge. I went to trade school and got an associate degree later on. Vincent, he stayed right here. He'd go live with friends in New Orleans sometimes, making good money as a stevedore. Yep, those were the days. After four years we had seven thousand dollars saved between us."

"But ten thousand was stolen," Simon said.

"When folks saw how hard-working we were, several folks kicked in small amounts to invest," Papa Joe replied.

"Not so small back then. Even fifty dollars took a long time for folks to save. You know what wages for black people were like in those days." Olivia looked at her husband.

"You're right. But they knew we'd have good jobs for our people. Folks were looking forward to the progress a successful black-owned business would bring to our community. Our parents made up the difference until we had ten thousand dollars." Papa Joe fell silent.

"So that's why most of the black population was so mad. I thought it was just in sympathy because the Joves and St. Cyrs were highly regarded." Simon now understood why the anger had continued for years from more than just the investors. The entire community felt wronged.

"It was a terrible blow. White businessmen laughed at how us 'colored' couldn't trust our own." Olivia heaved a sigh.

"It was twenty more years until Henry opened his food distribution operation. Losing Estelle seemed to suck the wind right outta his sails, poor fella." Papa Joe shook his head.

"What was Vincent like?" Simon wanted a clear picture of the man whose supposed actions had so affected them all.

"Like I said, always laughing. Always had a funny tale to tell, half the time stretching the truth." Papa Joe smiled. "He could sing, too. Guess music is in their blood, eh?"

"And he was a handsome man." Olivia put in with a twinkle in her eye. "Tall, dark brown skin, and big muscles."

"That's enough of that now, Liv." Papa Joe wore a tight expression.

"What's good for the goose, Joseph," she quipped.

"Okay, you got me back." Papa Joe chuckled. "Anyway, he

was hard-working and loved his family. But he did have a thing for Estelle. Guess that feeling won out when it came down to it."

"Strange they just vanished without a trace." Simon rubbed his jaw. "You'd think somebody would have seen them."

"Well, they found the car. Another thing, seems like they said something about they bought passage on a ship out of New Orleans. Yeah, the sheriff told us they checked the port. Had their names on the log of some freighter."

"Then why didn't they find them?" Simon said.

"It was about eight months later. The police were checking for some guy off a ship who had stabbed somebody in the French Quarter. They were checking to see if he'd gone back to Colombia. When they saw the names on the log, they remembered them from a wire the sheriff had sent before."

"So they knew where they went." Simon felt a flicker of excitement.

"The ship went to several countries. They didn't find them. The captain claimed he couldn't remember where they landed or find his record book. Probably bribed him." Papa Joe grunted.

"So many dead ends." Olivia sat staring ahead deep in the past.

"Let me see, what was the name of that ship." Papa Joe frowned in concentration.

"Papa Joe, try hard to remember. This could be the key to ending a big mystery." Simon strained forward trying to help his grandfather's memory.

"Let's see was it *La Marie? Momenta?*" Papa Joe scratched his head. "Or lost something or other. Son, I can't think of it now." He said in an exasperated voice.

Simon felt a flush of warm contentment at the image of Rae, her hair spread on the pillow beside him. He wanted the past put to rest so they could build a future filled with love and happiness. The shadow of an old mystery would have to be swept away first though.

"That's okay. But keep trying. Once we find out exactly what happened, we can move on," Simon said in a quiet voice.

* * *

"How are things?" Ellis Mouton gazed at him intently. "I'll have coffee, thank you," he said to the pretty receptionist at his elbow.

They sat around a polished oak table in a small conference room just off Darcy's office. A window with green drapes faced a lovely courtyard filled with plants. The dark green chairs had a paisley pattern. Darcy used this room for meeting with clients and top-level staff.

"Fine." Darcy smiled at him with confidence.

They regarded each other for several seconds. Ellis was about to speak when the receptionist came back with a tray bearing cups, sugar, and cream.

Darcy flashed a smile that made her blush with pleasure. "Thank you so much, Shanice," he said.

Ellis raised an eyebrow at them. "Working hard, I hope. Pantheon should require all your attention these days." His face did not change, but his tone was peevish.

"I'm on top of it." Darcy's lips lifted in a satisfied look.

"I see." Ellis glanced at the door through which Shanice had disappeared. "I've been thinking. Maybe this venture with Pantheon is not for me." He took a sip from his cup.

Several seconds passed. Darcy sat very still. "Explain."

"You can't get the property that would most suit them. There will be delays and they could well pull out. Will all the problems Shintech is having, other companies are skittish about making major investments." Ellis looked out the window.

"Pantheon is still interested." Darcy kept his voice level. He leaned toward him. "I spoke to them only two days ago."

"I need more assurance than that for my father and uncles."

"Such as?" Darcy gave him a wary look.

"I want to attend your next meeting with them," Ellis said.

"No problem. Anything else?" Darcy smiled at him.

"Give me a complete report on what your contingencies are now that different property must be used."

"You'll have them by close of business today." Darcy looked

relaxed again. "We've worked well together so far, Ellis. I want to do whatever I can to make you feel at ease."

Ellis shot him a sharp glance. His poise slipped. "So far you've fallen short. It took you too long to inform me that the Dalcour woman would not sell. Seems all your intricate planning has been for nothing," he snapped.

"Maybe, maybe not."

"Oh?" Ellis studied him through narrowed eyes. "Your mind never stops thinking of ways to get what you want."

"Never." Darcy put down his cup. "The plant will be built. We'll all make a nice profit. Count on it."

"I'm counting on *you*." Ellis put a hand on his knee. "And I intend to get what I want, too."

"We'll all get what we want, Ellis." Darcy stared into his eyes with confidence.

"Just be sure you're objective. I understand this Rae Dalcour has a special . . . interest for you." Ellis tensed.

"All you need to know is that Pantheon still wants to do business." Darcy's voice held an understated sharp tone.

"So it's like that, is it? I thought we—"

"Business, Ellis. We're still in *business*. Let's keep the proper perspective." Darcy pushed his chair back and stood. "I'll have Shanice start working to print out my alternative proposal for Pantheon."

"Don't forget how important Charter Enterprises is to its success." Ellis stood close to him.

"Ellis, don't even try it. I know how badly your family businesses have been doing for the past two years. You wouldn't have had the chance to bounce back if it hadn't been for me. Now, let me get back to work." Darcy's charming smile flashed back on as though he'd flipped some inner switch. "We don't want to waste a minute pulling in all that cash, now do we?"

Ellis was pale. "Be very sure you know all the rules in this game."

"Your concern is touching, but I'm always careful to know just which move to make and the right time to make it." Darcy opened the door leading back into his office. "Shall we?"

* * *

Rae walked past St. Anthony Catholic Church. How she loved the cool interior when she was a little girl. St. Anthony Grade School was in the next short block from it. She was enjoying the sunshine and laughter of children playing at recess. She sat on a wooden bench beneath a large oak tree watching little girls in identical navy blue jumpers kick a ball around the grass field next to the school yard.

For once, she was taking a break from the constant task of getting the dance hall ready. In a few short days, Memorial Day weekend, she would get a taste of being an entrepreneur. As word spread of her plans, she got more friendly greetings from folks when she came into town. Rae felt a kind of peace at being home that she'd never had growing up. From now on, she would learn to enjoy life. She smiled at the image of Simon sitting on her back steps, the brown skin of his muscular arms painted with sunlight. Who would have thought life in Belle Rose could be so sweet?

"I want to talk to you." Toya stood in front of Rae.

Maybe not that sweet. Rae heaved a deep sigh. "What could you possibly have to say to me? Thought up some new insults?"

"Normally I wouldn't waste my time," Toya said with a sour expression. "But you've gone to great lengths to cause trouble for me."

"As much fun as that is, I've had more important things to do." Using a sales flyer from the grocery store, Rae fanned herself with a lazy motion.

"Like sleeping with my husband." Toya's face was hard as stone.

"Ex-husband, sugar."

"What is it with you Dalcours anyway? You seem to have a sexual obsession with the Jove family. Your grandfather ran off with my grandmother, you slept with my brother, and now—"

Rae shot from the bench and Toya jumped back. "You've got it backward. Your grandmother had a bad case of hot pants. I don't remember anybody saying she was kidnapped."

"Of all the nerve!" Toya's mouth worked in frustrated anger.

"As for my. teenage fling with Darcy, we both had a good time disobeying our parents. And Simon, well now that's a different story." Rae grinned and lifted her shoulder.

"Just like the rest of your family, you don't care who you bring down," Toya said.

"What are you talking about?"

"You decided you wanted Simon so you went after him. Never mind that his business could suffer because of you."

"That's a load of crap." Rae waved a hand at her.

"Simon's business has done so well because old family ties connected him to some of the most successful black businessmen in this state. They could begin to doubt his judgment in getting mixed up with you." Toya lifted her nose in the air to stare down at her.

"People aren't that narrow-minded," Rae snapped. Toya's words nudged alive her fear that she could hurt Simon.

"You know I'm right." Toya smiled at her in triumph.

"Simon is established. They'll do business with him based on his reputation. We've already discussed it." Rae brushed back her hair. "Anything else?"

Toya stopped smiling. "Leave him alone. He's mine," she snarled.

"Excuse me?" Rae smoothed the short denim skirt down over her hips. "Simon isn't your property, or mine for that matter. He does what he wants. And right now, he wants me." She gazed. into Toya's malevolent stare with a half smile. "Get over it."

"You'll be very sorry," Toya hissed. "I'm warning you."

"Threats only make me angrier, Toya. And when I get really angry, I bite." Rae spoke in a low voice heavy with warning.

"We'll see." Toya spun around and stormed off.

Rae let out a long breath. "I'm not going to let that hussy spoil my day."

She went on with her errands, setting a leisurely pace in an effort to recapture the mood before her encounter with Toya. Still, the menace in Toya's last words stayed with her.

Eleven

"Hey, Rockin' Good Times. I like that name."

LaMar, wearing designer casual clothes, sat across from Rae in the dance hall sipping root beer. They agreed to meet there so Rae could continue her preparations for the opening. Garret Collins, the bartender she'd hired, was busy stocking the bar and kitchen. He had been friends with Andrew since first grade. Rae took a break and let him deal with the arriving delivery men.

"Daddy said any time there was a party or picnic, my grandfather used to say 'Come on, we gonna have us a rockin' good time.' " Rae smiled at the memory.

"Well, I'll be here. So will my pals from New Orleans." LaMar snapped his fingers in time to music coming from a jukebox.

"Hope we have a nice crowd," Rae said.

"Don't worry, it's going to be a hit." LaMar took a swig of root beer.

Rae looked around. She was very pleased with the work done on the interior. Driftwood, treated and finished by a local folk artist, hung on the walls. There were cypress wood shelves with pecan shell figurines in one corner. The walls were decorated with posters from the fifties and sixties advertising blues and zydeco artists.

"Cross your fingers nothing goes wrong." Rae frowned. The encounter with Toya three days ago left a bad taste in her mouth still.

WE INVITE YOU TO JOIN THE ONLY BOOK CLUB THAT DELIVERS HEARTFELT ROMANCE FEATURING AFRICAN AMERICAN HEROES AND HEROINES IN STORIES THAT ARE RICH IN PASSION AND CULTURAL SPICE...

And Your First 4 Books Are FREE!

Arabesque is an exciting contemporary romance line offered by BET Books, a division of BET Publications. Arabesque has been so successful that our readers have asked us about direct home delivery. Now you can start receiving four bestselling Arabesque novels a month delivered right to your door. Subscribe now and you'll get:

◇ 4 FREE Arabesque romances as our introductory gift—a value of almost $20! (pay only $1 to help cover postage & handling)

◇ 4 BRAND-NEW Arabesque romances delivered to your doorstep each month thereafter (usually arriving before they're available in bookstores!)

◇ 20% off each title—a savings of almost $4.00 each month

◇ FREE home delivery

◇ A FREE monthly newsletter, *Arabesque Romance News* that features author profiles, book previews and more

◇ No risks or obligations...in other words, you can cancel whenever you wish with no questions asked

So subscribe to Arabesque today and see why these books are winning awards and readers' hearts.

After you've enjoyed our FREE gift of 4 Arabesque Romances, you'll begin to receive monthly shipments of the newest Arabesque titles. Each shipment will be yours to examine for 10 days. If you decide to keep the books, you'll pay the preferred subscriber's price of just $4.00 per title. That's $16 for all 4 books with free home delivery. And if you want us to stop sending books, just say the word.

See why reviewers are raving about ARABESQUE and order your FREE books today!

WE HAVE 4 FREE BOOKS FOR YOU!

FREE BOOK CERTIFICATE

Yes! Please send me 4 *Arabesque* Contemporary Romances without cost or obligation, billing me just $1 to help cover postage and handling. I understand that each month, I will be able to preview 4 brand-new *Arabesque* Contemporary Romances FREE for 10 days. Then, if I decide to keep them, I will pay the money-saving preferred subscriber's price of just $16.00 for all 4...that's a savings of almost $4 off the publisher's price with no additional charge for shipping and handling. I may return any shipment within 10 days and owe nothing, and I may cancel this subscription at any time. My 4 FREE books will be mine to keep in any case.

Name _____

Address _____ Apt. _____

City _____ State _____ Zip _____

Telephone ( ) _____

Signature _____ AR1098
(If under 18, parent or guardian must sign.)

"You having problems with the locals?" LaMar nodded at her. "Savannah filled me in on some recent history. Toya Jove is a mean piece of work."

"We do seem to keep getting in each other's way." Rae mused on the irony that she should come to love Toya's ex-husband.

"The Jove family is quite interesting. Henry Jove's great-great-grandfather, Harbin, was brought to this parish as a slave. He'd been sold right off the docks in New Orleans not three days after arriving from Santo Domingo. Seems he earned favor by curing his master's only son of a deadly fever."

"Hard to think of any Jove being selfless," Rae snorted.

"In gratitude, Jean-Luc Bienville set him free and gave him a large tract of land. That's how they got to be an old-money family." LaMar leaned forward. "They've got a long history of being devious, even ruthless."

"No!" Rae's eyes went wide in mock amazement. "I never would have guessed."

"There are some old accounts that say Harbin made the boy sick, then cured him so he could be rewarded. You know how male heirs were prized back then."

"Now that sounds more like it. How in the world did you find out all this?" Rae stared at him in open admiration.

"The Joves donated old family papers to the Armistad Museum in New Orleans. I have a passion for researching family history. And your Tante Ina gave me a lot of juicy stuff." LaMar grinned.

"So the Joves will do anything to get what they want. Well, Toya came by it honestly."

"Let's fast forward. Estelle Fazandes was not just pretty, she was gorgeous. She met Henry in college. He fell hard, and they got married about a month after they graduated. And they would have lived happily ever after except—"

"Estelle liked variety when it came to men," Rae put in.

"Right. Henry was so nuts about her, he blamed it on the men. He got into a few fist fights from what I understand."

"Pawpaw Vincent was one of those men. The papers I found prove that." Rae wore a frown of dismay.

"Hi." Simon came in. "How are you?" He shook LaMar's hand.

"Simon St. Cyr, meet LaMar Zeno, ace private eye." Rae winked at LaMar. "He found out all kinds of neat stuff. Though I don't know how it's going to help us find Pawpaw."

"I might have something. I talked to my grandfather and he told me a few things," Simon said. He sat next to Rae.

"Fantastic! The next best thing to me being able to interview one of the principles in this drama." LaMar looked eager. "Tell us everything."

Simon ran through his grandfather's account of the events. Rae and LaMar sat listening without interrupting for several minutes.

"Too bad he can't think of the name of that ship," Rae said.

"I can track it down." LaMar wrote the names down on a small notepad. "When I get some leads, I'll let you run them by Mr. St. Cyr. He might recognize one."

"Good idea. Just give me a call."

"Well, I gotta go. I'll see you this weekend." LaMar put on his sunglasses. "It's going to be a blast, babe. Don't worry." He strolled out, waving to Garret as he left.

Simon came back from the bar with a can of soda. "Your cousin was right. LaMar is good at what he does."

"Yeah." Rae tapped on the table.

"Okay, tell me what's bothering you." Simon grabbed her hand to stop her nervous movement.

"I'm getting a funny feeling about all this." Rae looked at him. "I don't want you to have problems because of me, Simon."

"Forget that. I can take care of myself." Simon put an arm around the back of her chair "Don't let Toya tell you different."

"How did you know?"

"This is Belle Rose, remember? Miss Essie was downtown to see Doctor Picard. She saw you talking and could tell you weren't having a friendly chat. She told Mrs. Broussard, who has coffee with the second cousin of my grandmother's best friend, who told . . ."

"I get the picture." Rae grinned at him. Still she wondered

if their affair had moved too fast. She grew serious again. "Maybe we should take it slow."

Simon studied her for a few seconds. "Are you having doubts because of family conflicts or because you're not sure your feelings for me are real?"

"My feelings for you are the best thing that's ever happened to me." Rae touched his face.

"Then you doubt me." Simon took her face in his hands and kissed her.

"Reputation is important to your family."

"I don't care if your grandfather had a harem, fifty kids, and made his living swindling half the country. I love you."

Rae looked into his deep brown eyes. All her misgivings were gone in an instant. "Be careful, Simon St. Cyr. With sweet talk like that you just might have me on your hands for a long time."

"That's the idea." Simon kissed her again. "Now give me the grand tour."

They walked through the dance hall looking at all the renovations. As an added attraction, Rae'd had a porch built along one side facing the bayou where several tables would be set out. Old fashion rocking chairs were placed on one end so patrons could relax outside with their drinks. They were standing there when Marcelle and her husband arrived.

"Hey, cher. You got this place looking good." Freddie kissed Rae and shook hands with Simon.

"Gee, Freddie. Haven't seen much of you. You're always at work," Rae said. She gave his beefy arm a playful swat. "Marcelle's got you trained right."

"Humph, keeping all them mouths fed is a job. But they're worth it." Freddie stuck his chest out with pride.

"Besides, I'm going to work part time for Mr. Thibaut. Bookkeeping," Marcelle added. "Between the two of us, we'll feed, clothe, and educate those little darlings." She hugged her husband's arm.

"And you're going to help me, too. Bookkeeping is not one of my skills." Rae shook her head.

"You've got so many other assets, no one will notice." Simon seemed to forget they were not alone.

Marcelle nudged Freddie. "Child, you two make a nice couple. Don't they Freddie?"

"Got this town buzzing. They say— Ow! What'd you do that for?" Freddie rubbed his side where her nudge had turned into a jab.

"Just, hush," Marcelle shot back.

"Quit beating up on your husband, Marcelle. We know we're a favorite topic of conversation around town these days." Rae chuckled.

"And we don't care," Simon said with a pointed look at Rae. "What 'they' say is not important."

"You're right about that. Bunch of gossiping people with nothing better to do." Marcelle gave a curt nod.

Freddie turned a look of injured pride on Marcelle. "What I was gonna say before Marcelle punched me was lots of folks are downright thrilled Rockin' Good Times is about to open."

"Really?" Rae was surprised.

"Yeah, they saying this is sure to help black folks around here. Mr. Hilton is going to open up a snowball and po'boy stand on his property. Things are happening in this town." Freddie shrugged. "A couple of guys I work with are thinking of some part-time businesses they can run for the tourists."

Simon put an arm around Rae's shoulders. "See. What happened years ago will be quickly forgotten."

"Oh, yeah," Freddie agreed. "When money flows, a lot can be forgiven."

"Freddie!" Marcelle tried to look stern at his candid assessment.

Rae grinned at them. "Freddie is right. Pawpaw Vincent might have a statue in the middle of town if the money is right." Rae laughed out loud and the others soon joined in.

The pace of work became frantic as the opening day approached. Rae grew more anxious as each passing hour brought her closer to what she came to think of as the big showdown. She sat up late into the night trying to think of all the things that could go wrong. Rae made a list of contingency plans. The dance hall would open Friday evening. Dinner would be served in one section and the lounge would be open. Thursday night

Rae walked through the dance hall for the fifth time to make sure everything was the way she wanted it to be.

"We all set up, cher," Garrett said. He stood leaning against the bar. "Plenty to drink, kitchen is perfect. Sarah and Jack will be here at two o'clock sharp to start getting ready for dinner."

Jackson Leblanc and his wife would work in the restaurant with two part-time wait staff. Rae had been able to hire two local kids who were seniors in high school. Both were from poor families and needed extra money to further their educations.

"Sounds good," Rae called back from the other side of the lounge. She checked the tables to make sure each one was neat.

"Rae, it's going to be fine." Garrett gave her a pat on the shoulder. The older man had a calm manner that made him seem like a kindly uncle.

"Garrett, you and Jackson have been great these last few weeks. You saved me from making some big mistakes." Rae smiled at him.

"Shoot, that ain't nothing," Garrett said in his easy drawl. "Glad to do it. We're gonna have this place on every tourists guide before next summer. Watch what I'm saying." He winked at her, then walked off.

"I hope you're right."

Rae looked at her watch. Eight-thirty. Maybe she should call the band LazyDaze, to confirm they would be here Saturday night for her first big dance. Her stomach fluttered at the thought. *This is it, girlfriend. Make or break time.* She'd put ads in the student newspapers at Southern and Southwestern Universities and LSU. Rae figured that college students could make up a big part of her weekend business if she offered the right entertainment. With large multinational companies having offices located along the petrochemical corridor, she hoped that the restaurant could have a booming lunch trade eventually. The next few weeks would tell the tale. But this weekend would be a critical first step.

"Maybe we should go over the lighting once more." Rae was filled with nervous energy. She started toward the raised stage area where performers would be positioned.

Garrett had started back through the double door leading to the restaurant. He turned around. "Rae, it's all perfect. I gotta go. Cheré is keeping supper warm."

"You go on. I can do it." Rae's attention was on the microphones.

"You oughta go home. Don't stay out here by yourself. It's dark and you're over a mile from the gas station or Mr. Norvelle's house on the other side."

"I'll be fine once I lock the door. The flood lights are on. Now go on before Cheré calls here fussing." Rae crossed the room. She followed him around to make sure all outer doors were locked.

"Maybe I will stay." Garrett paused at the front door. He frowned into the darkness that crowded just beyond the light from the powerful lamps outside. "Cheré won't mind if I call and let her know."

Rae pushed him out the door. "Will you go home. I promise to leave within the next thirty minutes. Look, my car is right near the door. Okay?" She pointed to her Honda Civic.

"I'm gonna call back here, too." Garrett shook a finger in her face.

"Wonderful. Now, good night." Rae waved him on his way. She watched his red pickup pull off, taillights fading down the highway.

Rae sighed with relief. The truth was she wanted to be alone at the dance hall. As she walked through it, the enormity of what she'd accomplished hit her. For weeks she had put one foot in front of the other, not stopping to think about the difficulty of her task. Rae had been afraid that facing it all would have paralyzed her into despair that she could not do it. Instead, she'd taken this journey one step at a time. She touched the smooth wood of the chairs. The whole place smelled new, like polish and lemon. Rae had even managed to salvage a few of the items that had been in the attic at home. Old kerosene lamps and colorful tins from Monmon Marie's grandmother. Lucien had used a few to decorate the dance hall years before.

"We did it, Daddy," Rae said. She turned in a circle. "I hope this is just the beginning."

A peaceful feeling came over her. Rae stood listening. Was that a soft chuckle? She could have sworn it sounded like . . . no, she was just tired. "Now I know it's time to go home." She rubbed her eyes.

Rae turned off the lights in the dining room and headed for the lounge. She got her keys from the small office. There was a whispering sound that made her pause as she neared the front door. The thought that she should not leave just yet popped into her head for some strange reason. A loud thud to her right made her heart pound. Someone was outside. Footsteps tread softly on the wooden porch, apparently in an effort to be quiet. Suddenly Rae could distinguish an occasional creaking sound separate from the other night noises. She eased over to the nearest window and looked out. Nothing. There were scratching sounds, like clawing on the outside walls. Rae jumped back hoping they had not seen her. If they broke the glass and crawled inside, could she make it to the phone across the room in time? The scratching sounds grew louder.

Terror made her freeze with indecision for an instant. Then fear gave way to fury. How dare they! Rae looked around for something to use as a weapon. She ran to the bar and pulled out an ice pick. A knock on the front door behind her boomed through the building. Rae crouched down.

"Rae, open up. It's me," Simon called out.

Rae crossed the floor on shaky legs. "Oh, Simon." She flung the door ajar and hugged his neck.

"Hmm-umm." Simon buried his face in her hair. "I missed you, too. Hey, you're shaking like a leaf. What happened?" His grip tightened.

"You scared the life out of me walking around like that on the porch." Rae recovered and gave his arm a swat. "You almost got this up your nose, buddy." She showed him the ice pick.

Simon went rigid. "I wasn't on the porch. Stay here." He pushed her inside.

"No! Simon don't—"

"It's okay. I'll be right back." Simon pulled the door closed between them.

Rae yanked the door open again. "Simon, come back," she whispered. She stamped a foot in frustration.

He was gone around the corner of the building when she looked out. She strained to hear any sound through the chirping of crickets and cicadas. Minutes dragged by like hours. A long shadow was thrown onto the cypress wood to her right. Rae began to back up, the sharp tool held high over her head. When Simon appeared she took a deep breath.

"Didn't I tell you to get inside?" Simon put both hands on his hips.

"And leave you out here with some crook? No way." She hefted the pick. "I was going to jab anybody that laid a hand on you."

Simon took the ice pick from her. "Thanks Wonder Woman. Next time, be sensible and call the sheriff," he teased.

"You could've been in big trouble while I was doing that. Not to mention it would take them at least twenty minutes to get here." Rae brushed dust from her hands.

"It was probably some teenage burglar who got scared off when he realized you were inside." Simon tried to reassure her. "I'll call Sheriff Thibodeaux to have a look around."

Rae put a hand on his arm. "Why call him if it's nothing?"

"He could have a deputy patrol this way if he knows you're having prowlers already." Simon did not look at her.

"Tell me what you saw." Rae's fear spiked up again.

"There are footprints in the fresh dirt around the flower beds and . . . someone spray painted a curse word on one wall." Simon struck the bar with his fist. "I just wish I could have gotten my hands on the punk."

"I'm glad he was gone." Rae wrapped both arms around him.

Simon called the sheriff's office. As Rae predicted, it took over twenty minutes for a deputy to arrive. After looking around, Deputy Wilson came back inside and accepted a cold soft drink.

"Tell ya what, ain't much we can do except keep an eye on the place. Nothing been stolen. Just be careful out here alone at night, ma'am." Deputy Wilson swabbed at his smooth, dark brown face with a large handkerchief.

"I've all ready told her she shouldn't work late by herself," Simon said. They both looked at Rae with stern disapproval.

"I get the message," Rae grumbled. She did not like being treated like a naughty girl. "Oughta be able to be in your business." Still she knew they were right.

"Good night y'all. I'll make sure to put this place on our stops for this part of the parish. Best I can do. Of course, we do monitor security systems at the station for a fee." Deputy Wilson strolled out.

"An alarm system hooked to the station. Sounds like a great idea. We'll do it." Simon shook his hand.

"Simon, we have to talk." Rae was irritated with him for being so high-handed. Besides, she was on a tight budget.

"I know a guy who has a security company. I'll call him in the morning." Simon spoke to Deputy Wilson.

"Good deal. Now since y'all sure the place is locked tight, why don't you follow me out."

Deputy Wilson waited patiently for them. He gave Simon a final wave as he passed them on the highway to continue his night patrol. At Rae's house, Simon sat tense on the sofa. He seemed still on edge.

"I'll call Matt in the morning. He can have that system installed in no time." Simon gazed around the house. "Put one in here, too."

"Let me think about it." Rae went to the kitchen to fix coffee with Simon close on her heels.

"I want you to have as much protection as possible." He sat at the small table. "Matt will work fast when I tell him it's urgent."

"I don't know. I think once the dance hall is open, we won't have a problem. There will be people there a lot." Rae tried to sound confident.

"But not around the clock. No, Rae. The alarm is the best solution." Simon crossed his arms.

"That's a business decision that I have to make," Rae snapped. "It's my dance hall after all." Her hand holding the coffee pot was shaking. She put it down fast.

"Come here, baby." Simon got up. He pulled her to him into

a warm embrace. "You don't have to put on a tough act for me. I'll pay for the alarms and the monitoring fee."

"No. I've got to do this myself." Rae shook her head.

"Rae, don't shut me out. Let me take care of getting the alarms," Simon murmured.

Rae pushed away from him gently. "You're sweet to want to help me, Simon. But I can't let you do it."

Simon looked disappointed. "You won't change your mind, I can see it on your face."

"Let me think about it some more. And if I decide to get the system, I'll pay for it." Rae spoke in a firm voice. "In the meantime, the sheriff will increase patrols and we've got flood lights."

"I'll bring you some of Matt's brochures." Simon was not about to give up.

Rae sighed. "Okay. Seems not everyone is thrilled with me." The thought of someone waiting in the dark to strike at her sent a chill up Rae's spine.

"Thank goodness I decided to come out there tonight when you didn't answer at home." Simon hugged her tight again.

"My hero." Rae snuggled against his chest.

"Not so great a hero. I didn't catch the bad guy." Simon lifted her face to look into her eyes. "If he'd hurt you . . ."

"Nothing happened, sugar. Like you said, it was probably some kid who got scared and ran."

"Even kids carry weapons these days. I'll bring those brochures tomorrow. And I'll check the locks on your doors here. They look pretty old. At least let me replace them." Simon looked around the kitchen with a critical eye.

"Fine." Rae smiled at him in an effort to smooth the worry from his face. "Now let's relax."

At his urging, Rae got out her guitar. She sang a medley of ballads, both blues and zydeco. Then they listened to soft music as they talked. With the windows open, they enjoyed the humid air that stirred the curtains. Even at this distance they could smell the bayou, crushed wet grass, and water. Now Rae was comforted instead of threatened by the darkness. Despite her show of strength, she was grateful to have Simon hold her through the night.

Memorial Day was a smashing hit at Rockin' Good Times. The crowds were thick even when they opened at noon with lunch. College kids mixed in with retired folks from the area, the upwardly mobile out for fun, and tourists. There was laughter inside and out. Picnic tables were set up under the shade oak and sycamore trees on the property behind the dance hall.

Jamal took a long drink of his beer. "This place looks fantastic." He bounced to the beat of rhythm and blues music flowing into the lounge.

Jamal and Wes had brought the band to town for the weekend celebration. It had been Wes's idea to get the renowned blues artist Kenny Neal. In a few hours, they would have a jam session with Kenny that was sure to delight the crowd. Until then, the guys were enjoying hanging out.

"Say, is that fine lady going to be here?" Wes craned his neck to scan the crowded room.

"You were in town maybe two days and found a woman?" Rae laughed. "Haven't learned your lesson yet."

"Yeah, but she was special. I'm talking about that graceful Nubian queen you were talking to that day. The one with a walk that lit fires as she passed." Wes closed his eyes.

Simon joined them in time to hear his description. "One of our lovely ladies has captured your heart, eh?"

"With Wes, what she's captured is a bit lower." Rae gave a snort.

"Tell me her name. She was magnificent, her beauty outshone the sun. You know, Rae, you talked to her downtown right before we left. I hope she comes tonight." Wes looked around again.

"Toya? Please. She'd rather jump in a pit of snakes than come here," Rae said. Then a wicked gleam lit her eyes. "Of course, it would be nice to rub my success in her face."

"Rae, be nice. Toya probably won't be here. But then she's into jazz." Simon spoke to Wes.

"Humph, Toya won't be here because she's a stuck-up—"

"Stop. You're talking about the woman I love." Wes held up a palm. "I won't hear her insulted."

"Come on, man. You're tripping. Let's go get some of that great food." Jamal pulled Wes over to the table where Sarah had set up free hors d'oeurves for the patrons. Hot wings and tiny barbecue sausages were piled high.

When they were gone, Simon turned to Rae. "Toya is not so bad, Rae. Really," he said at the look she gave him.

"I've known her all my life." Rae thought of the arrogant walk Toya had mastered even as a small girl. "If she was so wonderful, why aren't you still married to her?"

"Just because our marriage was a mistake—"

"A disaster from what I heard," Rae snorted.

"We both made mistakes." Simon squinted at her. "Gossip is rarely accurate. Something you should know."

"Point taken. But I know firsthand what a witch she can be. So there." Rae dared him to refute her personal experiences.

"Haven't we talked about the injustice of holding the past against people?" Simon raised an eyebrow at her.

"Yeah, but . . ." Rae squirmed under his scrutiny. "Okay, I'll be good. If she shows up, I'll greet her with open arms."

"Sure you will."

"Hey, if Toya walks in, she'll be overwhelmed by the hospitality." Rae batted her eyelashes at him.

Simon's lip lifted at one corner. "Really?"

"You betcha," Rae tossed back. She leaned against the bar.

"Well, now is your chance." Simon jerked a thumb at the door. "Do your stuff."

Rae's mouth dropped at the sight of Toya strolling in on the arm of a handsome man. Darcy followed them a few seconds later. "I can't believe it."

"Excuse me, Miss Hospitality, time is awasting. Get over there and let your little light shine." Simon put a hand over his mouth to hide his wide grin.

"Hello there." Darcy walked right up to Rae and kissed her firmly on the cheek. "Congratulations. This place is fabulous, babe. Hi, Simon," he added as an afterthought, without taking his eyes off Rae.

"Yes, it is very . . . unique." Toya swept a hand around in the air regally. "Of course, beer and boiled crawfish go over big with most people around here." She sniffed as though the offending smell of both hung heavy.

"Right. I love good food, good drink, and jammin' tunes. This place is hot." Toya's gentleman friend obviously did not share her view. He moved to the beat of a pop tune. Turning around, he cast an appreciative eye at a group of college girls in shorts and T-shirts.

"Colin, grow up," Toya snapped.

Colin did not hear her. "Love that music. Hey, you forgot to introduce us. I'm Colin Dexter." He nodded to Rae and Simon.

Toya lifted chin. "Colin Dexter the Third, of the Dexters of Lafayette. Dexter Industries."

"Nice seeing you, Colin." Simon smiled at him. "How long has it been, man?"

"Last summer you beat me at the fishing rodeo. I'll get you this time, brother." Colin pointed a finger at him.

"In your dreams." Simon laughed.

"You two know each other?" Toya wore a look of chagrin.

"For a long time," Colin put in before Simon could answer. "Best contractor in south Louisiana, black or white." The good-humored man slapped Simon on the back.

"Thanks, man."

"Say, I was worried you would be mad about me dating Toya," Colin said in a low voice to Simon. However, his comments were still audible to Rae and Toya. Colin glanced at Rae. "But I guess not."

"Let's go." Toya jerked him away.

"All right." Colin, still having a good time, was not in the least disturbed by her behavior. "See you around Simon. Nice meeting you, pretty woman," he called back.

Toya's mouth was turned down in a sour expression when she looked back at a grinning Rae. She whipped her head back around and stomped off.

"That went well," Rae quipped. She could not suppress the catlike smile of satisfaction spread on her face.

"Now that you're a hit, you can afford to be generous." Simon gazed at her. "Toya is not a happy person."

"Tsh, and seeing my success makes it worse. I'm so-oo sad about that." Rae wore a fake forlorn expression.

Simon looked at his ex-wife. "Toya hasn't had the perfect life she likes to pretend."

"Why are you always making excuses for her?" Rae did not like his tone. "Anyone would think there's still something between you. Maybe her wish for a reconciliation isn't so one-sided." She faced him.

"Now that is a paranoid delusion, sweetness. I may have sympathy for Toya, but our divorce is a happy one in my opinion." Simon covered her mouth with his, brushing his tongue along her lips. Cat calls and whistles came from those nearby.

"Cut that out," Rae said. She put up a halfhearted struggle to break free.

"I crave you day and night. You're in my heart, mind, and body. Any more questions?" Simon held onto her in a solid grip.

"That covers it," Rae whispered. She shook herself from the clutches of a romantic haze that was fast taking over. "I've got to get back to work. It's going to be a long day."

"I'll be with you until the end." Simon winked at her.

The weather was perfect, sunny with a slight breeze blowing off the bayou. Just as Rae and Garrett expected, customers enjoyed the choice between indoor and outdoor festivities. Andrew was having a great time playing host so that Rae could mingle with what she hoped would be a substantial repeat crowd. Jamal brought a fast-paced song to an end with a flourish of his bass guitar. The crowd applauded and yelled in appreciation.

"Y'all look like you having a fine time. I'd say our hostess is doing a real good job of making everybody happy. Let's hear it for Rae!" Wes said into the microphone. A loud drum roll ended in the clash of cymbals.

"There you go!" Marcelle yelled out. She grinned. Numerous voices echoed their approval.

"Now Rae's been playing the role of businesswoman well. But we know something she plays even better. Don't y'all wanna hear one of the best blues musicians around?" Wes waved his arms to whip up enthusiasm. He was rewarded with loud shouts.

"Come on up here!" Wes beckoned to her.

"No, I've got other things to do," Rae protested even as Simon and Marcelle propelled her on stage. Her mother and brothers only laughed when she begged to be rescued.

"Come on now, play my song so I can show these kids how to really party," Tante Ina shouted. She and Uncle David did a two step then she turned to Rae. "You know what I wanna hear."

Urged on by the crowd, Rae gave in. "This is one special love song just for my sweet Tante Ina and Uncle David. And for everyone who has been lucky enough to find a one of a kind love." She looked at Simon standing near the stage. He wore a secret smile with a message that went straight to her heart.

The crowd became quiet. Rae thrummed the electric guitar. She brought cheers from the crowd when she launched into her version of the Fats Domino hit, "Ain't It a Shame." She and Jamal sang a duo, taking turns singing lead. Couples paired up to dance.

Rockin' Good Times had opened with a bang. The day went on without any major problems. When the bands took a break, the jukebox provided background music. The employees pitched in and took turns resting for short periods. Rae had tears in her eyes from time to time thinking of how wonderful the entire weekend had been. If only Lucien could see it. She sat on the edge of the porch enjoying the late evening shade after a hectic day when her mother sat next to her.

"Things been just beautiful today, cher." Aletha hugged her shoulders. "Andrew said it's been jumping since you opened Friday night."

"Yeah, Mama. I never expected it, to tell you the truth." Rae gazed around her. "I thought folks would stay away. But look at this crowd." There was awe in her voice.

"You did some hard work getting publicity, darling. This ain't no accident. Besides, down here we're always looking for an excuse to party." Aletha laughed.

"This is a dream come true, Mama." Rae leaned against her mother. "Lucien's dream."

"You've done your daddy's memory proud," Aletha said in a soft voice.

"You think I made up for all those times I said bad things to him," Rae whispered. She sounded like a little girl. "When we talked last year he claimed he didn't even remember half of what I'd said. But I . . ." Her voice broke.

"You ain't never had to apologize to Lucien, Raenette. There wasn't nothing you coulda said or done that would stop him from loving you. Nothing." Aletha dabbed at Rae's eyes with a cocktail napkin. "Shucks, he used to tell jokes about his saucy baby girl."

"Oh, come on." Rae sniffed a few times.

"I'm not lying. His favorite story was that time you snuck out to the dance down to the Bayou Boogie. Remember?"

"Do I? Daddy stormed into the high school gym and embarrassed me something terrible." Rae laughed out loud at the memory of how furious she was at the time.

"Yeah, and your so-called boyfriend tried to hide out in the restroom. Lord have mercy." Aletha slapped her thigh.

"Poor Keith. He was scared out of his mind my crazy daddy and older brothers were going to kill him." Rae sat up straight. "Thank you, Mama. You always know just what I need."

"That's what Mama is here for, cher. Don't care how old you get." Aletha kissed her forehead. "Now go find that good-looking man and dance."

Rae kissed her cheek and went in search of Simon. She found him chatting with Andrew and Baylor near the bar. "May I have this dance?" Rae said.

"I thought you'd never ask," Simon said with a gleam in his brown eyes. He led her onto the dance floor.

"This is one heck of a party. Congratulations, baby," Simon murmured close to her ear.

"It's all so fantastic. I'm scared it's too good to last." Rae looked up at him.

"Every business has bumps along the way. Some are little and some big. Just be ready for them."

"No, I mean most of my life nothing good like this ever seemed to happen for my family. Or if it did, then something bad took it all away." Rae glanced around with a tinge of anxiety.

"You sound a bit superstitious. Not at all like the tough lady I know."

"Sometimes it seemed my family was cursed. Even my uncles and aunts used to say so."

"Don't let old memories spoil a fabulous new day." Simon put a finger under her chin. "You're a smash hit, a talented musician and one heck of a kisser. A renaissance woman."

Rae let herself get lost in his brown eyes, sparkling with the reflected lights strung around the walls inside the dance hall. "You're right. Now I have it all." She rested her head against his solid chest.

Across the dance floor, Toya and Marius watched. Marius had come later with a tall, stunning college student. Darcy was sitting at a table with several old friends, but his gaze was on Simon and Rae.

"Look at her clawing at Simon like a cat in heat," Toya said in a voice hard with animosity. "Slut."

"At this rate, she'll be an economic force in no time." Marius gestured with the drink in his hand. "This place is almost as good as striking oil. With the college kids and tourists, she'll be a wealthy woman within three years."

"Not if I can help it." Toya faced him. "You've got a stake in this, too."

"Unlike you and Darcy, hormones don't drive my business actions. But you're right. We need her land." Marius looked relaxed. "Don't worry. Soon Ms. Dalcour will be glad to sell."

"Why? She won't need the money." Toya tapped a long fingernail on the side of her daiquiri glass.

"She will." Marius wore a nasty grin. "Trust me, she will."

Twelve

"Mr. Henry, how are you?" Simon shook hands with his former grandfather-in-law. Despite his divorce from Toya, he and Henry had always been on good terms. Still, he was puzzled at the reason for this visit. "Sit down. Nola, get Mr. Henry some coffee please."

Simon was thrown off by Henry's sudden appearance, or he would never have assumed Nola would fetch coffee. She was firm in what she would and would not do. Yet Nola wanted to linger as she was just as curious to learn more.

"Certainly. How's Miz Cecile?" Nola beamed at the older man as she prepared two cups for them from the pot on Simon's credenza. "You tell her I said hello." She hovered near the door after handing them both a mug of fresh dark roast coffee.

"I sure will," Henry replied. He dipped his head to her in a slight bow.

"Sure y'all don't need anything else?" Nola came back into the room.

Simon eyed Nola. "No, thank you." He gave a silent signal to leave.

"All right." Nola's mouth turned down with disappointment. The door closed softly behind her.

"So how have you been?" Simon sat in the chair beside Henry rather than behind his desk.

"Good. Can't complain." Henry settled into his seat with the coffee. "And you?"

"Very well, thank you." Simon felt a rush of contentment. In fact, things were perfect, in his view.

Henry studied him for a few moments. "Son, what I'm about to say might make you throw me out of here."

Simon smiled. "I can't think of any reason I'd do that, Mr. Henry. Even when I was married to Toya, we got along pretty well."

"Yes, but I know my granddaughter's ability to stretch the patience of a saint." Henry fixed him with his well-known sober stare. "I'm talking about all this business with the Dalcour girl."

"I don't know what you mean." Simon tensed.

"Son, it's your father's and grandfather's place to give you advice on your personal life, but I have to say getting involved with that Dalcour girl is—"

"Stop right there, Mr. Henry. My personal life is not open for discussion," Simon cut him off. A few seconds of heavy silence followed.

"Fine. I didn't mean to offend. But I've known that family longer than you, son. They've got some serious problems. Maybe it's not her fault who her grandfather was, or her father." Henry waved a hand.

"I don't think I want to hear it." Simon put down his coffee mug. Suddenly his taste for anything was gone.

"I've never known you to be this closed-minded, son. Before you judge me, listen to what I have to say." Henry leaned forward.

"I have a closed mind? You sit here condemning a young woman based on fifty-year-old events. You don't even know Rae or her family." Simon tried to contain his temper.

"Oh, I know enough, believe me. You do know she was . . . involved with Darcy at one time. There was always talk about her back in those days." Henry wore a grimace. "Her grandfather was the same way."

"Don't say any more, Mr. Henry." Simon could feel the pressure building. In a few moments he might say something very ugly to this man he'd known all his life. "Is there any other reason for this visit?" He stood up.

Henry rose to face him. "I thought we knew each other well enough that you would listen to reason. But at least consider the business aspects for our families. That property is important to both our companies, Simon. To sacrifice real economic development for a juke joint is crazy. Think of our community."

"The Dalcours have a right to decide whether to sell their property."

"She's being stubborn out of spite." Henry put a hand on Simon's arm. "Since you're close to the girl, talk to her. Maybe there is some advantage to your being on good terms with them. I want that property."

"I'm not going to use my relationship with Rae to change her mind." Simon moved away from him.

"I was young once, Simon. I know how it is to be single and carefree. After your fling is over, that property will still be vital." Henry persisted in pressing home his logic.

"You've made one too many assumptions. What happens between Rae and me is private." Simon spoke louder as he went on.

"Don't be a fool!" Henry shot back in a taut voice. "You're from one of the oldest families in this parish. The Dalcours are descended from fieldhands. You have a duty to the St. Cyrs and, yes, to the Jove family."

"That's nineteenth-century nonsense." Simon lowered his voice when a cautious knock sounded on the office door. "No wonder Toya thinks the way she does. This obsession with family background is disgusting."

Nola opened the door just enough to stick her head in. She peered from Simon to Henry. "Everything all right?"

Simon turned around and went to stand behind his desk. He started gathering up a stack of blueprints. "Goodbye, Mr. Henry."

"We'll discuss this again, Simon." Henry held himself stiffly, his face etched with deep lines.

Simon returned Henry's fierce gaze with one of equal resolution. "No, we won't."

Henry stalked out of the office without returning Nola's goodbye. She flinched when the outer door slammed. "Oo-wee, things got loud in here. Mr. Henry's not too happy about something." Nola looked at Simon expectantly.

"Pompous bag of wind." Simon threw down his ink pen.

"Yeah, who does he think he is?" Nola threw a glare in the direction Henry had gone. "Think their you-know-what don't stink."

"The man is caught up in the past." Simon wanted to do more than throw something. The veiled insults to Rae made him furious.

"Un-huh. Just cause his slutty first wife took off. Course he was jealous and mean." Nola spoke in a confidential manner even though they were alone. "But then, she liked to roam, as the old folks say."

"Now is that nice?" Simon scolded. Still, he could not help but be amused.

"I'm reporting facts." Nola shrugged. "Anyway, don't let him get you upset. Most of the town loves how she's bringing folks in to spend money. The dance hall is a big success."

Simon had to agree. There was an increase in the number of people strolling around downtown during the past weekend. He was sure more than a few were either headed for the Rockin' Good Times or on their way out. The owners open did a brisk business.

"My friend Darlene has an antique store on Front Street. She's so happy, she's ready to fight anybody who says a word against Rae. But looks like she isn't the only one." Nola's arched eyebrows went even higher.

"She's pretty special." Simon wore a faint smile. His anger at Henry's words was fading. "I'm sorry I had to get into an argument with Mr. Henry. I can understand his bitterness even after all this time, but he was out of line."

"Well, forget him. Let him stay back in the old days while the rest of us enjoy all the good stuff happening now." Nola gave him a thumbs up signal as she left.

Simon sighed. She was right. The present was too wonderful, the future too bright to let anything or anyone spoil it. He soon was so immersed in his next task, preparing a bid to build low-rent housing for the elderly, that he forgot Henry.

* * *

Rae never felt so good lugging a weighty bag. The receipts from the dance hall gave her a healthy cash flow. Though the crowds for the last two weeks never matched the opening weekend, she had not expected they would. But the coming summer months looked quite promising. She chatted amiably with the bank teller who handled her deposit.

Leaving the bank, she stopped by several shops to network with other small business owners. Three black women entrepreneurs had suggested they get together monthly to share ideas and problems. Rae was thrilled for the chance to make new friends. Marcelle had joined them for the first meeting since she was self-employed as a bookkeeper.

Rae came out of Darlene's antique shop. She collided with Henry stomping down the sidewalk.

"Oh, excuse me," Rae said. She noticed the pinched look on his face. "You okay?"

"Seems you have a talent for getting in the way," Henry snarled.

"Good morning to you, too." Rae squinted at him. This was closer than she had ever been to the man. Rae studied the expensive white shirt of soft knit cotton and olive green pants. Even in casual dress, Henry Jove looked as though he were on his way to a corporate boardroom. Rae did not feel intimidated in the least by the hostile look stamped on his nut brown face.

"Young woman, you've always been too clever for your own good. That dance hall will only lead to a lot of drunken idiots falling into the bayou." Henry brushed off his pants as though contact with Rae had soiled them.

"You mean your relatives from out of town are coming in soon?" Rae knew her response was childish, but he had opened the old wound of being an outcast.

"Very funny. You won't be laughing when folks realize that hole in the wall is costing them tax money." Henry glared at her.

"What?" Rae put both hands on her hips.

"We'll need more sheriff's deputies to round up the drunks, more ambulances to scrape them off the highway, and more trash collection." Henry sneered at her.

"Get out of my way." Rae resisted the urge to slap the superior look from his face.

"You won't stand between us and industrial development for long, girl. That property should have been sold to Simon."

"Simon and I have an understanding. And it's none of your business," Rae shot back.

"Darcy and Simon had plans for that property that could have meant hundreds of jobs for black people. But you were too selfish and ignorant to see it." Henry grew more incensed with each passing moment.

"That's a stretch. Operating a recreational area wouldn't have meant hundreds of jobs," Rae said.

"Simon didn't tell you? That was just for the short term. Eventually most of the property was going to be part of a new plant." Henry nodded with satisfaction when Rae looked stunned. "Darcy was going to make it happen."

Rae recovered. "Darcy? So he lied to Simon. You forget, I know your grandson. Nice try." She turned to leave.

"I'm not finished, young woman." Henry blocked her way.

"Look, your first wife preferred other men. Is that my fault? Maybe she was screwing my grandfather. It's been fifty years for crying out loud, get over it!" Rae threw the words at him like well-aimed arrows.

"Shut your dirty mouth, swamp trash!" Henry balled both his fists. His faced twisted.

"Grandfather, what is she doing to you?" Toya crossed the street from a fancy women's boutique.

"Vincent Dalcour was a lying no-good—" Henry stumbled back against the wall of the store front. He clutched his left arm.

Rae did not like the ashen cast to his skin. "Take it easy. You look like you need a doctor."

"Grandfather, come over here." Toya led him to a wooden bench. She patted Henry's hand and accused Rae at the same time. "Now see what you've done?"

"Mr. Henry, getting worked up over old grudges isn't good for you at your age." Rae was concerned about him. He did not look good at all. "Let's call a truce. I mean, we both said some nasty things that we shouldn't have—"

"Speak for yourself," Henry said. He seemed to be gathering his strength. "I told the truth."

"Just go away," Toya put in.

"No problem. By the way, I've hired a detective to find out what really happened to my grandfather. I can take the truth. Can you?"

Rae made it a point to stroll away without hurrying. She looked back to see them walking slowly down the street. A few people offered to help. She could hear Henry insist he was fine. All the concern she'd felt for the stubborn man was gone.

It's true what they say. Success is the best revenge. Rae wore a grim smile as she threw one last glance at the pair.

Rae was so busy with the dance hall that she had not thought about the investigation for days. She was inundated with all the details of running a business. Even with able assistance from Garrett, there was so much she had to do herself. When LaMar called, she felt a flutter of excitement mixed with anxiety. He gave her a few details but was reluctant to say more until they met. That he suggested her brothers be there was even more intriguing. The next day they were all sitting in Rae's living room. LaMar got right down to business after introductions were made.

"LaMar has done a great job so far." Rae looked at him expectantly. "But he's playing the part of the mysterious private eye." She raised an eyebrow.

"Some news should be given in person." LaMar glanced at them all. "I've traced your grandfather to Uruguay . . . I think."

"Uruguay? What the hell would he be going there for?" Andrew blinked at him.

"Wait a minute now. What you mean you think?" Neville said.

"Is he there now? What does he look like? Is Estelle with him?" Rae shot out the questions. Her mind all ready raced ahead trying to figure out how she could leave the dance hall and travel to this exotic place.

"Hold up, one at a time. Let me start at the beginning. I found old records that show a couple got passports to travel there and bought passage on a freighter. They were to work off part of the cost."

"But why didn't the authorities know he was wanted?" Neville frowned.

"Somehow all this slipped through the cracks. Maybe they never considered they would try to leave the country. Or they could have paid hush money." LaMar shrugged. "Anyway, there is nothing that indicates they didn't go on the ship."

"But nothing to prove they did," Rae put in. This all seemed too farfetched. Somehow she had a feeling something was wrong.

"No, that's why I said I think that's where they went." LaMar looked at Neville who nodded.

"But why Uruguay?" Andrew scratched his head. "I mean, what would Pawpaw Vincent know about anyplace farther than Houston?"

"Maybe he paid more attention to geography in school than you did, Andy," Neville quipped. "Lot's of black folks left, going to other countries for better opportunities. Don't forget what it was like back then for us."

"Right," LaMar added. "Quite a few Latin American countries had economic booms in the early twentieth century. Uruguay was quite prosperous until the late sixties. Black people left America to settle there and in the Caribbean."

"Doesn't feel right," Rae said.

"That's what I'm saying," Andrew added. "Something's strange about all this."

"The other thing is this, they could have gotten off in another country. Brazil for one. If so, it would take a lot of looking with little chance of finding them." LaMar sat back and looked at all three.

Neville grunted. "In other words, a lot of money."

"So we gotta decide if we can afford it and how bad we want to find them." Rae drummed her fingertips on the sofa arm.

"Rae, I know you wanna keep your promise to Daddy. But you've already invested several hundred dollars." Neville shook his head. "You've got the dance hall that needs tending."

"The cash flow so far is good." Rae reviewed all the options.

"But you've got big expenses remember." Neville frowned.

"You went over the books with me. We're pulling in a nice profit." Rae sat forward. She was ready to debate continuing the search.

"I know but . . ." Neville rubbed his chin.

"Hey, I paid you back a nice chunk already." Rae tapped his arm.

"It isn't about that," Neville replied. "I knew the first few days I'd be getting my investment back. You don't have to rush."

"Trisha slipped up and told me about the second mortgage, Neville. I made her go down and make a big payment on that loan." Rae wagged a forefinger at him. "Within the next few months, I want it all paid off."

"Doggonit, that woman will never tell a lie." Neville looked sheepish.

"Thanks for wanting to help, big brother." Rae kissed his cheek.

"I told Daddy I'd make sure you both stayed straight. Ain't had much success with that one." Neville pointed to Andrew with a wry smile.

"Watch out, now." Andrew gave him a playful swat on the shoulder. "So what we gonna do?"

Rae looked at Neville then Andrew. "I really want to keep looking. But to be practical, let's set a time and money limit."

Neville thought for a few seconds. "Okay, sounds reasonable."

With guidance from LaMar on the cost and probable time, they decided that he should continue for at least another six weeks. They negotiated a flat fee that included LaMar taking a trip to Uruguay or whatever South American country seemed most promising.

"We might be close to finding out what happened. I just have a feeling . . ." LaMar lifted a shoulder. "I can't explain it."

"Yeah, just like for some reason it doesn't feel right that pawpaw would go away like that. Daddy and Tante Ina said he was crazy about his children." Rae tried to explain the tinge of uncertainty in her gut. "And he'd played around with other women before Estelle."

"Don't forget the money," Neville said with a somber expression. "The money went with them."

"Then at least we can put all these questions to rest." Rae sighed. "Either way, I'd like to know if he's alive. I want to meet him."

"And her, too," Andrew added. "Wouldn't that be something? To be able to get it straight from the horse's mouth." He gazed at them.

"The plane couldn't get me there fast enough," Rae said. Goose bumps rose on her arms at the thought of it.

"Who the hell do you think you are, boy?" Henry yelled at Darcy. "I built Jove Enterprises into a multimillion dollar operation before you were out of diapers."

"Grandfather, calm down. You haven't been feeling well." Toya hovered next to his chair.

They were in Henry's spacious den. A golf match played out on the big screen television in one corner. Cecile waved the housekeeper out and closed the door.

"Henry, if you won't see Dr. Picard, you should at least get some rest." Cecile tried to plump a pillow behind his back.

"Get away from me, woman!" Henry threw it onto the floor. "I don't need you pawing at me all the time."

Cecile drew back, her face pale. "I just thought—"

"Then don't think. I end up worse off every time you do," Henry snarled. They stared at each other in silence for a few moments.

Darcy cleared his throat. "Pantheon needed an answer, Grandfather. They wouldn't wait around forever to know exactly what to expect from us." He spoke in a measured tone.

"Don't talk to me as if I'm senile." Henry turned his wrath back on Darcy. "I have to hear what's going on in my own company secondhand at a damn Chamber of Commerce luncheon."

"Calm down. I'm sure Darcy knows what he's doing." Toya tried to soothe Henry. She glanced at her brother from the corner of her eye.

"Be quiet, Toya. Darcy, tell me everything." Henry glowered at him.

"Pantheon was not happy about the change. It was touch and go for a while." Darcy looked pleased with himself. "But I'd done my homework. I bought old man Trahan's property. He died last month. After I found his son in Atlanta, he was happy to sell at a good price."

"Lloyd Trahan sold his family's property that easily? I don't believe it." Henry fixed Darcy with a discerning gaze. "What else did you throw in besides money?"

Darcy stuck out his chest. "I made a few phone calls so his industrial pipe company will get some of Pantheon's contracts."

"Good thinking," Henry admitted grudgingly. "But there's something else."

"Yes, er, there will have to be some dredging along Bayou Pigeon," Darcy said.

"Haven't I told you plainly how I feel about that?" Henry sat forward.

Darcy lost his confident look at the gathering storm in his grandfather's eyes. "Studies show it won't affect the water flow. At least look at the reports, Grandfather."

Henry was silent while the others seemed to hold their breaths. "All right. I'll take a look."

Darcy looked relieved. "Great. The deal will certainly fall through if we don't make barge traffic possible. And we need to build a road through a section of our land near Bayou Latte to—"

"What?" Henry's head jerked up.

"Those woods about seven miles down between Bayou Latte and Palcour Landing. With the change, we'll need a road to the back of the plant for delivery from the barges." Darcy wore a looked of confusion at the effect of his words.

"No, no, no damnit!" Henry rose from the chair, his eyes wide with rage. "Tha-that's prime hunting land. I won't have it disturbed," he shouted.

"A road in that location is critical." Darcy stared at him in shock. "We started two days ago."

"Then you can just stop." Henry advanced toward him. "Did you hear me?"

Darcy's expression hardened. "No."

"What did you say, boy?" Henry said in a raspy voice.

"It's time you really retire. I'm going to take full control of the company and I'll make the decisions. I'm CEO now."

Henry raised a clenched fist. "Stay away from that property. I'll have you thrown out of my office . . . My company—" Henry swayed in a wide arc, his eyes glassy.

Toya jumped up to grab him on the right while Darcy moved quickly to his left side. Cecile let out a squeal of distress. The left side of Henry's mouth twisted sideways. He slumped down onto Toya knocking her to the floor.

"Call an ambulance! Oh Lordy, Henry! Henry!" Cecile wailed.

"I thought he was going to hit me." Rae leaned against Simon. They sat in his town house sipping wine.

"Yeah, well he's not too happy with me either." Simon wore a look of sympathy. "I never realized he was still so angry. You'd think it all happened last week."

"Well Henry Jove has taken carrying a grudge to a whole new level, cher. The man is a little scary with this obsession. Estelle must have put some kinda voodoo love spell on my man."

"Let's forget about him and everyone else. For the first night in weeks, I don't have to share you with a hungry, thirsty crowd." Simon hugged her to him. "I just want us to concentrate on each other."

Rae pressed her mouth against his, her tongue tasting his sweetness. "Uh-huh, you got it," she mumbled.

She strained against him, relishing the feel of his hands on her breasts. Fire raced through her pelvis. A week had passed since they had made love. In short order, both had shed their clothes and lay on the thick carpet. Simon pulled her on top, astride him, in one motion. Rae felt an urgency. She did not want to go slow. Simon responded with the same intensity. Rae moved up and down fast, her hips pumping as he gripped her waist. Simon came with a loud cry, his body arched, lifting her high. The sensation of him growing even harder inside her brought the sharp, sweet pain of her orgasm. Rae gasped for air as she gently rolled to lie beside him.

"Whew! That was so good," she panted. Rae sighed at the whisper of chilly air from the vent above that washed over them.

"What got into you?" Simon's chest rose and fell rapidly.

"You," Rae said with a giggle. She stretched. "Good thing this carpet is so soft."

"Come here." Simon grabbed at her.

Rae wiggled away. "No, I wanna cool off first. Then we'll take another ride."

"Better get my Wheaties," Simon said with a soft moan.

Simon retrieved a pair of pajamas. Rae wore the shirt and he the pants. They listened to a variety of music on his compact disc player, from hip hop to Mississippi Delta blues. They had settled in for a cozy night of intimacy, and the ringing of the telephone was a jarring intrusion.

"Ignore it," Simon mumbled. He rested his head against Rae's neck as they snuggled on the sofa. The answering machine clicked on with Simon's voice prompting the caller to leave a message.

"Simon, Grandfather is very sick. We're at the hospital and he's in intensive care," Toya rasped in a tearful voice. "Please come. The doctor said he might not make it. Simon, please," she sobbed. Then there was a click as she hung up.

Simon and Rae sat stunned by the news. Then Simon stood up.

"I have to go. You understand, don't you?" Simon gazed at Rae.

Rae sat up. "Yeah, sure." The sweet mood they'd shared was gone.

As Simon took a quick shower and dressed, she sat thinking of her last encounter with Henry Jove. He had always seemed so powerful, so in control. Of course, he was only human like everyone else. It would be sad if he died just when LaMar was on the verge of finding out the truth about Pawpaw Vincent and Estelle, especially as it might turn out that Henry was right all along.

Rae went into the bathroom and showered and dressed hurriedly while Simon waited. They walked out together. Rae got into her car.

"I'll call you later, babe." Simon leaned down and kissed her forehead.

"Okay."

Only moments ago the night had been magical, a velvet comforter that wrapped them in love. Now there was an ominous feel to the blanket of darkness on the rural highway as Rae drove home. The descending sense of gloom puzzled her. Though she felt sorry for Henry Jove despite their harsh words, there was something else. A palpable shift in the atmosphere seemed to signal dire events. Maybe digging into the past had released some kind of negative energy. Rae tried to shake off her morose musings. Unable to sleep, she stared at the television most of the night without really seeing it.

Thirteen

"Over here, Willie," a deep voice shouted. The work crew boss gestured to the man operating a dump truck.

Bright, hot sunshine beamed down on the men. The work had begun early enough, but now at only ten in the morning their shirts were soaked with sweat. In spite of the heat and humidity, the men kept up a steady pace. They took turns drinking water from the big round coolers they carried with them. For three more hours they worked clearing the thick vegetation in preparation for putting in a road. Onlookers who lived or worked near Bayou Latte wandered over to watch off and on. Even birds, disturbed from their usual quiet routine, perched high in the trees to observe the activity below.

The sandy dirt was scooped up into huge piles that would later be used to build up the levee along Grande River. Large rocks would be broken up to be used as gravel for road beds or concrete mix. Nothing would be discarded. Yet even the clank of machinery did not spoil the beauty of the scene. Bayou Latte, which flowed along for miles, was surrounded by lush green grass. Wide palmetto bushes sprouted as they had in the sub-tropical land for centuries. Tall oaks, white ash, and maple trees formed a canopy for the forest floor. A breeze stirred their leaves high up but did little to cool.

The sparse audience shared a cordial companionship with the men working. Light banter went back and forth as all enjoyed the day. Dump trucks lumbered away hauling their loads, some of which would be placed on barges.

"Hey, Gus!" A workman shouted. "Come over here, man. Looka this."

The foreman strode over to stare down at ground. "What the— That's probably some deer or something."

With a slow shake of his head, the worker disagreed. "I hunt, man. That don't look like no deer bone to me."

An hour later, the men sat around eating their lunches and waiting. Deputy Wilson and Sheriff Thibodeaux stood staring down at the bones laid on the ground.

"Best we call the state police on this one, Kedrick," Sheriff Thibodeaux said. He squatted down and took off his sunglasses. "This might be nothing, then again . . ."

Andrew sat down at the bar and ordered a sandwich for lunch. "Hey, Garrett. They was digging over by the bayou and found some human bones. Got everybody spooked."

Garrett, getting ready to open for the evening, stopped arranging glass beer mugs. "Say what? Man, you gotta be kidding."

"I'm telling ya. My boss was down there when one of the guys dug them up. Folks already wondering who it could be." Andrew grinned when Sarah brought him a po'boy. "Thank you, ma'am." He handed Garrett a five dollar bill.

Garrett gave him his change with mechanical movements, his forehead wrinkled. "Can't be nobody from round here. We'd have missed them by now. Tell ya what, it's one of them drug dealers I bet."

"You think?" Andrew took a bite of the fried catfish and French bread.

"Sure. They use these bayous to smuggle drugs. Bet one of his business partners decided he didn't wanna share the profit."

"Or maybe he one of them gang members from Lafayette or New Orleans. Folks love to come out here and dump their trash." Andrew gave an grunt. "Drugs and gangs, just another form of pollution."

Sarah lingered to join in the conversation. "They ain't the

only ones that kill people." She dropped her voice. "Miss Zenola says voodoo's still practiced round here."

"Don't talk foolishness," Jackson, her husband, came from the kitchen wiping his hands on a towel. "That ain't how voodoo folks kill."

"He oughta know, his mama one of them," Sarah mumbled to them before he got close.

"Besides that, they use spells to make folks get sick and die. They wouldn't need to dump a body." Jackson took a seat on one of the bar stools.

For the next few minutes a lively debate ensued. Sarah insisted there was some evil magic being practiced. Garrett favored the more earthly sins of crime. Rae walked in on them discussing gossip and developing theories.

"What is all the commotion? I can hardly think back in my office." Rae sat down at a table with a sandwich and soft drink. "Sounded like a room full of people in here."

"Child, they found a body in the bayou," Sarah blurted out, foiling Andrew's effort to tell her first.

"Humph, more good news. Now we find out our backyard is a cemetery." Rae was fast losing her appetite.

"Yep, Belle Rose is jumping here lately." Garrett went back to work as he talked. "If old Henry dies, this town won't be the same."

Rae felt a shiver down her back. She did not like to think of that day she was confronted by the self-righteous patriarch of the town's most prominent Creole family. He looked ill after their heated exchange.

"Guess his bad temper finally did him in. Rae let him have it the other day. Right, baby sister?" Andrew threw a glance at her. "Say he had smoke coming out of his ears."

"Hush, Andrew," Sarah whispered.

"What did I say?" Andrew looked baffled. An uncomfortable silence descended.

Garrett rattled several bottles. "Uh-oh, I'm going out back to the store room." He darted away.

"I got to start marinating my meat for tonight." Jackson followed him.

"Hey, everybody's acting like I stepped in something," Andrew lifted both hands. "What's up?"

"Rae, don't you listen to ignorant gossip. You ain't caused the man to have that stroke." Sarah gave Rae a maternal pat before leaving. She shot an admonishing look at Andrew. "You're gonna learn to let your brain guide your mouth one of these days."

"Aw, come on. Rae knows she didn't make the old man sick." Andrew pulled out the chair next to her and sat down. "Ain't that right?"

"Yeah, well the talk is I pushed him over the edge." Rae lifted a shoulder. She traced an invisible line on the table cloth.

"At his age, anything can go wrong. The man is seventy-seven, Raenette." Andrew put an arm around her shoulder. "He's already cheated the grim reaper longer than many."

"Henry Jove is the last person I'd loose sleep over, Andy. But I don't wanna kill the man either." Rae rubbed her eyes.

"Pooh-ya! One conversation ain't gonna kill that mean old goat."

Rae patted his hand. He could always tease her out of a blue mood. "Yeah, you're right."

"Sure I am. Not even you got that powerful a personality." Andrew poke her in the ribs. "Though you could raise Mama's temperature with them tricks you pulled."

"All right, let well enough alone." Rae tried not to laugh.

For the rest of the day hard work was a comfort, allowing Rae to avoid thinking of the Joves. She completed an inventory, worked with Marcelle on the books, and paid sales taxes. The dance hall closed at midnight. Garrett soon proved his skill and became her manager. This meant that eventually Rae would not work sixteen-hour days. Yet tonight, she welcomed it. Only a few days ago, the dance hall was a barrier to being in Simon's arms. Now she fought a fear that he would be drawn away from her. Working late meant she could delay going to an empty house. All she heard was his tired voice on the phone telling her that Henry Jove's condition was still critical. The weekend came and Rae could stand it no longer.

"Garrett, you mind if I take Saturday off?" Rae's nerves were raw. She'd not had a decent night of sleep for several days. "Andrew will help. Neville will be down Saturday night."

"Bet Andrew jumped at the chance." Garrett grinned. "Surprised me, but Andrew's got a gift for running this place. Why don't you let him take some of the burden off you?"

Rae thought of her carefree brother. Despite his laid-back attitude toward work, playing host was his strength. Garrett was right, Andrew showed an understanding about cash flow and balance sheets that was more than a surprise, it was an outright shock.

"Think I can persuade him to quit his day job at Ventre's?" Rae raised an eyebrow.

"Only reason he'd say no, is if you don't ask him," Garrett quipped.

Of course, Garrett was right. Andrew wore a wide grin when Rae broached the subject.

"Now I gotta give Mr. Ventre notice. He'll probably let me work some anyways. Me and Garrett switching days as manager is a fine idea." Andrew stuck out his chest. "The Dalcour family enterprise is on its way."

Rae tried to share his bright outlook. Once he was gone, the gray fog of gloom settled back over her.—Not even the clear blue sky with puffy white clouds helped. Rae strolled along the river downtown trying to leave it behind.

"Rae, I've been looking for you," Simon called to her. He crossed to the small park behind city hall. "Just so happened I came to the office for something and saw your car."

"Hi, baby. How are you?" Rae pulled him close. He felt so good.

"Sorry I haven't been by in the last couple of days."

"You don't have to explain." Rae placed her fingertips on his lips. "Is it bad?"

"He's stable at least. But his left side is paralyzed and he can't talk. At least not so you can understand him."

"What does the doctor say?" Rae tried to visualize the formidable man unable to command his own body.

"Dr. Picard had the neurologist examine him The next few days are critical."

"Even though he's not exactly one of my favorite people, I'm sorry this happened." Rae took a deep breath. "How is the family holding up?"

"Darcy is fine." Simon frowned, disapproval on his face. "He's been at the hospital, but his biggest concern seems to be getting the sheriff and state police out of his way so his precious road can be built."

"Man, I forgot about that. Seems we have a murder mystery on our hands." Rae sat down at a picnic table under a sprawling oak tree in the tiny park.

Simon put an arm around her waist as he joined her on the wooden bench. "Darcy didn't even let the fact that his grandfather had a stroke the night before keep him from going out there the next morning."

"From the what they say, this plant is going to help make the Joves even richer." Rae gazed out over the sparkling water. "Darcy wouldn't let anything get in the way of that."

"Yeah, guess you're right."

"The apple doesn't fall far from the tree either. Mr. Henry is just as single-minded about making money." Rae glanced at Simon. "I shouldn't have said that under the circumstances."

"No, you're right again. But the strange thing is, Mr. Henry wasn't too happy about something connected to the deal." Simon looked at her. "He was in the middle of a tirade about his property when he had the stroke."

"Henry Jove didn't want to make more money? Now that is strange." Rae leaned against Simon. "He sure could get worked up. Mr. Henry tore into me a couple of days ago and—"

"My grandfather wouldn't be lying in a hospital right now if you hadn't come back to town," Toya cut in. She stood several feet away to their right with a stony face.

Simon turned to face her. "Mr. Henry was at risk for a stroke because of his heart and high blood pressure. Rae didn't have anything to do with it."

"The doctor said stress plays a factor." Toya jabbed a finger at Rae. "She has deliberately provoked us by digging up the past and opening that sleazy dive."

"You're delusional." Rae did not try to curb her anger. She

was tired of Toya's attitude being thrown in her face at every turn. "I guess that thunderstorm we had the other night is my fault, too."

"Grandfather was doing just fine until you provoked him! Why couldn't you go back to bar hopping with that straggly band of yours?" Toya snarled. "Your grandfather stole from him and now you're here to drive him to the grave."

"Toya, stop it!" Simon said in a clipped voice.

Seeing the look on his face, Toya went from being wrathful to acting like a helpless female in the blink of an eye. "I don't know what I'm saying or doing right now. I'm beside myself with worry. Could I talk to you privately?"

"He just came from the hospital. He does need to rest sometime," Rae said through clenched teeth.

Toya ignored Rae. She dabbed at her eyes. "Grandfather isn't doing much better, and Darcy keeps leaving to take care of business. Grandmother Cecile has gone to pieces." Her voice broke.

Simon turned to Rae. "I'm headed to my office anyway, so . . ."

"You're not fooled by that act, are you?" Rae muttered.

"That's not fair. Toya is real sensitive," Simon whispered. "Especially when it comes to Mr. Henry. I won't be long and then—"

"Right. See ya," Rae cut him off and stood up.

"I'll come by later. Let's plan to sit out on the porch at the dance hall. Just you, me, and a breeze off the bayou. Okay?" His eyes pleaded for understanding.

"Sure." Rae gave him a weak smile.

Her stomach roiled at the sight of them together. They were from the same world. Simon, in his expensive casual clothes from his shirt to his shoes, looked natural beside Toya. Why did she get the feeling that Simon was walking away from her in more ways than one?

Ellis Mouton formed a steeple with his slender fingers. He seemed intent on the antique limited edition Audubon print of a Louisiana brown pelican that hung on his office wall. Darcy sat in a casual pose, seemingly undisturbed by his silence. Mouton's senior vice president, Carl Waguespack, fidgeted.

"How much longer will there be a delay? We can't afford to let one more thing put off this plant being built. The Pantheon people are getting restless," Waguespack blurted out finally.

Darcy examined his neat fingernails while seconds ticked by. "Sheriff Thibodeaux says only another day."

"I think there are too many complications. Now we have a murder investigation to contend with, of all things. It's just been one problem after another." Carl looked at Darcy as though this latest development was his fault.

"I've spoken to Raymond, one of the project managers at Pantheon. He's going out with the civil engineer to walk through the layout. They're going ahead with their schedule. Building starts Monday." Darcy glanced at Ellis then back at his hands.

"Finding a body didn't at least cause a tiny ripple?" Ellis raised a dark eyebrow at Darcy.

"Oh there is some passing interest. But it doesn't have any impact on their plans." Darcy lifted a shoulder.

"What about the road? That certainly does impact the new plant, Mr. Mouton," Carl said. "It's a crime scene and could be tied up longer depending on what the police find."

"Not according to what the state police told Sheriff Thibodeaux. Those forensics folks are pretty thorough these days. They'll gather what they need, then the real investigation begins in a laboratory." Darcy beamed a smile at Ellis. "Naturally, I've discussed this with him in some detail."

"So a little thing like murder shouldn't stand in the way of commerce?" Ellis studied Darcy with an amused gleam in his dark eyes.

Darcy's tilted his head a bit. "Since it doesn't concern us. Why should a multibillion dollar company vital to the parish economy be hampered?"

"Ah, I see." Ellis gazed at Darcy with open admiration.

Carl's thin mouth was a tight line as he glanced at Darcy. "I think we should go with our alternative plans. We can't afford to find out later on, after construction has begun, that there are other complications."

"There won't be any other complications. In the unlikely event that there are, they'll be dealt with with the same efficiency as we've handled others." Darcy's smile grew stiff, his voice held an edge.

"Mr. Mouton, the Trosclair property is still on the market." Carl spoke to Ellis in a tone that dismissed Darcy.

"You've been discussing plans that don't involve Jove Enterprises?" Darcy said. His full lips curved up, but the expression was no longer one of satisfaction.

"We have extensive experience with major projects. It is our standard operating procedure to develop contingency plans." Carl spoke as though instructing a dense child. His voice dripped with barely suppressed condescension.

"Jove Enterprises has acted in good faith. My company has gone to considerable expense in this venture. Not to mention I set up the deal with Pantheon. Now you think you can cut me out?" Darcy no longer looked like the bored young man playing at big business. He had a cold knife-sharp quality.

"We have no contract with Jove Enterprises." Carl stared at Darcy.

Darcy leaned forward in his chair. "Ellis, I'll give you complications you never dreamed possible if you make even one tiny move to cut me out of this."

"With the extensive Trosclair property, we could go ahead with the plant regardless of any other . . . developments." Carl nodded at Ellis. "It's certainly a viable solution."

"I'd be careful bragging on your plans, Carl." Darcy threw him a disdainful glance. "The dust hasn't settled from that disaster you orchestrated with the Delta Corporation."

"That wasn't my fault. Everyone knows the environmentalist had no solid evidence that our process was harmful to the wetlands," Carl burst out. His face turned red with ire.

"Really? Of course, the fact that the company had scores of clean water violations with heavy fines in another parish didn't help. Too bad you didn't have a contingency plan for that," Darcy retorted.

Carl looked ready to explode. "Now you wait just a minute. Who do you think you are? I—"

"Carl, calm down." Ellis spoke in a mild tone.

"But, Mr. Mouton, he's questioning my competence," Carl protested. He drew himself straight. "My family has been in business for seventy years in this parish."

"Skill in making the big deals must have skipped a generation," Darcy said with sarcasm.

"One company doesn't make you a corporate giant!" Carl shot back.

Ellis stood up and came around his desk. "Carl, let me talk to Mr. Jove alone." He ushered the outraged man through the door. "I know, I know." The two men spoke in muted voices in the outer office for several moments.

"Soothed his wounded pride?" Darcy sat once again in a relaxed pose.

"You really shouldn't provoke him." Ellis sat next to Darcy.

"Carl made it plain what he thinks of me. Now he knows what I think of him. The man is a snob and a bigot."

"He's a product of his upbringing. You could say he can't help what he is, Darcy." Ellis leaned toward him in a confidential manner.

"Bull." Darcy gave a grunt. "Forget him anyway." He waved a hand to dismiss the subject.

"You're right. The important thing is how does Pantheon really feel. First Raenette Dalcour wouldn't sell her land and now a body is found in the path of their new road." Ellis stared at him hard. "Tell me the truth."

Darcy returned his gaze without a hint that he was tense. "Naturally smooth sailing would have been preferable. But they've spent a lot of money on making this site work. Going to another location would be even more problematic."

"I see." Ellis did not seem totally convinced.

"Ellis, that flap Carl caused with Delta was only one in a series. A reporter in Baton Rouge has written a scorching set of articles about companies that skirt environmental rules and spoil Louisiana's precious landscape," Darcy said.

"Yes, I know. Carl should have done a better job researching Delta," Ellis pursed his lips.

"That's an understatement," Darcy quipped.

"But I'm not sure it means anything to us."

"Locating near a town that welcomes them and where we've done comprehensive environmental studies is ideal for Pantheon." Darcy straightened his silk tie. "They're committed to making it work."

"You're dancing on a tight wire, Darcy. One strong wind and you could fall."

"This plant is a go. Don't you worry." Darcy looked certain of his words.

"But, I do." Ellis spoke in a soft voice. "I need assurances that there are no more ugly surprises."

"There won't be." Darcy started to rise, but Ellis put a restraining hand on his arm.

"You seem very sure of yourself. I hope you're right."

Darcy stood up. He brushed the sleeves of his jacket. "I am. Just make sure your second banana stays out of my way. You know I deliver."

"Yes, and our association will continue as long as you do." Ellis was all elegance and grace as he walked back around his large desk. "Keep that in mind." The implied threat was clear.

"Oh, I know exactly who I'm dealing with on all sides, Ellis. That's how I've been so successful at what I do." Darcy flashed a handsome grin before sauntering out.

"Monmon Cecile, Grandfather prefers more sugar in his tea," Toya said. She smiled at Henry who nodded.

"The doctor says he should restrict certain foods. I know what he needs." She stepped in front of Toya blocking her view of Henry. "Here now take this."

"Cecile, I'm sick not dea-d." Henry's voice slurred yet he clearly communicated his annoyance.

"Grandfather should be up and around in no time. He's bounced back better than expected." Toya scowled at her step-grandmother's back.

"Thank you, cherie," Henry said with a wink to his grand-daughter. It took great concentration for him to raise the cup to his lips. He looked tired from the effort.

"Well, for now he's not on his feet. You're still paralyzed on the left side, you need speech and physical therapy. And I've got to do most everything for you." Cecile sat with her hands folded in her lap. She looked pleased at his state. "At your age, you're not going to do much bouncing. I'll see to it things are taken care of."

Toya sniffed. "I'll be checking on you every day. I'm so glad you're finally home. Almost a month in the hospital must have been terrible for you."

"It's what he needed. They kept him in the rehab unit so he could get intensive therapy. The doctors knew right," Cecile answered before Henry could stammer out a response.

"Grandfather," Toya said in a tight voice, "would you like me to take you riding later? I know how you hate being cooped in the house."

"I don't know about tha—"

"Ce-Cecile!" Henry snapped. "I ca-an speak for myse-self!" He stared at Cecile until she clamped her mouth shut. "I'd love to, darl-lin."

Once Toya was gone, Cecile turned to Henry. "Make no mistake, you need me Henry. I've done much for you all these years. Suffered for you, too."

"I kno-ow that Cecile." Henry looked straight ahead. "I-I know."

"I've been loving you since I was ten years old, long before you set eyes on her. Wasn't I good to you?"

"Ye-es." Henry closed his eyes. "I'm so ti-red, Cecile. *Sa fini pas.*" (It never ends.)

Henry looked like a shadow of the proud man-in-charge he'd been a few short weeks ago. Now for the first time in his life, he looked old. He rested his head against the large pillow placed behind him.

Cecile put a hand over his gnarled knuckles. *"Non, c'est fini.* As I've done before, I will take care of you."

"Maybe it's for the best." Henry rubbed his eyes.

"Darcy has gone too far. Marius should take over." Cecile glanced out the corner of her eye.

"I need to r-rest now." Henry seemed not to have heard her.

"I know you do, dear. But Marius must be placed in control soon before Darcy does more damage. Look what has happened in the last month." Cecile spoke in a soft but insistent voice.

"I-I'll think about it later. Help m-me to my room." Henry struggled to stand. He gripped a heavy wooden walking cane with a carved handle.

Cecile did not move to help him. "Henry, sit down." Her voice was firm.

Henry looked at her sharply. "Yes, wh-what is it?"

"No matter how you feel about him, Marius must be in charge. This cannot wait. You'll feel more at ease once it is taken care of, cher." Cecile didn't quite succeed in hiding the calculating purpose behind her smile.

"Is that a fact?" Henry sat very still.

"Yes, as always we will be the ones you can count on." Cecile lifted her chin. "He is the best of what comes from the union of the Jove and Thierry families."

"So, I should listen only to you and Marius now." Henry stared at her. There was a gradual hardening of his expression that Cecile, intent on gaining ground at last, failed to notice.

Cecile nodded. "Marius has done much for you with little thanks, as have I. It's time we get more consideration." She softened her tone. "But you are generous with our children to an extent."

"I see."

"But Darcy has to be put in his place."

"And you will tell me wha-at that place is I suppose?" Henry's eyes were slits.

"He can still be active in the business in some capacity." Cecile nodded to herself as though deciding the matter.

"How kind of you and Marius." Henry wore a fierce smile. "I mean, to let him continue in the company at all."

"He has some skills I think," Cecile said.

"What if I don't a-a-gree?" Henry kept his tone mild.

Cecile gazed at him intently. "He chose the spot for the road without consulting you. It's going through the old Auguste's Field, the one your grandfather planted years ago. Remember it was a favorite meeting place for young lovers back—"

"I know my own pro-perty. I won't discuss it."

"Marius should be made the boss." Cecile spoke in a low voice.

"You think I am now so feeble, you ca-an hold some power over m-ee?" Henry glowered at her with all the old power. "Think again, woman."

"This is the least you can do for me, Henry. I've sacrificed for you as no other woman would have."

"For your own selfish ends," Henry shot back.

"Selfish? If it's selfish to love with all my heart, to want to be with you, then I am selfish." Cecile grabbed his left wrist.

"Al-w-ways some payment is due for your devotion." Henry plucked her fingers from his skin as though repelled by her touch.

"Don't say it like that," Cecile whined. "I only want you to care for me the way . . ." She took a deep breath.

"You are still jus-st as foolish," Henry said. He studied her for a several minutes. "Well, I thought to speak to-o Darcy about his actions. We'll see wha-at he ha-as to say for himself."

"And Marius?" Cecile's eyes gleamed.

"I haven't decided." Henry tried to flex his left hand. "Both of the-m are probably making pla-ns to take my place. Bu-t I'm not go-ne yet."

"What of the . . . delay on the road?" Cecile watched him.

Henry sagged again, the strength seemed to seep from him bit by bit. "So many years have passed."

Cecile looked grim. "Nothing will happen. Don't worry." She stared out the window as though she could see across the miles to the field. *"J'ai pas apris grand chose."* (I did all I could do.)

"Merci beaucoup, Cecile." Henry let out a long breath. "You never wavered when I needed you most. When Estelle . . ." He grimaced, still feeling the pain of Estelle's betrayal.

"My love for you made everything simple. I wanted you more than anything in the world." Cecile spoke with a dark fervor. "Anything."

"I'll go si-t on the porch for a whi-ile." Henry moved away from her. "Alone," he added when she started to follow him. "I can ma-make it o-on my own." He seemed eager to leave her.

"That's good. The therapist said you should try to do more." Cecile watched his shuffling progress. "But go slowly. I'll check on you in a minute."

"No-o need." Henry kept going without looking back.

"Oh, yes, I'll be right here, cher," Cecile called after him. "I'll be here until the end," she murmured.

Fourteen

"You're pretty good at keeping the books."

Marcelle flipped through the stack of spreadsheets that Rae kept so they could do the books at the end of each week and month. They sat in Rae's office at Rockin' Good Times.

"That small business accounting course at the university sure helped," Rae said.

"Yeah, I wish Mr. Thibaut had learned as well as you. Bless his heart, he can sure fix air conditioners. But when it comes to his books? Pooh-ya!"

Rae tucked a stray tendril of hair back inside the elastic cloth band that tied her thick locks. "Now, if I can just get a new computer. I saw an ad for accounting software designed for restaurants and lounges. That would make both our jobs easier."

"Doing the books, taking classes, booking entertainment, and even playing every once in awhile. You trying to set some kinda record?" Marcelle shook her head.

"I'm just doing what needs doing, Marcelle. I'm a business-woman now."

"Rae, you're running yourself ragged. Let Andrew take over some." Marcelle glanced at her. "Or are you trying to keep busy for a reason?"

"Sure I'm keeping busy for a reason, I've got a dance hall to operate," Rae shot back.

Marcelle raised a dark eyebrow and watched her for several seconds. "Simon been real occupied lately I hear."

"Simon is a caring, responsive man." Rae tugged at her hair.

"True."

"Of course, he's going to try and help the family all he can. Henry Jove helped him start his business." Rae slapped the stapler hard on a stack of forms.

"Yeah, put up money not long before him and Toya got engaged, they say." Marcelle pretended to study the spreadsheet in front of her. "Toya got the old man to get up off more money than he'd planned. Her and Simon were quite a pair."

"Oh, they were?" A loud smack punctuated her words as Rae hit the stapler again on several papers.

"Yeah. Honeymoon in Jamaica, vacations every year to some great place. Something else, I tell you."

Rae attacked several more sheets with the stapler. "Damnit! This cheap thing." She cursed at the twisted staples she had to pry from the mangled corner of an invoice.

"If you stop beating up on it, you might do better," Marcelle replied mildly.

"Nice try, Marcelle." Rae pointed a finger of accusation at her. "But I'm not going to let you play me."

"What? What did I do but mention . . ." Marcelle wore a wide-eyed innocent look.

"Don't give me that 'Who Me?' act. You're trying to get me going by mentioning how Simon is spending a lot of time with the Joves. Which means Toya probably has her pointy talons digging into his flesh at every opportunity," Rae said through clenched teeth.

"She's a mess now," Marcelle agreed.

"But, I'm not worried. If he wanted that well-groomed alley cat in his life, he could have had her any time." Rae squared her shoulders and tried to sound more secure than she felt.

Marcelle abandoned any pretext of interest in the figures before her. "Don't sit stewing. Call the man. Have him come to your house every day."

"I don't feel sorry for myself," Rae protested with heat. "I can live without a man, thank you very much."

"Yeah, but who in the world wants to?" Marcelle retorted. "Don't talk stupid."

"Simon knows where I am. I'm not going to chase him down. We see each other regularly."

"But Toya is seeing him, too. Why Darcy or his children can't help is what I wanna know." Marcelle folded her arms.

"Darcy devote more than token attention to anyone but himself? Don't make me laugh. And Henry's other children live out of state." Rae tapped the stapler with a forefinger. "Simon and Henry got along good. I never knew how good until now."

"Which means Toya is going to ooze back in if she can." Marcelle leaned across the table adjacent to Rae's desk. "I'm telling you, cut her off at the pass."

"Will you stop." Rae waved a hand at her.

What she did not tell Marcelle was that she'd thought some of the very same things for the past few weeks. Yet Rae did not have any intention of turning into one of those clinging lovers who hurled jealous accusations. She had left more than one man who tried to smother her, she was not about to imitate them. Though she had to admit, now she understood how they felt. Rae had never felt this kind of love before. When they were apart, wanting to be with him was like a gnawing hunger only he could satisfy. No wonder numerous blues love ballads described it as a sickness. Sure Rae wanted to shout that Toya was a witch who used people. But she clamped a lid on the impulse that surged each time he said her name. Simon would think she was an immature harridan, no better than the woman she assailed, and he'd be right.

"Just saying you oughta take out some love insurance." Marcelle went back to her work.

"Marcelle I—" A knock at the door cut off Rae's response. "Come in."

"Hey, hardworking people. Sure I'm not interrupting?" Simon came in.

Rae sprang from her chair and wrapped herself around him. "Definitely not."

Simon fitted his body to hers in welcome. "Hi, baby." He gave her a quick kiss on the lips then stared into her eyes. "Been missing you bad," he whispered.

"Me, too." Rae closed her eyes. She felt shaky with relief to see him just at a moment of feeling the most uncertain. His arms around her were an effective defense against all doubts. Rae purred at the sensation of his hard body.

"Ahem, I'm kinda young to be witnessing this hot stuff," Marcelle quipped. "Maybe I better leave."

Rae blushed when she realized how close she'd come to embarrassing herself in front of her friend. She stepped back before her hands moved on their own to some delicate place on his fine body.

"Stay right there." Simon grinned at her. He turned back to Rae. "We'll have plenty of time later. Tonight, pick you up at six," he murmured close to her ear before kissing her cheek.

"I'll be ready." Rae felt the heat flare again in her chest.

"You better be," Simon said with a wink. He stepped back from her. "I don't want to stop progress at the hottest place to party outside of New Orleans." Simon spoke in a normal tone.

"*Mais* yeah, cher. It's a bayou kinda thang." Marcelle snapped her fingers and bounced to the beat of music coming from the FM radio station playing over the sound system.

"Things are going great, Simon. Better than I ever dreamed." Rae's spirits soared.

The dance hall had become a popular watering hole for young professionals in nearby Lafayette, Baton Rouge and Lake Charles. Rae also catered to those wanting family entertainment by having outdoor celebrations with activities for the kids. She threw herself into participating in campaigns to curb teen use of alcohol and to encourage responsible adult drinking. The result was a growing core of loyal customers who spread the word about her Friday night Swamp Groove Jams. On Saturdays, she usually had some popular band that kept the dancing and listening crowd shouting for more.

"This place looks better and better. I like how you had that old buffet set up. Where did you find it?" Simon said.

"Tante Ina got it for me at her friend's house. It was falling to pieces, but it's a classic. So since Mr. Calvin is doing some finishing touches around here, he said he'd fix it up." Rae smiled. "He did a beautiful job."

"Sure did. Hey, when is he going to be through?" Marcelle put in. "Can't have much work left."

"There isn't. But he said it wouldn't keep the place from opening." Rae sat on the edge of the desk. "He's working on the other half of the restaurant."

"I thought that was gonna be a bigger office." Marcelle looked around the room no bigger than a small bedroom. "We need extra space."

"We need space that can bring in money," Rae retorted. "I want to pay Neville back as quickly as I can. He went out on a limb for me."

Simon smiled at her and brushed a wisp of dark hair from her forehead. "I'm sure he's willing to be patient for his baby sister."

"But I'm not. Neville, bless him, overcame some real reservations. I'm going to see he and Trisha get every penny."

"I'm sure you will, cher." Marcelle beamed at her.

"So am I." Simon stared at her with a warm glow in his eyes. "Well, I gotta get going. I'll see you later, sweet thing."

"Bye, babe." Rae pressed his large hand to her cheek.

"Bye, Marcelle," Simon said with a wave on his way out.

"Bye now." Marcelle sat staring at Rae with a smirk for several minutes.

"What?" Rae went back to sit behind her desk. "Why are you gawking at me with that silly look on your face?"

"You're in charge, girl. Go ahead and show us how it's done." Marcelle snickered,

"All right, you." Rae tried to suppress a catlike smile of satisfaction that broke through anyway.

"My man got a serious-to-the-bone-Love Jones." Marcelle snapped her fingers twice. "Now deal with that, Miss Toya."

Rae could not resist. "Suck swamp mud, hussy." She giggled with the glee of a teenager.

The two friends laughed hysterically until tears flowed. Tales of youthful adventure flew back and forth for hours as they enjoyed the day and companionship. After lunch they sat out on the porch of the dance hall, each with a glass of iced tea.

"How did I ever get along without you, and all this?" Rae

gazed out over the vibrant mix of bright colors. Lush growth, encouraged by heat and moisture, crowded along the highway and at the edge of the cut lawn surrounding the dance hall.

"You had a great musical career going, for one thing."

"But deep down I knew something was missing." Rae rested her head back against the wooden rocking chair. "Still, I never would have thought it was here."

Marcelle gently rocked back and forth. "Strange because I never thought of living anywhere else."

"Well, you never had the trouble I had. Not that I didn't help it along myself." Rae wore a half smile.

"My family ain't exactly on the Creole social register. Lord, but you and Mr. Lucien did keep things hopping around here." Marcelle chuckled. "Did I mentioned how glad I am you're home?" She patted Rae's arm.

"Yeah, but once more won't hurt." Rae sighed.

"Looks like Raenette Dalcour is on her way to being a leading town citizen," Marcelle said, with a mischievous twinkle in her eyes.

Rae gave an exaggerated shiver. "Please, let's not take it too far. You make me sound like I'm going to join Miss Cecile's society club."

"You know what I mean. The old days of hard times and people looking down on us are over." Marcelle hummed a Creole lullaby.

"It would be almost perfect except for dead folk turning up where you least expect them to." Rae wore a slight frown.

A cloud floated across the sun, dimming the bright sunshine. She wondered if such a brutal act of violence close by was a sign of trouble to come.

"I'll bet it's a deer or cow, something like that. Even if those bones are human, I'll bet it's some drug smuggler. Nobody from around here." Marcelle did not stir from her relaxed pose.

Rae squinted into the distance at the fluffy white cloud now floating on its way. Sun rays washed the landscape again with radiance, "I suppose you're right. Yes, life is good."

* * *

"Good afternoon." Simon stood awkwardly in her back door. "I can come back if you want." He gazed at three sets of eyes examining him.

Rae sat with LaMar, Tante Ina, and Andrew. LaMar was about to give them his latest report when Simon arrived. They had become so comfortable, Simon was now used to walking around the back if he thought Rae was in the kitchen.

"No, come on in." Rae shot an anxious glance over her shoulder.

Andrew and Tante Ina wore closed expressions while LaMar looked curious at the change in atmosphere this newcomer brought. Though her family had met Simon at the dance hall, this was the first time any of them had been in such close contact with him. Andrew had treated him with guarded, stiff courtesy in public. Rae had no time to caution her relatives to be polite.

"I'm a little early. I could go take care of a few errands . . ." Simon spoke in a low voice.

"Stop fidgeting." Rae planted a firm kiss on his cheek. "Simon, this is LaMar Zeno. He's the private investigator I told you about. You know my sweet Tante Ina and Andrew."

"Nice to meet you. Andrew, Miss Ina." Simon shook hands with the two men and nodded to Tante Ina.

"Sit right here." Rae pulled out a chair at the table. She perched on a kitchen stool next to Simon. She gave her aunt and brother a "You better behave" look.

"How's your pawpaw and monmon, Simon." Tante Ina nodded to him.

"They're fine, thank you," Simon said.

"Tell Olivia I said hello. I'm gonna try and be at the Women's Auxiliary meeting next Tuesday." Tante Ina flashed a smile. "That Liv always comes up with the best ideas for the taste fair."

Andrew seemed to take her cue. "Some party when the dance hall opened, eh? You been all right?"

"Fine, just fine." Simon nodded at him.

"LaMar was about to tell us some news." Rae looked at Tante Ina and Andrew. "I didn't tell y'all Simon helped me. He got some information from Mr. Joe that really did give LaMar some good clues on where to look."

"That a fact? Thank ya, man." Andrew broke into his familiar charming smile.

Tante Ina hopped up. "Here, son. Have some cola. I brought over tea cakes, too." She ignored Rea's protest that she should not move. "Pooh, I'm right here at the ice box."

The tension gripping Rae's neck began to ease. Of all people, she'd been afraid that Tante Ina would have trouble accepting Simon. Yet she now realized her error. Both Tante Ina and Andrew were the most open, warm people she knew. They were willing to get to know Simon, not reject him because his name was St. Cyr. The ultimate proof was that Tante Ina was fussing over them all serving food. *Simon, babe, you're in.*

"Now we fixed up." Tante Ina checked to make sure everyone was served at least one tea cake and a beverage of choice. "LaMar, sugar, tell us what you done found out."

LaMar took a deep breath. "What I've discovered so far isn't promising or good news."

Tante Ina leaned forward with both plump arms resting on her table. "You mean it's all true? *Salleau prie!"* (Doggonit!)

"You found them?" Rae strained forward. Her heart thumped at the thought that she might meet the two legends of Belle Rose.

"Well, I'm pretty sure they bought tickets for that freighter. I found out that Estelle had an uncle in New Orleans. Her family goes back to the late eighteenth century in Creole society." LaMar unzipped a black leather portfolio. Inside was a light green legal pad filled with notes in his neat handwriting.

"Yeah, Estelle and her whole family was something else. The Fazandes looked down on everybody, even the Joves." Tante Ina made a rude noise to show what she thought of Estelle's family.

"Well this Uncle Alphonse is the one who probably helped her get passports. He wasn't much older than they were and he was considered really eccentric. I can't find anyone connected to the ship who might know a way to prove they got on. So I went on the assumption that since they were never found, they must have made the trip." LaMar flipped a page of the notepad.

"But why leave the country?" Andrew scratched his head.

"The freighter went to South America. There were countries there that offered more opportunities to people of color. But here's the kicker. They could have gone to the one of the Caribbean Islands, too." LaMar looked at him and nodded slowly.

"This is gettin' crazier by the day." Tante Ina waved a hand.

Rae blinked at him. "Don't tell me, the ship made stops at the islands."

LaMar turned to her. "You got it. They stopped at Puerto Rico, Trinidad, and Jamaica. Then went on down the coast of South America ending up in Bolivia."

"So he did run off with Estelle." Andrew sat back in his chair. "That old rascal."

"He wasn't old when he did it, Andy," Rae said. Still she understood what he meant. She, too, had grown up with the image of an older man like the grandfathers they knew in other families.

"It looks that way." LaMar looked at his notes again. "And they would have needed more than a few dollars to do it. I hate to say this, but . . ."

"Yeah, I'm thinking exactly what everybody in town was thinking back then." Andrew folded his arms across his chest. He looked at Tante Ina and Rae. "And they didn't know as much as we do now."

"Looks like they had it right all along," Tante Ina said in a small voice. "Even though I suspected it, deep down I always hoped it wasn't true. Mama never said a word, but she was so bitter."

"Of course, you won't know for sure unless you find out exactly where they went," Simon put in cautiously. "I mean, they should get a chance to tell their side."

"What are they gonna say? Love made it right?" Andrew made a grunting sound to show what he thought of that statement.

"I'm just saying, although it's a long shot, there could be another explanation." Simon shrugged. "You never know."

"Thanks, cher. But I gotta agree with Andrew." Tante Ina patted his hand. "Rae, quit throwing good money after bad. Looks like we got our answer."

"Simon is right. I at least want to hear what they have to say." Rae's full mouth was set in a determined line.

"Sugar, you've done what Lucien asked. He wanted you to find out the truth. Now, I know this ain't what he would have wanted to hear. Shoot, he probably wouldn't have believed it. But you can't spend all your money," Tante Ina said.

"But—"

"Tante Ina is right, Rae. We got to think about the dance hall now. Let's at least build that up for this family." Andrew looked at her.

Simon took Rae's hand. "LaMar, what do you think?"

"Well . . ." LaMar rubbed his chin for several seconds. "I have to be honest, this little mystery has led me down some intriguing paths. But I have to agree with Miss Ina and Andrew. The logical thing to do, based on circumstantial evidence, would be to end the investigation."

"I hear a 'but' in your voice." Rae sat forward. "Come on, LaMar, spill it."

"Maybe I'm imagining things, but it's all too . . . neat, I guess is the word." LaMar pushed the notes aside. "Look, two lovers in a fit of passion plan their getaway. They steal money and dash off one hot summer night."

"You could write one of them romance books, cher." Tante Ina grinned at him.

"I'll keep that in mind." LaMar chuckled. "Anyway, they get to New Orleans, board a ship and poof! They're gone forever. The trail is clear up to a certain point. Why didn't more people see them? It was in the newspapers at the time."

"They were careful. Maybe they had friends helping them along the way," Rae put in.

"And not one of them talked? No neighbors noticed anything?" LaMar shook his head. "Somebody *always* talks in my experience. Even career criminals slip and tell somebody."

Simon wore a slight frown of concentration as he digested his words. "Yeah, I see what you mean. Another thing, there was a reward offered of five hundred dollars for information."

"You right," Tante Ina put in. "I remember that now. But none of the tips they got turned out to be worth much."

"Papa Joe said it was mostly folks who didn't really know anything, but were just after the money," Simon said.

"Mais yeah. Five hundred dollars could get you a car and down payment on a house back then," Tante Ina said.

"But didn't Mr. Henry's daddy withdraw that reward only a month later or so?" Andrew gazed around the table.

"What?" LaMar's head jerked up.

"Daddy always said that's one thing that made him real suspicious. You lose ten thousand dollars, why would you offer a reward then cancel it?" Andrew lifted a shoulder. "Course, I hear the old man was stingy."

"Not only that, he wouldn't have given two pennies for Estelle," Tante Ina retorted. "For all her fine family, old man Jove and especially Henry's mama didn't think much of her."

"Papa Joe said they weren't happy with Mr. Henry's choice of a wife at all," Simon put in.

"Then that could be the explanation." Andrew looked at everyone. "Right?"

Several seconds ticked by as they all pondered the tangle of facts. LaMar had done a great job of tracing what seemed an invisible trail. There was no conclusive answer to all the questions, yet everything they knew pointed to a likely explanation.

Rae slumped in her chair. "Yes. It could."

"Babe, it's up to you. How badly do you want to find out the whole story?" Simon put an arm around her chair.

"Yeah, cher. I gotta admit, it sure is interesting to find all this out after wondering about it for the last fifty years. But the only mystery left is where they went and what happened to them since then." Tante Ina sighed.

"True. Do we wanna find a man who maybe don't wanna hear from us?" Andrew said.

"Daddy wanted me to find out the whole truth. Seems to me, we're right back where we started." Rae tapped the tabletop with her forefinger. "I want to keep searching, LaMar."

"Tell you what, I've got to go down to St. George's on another case. It's just a short hop to Trinidad from there. So the entire cost won't be charged to you," LaMar said.

"Thanks, LaMar. Anything else you need to do, do it." Rae said.

"I'll check with you before proceeding in any way that will

exceed my daily rate." LaMar zipped his portfolio and stood up. "I'll send you an itemized list of expenses for my trip. Y'all have a good evening."

"Sounds good." Rae walked him to the back door.

"Well, that's that. We're gonna go after the facts." Andrew smiled. "I feel like I'm in one of those mystery movies on the 'Late, Late Show.' "

Tante Ina did not share his humor. "I got a bad feeling. My grandmama used to say watch out when you get a shiver up your spine on a hot day. Something bad gonna happen." She looked grim.

"Aw, come on now." Andrew pinched his great-aunt's plump cheek. "Just cause they found somebody's bones and Pawpaw Vincent might be a thief, no need to get superstitious."

"Is that your idea of lifting our spirits, Andy?" Rae teased.

Andrew's wide, boyish smile beamed. "Look, business is great and it's a beautiful Wednesday evening. Y'all gotta quit looking for reasons to have a long face."

"You and your happy face can take me on home, Andrew Paul Dalcour." Tante Ina gave his ear a pull. "Let's leave these lovebirds alone." She rose from her chair.

"Y'all don't have to rush off," Simon protested with a blush.

"That's right. Stay and chat awhile," Rae added.

"No, my club is meeting this evening at six thirty over to Bea's house. Goodness, it's almost five. Come on here, Andrew." Tante Ina gave Rae a hasty peck on her check. "Bye, y'all. I got finger sandwiches to fix."

"I'll get you home in plenty of time, tante." Andrew followed her out with his long-legged stride.

"If you're thinking about speeding, think again. Wonder you ain't wrapped your fool self around some tree . . ." Tante Ina's strong voice trailed off. As she walked down the side of the house, her voice and Andrew's could be heard in a good-natured argument.

Simon put an arm around Rae's neck. "Satisfied with your decision?"

"Truth is I'm beginning to wonder if I want to know the

whole story. It could be worse than any of us has imagined."
Rae leaned on him for emotional as well as physical support.

It was disturbing to think that her grandfather was not at all
the man Lucien kept alive in memory. Her father had been insistent that his children listen to happy stories about the big,
handsome man. Yet Lucien had only been seven years old when
Vincent disappeared. A child's idealized image of the father he
adored could be far from the reality.

"Who was the real Vincent Dalcour? That's as big a mystery
as what happened to him," Simon mused.

"Yes. Deep down I believed Daddy's view of him all these
years. And now . . ." Rae shook her head.

"Well, Mr. Henry sure does go on about him. Toya says . . ."
Simon's voice trailed off at the look Rae gave him.

"How is Miss Center of the Universe these days?" Rae
snapped.

"Come on now." Simon wriggled under her hard stare. "Visiting Mr. Henry I'm bound to see her. He's her grandfather you
know."

"Hmm. Just why are you always over there anyway? Yeah,
yeah, I know you got along with the man and still do, but it's
not like he's *your* grandfather." Rae knew she sounded a bit
childish. But the thought of Toya prancing around Simon irritated her to no end.

"Actually he has been like a second grandfather since I was
a kid. My mother's father died before I was born. Mr. Henry
and Papa Joe took me fishing and camping, stuff my dad isn't
too crazy about." Simon smiled. "Dad and I love to visit librar-
ies and museums, something that mystifies Papa Joe to this
day."

"Which is how you and Toya ended up together."

Rae did not like the direction of this discussion at all. She
could not compete with the strong ties and memories between
the Jove and St. Cyr families. No doubt Toya would remind him
of that fact.

Simon nodded. "We've known each other all our lives. But
we didn't start dating until after I was a senior in high school.

Then I left the state for college. We started seeing each other again when I came home after graduation."

"And sugar daddy Henry helped put you in business after Toya reeled you in. Nice." Rae wore a sour expression.

"What does that mean?" Simon frowned.

"Toya has her hooks ready to sink into you. All you have to do is keep hanging around old Mr. Henry enough." Rae snorted. "Men are so gullible."

"Don't be silly." Simon waved a hand with a crooked smile.

Rae bristled at his easy dismissal. "Mr. Henry might even be in on it."

"Sure. That stroke was just a ploy to get me and Toya back together." Simon shook his head slowly.

"Or is it that you wouldn't mind another go with her?"

"Cut it out, Rae," Simon said in a tight voice.

"It's all real cozy, I'll bet. Just like old times." Rae felt that old familiar lump of resentment at being an outsider.

"Don't do this to us, Rae," Simon warned. "I had enough of suspicions and temper tantrums when I was married to Toya."

A tense silence stretched between them as Rae fought her natural urge to unleash another verbal barrage about Toya. When she was younger, she would have done just that. Now she knew that relationships could be easily damaged forever with words that are not easily taken back. Simon was right, this conversation was leading to one of those deadly arguments that escalate and leave scars. Rae bit back the anger.

"Forget what I said. I'm just worn out from work." Rae inhaled deeply.

"Honey, I'm not stupid. I know Toya takes every chance to bait you." Simon's tone softened. He took her hand. "Mr. Henry is still bitter against your family. But look at all you've accomplished. You came home a successful musician and started a dance hall that's taken off."

"But I'm not just another business person in this town. I'm a Dalcour. Truth is, I do feel like I've got something to prove to the Joves and everybody else."

"You've got too much on your shoulders right now. Let's relax and let go of troubles for a few hours."

Rae liked the way his large fingers laced through hers. She was relieved that they had avoided an argument about Toya. "I'd like that," she said softly.

Simon massaged her shoulders with strong hands causing her to squirm with pleasure. "I love the scent of jasmine in your hair."

"That feels so good." Rae bent forward to let him rub her back also. The tension drained from her body.

"This would be better if you were lying down," Simon murmured.

Without another word passing between them, he led her into her bedroom. Rae undressed, leaving on only the dark red lace bra and matching satin panties she wore, while Simon stripped down to only his briefs. Simon took control, directing her to lie across the bed on her stomach. Straddling her, his hard fingers kneaded her flesh. He started at her neck. With a slow tender touch, he moved down her body. He was breathing rapidly by the time he reached her calves.

Rae turned on her back and pulled him on top of her. "Massage over," she said. The need to have him inside her was like a hot iron stabbing through her hips.

Their lovemaking was fast and frenzied. Rae raked his back with her fingernails urging him not to be gentle this time. His body crashed against hers with each solid thrust of his hips. She needed him with a fierceness that was frightening. Rae clung to his body drinking up the rush of pleasure and security he gave. Both lay gasping for air afterward, stunned by the force that had seized them.

"It will be all right, darling. I'll make it so," Simon whispered in a raspy voice, his face buried in her hair.

Rae maneuvered to fit her body to his spoon fashion. "Thank you, baby," she murmured. All traces of the storm that threatened to overtake them was gone. Yet a small part of her still worried that more was to come. *No, I won't let Toya drive a wall between us. I'll learn to keep my mouth shut, no matter what she does.*

* * *

Cicadas and crickets sang out their insect chorus in seeming honor of the onset of hot summer nights in the bayou. Darkness, the ink blackness of being out in the country away from city street lights, hung like a curtain along the highway. A late model blue truck puttered along. It approached the dance hall and slowed. The glow from the end of a lit cigarette flared as the driver took a pull. He blew out a long stream of smoke.

"You sure ain't nobody there? It's got lights on inside," the driver rumbled.

"Since you screwed up last time, she been leaving lights on." A thin, wiry man with a scruffy beard shot a baleful glance at him.

"Me? It was your idea to scare her. We was just supposed to wait until she left then trash the place." The driver flicked the cigarette away and lit another.

"You had to tromp around like big foot letting them know we was along the side of the place," Scruffy beard snapped back at him.

"Hey you was—"

"Just shut up. Let's do this and get it over with." Scruffy beard looked around. "Somebody might drive by."

The driver grinned. "Ain't nobody coming out here this late on a Wednesday night. Deputy way over to Gator Bend on the other side of Grande River. Good idea I had for my brothers to fake a fight at Ida Mae's bar. We got plenty time to have us a drink even."

"You on a job with me, we stick to business. Got that?" Scruffy beard glared at him. The menace in his eyes was unmistakable.

"Yeah, sure," the driver answered quickly. "Whatever."

"You got all the tools?"

"Right here, man. Relax. I wasn't an electrician for nothing. I'm gonna make it look good."

Scruffy beard gave a snort. "You was Mr. Ardoin's assistant."

"I was his apprentice," the driver corrected him. "He said I was the best, too."

"Okay, master electrician. Let's go."

* * *

"Good morning everybody," Rae called out her kitchen window. The singing birds seemed to return her greeting.

It was a beautiful day so far. Rae helped Simon get off to an early start by serving him coffee. Simon had only just left for home so he could shave and shower before going to his office. Every muscle in her body was relaxed after the wonderful night they'd spent together. The jangle of the telephone jarred the peaceful daydreams she had sitting on her back steps sipping hot tea.

"Who has the nerve to call my house this early?" Rae went inside. "Hello and good morning," she answered still in high spirits. The smile faded from her face. "Oh, no. My, God, how bad is he hurt?"

Fifteen

"Marcelle, it's just awful." Rae met her at the door to the waiting room of the small Grande River Hospital. "Mr. Calvin went out early this morning to finish some work at the dance hall. He was overcome by smoke and—" She broke off when a doctor came out.

"Mrs. Johnson?" The tall red-haired physician looked around the room.

"Me, I'm his wife Elda," a plump woman answered. She wore a yellow jacket with Jay's Supermarket in blue letters above the chest pocket.

"He's got some third-degree burns on his legs and his lungs are damaged from the smoke. Come over here so we can talk." The doctor led the anxious woman away to a smaller waiting room separated from the big one by a wall whose upper half was made of glass windows.

"Girl, what happened?" Marcelle sat down next to Rae.

"A fire started at the dance hall early this morning while Mr. Calvin was working. He got there about six. He liked to get started early before it got too hot." Rae stared at Mrs, Johnson and the doctor.

"How did a fire start? "Marcelle held her hand.

"I don't know. The fire chief says it'll take maybe a few days for them to find out."

"This is terrible. Poor Mr. Calvin. I'm gonna call Mama." Marcelle searched in her large purse for a coin. "Her and Miss Elda been friends for years."

Marcelle went over to the pay phone. Rae sat in misery. The sight of the still-smoking wood kept playing in her head like a video tape. The smell of burning was still on her clothes. It was the smell of a dream dying and a nightmare being born.

"I'm gonna pick up the kids later so Mama can come over to sit with Miss Elda awhile." Marcelle sat down with a sigh. "Lord, Mr. Calvin is the sweetest man. Remember how he used to give us pieces of his homemade pecan candy?"

Rae felt the start of tears at the corners of her eyes. "This is my fault."

"Don't talk silliness." Marcelle clucked and patted her hand.

"I pushed the workers too hard. I've been rushing to make the place profitable. Mr. Calvin wouldn't have been working if I hadn't said how much I wanted it finished." Rae sniffed.

"The fire was an accident. You can't beat yourself up about that."

"Maybe it was an accident, maybe not." Rae dried her eyes with a tissue Marcelle handed her. She felt anger growing inside her.

"You mean . . . But who would want to do something so low down?" Marcelle's eyes were wide.

"There are still plenty of people around here that don't like that I'm doing well." Rae thought of Toya Jove for one. But she was not alone.

"Well, if it wasn't an accident, Harold Frey will find out," Marcelle said with a sharp nod of her head. The whole community was proud the first full-time fire chief was a black man.

"I hope so." Rae stood up. "I'm going back out there. Might as well see how bad it is."

"I'm going with you." Marcelle followed her out.

Marcelle's Chevy Cavalier rolled up beside Rae's Honda onto the gravel lot next to the dance hall. Firemen still picked through the rubble looking for hot spots. The water used to douse the fire was all but dried up by the noon day sun. Rae and Marcelle walked around to the back. The firemen would not let them enter the rest of the dance hall even though no fire had reached the lounge.

"Ma'am, please. I know you want to check on your business, but you gotta let us make sure it's safe." A tall blond man wearing a tan T-shirt and cap waved them back.

"Here comes Harold." Rae wiped her hands on her Levi jeans and walked toward him.

Harold Frey, with his barrel chest, was built like a weight lifter. He dipped his head at the two women. "Hi, Rae. Sorry about this."

"Buildings can be replaced. I just want Mr. Calvin to be okay." Rae brushed her hair back. "Do you have any idea what might have happened?"

"From the burn pattern, looks like it started in a wall near the breaker box. Now this isn't official, but it might be from a short." Harold wiped sweat from his dark brown face. "Tim has got to do more investigating." He gestured at the blond-haired man who'd spoken to them.

"But the wiring was redone completely." Rae looked at him with a frown.

"Who did the work? We'll want to talk to him. Routine," Harold added at Rae's questioning look. He left after taking the business card Mr. Ardoin had given her.

"What's that about, I wonder," Rae said, watching him walk over to Tim.

The two men stood talking for a few moments, then stepped into the charred portion of the room where Mr. Calvin had been working. Tim called out to another fireman wearing the uniform of the arson squad.

"Routine, like he said. What else?" Marcelle glanced at her watch. "I gotta go get my kids. Thank goodness I don't have work today. I'll call you later."

"Okay." Rae stared at the building hard. A lump of disquiet was heavy in the pit of her stomach. She would stay until Harold said she could go in for a least a quick look around.

Andrew pulled up in his truck. "Rae, ain't this something? I just come over from the hospital." He wore a somber expression.

Rae's heart thumped "Mr. Calvin?"

"He's holding his own. Doctor says he'll recover, but it will take a while. He got burned bad after he passed out from the smoke." Andrew rubbed his jaw.

"Yeah, his legs." Rae shuddered at the pain he must be in.

"Miz Johnson says he'll need some skin grafts they're pretty sure. He doesn't have medical insurance, Rae." Andrew said.

"Our policy ought to cover it, don't you think? I better have a talk with Tony." Rae sat on the fender of Andrew's truck. "I don't want them to have to worry about money along with everything else."

"Yeah." Andrew tugged on the front rim of his cap and squinted at the dance hall. "What a mess."

"Seems like folks around here are right. Nothing but bad luck follows me." Rae stared at the ground. "I should have gone back to Houston."

"Then it must be riding my rump, too. I helped you every step of the way, little sister." Andrew nudged her with an elbow. "Come on now. We've been through rough spots before. We'll make it."

"I won't be able to finish paying Neville back so soon." Rae wished her older brother were here. She could use his common sense approach to reassure her.

"I called him at work. He's coming later this afternoon. Only thing he cares about is that you're okay." Andrew put an arm around her shoulder.

"I've got the best brothers in the world." Rae gave him an affectionate look.

"Ah, well." Andrew grinned. "As for folks that still don't like you, to hell with them."

"Yeah," Rae chimed in. She was feeling strong again.

"Dalcours have been bouncing back since before the Civil War." Andrew stepped back to look at her. "You ain't never let what they said stop you before."

Rae sat straight. "I'm going to get this place open again. I did it once, I'll do it again."

"Let's go find Tony. Sooner the policy gets processed, the

sooner we're back in business." Andrew pointed for her to get in his truck.

"We might even be able to open the lounge part if the building inspector says it safe," Rae said. She got in on the passenger-side and slammed the door shut.

Andrew's ancient truck started with a rattle. "Now that's what I wanna hear. Dalcour ingenuity."

Toya sat on the covered patio of her spacious home gazing at the waterfall in the center of her garden. She sipped a marguerita. "Marius, tell me again how bad it looks." A feline smile of pleasure was stamped on her face.

"I'd say even in the parts that weren't damaged by fire, the smell of smoke and the water damage will keep the place closed." Marius wore white shorts, a white cotton shirt with green stripes, and Perry Ellis sunglasses. He crossed one ankle over his knee.

"Ah, what a great weekend," Toya said with a sigh. She stood up and smoothed down her denim minidress.

Her leather sandals slapped on the stone floor as she went to a table. A tray with a pitcher of wine punch and a tray of snacks were arranged neatly. Her Saturday afternoon patio party was in full swing when Darcy arrived an hour later. Toya's schoolmates and old friends, all expensively attired in the latest casual wear, milled around chatting. Darcy marched through them without returning one greeting.

"I need to talk to you," Darcy muttered to Toya. "You, too." He pointed a finger at Marius. Without waiting for replies, he spun around and headed into the house.

"Darcy, Shaunice is hurt. You didn't even speak to her. You know how she feels about you." Toya shut the door to the sun room, behind them.

"Man, what's up with this?" Marius took off his sunglasses.

"Which one of you is responsible?" Darcy faced them.

"Not me." Marius held up both palms. "Sure I picked up the crushed iced, but Toya planned the party."

"Rat," Toya quipped. She flounced down onto a rattan chair with flowered upholstery.

"You know damn well I'm talking about the fire at Rae's dance hall." Darcy looked at Marius. "I told you not to get involved in this."

"That land would allow us to sell to another corporation for development," Marius shot back.

"Oh really? We'd have to fight the police jury, the environmentalists, and probably most of the local businesses that depend on tourism." Darcy threw his car keys down hard.

"They couldn't stop us," Marius replied.

"A plant would have to get all kinds of permits and licenses, you idiot." Darcy paced in front of them.

"And we'd get them. Grandfather has contacts . . ." Marius lifted a shoulder.

"Grandfather, in case you haven't noticed, shows little interest in business since the stroke. Or anything else for that matter. He's left everything to me. Got that? Me!" Darcy slapped his chest.

"Don't think you're going to steal the family company from me, cousin." Marius walked up to him. "I've put a lot on the line for years."

"You mean you've been working at the company since you barely squeaked out of college." Darcy brushed past him, bumping him aside. "Face reality. I'm in charge of Jove Enterprises and that's not going to change."

Marius grabbed his arm. "Grandfather has the final say. He's not exactly thrilled with the way you've handled things so far. Digging up that property got him so steamed, he stroked out."

"That's bull!" Marius shouted.

"Don't get your hopes up, cuz. He's still alert enough to bust your plans. The old man isn't dead yet!" Marius glared at him.

"You idiot." Darcy shoved Marius so hard, he almost went over a love seat.

Marius caught onto the furniture before hitting the floor. "I'm going to finally kick your—"

"Stop it! You're making a spectacle!" Toya stepped between them. She walked to the glass door quickly and stuck her head out at the staring guests. "Nothing serious folks. Just a little family squabble. No need to worry."

Darcy backed away from Marius, straightening his shirt. He went to a small refrigerator behind the wet bar and got a can of soda. "So it was you."

"I was nowhere near the place the morning of the fire." Marius brushed dust from his shorts. "But Grandfather will be pleased when he finds out how *I* made getting the Dalcour property possible."

"She has insurance, Einstein." Darcy gave him a contemptuous look.

"That won't pay in case of arson." Marius wore a vicious smile.

"You moron. That won't work." Darcy stared at him.

"What's the matter? Your little girlfriend stirred old feelings?" Toya put down her drink. "Well tough!"

Darcy rubbed his jaw. "You went along with him on this?"

"I was having with breakfast with friends when the fire started," Toya said with smirk. "She'll be too busy sifting ashes to chase Simon now."

"Then you're as stupid as he is, Toya. Simon was through with you long before Rae came back home," Darcy said in a merciless tone.

"That's not true! He's too trusting to see what kind of a woman she really is." Toya's eyes blazed.

"Oh, he knows exactly what kind of woman she is. If I know Rae, she's got him begging for it," Darcy said.

"Shut up," Toya spat. She turned her back to him.

"As for the property, I've already spoken to Grandfather. He doesn't care about the road being built now. In fact, he told me the deal with Pantheon will finally give the family financial security he wants us to have." Darcy crossed his arms.

"That's not what he told me." Marius blinked at him, with a slight grimace.

"You just got yourself involved in a felony for nothing, Marius." Darcy raised an eyebrow at him. "I hope your hired hands can keep their mouths shut."

Marius tried to strike a casual pose. "Like I said, I didn't have anything to do with it." The anxiety across his sharp features was evident.

"Hmm, you better work on that act a bit more. Your voice cracked just a little toward the end." Darcy smoothed his dark, glossy hair with one hand. "Have a nice party." He sauntered out.

Marius stood in frustrated fury. "One of these days I'll make him sorry."

"Oh, grow up," Toya snapped. "Are you sure those two knew what they were doing? I don't want anything traced back to me." She chewed on her bottom lip.

"Don't listen to Darcy." Marius twisted his hands together. "We're covered."

"I hope so." Toya dabbed at perspiration on her forehead. "I certainly hope so."

I've always hated Monday mornings. Now I know why. Rae watched the insurance agent squirm in his imitation leather chair. She stared at him for several seconds before speaking.

"What do you mean there's a small problem?" Rae asked. "Last week you told me the papers would be processed fast so I could get the dance hall back in shape."

Tony Baranco shuffled papers on his desk. "Ahem, well I talked to Chief Frey and he says his arson people have some questions about how the fire started."

"It was the wiring, wasn't it?"

"Yeah, but it looks like maybe somebody might have tampered with it and put some accelerant around the wall." Tony offered a sickly smile. "But, that's not for sure. The fire burned pretty hot and it's hard to say for certain when the evidence goes up in smoke."

"Well there was that incident about a month ago. Where somebody was creeping around the place late one night." Rae went rigid with anger. "Are you implying I set fire to my own business?"

"Now, take it easy." Tony sought to diffuse a rapidly deteriorating situation. "The company has the prerogative of delaying payment until our investigator can—"

"Why in the world would I set a match to a business that's raking in cash like crazy? What's my motive?" Rae demanded. She stood up and placed a fist on one hip.

"Calm down, ," Tony stammered out. "We need to find out the truth. We're not accusing you of anything."

"Not yet, but I'm sure it's coming." Rae wanted to sweep everything from the top of his desk onto the floor, she wanted to scream. *So that's why folks were looking at me funny for the past day or so, whispering when I walked past.*

"Now, that's not true." Tony blinked at her rapidly. "We're working to find out as much as we can, something I'm sure you want."

"Okay, investigate. But when the truth comes out, I want my money fast. You got that?" She stabbed a finger at him as though aiming at the tip of his nose.

"Sure, Rae. Listen, you know how people talk in this town. They take one little thing and by the time it makes the rounds—"

"Bye, Tony. I expect to hear from you real soon." Rae swept out the room.

Once outside in his parking lot she put on her sunglasses. Her next order of business was to find Harold Frey. Rae rubbed her bare arms. She felt a chill that did not come from the air conditioning.

"Hi, Rae. How's it going?" Harold Frey ambled into his office.

"What is this about arson? Why didn't you see fit to tell me before spreading it all over town? Tony doesn't want to pay off on my policy," Rae blurted out in a rush. She stood with her feet planted apart, both hands on her hips. The tank shirt and denim skirt she wore felt stuck to her skin from a cold sweat of outrage.

"Whew, one at a time." Harold held up one meaty palm. "First, Tim said it could be the wires weren't done properly *or* it could be arson. There is a residue that he thinks could be some type of chemical used commonly as an accelerant."

"Accelerant?"

"A substance used to make a fire spread fast. Anyway, it could just as easily be faulty wiring. You did get that place up kinda fast. And some of that wiring is pretty old." Harold spoke in a calm, measured tone.

"So I'm either an arsonist or I put my staff and customers at risk because of greed. Nice. Real nice." Rae shook her head. "I should have known better than to try and help this rotten town."

"Hold on now. Nobody said this is all your doing. It's under investigation." Harold sat on the edge of his desk.

"People in this town have all the information they need. I'm guilty either way." Rae raked fingers through her tangle of dark hair. "How long before you know for sure?"

"We're waiting on test results from the state police crime lab. Should be another week or so."

"Great. Another few days of going broke." Rae's head began to pound.

All sorts of thoughts crowded in at once. At least she'd paid back Neville part of his loan before this disaster. What would she tell her employees? Garrett quit a great job in Lafayette so he could work close to home. Now what would he and the others do?

Harold took a deep breath. "I'm hurrying as fast as I can, Rae. It's not all in my control. The tests take time. Tim has to carefully examine evidence."

"Right." Rae pressed fingertips to her temples.

"I promise you, if there is anything more that can be done to move this along, I'll do it. We're not out to get you no matter what some wagging tongues may be saying."

"But why didn't you call me?"

"I just tried. You weren't at home. And Tony was out at the dance hall with the insurance adjuster late yesterday. He probably talked to my guys. That's routine."

"Well the word is out, I'm a crook." Rae frowned. This was familiar territory for the Dalcour family.

"You know how hard it is to keep news from spreading in Belle Rose."

"I've been the lead story for local gossips most of my life. You bet I know," Rae said with a grunt of distaste.

"Look, I don't want this town to lose the money Rockin' Good Times was bringing in from sales taxes." Harold put his head to one side. "Hell, we could use some new equipment." He wore a half grin.

"At least you don't think I'm poison. That makes three of us, counting Andrew."

"Garrett, Jackson, and Sarah are on your side, too. And from what I hear, nobody even hints nasty stuff about you without those four jumping down their throats," Harold said.

"They're good people." Rae's eyes stung at the thought of them defending her.

Harold's bushy black brows went up. "Don't forget Simon."

"No, I can't forget him," Rae said in a soft voice.

Simon had been a constant source of encouragement and support for the last five days. It seemed he had a sixth sense, calling at some of her darkest moments. He even offered to help with the rebuilding of Rockin' Good Times. With his crew and an architect friend helping, at least the lounge and dance hall section could open. The restaurant could be completed within three weeks of settling the insurance claim. That is, if the claim was settled.

"I'll call you the minute I know anything definite. And I'll try to keep my staff from talking to anyone but those in authority." Harold stood and folded his big arms.

"In authority?"

"Well, if it's arson, the sheriff and DA get involved." Harold waved a hand in a effort to allay concern etched on her face. "But we have no firm evidence of that yet. Don't worry."

"Sure, don't worry," Rae mumbled as he ushered her out the door. "I could go broke and go to jail, do not pass go. This isn't a Monopoly game, you know."

"You're overreacting. This is all a part of every fire we look into. Routine stuff, okay?" Harold walked her to her car.

Rae did not feel better at all despite his cheery wave goodbye as she drove away. Being the subject of gossip she was used to, but a crime suspect? Routine did not describe this situation at all from where she stood.

"Harold's a fair man, Rae. He wouldn't lie to you. If he says not to worry, then don't. At least not about being locked up for arson," Marcelle said in a light voice as though she was not talking about jail time for her best friend.

"I guess," Rae said. She sat with her eyes closed, enjoying a rare moment of peace.

It was nice to be away from the nerve jangling task of cleaning up the dance hall, securing the inventory, paying her employees, and all the other painful details of a businesswoman in crisis. Even more, Rae was relieved that she could push away the image of her charred dream for at least a few blessed hours. It did her good to remember that people were more important than wood and plaster.

Marcelle had baby Felicia nestled in one arm happily sucking a bottle of formula. They sat on her front porch in the late afternoon shade. A slight breeze from ceiling fans above helped to cool them along with being in the shelter of oak and white ash trees. The faint voices of her three boys, yelping with exuberance as they played in the woods with friends was oddly comforting to Rae. Sweet, joyous innocence.

"Sure. Harold can be trusted. Not like some of these two-faced folks."

"If you say so." Rae tried not to think about the Dalcour name once again being bandied about.

Marcelle cooed at the baby as she flipped her up onto her shoulder. A tiny burp sounded. "You bet I say so. Besides, most folks can't wait for Rockin' Good Times to reopen."

"Harold said as much, too." Rae breathed in the smell of cut grass and honeysuckle.

"That's what I'm talking about. Now let's round up the wild bunch and go see how Mr. Calvin is doing."

After Rae's coaxing and Marcelle's threats finally succeeded in bringing the boys back to the house, they piled into Marcelle's car. They left the children with Marcelle's mother-in-law. The

ride to Grande River Hospital was silent and glum. Mrs.
Johnson was standing just inside the entrance chatting with a
nurse. Her expression hardened at the sight of Rae approaching.

"Hey, Miss Elda. How's Mr. Calvin? Mama's coming by
later." Marcelle gave her a kiss on the cheek.

"Thank you, baby. He's doing a little better than he was. But
he's got a long way to go." Miss Elda did not look at Rae.

"Don't you worry, Miss Elda. I'm going to make sure y'all
have what you need." Rae placed a hand on her shoulder.

"That's the least you can do. You put him here in the first
place," Miss Elda said through clenched teeth.

"What?" Rae froze.

"Now, Miss Elda, that's not so." Marcelle stared at her in
astonishment.

"Calvin told me how you was looking for cheap wiring and
stuff. Poor man was bragging on how smart you was. But you
was cutting corners." Miss Elda's voice went up causing a small
curious crowd to gather.

"Everything we did passed inspection." Rae was numb.

"So? I've heard the talk. Tony Baranco don't wanna pay off
that policy." Miss Elda pointed a finger at Rae. "That building
was meant to burn because you built it cheap or you got somebody to burn it. Either way you're the reason my husband almost
died. He might never work again." Her bottom lip trembled.

"Come on, Miss Elda. You can't go see Mr. Calvin all upset."
A nurse's aide in a bright blue uniform put an arm around her.
"It isn't worth all this," the short brown woman looked at Rae
with dislike in her eyes. She tried to lead Miss Elda away.

"You're gonna pay for this, Rae Dalcour. Trouble, that's what
you've been since you could walk and talk. Trouble," Miss Elda
said. Tears streamed down her face.

The aide finally got her to leave the lobby. Miss Elda, head
down, sobbed and leaned against the woman as they walked
down the hall. Rae was rooted to the spot. A group of six or
seven people lingered, exchanging whispered comments on the
scene they'd witnessed. More than a few of the glances at Rae
were hostile.

"She's under a lot of strain. She didn't mean it, Rae," Marcelle said in a weak voice. Her distress grew when she looked beyond Rae. "Oh, no."

"Now maybe folks will listen when I tell them you're a walking voodoo curse." Toya wore a triumphant, unpleasant smile. Her eyes glittered with ire. "You see what I've been saying, Simon?"

Rae spun around, sickened that Simon had heard those horrible accusations. Of course, Rae knew she was not responsible, that the things Miss Elda said were not true. She felt the old familiar feeling of being an outcast treated with scorn unjustly. Simon stood close to Toya, their arms touching. What was that look in his eyes? Pity? Rae did not need his pity. Fury began to build. She turned to face Toya.

Marcelle glanced at Rae with concern. "Don't go there, girl," she muttered.

"Lies being told about me is nothing new. Someone has been feeding Miss Elda dirty gossip that's got nothing to do with the truth." Rae's voice shook.

"Toya, Mr. Henry's doctor needs those hospital files. Why don't you go get . . ." Simon gave Toya a gentle push in the direction of the administration wing.

Toya did not move. "Miss Elda is finding out what I knew all along. What the rest of this town is going to know, you're no good."

"I've got as much right to live here as you do." Rae stared at her. "You've got some nerve judging me. Backstabbing and lying are your *good* points."

"Sure, go ahead. But your smart mouth won't get you out of this so easily," Toya shot back.

"Let's at least take this outside. We've got a growing audience here," Simon mumbled. He glanced at Marcelle with a look that cried "Help!"

Marcelle gripped Rae's arms and marched her out the automatic doors into the glare of sunshine. "Let's get out of here."

Toya followed them out to the hospital parking lot. She broke away from Simon to face Rae. "Can't you take a hint? Get out of town."

"Like hell. I decide where and when I go," Rae said in a low, dangerous voice. "Now get out of my face."

"Nobody really wants you here. Not even Simon. He's just fooled by your flashy act." Toya gave her a glance from head to toe. "You're something different for him to sample."

"He's been taking more than samples, honey," Rae tossed back.

"Rae, don't provoke Toya like this," Simon spoke up quickly.

"Take Toya inside, Simon. Rae, let's go." Marcelle tried to head off an explosion with little success.

Rae shook loose from Marcelle's hold. "What's really bothering you, huh? That I busted up your pitiful plans to get Simon back? News flash, sugar, he ain't coming back. Not now."

"The novelty will wear off. Simon is used to class." Toya tossed back her head, causing her styled hair to bounce.

"Which is why he's not with you." Rae took a step to stand inches from her face. "Take a good look. Yeah, it's me. I've got your man and it's eating you up. You still haven't learned not to mess with me."

"Sleeping with Simon isn't going to get you on top of the social ladder," Toya snarled.

"Seeing your eyes bulge out is reward enough, honey. I've got your man and there's not a damn thing you can do about it," Rae said in a raspy, taunting voice.

"Witch!" Toya shrieked.

She lashed out with her long fingernails in an attempt to claw Rae's face. Rae grabbed her hand in one motion and slapped her hard with her free hand. Toya kicked Rae's ankles trying to dig the heels of her pumps into flesh. The thick denim jeans Rae wore protected her legs from serious injury. Rae swung at Toya's head but missed when Simon snatched her back. Marcelle tussled to get her arms around Rae. She yanked Rae back while Simon managed to wrap both arms around a screaming Toya.

"Let me go, Marcelle," Rae shouted. She strained to break free. "She's overdue for a butt whipping."

"No!" Marcelle tightened her grip. "Listen to me! Listen." She shook Rae hard. "Don't give her the upper hand by getting down in the dirt with her. Walk away."

"But Marcelle, she—" Rae's breathing was rapid.

"She'll be even more aggravated if you're cool, calm and collected. Just walk away," Marcelle said close to her ear.

Rae gradually slowed her breathing. She nodded to Marcelle that she was under control. With a great show of haughtiness, Rae smoothed down her red silk camp shirt, tucking the loose ends back into the waist of her jeans. Toya still huffed with wrath. Simon shook a finger at her as he lectured. He glanced over his shoulder at Rae and Marcelle.

"Ileen, make sure she stays here." Simon strode over to talk to Rae.

Ileen, one of Toya's pals from another old family, eagerly agreed. She looked thrilled to be an eyewitness to what was sure to keep Belle Rose buzzing for weeks.

"Good thing I was here visiting a friend," Ileen said with relish.

"I'd liked to smash her face in," Toya spat out.

"Remember who you're dealing with, dear." Ileen threw a disdainful look at Rae and Marcelle. "Don't soil your hands."

Simon marched toward Rae and Marcelle with a grim look. "I'll see you later." His jaw muscles worked.

"Yeah, yeah. Don't think I didn't notice you all up in her face," Rae flung at him. Her anger simmered just a few degrees from boiling over again.

"Don't you think one nasty scene a day is enough?" Simon looked off into the distance as he spoke in a low, controlled voice.

Marcelle stepped between them, cutting off another remark from Rae. "Yeah, we all need to take a deep breath and cool off. Come on, Rae." She used her body to push Rae ahead of her to the car. "See you, Simon."

Rae watched a stony-faced Simon go to his car across the parking lot. She fought the urge to kick and scream in frustration. *So that's how it is.* A picture of Simon standing close to Toya was stamped in her head. It was obvious that on some level he still cared about her. To hell with them both!

"Drop me off at the dance hall," Rae said. At least there she could do something to work off this tension.

"How are you going to get home?"

"Andrew is supposed to be there. Garrett, too. If not, I'll walk home."

"Maybe you should anyway. A brisk three-mile walk might work off that temper," Marcelle said with both dark eyebrows raised.

"Don't you start in on me, too."

"Rae, Miss Elda is upset. She'll calm down once she has time to get some rest." Marcelle pulled onto the dance hall parking lot.

Rae sighed. "Not if folks keep feeding her lies. I can't much blame her. How would you feel if somebody told you Freddie got hurt because his boss made him work in an unsafe building?"

"I know, but—"

"Having folks believe the worst about me is nothing new." Rae turned her face away. "But this . . . I wouldn't do anything to hurt Mr. Calvin or anybody else working on the dance hall."

"I know," Marcelle said in a quiet voice.

"And set a match to Lucien's dream? Never. Just the thought makes me sick to my stomach."

"I know that, too. Remember what my aunt used to say?" Marcelle tapped her arm.

"Miss Shirley?" Rae smiled at the memory of Marcelle's independent aunt. They had idolized her as young girls.

"Yep, she wore what she wanted and did things that kept the women in this town flapping their lips. When Grandmama would fuss, Aunt Shirley would put her hands on her hips and say—"

"I don't care what the people say, cause the people don't run my business," Rae finished with a laugh.

"You got that right. We know you didn't put money ahead of safety or set fire to the dance hall." Marcelle leaned toward her. "And Harold doesn't believe it either. He'll find out the truth."

"Like they found out the truth about Pawpaw Vincent? If that fire was set, they'll have to find proof somebody else did it, or this town will forever believe it was me." Rae bit her lip.

"Rumors don't mean a thing."

"Business at the dance hall could suffer for months, even more. I can't hold on that long." Rae closed her eyes. "And if the insurance company won't pay, that's the end of Rockin' Good Times."

"Fight back, and I don't mean with Toya either," Marcelle said with a twinkle in her eyes.

"Lord, I can just imagine what a sight that was. Me acting like a crazy person, screaming and kicking." Rae put her head in her hands.

"One thing about it, Miss Toya is gonna cross the street when she sees you coming." Marcelle giggled. "Sugar, *I* felt that slap you gave the hussy."

Rae grinned at her. "I've wanted to do that since we were in the fifth grade." Then the thought of being under suspicion sobered her. "Much as we hate it, Toya does have power in this town. In the parish even."

"Not enough to have you charged with a crime you didn't commit." Marcelle's eyes glittered with defiance. "And just let them try it. My cousin Phillip in Baton Rouge is one of the best darn lawyers around."

"Great, now we're lining up my defense team." Rae shook her head. "Lucien, you got me into this fix, so you better help get me out." She gazed around as though expecting her handsome, rebel father to appear. A series of loud thunderous knocks, like wood being hit, caused both women to jump and grab hands.

"Wha-what was that?" Marcelle whispered.

Andrew came from around a corner of the dance hall with a couple of the carpenters. The men waved at them. Rae and Marcelle exchanged a glance then burst out laughing.

"Girl, we're losing our minds." Marcelle gasped for air and wiped tears from her eyes.

"You should have seen the look on your face," Rae spluttered before becoming incoherent as giggling took control again.

"Me? Your eyes were big as plates." Marcelle took a deep breath.

Rae patted her face with a tissue from the dispenser in Marcelle's car. "I must be crazy laughing at a time like this."

"Lord have mercy, it's the stress." Marcelle fanned herself.

"If you say so." Rae shook her head with a slight smile.

"And I'll tell you what, we're gonna beat this just like we beat all the tongue wagging before. You wait and see." She reached over to hug Rae's neck.

"Did I ever say how lucky I am to have you for a friend. You've always been right there when I needed you most." Rae held onto to her a while longer before pulling away.

"Shoot, I wasn't gonna miss all the fun." Marcelle chuckled.

Rae got out of the car and waved goodbye to her as she drove off. As usual, Marcelle had helped to lift her up when she was slipping down into dejection.

"Hey, little sister. We got good news." Andrew beamed at her.

"I could use some." Rae greeted the other two men.

"We figure it'll take a week tops to rip out the burned wood and put in some new. In fact, Kirk here thinks we'll come out better."

Kirk nodded. "Yeah, we gotta buy lumber so we can put up that patio overlooking the bayou. Won't cost hardly more than a few deals extra since we're buying a big load."

"That'll be great for private parties," Andrew added. "And now we don't have to wait."

"If the insurance pays, that is." Rae looked glum. "Thanks, guys."

Andrew waited until the two carpenters had gone back to work before speaking. "Let's go on with the work."

"You kidding? Andrew, I don't have the money." Rae threw up both hands.

"I talked to Neville and he agrees. I've got a few hundred I'm willing to invest, Tante Ina and Uncle David have got money, too. We're going ahead."

"I can't ask you to do that." Rae felt a swell of emotion. "You're risking everything you have."

"It's our decision. And the insurance company is gonna pay up." Andrew spoke with confidence.

"That's not what Tony says."

Andrew looked around and lowered his voice even though it was obvious they were alone. "Kirk's brother-in-law's cousin is a mechanic at Pop's Garage. He the only one knows how to work on the fire truck. He told Kirk he overheard some of the firemen talking. They say it's gonna be hard proving it's arson, let alone who did it."

"Really?" Rae's hope flared then went out with a puff. "Hold up, this is third- or fourth-hand information. Until we hear it from Harold or Tony, don't count on anything."

"I'm telling you, the insurance company is gonna cough up in the end. We got it made."

"Maybe." Rae felt a flicker of optimism. Harold was a smart man not likely to jump to conclusions.

"Truth is, I don't think Harold is dumb enough to believe you'd burn this place down. He smells a rat." Andrew nodded as he gazed at the dance hall.

Rae studied her brother for a few seconds. "You're ready to make a stand."

Andrew looked at her with a sober expression. "Even if the insurance doesn't pay, we're going to rebuild. We can't let them wipe their feet on us, Rae."

Looking at him, Rae felt a strange tingle. It was as though Lucien was speaking through his son. She had never thought of Andrew as taking anything too seriously. Nor had she ever thought of Lucien as heroic. But she was wrong. Just as she'd been wrong in thinking Neville had nothing but contempt for their father and would never help her revive his dreams. Rae slapped her hands together.

"Then let's get moving, man. We've got a lot of stuff to do." Rae smiled at him.

When he put his arm around her shoulder, she felt all her misgivings shrink to nothing. They talked about lumber, wiring and other details as they walked to where the carpenters were working. In the back of Rae's mind was the thought of seeing Simon again. He'd been right to be disgusted with her behavior. She would apologize for making a scene. Rae savored the anticipation of feeling warm and loved in his arms. In spite of all that had happened, she still had reason hope she could make a life here.

Sixteen

Rae sat on her front porch that evening. The ugly confrontation with Toya earlier was put in perspective. Marcelle was right. It was natural that Miss Elda was upset at such a difficult time. Rae was amazed then thrilled when she got home to find over a dozen phone calls from folks around expressing support for her to reopen the dance hall. She had reason to see a distant light at the end of this dark tunnel. When Simon drove up, she sprang from her rocking chair feeling renewed.

"Hi, babe." Rae met him halfway as he walked across the front yard. She pecked him on the cheek. He did not smile or lean toward her.

"Hi." Simon followed her onto the porch. After refusing a drink of tea or soda, he sat down.

After several minutes of awkward silence, Rae spoke up. "That breeze feels good. Nice end to a hot day."

"There's more than one reason to be glad this day is over." Simon seemed intent on some far off object.

"Listen, Simon, about what happened . . . I'm sorry for letting Toya push me over the edge. The witch got the better of me, and that hasn't happened often." Rae lifted a shoulder.

"Is that a fact?" Simon continued to look straight ahead.

"Sure." Rae wore a slight smile. "I made getting back at old Toya into a fine art since seventh grade."

"I see."

"Damn straight. Toya went out of her way to treat me like garbage. She and her girlfriends would stand in a group making jokes about me. Even after she went to that fancy private school, when she came home on holidays it was the same thing."

"So you learned to get back at her," Simon said in a quiet voice.

"Did stuff that drove her nuts." Rae gave a short laugh. "This one time I—"

"Is that what I am? Your adult version of payback?" Simon cut her off.

Rae stared at him with a puzzled expression. "What are you talking about?"

"I'm talking about what you said to Toya. It sounded to me like your main motivation for seeing me is to get revenge. Is that why you were so . . . friendly when we first met? Because I was Toya's ex-husband?" Simon looked at her directly for the first time.

"Don't be ridiculous." Rae tried to smile but it faded at the anger that made his dark brown eyes sparkle. "Look, I admit that making Toya crazy with jealousy is fun. But once I got to know what kind of person you are . . ."

"And how long did it take, Rae? The first time we made love? Or the second?" Simon's knuckles stood out as he gripped the arm of the rocking chair. "Just when did I become a person to you?"

"That's not what I meant. Stop twisting this all around," Rae said in exasperation.

"Explain it to me then," Simon said.

"Okay, so I despise Toya. Big surprise considering what her family has done to mine for fifty years! Yes, I enjoyed how seeing us together made her miserable. I plead guilty."

"I thought you were different from what people said about you. She's selfish, loves to break rules just for the hell of it, is what I was told. A user, anything to get what she wants." Simon gazed at her without a hint of warmth.

"One fight with Toya and this is what I get?" Rae shook her head. A ball of hot fury burned in her chest. "No, I don't buy it. What's this really about, Simon?"

"I don't have a hidden agenda. But it seems to me in a moment of anger the truth slipped out." Simon did not raise his voice. "More than you intended."

Rae jumped from her chair. "I've seen you petting up Toya for the last month or so. Mr. Righteous! I see through your game."

"What game?"

"You're using this as an excuse to pick a fight, just like you've been visiting Mr. Henry as an excuse to see Toya."

"Now you're twisting things." Simon stood up. "Everything that's happened, this fighting with Toya, rushing to get the dance hall open, it's all to show up everybody, right? To thumb your nose at the society folks." Though he still did not raise his voice, his words were amplified. They seemed to bounce off the trees, echoing with condemnation.

"Yes! Is that what you wanted to hear? I want to rub their noses in the fact that a Dalcour beat them at their own game!"

"You're no different from Toya, you know that? All bitterness and spite." Simon pronounced a harsh judgment in a dry, hard tone.

"And I suppose you believe all the talk about me setting fire to the dance hall, too?" Rae's tenuous hold on her temper snapped.

"I didn't say that."

"You didn't have to, it's all over your face." Rae jabbed a finger in the air between them.

"I talked to Oliver Ardoin about the electrical work he did. The man cut some corners, and he says you knew it."

"So that offer to help was an excuse to investigate me. I guess Sheriff Thibodeaux will pull up, lights flashing, and take me away in handcuffs right about now!" Rae felt dizzy with fury. "You're good, I have to hand it to you."

"I wanted to help you get open again so you would hold onto your father's dream and keep your promise. I thought that's what was really important to you. Not getting back at the Joves."

"Sure you want to help me. I've been feeling the glow since you got here," Rae shot back.

"I don't believe for a minute that you set that fire," Simon said.

"Just that I got somebody else to do it." Rae managed to keep her voice steady. She was not going to let him see how much pain he was causing her. She would not!

"No," Simon blurted out. "Of course, not. But you might have made a mistake letting Ardoin use wiring made overseas."

"So, I'm not a criminal, just negligent. Well that makes all the difference in the world," Rae spat.

"You didn't realize or take time to check with me." Simon shook his head.

Rae glared at him for several seconds before answering. "I'm not a contractor, but working on stages for the past seven years I do know something about wiring. Oliver Ardoin is a jerk who tried to increase his profit margin by using material made in South America somewhere. But I caught it. That wiring is by the same company that's used in stage sound and lighting systems. It meets most safety standards," she said in a voice as cold as steel.

"It could have been better." Simon stared at her, then turned away. "Listen, I guess we've both said too much today."

"Understatement of the year," Rae muttered to herself. She gazed at him. "I don't much feel like having dinner now. You better leave."

"So that's it? I'm dismissed without any of my questions answered?" Simon turned to face her again.

Rae walked up to him. "You come over here and insult me then demand answers. Who the hell do you think you are anyway?"

"You've had an attitude for the last few weeks," Simon shouted back. "Every time you've seen me with Toya, you started sniping. I tried to put up with it, let it slide."

"Don't do me any favors," Rae shot back.

"I should have seen it before." Simon scoured her with a head to toe look that said he was repelled by what he saw.

"Maybe she's more your kind than I am. You deserve each other." Rae was breathing hard with the effort to keep the tears from falling. "Get off my property. Now!" She kicked open the screen door.

"So, this is the Rae Dalcour everyone tried to warn me

about," Simon said in bitter voice. He went through the open door without looking back.

Rae watched him stride across her front yard to his truck. His long powerful legs moved fast as though he could not wait to put distance between them. She wanted to scream some stinging last remark so he would not have the last word. Yet her throat seemed to have rope wrapped around it, choking off any speech. Part of her was still angry, another part was already in mourning for what she'd lost. The realization hit her like a blow in the midsection. Simon was out of her life.

"I was stupid for jumping into something with the guy anyway," Rae mumbled. "He wasn't my type. Bourgeoisie, lame creep." She tried to make herself believe, but there was no heat behind the words. Her voice broke and the tears finally came.

"I tell you, Harold, this is something else." Sheriff Thibodeaux threw his pen down in disgust. "We hardly have a petty theft in months and then Belle Rose gets a crime wave within two weeks."

"Yep, we seem to have hit an upswing in the last few weeks. Looks like life is gonna be interesting for a while." Harold eased down into the chair opposite the sheriff's desk.

"Humph, I *like* being bored," Sheriff Thibodeaux exclaimed. "Give me nice and quiet over interesting any day."

"I hear you, man." Harold grinned at him. "But interesting is what you'll get with a skeleton to identify and a suspicious fire to sort out."

"Lots of talk going round about this fire." Sheriff Thibodeaux leaned forward. "That why you come to see me?"

"Yep." Harold scratched at the stubble on his face and thought for a few seconds. "Tim says he's got a suspicion that fire was started but . . ."

"But what?"

"He can't prove it. The heat melted the wire coverings, so there's just no way to tell if they were tampered with. The flames were intense, there was just enough oxygen to feed it pretty good in that confined area." Harold tapped out a beat on the arm of the chair with his blunt fingertips.

"Then what makes Tim think it's arson?"

"He says those wires weren't the top of the line, but he can't find any good reason there should have been a short."

Sheriff Thibodeaux shook his head. "That don't mean there wasn't one. Still, Tim ain't no fool. Even if he is my crazy cousin's youngest."

"John, if Tim says it's suspicious then count on it. I sent him to the best training down in Baton Rouge. The boy knows what he's' talking about," Harold said with conviction.

"Then you want me to question Rae Dalcour? Guess she's got big insurance on the place." Sheriff Thibodeaux's blue eyes narrowed.

"I already talked to Tony Baranco. She's got the standard coverage, nothing out of the ordinary." Harold looked at his old pal. "It doesn't feel right, being her, I mean."

"Keeping to the simple explanation always works in crime, Harold. The one with the most to gain is the one most likely done it. I didn't need no fancy training to teach me that." Sheriff Thibodeaux nodded.

"Didn't Kedrick go out to the dance hall one night to investigate a prowler? Some in town would just as soon see the place closed and Rae leave," Harold said.

"Yeah, Deputy Wilson did file a report, but he didn't see nothing. We only got her word somebody was out there."

"But Simon was there, and there was some spray paint on the wall outside, right?"

"Simon didn't see nobody either. And she coulda put that paint on the wall to make her story sound convincing." Sheriff Thibodeaux was warming to his theory. He appeared excited at the prospect of solving one possible crime and restoring the peace in his small town.

"Nah, John. I don't buy it." Harold waved a hand at him.

"Aw, come on. From all I been hearin' lately, folks say she's been a bit wild all her life." Sheriff Thibodeaux stuck his chin out. He glanced at Harold as though his friend was being disloyal by not allowing him to wrap up at least one case in a neat package. "Maybe she decided getting her money without the hassle of running the place was easier."

"I've known Rae Dalcour all her life. She's got a temper, and a smart mouth for sure. But this just doesn't fit her."

"People change, man. She been out in the big city. Hanging with them musicians. Could be she's graduated from minor stuff to the big leagues." Sheriff Thibodeaux looked at Harold with the glint of a hunter scenting his prey.

"Rae is on a mission to keep a promise to her late daddy. I don't think she'd burn the place."

Sheriff Thibodeaux threw up both hands. "Things can't be simple these days," he said with a sigh. Much as he wanted a solution, he could not deny that he trusted his old pal's judgment.

Harold looked at him with sympathy on his dark brown face. "If it'll help any, Tim is hoping some real hightech tests at the state police crime lab will give us more."

"Yeah, yeah," the sheriff said without enthusiasm.

"Really, man. Those tests are so advanced these days. Same as with other forensic techniques." Harold tried to sound encouraging.

"Sure . . ." Sheriff Thibodeaux's mood lightened a bit after a few moments of thought. "Maybe we might just be able to find out how they did it. And that could point a finger at who did it."

"The state police crime lab is state of the art."

The ringing phone cut off a comment from the sheriff. He lifted the receiver then gave a grunt of satisfaction. "Speaking of which, this is them. Yeah," he said into the phone. "Un-huh. Un-huh." He was writing on a notepad furiously. "Say what? Pooh-ya-ee!"

"What?" Harold asked leaning forward eagerly. He wondered about the look of disbelief in the sheriff's face.

"Yeah, thanks." Sheriff Thibodeaux put the receiver down with a bang. "Thanks for nothing," he said with energy. He combed thick fingers through the sandy, thinning hair on his head.

"Is this about the bones they found?"

"This ain't been my week, Harold. Hell, this ain't my month."

"How bad can it be? Somebody we know?"

"Not unless it was in a previous life." Sheriff Thibodeaux looked at the ceiling.

"Huh?" Harold blinked at him. "What are you talking about, man?"

"Those bones been in the ground longer than you and me been alive." Sheriff Thibodeaux gazed at Harold with a look of resignation that things were going downhill fast. "Buried at least fifty years ago."

"So then what did you say?" Baylor took a sip of his coffee. He squinted at his friend even though the sun was not in his eyes.

Simon and Baylor sat having breakfast at an outdoor cafe in downtown Belle Rose. The two men watched a couple of tour vans loaded with tourists deposit passengers across the street.

"I said 'See ya' and left. That's what I said." Simon put his cup down with a thump.

"Uh-huh. Women are something else. They just love throwing stuff like that in each other's face. You know, 'I got your man, honey!' " Baylor said in a highpitched voice. He did a double snap of his fingers.

"Man, that's exactly what Rae said." Simon gave a grunt of contempt. "Like I'm some bone they've been fighting over."

"Who needs it? That's what I say. Which is the main reason I enjoy my freedom." Baylor pointed a forefinger in the air to emphasize his point. "After I pried Claudette's claws out of my butt, I said no more."

"This is my fault. Papa Joe tried to tell me. Grandmama Olivia tried to tell me. But would I listen? No!" Simon sat back against the chair and folded his arms.

"Hey, I don't need any more brick walls to fall on me. I've learned my lesson. Call me commitment phobic if you want. I don't care." Baylor was intent on his own romantic troubles.

"What's up with her anyway? I'm being for real and she's playing some game. I don't have time for that." Simon looked determined. "Forget her."

"Yeah. And I'm lucky I got Claudette outta my system,

brother." Baylor lifted his cup in a salute. "Who needs her throwing her stuff all over my house."

"Man, something should have told me I was jumping in too fast with Rae. I usually take my time, you know?"

"The way she woke me up early on Sundays banging pots in the kitchen and singing off key," Baylor said with a frown.

"Okay, I admit it. She had me fooled with those sultry eyes. Smiling at me like she's got some sweet secret." Simon looked like he tasted lemons. "She saw me coming."

"Hanging wet panty hose over the towel bar in the master bathroom. That used to drive me crazy." Baylor had a far away look in his eyes.

"I didn't know what hit me once she set her scheming sights on me. I was like a duck caught in hunting season." Simon seethed with resentment at being used.

"Claudette made the best blueberry muffins from scratch. Damn!" Baylor licked his lips. "And the way she . . . kissed . . ."

"Say, this is the woman who stomped on your answering machine after she listened to a message from an old girlfriend without letting you explain." Simon punched his shoulder. "Don't start caving in on me, man."

"What? Oh, yeah, yeah. One little lunch with Taneka and I'm the villain. So what if she's fine?" Baylor resumed his self-righteous tone.

"Women have no sense of proportion." Simon brought him back to their shared masculine outrage.

"Okay, and we did have drinks. But you don't destroy a brother's property behind that." Baylor held up both hands as if he was the epitome of reason.

Simon grimaced after a few moments of silence. "Not that Rae wasn't provoked. If anyone knows about Toya's spiteful ways, it's me."

"After ten long years, Claudette should have trusted me. Like I can't go out with an old friend from school. Humph, women!" Baylor shook his head.

"She's under a lot of stress these days, too."

Simon wished he could at least see Rae from a distance. He'd not seen or spoken to her for four days now. Maybe she would be in town on some errand. He craned his neck at the approach of footsteps only to be disappointed when an older woman appeared.

"Yeah, Toya has been through a lot with Mr. Henry being so sick."

"I was talking about Rae," Simon murmured. He stared at the beignets on his saucer. They were cold, along with his café au lait.

"Now, don't you start." Baylor signaled to the waitress and ordered them fresh coffee. "Rae played you, brother. A female hit-and-run artist. Used you for a revenge thang, man."

Simon felt a hot chill up his spine at the memory of her fingers on his skin. Having her wrapped around his body was such a sweet sensation. "But it felt good being used."

"Don't go there, man. Put it out of your mind. Okay, so she gave good love until your brain turned soft as Grandmama's grits. Don't think about it."

"Oh, sure, just like you've forgotten Claudette." Simon raised an eyebrow at him.

"Exactly," Baylor said firmly.

Simon let out a sharp laugh. "Let's face it, we both bumped into women who took us high and then dropped us hard. It's going to take time to move on."

"I guess." Baylor looked thoughtful.

Now he would never unravel the sweet mystery hidden behind her voluptuous smile and those big brown eyes sparkling with mischief. Though they had been lovers less than three months, Simon knew the memory of being wrapped in her soft arms would linger for a long time. Still, she was able to dismiss him without much effort. Rae Dalcour would not let anyone close to her. She took life and love only on her own terms. No room for compromise, no letting down her guard. He should have paid attention to what folks said about her. Simon summoned up the image of a vengeful Rae, face twisted with malice. An image he badly needed to counteract the hot desire to touch her that gnawed at him constantly. Her words, sharp and mean, played in his mind with the clarity of a compact disc. They had moved too fast, ignoring their differences in the heat of passion.

Simon breathed in deeply. "It's just as well, Baylor. Rae and I were bound to crash and burn. I'm a classic jazz and white wine guy. She's a blues and beer sassy lady. I would have bored her after awhile."

"True that," Baylor agreed. "You are kinda into the quiet life."

"You saying I'm a geek?" Simon scowled at him.

"No, no. What I'm saying is you like routine." Baylor's eyes went wide when he realized what he'd said.

"So I'm in a rut."

"No, I mean . . . Routine is good," Baylor blurted out. "Same old, same old is your thing."

"Say what!" Simon squinted at him.

"But that's good," Baylor put in quickly. "You're steady, I mean stable. Lighten up, brother."

"Sorry, didn't mean to get all defensive. After so many years of dealing with Toya, I thought I was through with this kind of rollercoaster ride." Simon pressed his fingertips to his eyelids.

"Look, man, Rae is way too volatile for your temperament. This breakup is for the best."

"Right." Simon put his sunglasses back on. Then why did he feel so wrong?

"Rae Dalcour, you're crazy! Letting that fine man walk away." Tante Ina pursed her lips.

"You were the one dogging out his family for being snooty." Rae sat at her aunt's kitchen table. Her mood was not helped by this unexpected reception.

"That was before I met him. Looka here, I've known you since you was in diapers. Don't tell me your eyes didn't light up soon as you heard he was Toya's ex-husband." Tante Ina held her coffee cup poised waiting for answer.

"I didn't—"

"Don't play me for stupid, gal." Tante Ina put her cup down. "I've seen you many a time get boys all whipped up just for the fun of it."

"I was a kid, for goodness sakes. I'd never do . . ." Rae's

voice died at the skeptical and wise look Tante Ina wore. "Okay, so I maybe it did interest me when I found out they'd been married. But that wasn't the only reason I went out with Simon," she added defensively.

"No, course not. He's one good-looking young fella. Still, that probably was lagniappe to you. Here you got yourself a way to get back at the Joves and the St. Cyrs. Bet you anything his granddaddy had a fit about him keeping company with a Dalcour."

"Maybe." Rae shifted in her seat and did not look at Tante Ina.

"That means he did," Tante Ina quipped. "And here you're having yourself a big time. Showing up folks with your new dance hall and running round town with a St. Cyr. Toya musta been gritting her teeth so hard they're down to nubs."

"Okay, so I had fun. I was overdue, Tante." Rae stared into the dark coffee she swirled in her mug. "Long overdue."

"Cher, I know."

"They'd say, 'What can you expect, that's one of Lucien's kids.' But I never let any of them tell me who I was or was not going to be," Rae said in a fierce voice.

All the bitter memories of her childhood came back in a flood. The snickers when she walked past after one of Lucien's famous drunken tirades about his father. The way girls like Toya whispered lies that made boys think she was promiscuous. Anger welled up inside at how much she'd had to endure. By the time she was fourteen, Rae had decided to strike back. At sixteen, all those girls secretly envied her. Boys fell over each other just to have her smile at them. They even began to defend her when the girls made nasty remarks. Rae would lure a boy to her, enjoying the game of making him lovesick. Then she would toss him aside without a backward glance. Yes, revenge became her weapon of choice. Now that weapon seemed to have blown up in her face.

"You got caught in your own trap. Ain't that right, cher?" Tante Ina spoke to her in a soothing voice full of sympathy.

Rae opened her mouth to deny it, but her voice would not work. A fist of anguish closed around her throat. Yes, it was true. Her first thought had been to make Toya burn with jealousy. Her little plan had not taken account of falling in love with Simon so hard or so fast.

"Okay, so I did get sort of attached to him. But that doesn't mean I can't live without him," Rae said, her voice rising. "He just wants the best of both worlds. Staying all up under Toya and her grandfather to keep his business afloat. It's sickening."

"You think so?" Tante Ina looked dubious at this explanation. "I hear he paid Mr. Henry's loan back several years ago. Got his own reputation now. Why, folks from all over Louisiana call him to—"

"Oh, who cares?" Rae burst out. "Can't we talk about something else?" She jumped up. "I'm going for a walk."

"All right, cher. It's a fine evening for a walk. Nice breeze, *mais* yeah." Tante Ina clucked like a mother hen.

"And stop looking at me like that," Rae said with a puff of frustration.

"Like what, sugar sweet?" Tante Ina put a comforting plump arm around her shoulder.

Rae's lip trembled at the old endearment, one Tante Ina used when she tried to ease the most painful hurts brought to her by one of her brood.

"Tante Ina, I wish I'd never come here. Wish I'd never heard of Simon St. Cyr." Rae put her head on Tante Ina's shoulder.

"I know, I know," Tante Ina said in a soft voice just above a whisper. "Come on and sit down. You're gonna stay here with me for a while." She held Rae in a maternal embrace and let her pour out the grief.

"You fools!" Marius paced back and forth across the concrete floor of the old garage. "I told you to make sure it looked like Rae Dalcour did it. Now they're saying it could have been accidental."

"Look, you wanted the place to burn. We done that." Scruffy beard scratched his face. "Ain't I right, Sly-Man?" He glanced at his partner.

"Yeah, Tyrone is right. We earned our money." Sly-Man grinned at Marius. "Time to pay up."

"The job isn't finished until they accuse Rae of arson," Marius snapped. "Now what are you going to do about it?"

Sly-Man's grin never faltered as he advanced on Marius. "Looka here, one way or the other we getting our money today."

"I don't think so," Marius said in a tight voice.

"Oh, yeah? What's it gonna be, slick?" Sly-Man held up both hands and took another menacing step.

Marius pulled a small automatic pistol from inside his suit jacket. "I'll tell you what it's gonna be." He mocked Sly-Man's uneducated speech. "You two have half of what I agreed to pay, which is a hell of a lot more than you're worth, by the way. You were paid to make the evidence lead to Rae Dalcour. Finish the job or they'll be digging up your bones on my family's property years from now."

"Aw, man, you mean that dude they just found . . ." Tyrone's eyes grew even bigger as he stared at the gun. "Daa-amn!"

"Say, looka here, ain't no need to be getting all hostile and stuff." Sly-Man stood frozen in place, careful not to move in any way that might make Marius feel threatened.

"Un-uh. Don't mess with me, all right?" Marius looked like he knew exactly how to use the gun and would not hesitate to do so. "We've worked well together before, but I expect results."

"Yeah sure, man. We know." Tyrone seemed eager to please.

"We can't go back over there now!" Sly-Man protested. "Between the sheriff's deputies and the firemen there's always somebody hanging round there."

"He's got a point, man," Tyrone agreed.

Marius gave a short grunt. "You're the so-called professional crooks. You figure it out."

Sly-Man shrugged. "What do you care anyway? She's having money trouble because of it. Insurance man giving her the runaround. I can tell ya, they'll tie up paying out so long she'll be broke."

"That's true, too." Tyrone's head bobbed up and down.

"They'll have to pay if there's no real proof she did it." Marius was unconvinced.

"And by then it'll be too late. I'm telling you, they ain't paying nothing as long as their investigators ain't satisfied. They gonna hold out long as they can." Sly-Man did not look nervous now. He watched Marius digest his words.

"Maybe. But I need some insurance myself." Marius frowned. He stared past the two men. "If I can get that property, the old man will give me control."

Sly-Man stole a quick sideways glance at Tyrone. "Hey, Rone, didn't we hear something about her leaving town?"

"Huh?" Tyrone looked dumbfounded. He blinked at his partner. When Sly-Man nodded at him, he perked up. "Oh, yeah, right. Sure did."

"Man, you could be getting that property sooner than you think," Sly-Man said in an ingratiating voice. "You sure did plan this one right."

"On target, that's what I'm talking about." Tyrone was now into the game. He watched his partner for a cue.

"She ain't for hanging round here no more is the talk. Ain't that what you told me, Rone?" Sly-Man moved closer to Marius.

Marius stared out a grimy window behind the two men deep in thought. "Grandfather won't forgive or forget the way Darcy ignored his wishes. With that property, I'll make a bundle with my own deal with Pantheon. Or maybe the Shale Technology people."

"Sounds like you're already moving ahead. You're smart." Sly-Man said.

Tyrone looked at Sly-Man then fell to the floor. Marius turned fast to point the gun at him. Sly-Man dealt a sharp kick to Marius's arm. The gun flew from his hand and clattered across the concrete. Tyrone bounced up and punched Marius in the stomach three times in quick succession. Marius bent double, groaning in pain.

Sly-Man leaned against an old rusty shell of a old yellow Ford Fairlane. "Now, I think we can talk better. Don't you?" He waved the gun in his hand.

Marius spluttered for few moments. "I ought to—"

"Looka here, I'm gonna be reasonable about all this. Maybe

we can do something to tighten up this job." Sly-Man lifted a shoulder.

"Say what? Sly-Man . . ." Tyrone shook his head with vigor.

"Hold up, now. I got me an idea how to do it so we don't have to stick our necks out." Sly-Man motioned for him to keep quiet. "Course we need some more what they call incentive." He wore a predatory smile as he looked at Marius.

Marius was still on his knees but he did not look the least bit intimidated. "No more money. Remember, I know where you boys live. You're going to jail next week if you don't pay up six thousand dollars of back child support." He pointed at Tyrone.

"How you know about that? Getting all up in my business!" Tyrone looked outraged.

"And Sly-Man, Pookie DeLarousse won't be happy when he finds out you've been making a profit at his expense. He's not the forgiving type. Anything happens to me, he gets a phone call." Though he was still in obvious pain, Marius smiled at the look of fear in Sly-man's eyes.

"What you gonna do, man?" Sly-Man licked his thick dry lips.

Marius stood up slowly with a wince. "I'm going to forget this little incident in the spirit of goodwill," He reached out his hand and waited.

Sly-Man gave him the gun. "Especially since we can bust your butt about several jobs in the last four years. Including the one over in Morgan City."

"Only if you fellas live to tell the tale. Remember Pookie." Marius tapped his temple with a forefinger. He chuckled. "Now that we've established that it's my world, tell me this idea you have."

Seventeen

"Rae, I gotta tell you . . ." LaMar sank down onto one of the chairs on her front porch. "I just don't think we're going to find out exactly what happened to your grandfather. It's been too many years."

"Nothing, huh?" Rae put down the tray with glass mugs of root beer on it. "That's my luck these days. Seems everything I do comes to nothing." The stab of pain she felt had more to do with Simon than her grandfather or the dance hall. She pushed thoughts of him away.

"If they went to Trinidad, then I can't find them. They could have gone anywhere in the Caribbean, eastern or western. Not to mention all of South America." LaMar took a deep gulp of the cold soft drink.

"Well thanks for giving it your best effort." Rae sat down in the chair next to him.

"I've got one more lead that could—"

"Forget it, LaMar. It doesn't matter," Rae broke in. "I've got enough dealing with the present, much less digging into the past." She stared off at the bright green foliage that lined the rural highway.

"Yeah, running a business can get hectic." LaMar took another sip of soda.

"Especially when it's been torched and the sheriff thinks you did it," Rae said with more than a trace of bitterness.

LaMar's dark eyebrows went up. "What? Tell me the details."

Rae was reluctant, but at his urging she described the events that had taken place since their last meeting. LaMar interrupted her several times to ask questions. He wanted to know details of how she opened the dance hall, offers to buy the family land, and her relationship with the locals.

"So that's about it." Rae rubbed her eyes. "It's just as well you're ending the search. I'm just about broke."

"Not to worry. You paid me for at least two more weeks." LaMar was silent for several seconds. "I've got an idea. Let me look into the fire."

"What?" Rae looked up at him.

"I could keep investigating what happened to Vincent, but finding out anything more is a long shot. You've got a more immediate problem, I'm paid for, so why not?" LaMar rubbed his hands together. He was already processing what he'd been told about the fire.

"But, well . . ." Rae wondered truthfully if she should just get the money refunded. She might need it soon, in the worst way. "The arson investigators are looking into it now."

"If they find evidence that seems to point to you, they're not likely to look much further." LaMar wore a slight frown. "And it sounds like there are several people who might definitely profit from the failure of your business."

Rae shrugged. "I didn't feel a lot of pressure to sell."

"Maybe they had a plan B." LaMar sat with his elbows on both knees looking straight ahead. "It's possible."

"Yeah, possible."

LaMar cleared his throat. "More than one person is interested in buying your land, right? Simon St. Cyr approached you first."

LaMar was suggesting that Simon's main interest was getting his hands on Dalcour property. Could he have been using her all along? Rae did not want to believe that she'd been so gullible. Had her vanity blinded her? Had they played on her desire to get back at Toya? It seemed entirely possible that Simon, Toya, and Darcy had coldly calculated how to use her need for revenge. What an idiot she had been! All her life she'd know that upper-class Creoles were notorious for sticking together.

"Until this moment I hadn't seen the obvious." Rae felt numb now. This new pain was too much for her senses. There were no more tears. "Simon showed up the night someone spray painted the dance hall. I should have been suspicious when he didn't bat an eye after I wouldn't sell him our land."

LaMar watched her face for several moments. "Is there something more you need to tell me? This seems to have hit you pretty hard."

Rae steadied herself. "Simon St. Cyr and I . . . We were . . . seeing each other," she said in a strained voice.

"Damn! Look, I'm sorry. I could be off base." LaMar's expression said otherwise.

"Or you could be on target. I let my ego and a little down-home charm from a good-looking man fool me." Rae thought of how Simon had rushed back to the Joves after Mr. Henry's stroke. "The ties that bind." Rae barked out a laugh that was contemptuous more of herself than of Simon.

"Tell me what you want me to do." LaMar waited with no sign of impatience or intent to sway her decision.

"I'm not going out like that," Rae said. She looked at LaMar with a hard expression. "Nobody is going to force me out of Belle Rose. We'll look into the fire."

"Good deal." LaMar started making notes at a furious pace.

"If it was arson, I'm going to grind the bastard responsible into the dirt. Whoever he is." Rae blocked out all feelings except the need for retaliation.

For another hour, LaMar questioned her in depth about everything that had happened to her since her arrival in Belle Rose for her father's funeral. The more she talked the more certain she became.

"I think I know how to flush the rats out of their nest," Rae said. "I'll go to the source."

"Maybe you should let me handle this. It could get tricky," LaMar said. "These guys could be capable of anything."

"Just hear me out, okay?"

Simon and Toya sat on the sofa in his office having coffee. Nola stared at Toya with open dislike stamped on her face. She handed Simon a phone message.

"You might want to call Mr. Hyde back soon," Nola said with emphasis. "Could be urgent."

"Thanks, Nola." Simon put the message down. "But I doubt it. We finished that job last month." He gave her a pointed look.

"Oh. Just trying to help," Nola said with a sigh.

"I appreciate it." Simon smiled at her with affection.

He knew she was trying to help him get rid of Toya. Deception was not his way. His lips turned down at the thought of how Rae had used him. When the door closed behind his secretary, Toya took up where she'd left off.

"Didn't I tell you she was no-good?" Toya wore a triumphant smile. "Didn't I say Rae Dalcour only thinks about herself?"

"Let's not get into this again," Simon said through clenched teeth. He tapped on the table with his fingers.

Why had he even mentioned he and Rae were no longer seeing each other? Of course, she was bound to find out. It was just a matter of how soon. Now he realized a delay would have been preferable.

"What happened? Another man I'll bet." Toya crossed her legs. "She was always loose."

"It doesn't matter why." Simon resisted the temptation to correct her assumption.

"Men are so sensitive about these things. Her behavior with other men doesn't reflect on your masculinity, dear." Toya leaned forward to put her hand on his arm.

"Toya—"

"But I've known her a lot longer than you. She's no better than an alley cat. She mates then moves on."

"Don't talk like that." Simon had a sour taste in his mouth.

"Sorry, darling. But you need to face the truth. Oh sure, she's charming in her way. But she's a wh—"

"Stop it right now!" Simon jerked his arm free of her hand. "Rae and I had an argument, but it had nothing to do with another man. She's not at all like that. She's . . ." A sweet, hot memory seized him unexpectedly.

Toya pressed her lips together and studied him. Resentment radiated from her. "Rae Dalcour still has some sort of hold on you."

Simon could not work up the will to deny it. He wanted to, but why lie? It seemed like forever since he'd seen Rae, though only a week had passed. The days were bad enough, but it was the sleepless nights that really took their toll. For hours he tossed and turned. Every caustic word spoken between them replayed in his mind like a recording. Yet his body still felt the traces left from being in her arms. He wanted to escape. Talking about it would only prolong the agony.

"I've got a long day ahead of me." Simon failed to add the words "Thank goodness." It meant he could put off going back to the empty house and loneliness. "Did you want to talk about something else?"

"Things will be right in no time." Toya moved closer to him. "Just wait and see. Anyway, Darcy says maybe he'll talk to Rae about selling her property now. With the fire and all, she might need money. For a good lawyer," she added in a gleeful voice.

"Rae would never set fire to Rockin' Good Times. It meant too much to her and her father." Simon was not defending Rae based on emotion. "She loved that man."

"Whatever. Who cares? The point is we can get that land for a song, now. It's perfect." Toya inched closer until their hips touched. "You can go forward with that park you wanted."

"You don't know if Rae will have to sell." Simon did not share her excitement.

"Whether they prove she did it or not, she's losing money big time with every day that goes by. She won't be able to recover." Toya looked pleased at the prospect.

"I hope she can. But if she wants to sell, I'll pay her a fair price."

"That's noble, darling, but don't pay more than you have to. Remember this is business. A fleeting liaison shouldn't make you forget that."

"I'll discuss it with Darcy when and if he brings it up. Not before," Simon said.

"But why wait? She's getting desperate for money, I just know it. All we'd have to do is make the least bit of an offer and she'd have no choice."

Simon felt a rise of revulsion. "Look at us, sitting here like vultures waiting for some poor animal to die so we can pick over the bones." He stood up. "I don't want to discuss Rae anymore."

Toya stood up, too. "Fine. Don't be upset with me. Rae is saying the Joves and St. Cyrs are the real crooks."

"What are you talking about?" Simon glanced at her sharply.

"She's got that private detective looking into the fire. He's been poking around. It's clear what she's up to." Toya lifted a shoulder. "Of course, it won't fly. Marius is certain about that."

Simon did not understand her last statement. "What's Marius got to do with it?"

"Hmm?"

"You said something about Marius being sure. Sure about what?"

Toya went still for a beat then recovered. "Oh, just that Marius doesn't think she'll be able to wriggle out of what she's done." She gave a brittle laugh. "Everyone knows what kind of woman she is."

"Do they?" Simon was deep in thought as he watched her fidget with her expensive handbag.

"Including Sheriff Thibodeaux. Well, what can you expect from a Dalcour, after all." Toya patted the smooth hair wound tightly into a swirl on her head.

"I see."

"Ahem, look at the time. I'm keeping you from important things. I'll see you later at Grandfather's for dinner." Toya gave him a lingering kiss. "Maybe we can manage to get away early."

"Maybe," Simon said in a distracted manner.

"Oh, Simon." Toya wore a delighted smile. "Thank you, darling. Maybe I'll do a little special shopping at Deidre's in the lingerie section." She tilted her breast forward to show more cleavage.

"Sounds nice. Bye." Simon did not hear what she said.

"Goodbye, cher." Toya swung her hips as she walked out of the office. She glanced back at him with a seductive smile to make sure he was watching.

Simon did notice. Only because he wanted her to leave so

he could make a phone call. Toya walked ahead of him and out the front door past Nola.

"Spider Woman's finally gone, thank goodness," Nola quipped.

"Yeah. Do you have Harold's number?" Simon stared at the closed door through which Toya had gone.

"The fire chief? Think so." Nola began flipping through the cards. "But we scheduled for him to inspect the building on Joliette Road already. I'll call him for you to double check."

"No, just give me the number." Simon watched her write the phone number down on a slip of note paper. "I'll make this call myself."

Sheriff Thibodeaux was not a happy man. "Tell me this again, Bob." He sat staring at his friend as though it was his fault.

"Look, John, you got the report. The bones are from a black male, between the ages of eighteen and twenty-nine with a broken collarbone that healed well." State Trooper Bob Bonnecaze sat in his dark blue uniform looking as though every hair was in place.

"And been there fifty years. How did she know that?" Sheriff Thibodeaux referred to Sarah Manley, the forensic anthropologist used by the state police.

"There was an old rusted watch, some buttons, and a belt buckle. Dr. Manley consulted with the Human Ecology Department at LSU in Baton Rouge. Some lady there is an expert in textiles, buttons, and such. They got lots of books on clothes made since way back before the Civil War."

"So from that stuff, she figures he was buried about fifty years back." Sheriff Thibodeaux pulled a large hand over his face. "Lord, but if this ain't a mess."

"Aw, come on, John. You haven't had a murder around here in fifty years. That's good news." Trooper Bonnecaze grinned at the sour look his pal shot him.

"I got a fire at the local dance hall that might be arson, but we can't pin it down. There's grumbling that we oughta arrest the owner, a woman. And now this." Sheriff Thibodeaux shook his head.

"Who's been missing for fifty years?"

"How should I know? I wasn't even born!" Sheriff Thibodeaux said with a grunt of exasperation. "I'll have to do some digging to find that out."

"Just ask some of the old folks around. They ought to know." Trooper Bonnecaze stood up and dusted off his already spotless hat. "Let me know if I can help any. Just passing through on my way to a meeting in Lafayette on crime scenes."

"Yeah, thanks. Sure hope we're on the tail end of this crime wave." Sheriff Thibodeaux walked with him out to the lobby.

"At least you get to test out those investigative techniques you learned up in Virginia at the FBI workshop. See ya." Trooper Bonnecaze gave him a hearty clap on the shoulder.

With a grim expression, Sheriff Thibodeaux watched the dark blue sedan with the state police emblem drive off. "Yeah, right. I'm just tickled to death about it." He winced at his unintended pun.

Rae strode into the elegant office suite of Jove Enterprises and stood in front of the receptionist. "I'm here to see Darcy Jove."

"Your name?" The young woman picked up the telephone receiver.

"Rae Dalcour. And no, I don't have an appointment."

The receptionist spoke low into the phone while Rae glanced around at the prints and plush furnishings. She was sure the murmured conversation included the best way to get rid of her. When the receptionist put down the phone, Rae turned back to her.

"Mr. Jove's secretary says if you'd just leave your name, she'll let him know you came by." The young woman smiled at her warmly. "I'll be sure he gets the message."

"Lisa," Rae said, reading the name plate on her desk. "Darcy and I go back a long way. Just point me to his office and I'll wait. This way, right?" She went toward a set of oak double doors at the end of a wide hall.

"Well, he has a tight schedule and I— Wait, miss, you can't go in there!" Lisa bounced up to follow Rae, then went back to call someone.

Darcy's secretary darted down a side hall to intercept her. "Miss Dalcour, Mr. Jove is not available."

"He's here, I can smell him," Rae said in a loud voice. "Come out here, Darcy!" she called.

"What the hell is going on?" Marius came out of his office. His eyes widened with surprise when he saw Rae. He soon recovered and plastered a smile on his face. "Well, fancy meeting you here."

"Marius, right?" Rae gave him a head to toe glance. "Yeah, I remember you. Out of prison so soon?"

Marius lost the smug smile. "What the hell does that mean?" He shot a look around to see who was listening.

"All those times Mr. Henry had to bail your backside out of trouble. Didn't you have to do time over that deal in Morgan City a few years back?"

"I've never seen the inside of a prison. Look, you seem to have made a wrong turn. This isn't a barroom."

"No, it's a snake pit. Now where's the head snake? Darcy, come on out of hiding!"

The doors to the conference room to her left opened and two men walked ahead of Darcy. "Pantheon should be pleased with the progress so far." He paused when he saw Rae glaring at him.

"No they won't. Not when they find out what crooks you all are," Rae said.

"Should I call the police?" Darcy's secretary asked Marius.

"Good idea. Call them now," Marius snarled.

"Show these gentleman out, please." Darcy did not show a sign of being upset. He murmured a few words to the men, who were staring with frank interest at the scene. The secretary bustled forth and made bright chatter, hoping to drown out any background noise from Rae.

Darcy straightened his tie and walked toward Rae. "Should I be glad you came to visit me?" He wore a charming smile

"Which one of you did it!" Rae snapped.

"Come in my office." Darcy opened the double doors and motioned her in. "Now let's talk in a reasonable manner."

"Sure, I can be reasonable. You tell Harold Frey and Sheriff Thibodeaux how you torched my business. I'll ask them to go easy on you during the sentencing phase of your trial. How's that?" Rae looked from him to Marius.

"Get real. Let's throw her out on the sidewalk." Marius stood with his arms down, both hands balled into fists.

"You want me out of town, but first you want me to sell my land. When sending Simon to romance me didn't work, you switched to the backup plan. I know you, too well, Darcy. Or was it Toya's brilliant idea? Yeah, she had a hand in it." Rae did not appear the least bit fearful.

"Not only will we have you thrown in jail for disturbing the peace, but I'll sue you for slander," Marius shouted.

"Judging from your reaction, I'd say you made all the arrangements. Sure, you're the one with criminal experience." Rae let out a short laugh when Marius flinched at her words.

"You b—"

"Get out," Darcy said. He moved between Rae and Marius.

"You heard him," Marius spat.

"I meant you. Go on. I'll handle it." Darcy looked at him.

"Are you going to let her accuse us of arson? Grandfather would have her arrested on the spot." Marius was puffed up with fury.

"Grandfather isn't here, is he? Now leave."

"Oh, no, I want you both to hear this. I'm not through with either of you. They can't prove who started the fire. I just talked to Harold. So I'm going to burn you the way you tried to burn me." Rae stood, feet apart, hands on her hips.

"The investigation isn't over." Marius blinked when Darcy gave him a furious look. "That's what I hear."

"Don't be so sure. Things aren't going quite the way you wanted." Rae looked at Marius. "You botched the job. I'm going to be back in business soon. Count on it."

"Big talk is fine, but with no insurance . . ." Marius wore a mean smile as he shrugged.

"Marius, I said get out," Darcy barked. He yanked open the door and shoved him.

"You're all talk, babe. All talk," Marius said before the door closed on him.

"You've really sunk low." Rae turned all her ire on Darcy now. "But I'm not going down, got it?"

"Rae, this is crazy. We had nothing to do with the fire." Darcy did not flinch or give one sign of guilt.

"You always were good at not showing your hand." Rae walked around the office. "Done well for yourself, too. Made Jove Enterprises even more profitable. All without getting indicted once."

Darcy shook his head as though with regret. "I know we have a bad history, but resorting to crime isn't my way. Jove Enterprises has grown through hard work and honest dealings."

"Tell me another story, Daddy," Rae said in a mock little girl voice. "Look, you and that slimy cousin of yours are on official notice. I'm going to get to the bottom of this, and when I do, watch out."

"If it was arson, I hope the authorities find the culprits. But it wasn't me." Darcy took a step toward her with his hands out. "I've done a lot of things in my life, but trying to destroy you is something I'd never do."

"Save it, Darcy. You'll need all your finesse when this gets traced back to your doorstep." Rae pulled the door open to find Marius still standing outside. "You both remember that!" She pointed to Darcy, then Marius, before stalking off.

Once outside, her look of irrational rage was replaced by one of calm calculation. Rae drove to a nearby public phone and punched in a number. The mobile operator made the connection after several seconds.

"Hi. I just stirred the pot. You can expect it to boil over real soon," she said to LaMar.

* * *

"Things are going very well. The road is being built just as we planned." Darcy sat across from his grandfather.

Despite his ill health, Henry Jove had proved tougher than even his family expected. Though still unable to drive, he had Marius take him to Darcy's office at least once a week. Physical therapy and medication helped him regain strength.

"Don't think I'm going to congratulate you. I didn't want that land spoiled." Henry glowered at him. "Deal or no deal."

"Fine. But you have to admit that we're going to make money hand over fist because of it. Pantheon is tickled pink, Grandfather." Darcy nodded at him.

"Humph. If you say so." Henry's frown softened at the mention of money.

"We could do even better with the Dalcour land," Marius put in. "We may get it soon. That fire at the dance hall was right on time."

"Forget it. Rae won't sell. So don't have any more thoughts of doing something foolish." Darcy sneered at his cousin.

"I'm not going to back down and let this opportunity slip away. Rae Dalcour is no sentimental favorite of mine," Marius snapped back at him. They regarded each other with hostility.

Henry scrutinized both his grandsons for several moments. "I'm sure Marius recognizes he's done enough for now."

"But we're close to having it all. With the Dalcour property we can attract more industrial development." Marius had the gleam of avarice in his eyes.

"I've always taught you boys one thing, know when enough is enough. You made a bold decision and escaped unscathed, I can admire that. But Darcy is right."

"Why can't you back me just once," Marius complained. "Those guys can—"

Henry held up a hand. "No details please. I said leave it be now." He looked at Marius sharply. "I won't argue the point."

Marius closed his mouth on another protest. His jaw muscles were tight. "Fine," was his clipped reply. He sat down hard and stared out the window.

Henry turned to Darcy. "The sheriff hasn't caused any more

delays about the bodies they found?" He sat very straight as the seconds ticked by.

Darcy lifted a shoulder. "No. Once they determined there was no more evidence to find, we were able to proceed. Of course, we're two weeks behind schedule. But that's no big deal. Trucks going to the plant can still take the old LaBauve Road."

"And he hasn't questioned you?" Henry fingers were tight around the curved handle of his walking cane.

"Sure. Just routine stuff about missing employees or any reports of suspicious activity on our land. He thinks it might have been some drug dealer killed and dumped out here."

"Nothing else?"

Darcy exchanged a glance with Marius. "No. You have any ideas?"

"Of course not." Henry sat back against the chair and smiled. "Now tell me all about the millions we'll make."

For twenty minutes Henry interrupted Darcy with sharp questions about the details of the Pantheon plant. It was clear to the two young men that the stroke had not dimmed their grandfather's mind. He issued instructions on how Darcy should proceed to protect Jove Enterprises even more.

"Now, I'll go visit my old friend Ivory Newman. He's semiretired now. We're going to the Black Chamber of Commerce meeting over in Lafayette." Henry rose with only a little difficulty.

"You want me to drive you?" Marius held onto Henry's elbow.

"Ivory is going to drive. And take your hands off me. I can walk three blocks down to Ivory's shop!" Henry moved with a stiff grace as he left.

Marius rubbed his chin as he stared at the closed door through which Henry had just gone. "Well, Grandfather has his own secrets."

"What are you babbling about now?" Darcy moved papers around on his desk.

"You know damn well he was trying to find out about the sheriff's investigation. He knows something about that skeleton. Maybe he even knows who it is," Marius said in a low voice.

"You've been watching too many old movies, son." Darcy did not look at him but put derision in his voice. "Now I have phone calls to return—"

"Then why did he say bodies?"

Darcy paused in the act of picking up the telephone receiver. "What?"

"They found a skeleton. One set of bones. Why did he think there was more than one?" Marius raised one dark eyebrow.

"He, uh, heard talk around town. That doesn't mean anything." Darcy pulled his hand away from the phone.

"Maybe, maybe not. But I think we need to stick together as a family." Marius brushed his slacks.

"Meaning?" Darcy's eyes narrowed to slits.

"Meaning I should get some support for my own projects," Marius shot back. "I'm tired of being treated like a flunky."

"You petty criminal slime ball. How dare you try to blackmail your own family!" Darcy jumped up from his chair. "You don't know a damn thing!" he shouted.

"Best keep your voice down, cousin." Marius shook a finger at him. "We don't want folks to come running and ask questions."

"I'll see you in hell before one bit of Jove Enterprises gets in your control!" Darcy only lowered his voice a few decibels.

"Despite what you think, I'm not dumb. I've already been thinking about who them dry bones could belong to," Marius said. "And don't make any bets that the sheriff wouldn't be willing to listen either."

Darcy gazed at him for several moments. "What do you want?"

LaMar sat down on a bar stool in the seedy juke joint. All around him, young black men wearing gold bounced to the beat of a loud song blaring from the stereo speakers. He ordered a bottle of malt liquor and looked around. LaMar was dressed in the same style as the other bar patrons, baggy Chicago Bulls T-shirt and red baggy sweat pants. Though their behavior did not change, he knew he was being watched.

"Say man, whacha want wid Pookie?" A tall man, no older than seventeen, stood off from LaMar.

"What you care? I ain't asked you nothing about it." LaMar took another pull from the bottle of malt liquor.

"You're in my world, punk. You've been asking around my hood. Say man, who're you? The FBI or something?" The young man did an exaggerated up and down look at LaMar. All conversation around them ceased.

"Nah, I'm the one what's gonna whup ass if anybody in here touches me." LaMar pulled out a revolver.

"Listen up!" A huge man who looked to be at least thirty with arms like barrels, pulled a long shotgun from nowhere. "I don't allow none of that in here. See that sign?" He pointed to a bright yellow neon that declared NO GUNS. "Yeah, you!"

"Hey, Teedie, you right. Man, we need to escort this punk on up outta here." Another teenager joined the tall one who still glared at LaMar.

"Give me the piece, man." Teedie held out a huge palm while balancing the shotgun in the other arm.

LaMar glanced around in a split, checking on the positions of other men in the bar and his exit options. "Sure. I didn't see the sign when I come in." He handed over the revolver without missing a beat.

Teedie still stood behind the bar. "Andre and Sharif, out. You both been looking for trouble since you come in." He waved the shotgun at the two young men who clearly were eager to be given the task of dealing with LaMar.

"Teedie, man, dis ain't right. He—"

"You know I don't believe in arguing." Teedie's expression deepened into a fearful scowl. He watched the two sullen teens walk out with rolling gaits designed to show the world they were gangsters worthy of respect. "Come with me."

"Listen, I don't want no trouble." LaMar held up both hands.

Teedie jerked his large head once and said nothing. LaMar kept checking his back as he walked ahead of Teedie across the bar, through a doorway and down a dark hall. At the end of it was a door. There was a click and the door swung open. A room, almost as large as the barroom up front, was filled with people.

There were women of all shapes, colors, and sizes jiggling and giggling. Men gambled and smoked. A white woman with blond hair passed LaMar, brushing up against him.

"I'm Heather. I'll be out here waiting for *you*." She ran her tongue over bright red lips.

"Cut that out," Teedie rumbled at her.

"I'm not gonna be here long enough," LaMar said with a grin. He shook his head as she strolled off putting every ounce of sway she could into her hips.

Teedie took him to yet another door, this one recessed in a wall and covered with padded fake red leather. He pushed through without knocking. A long sofa was against one wall. Two men were seated on it. Opposite them was a large oak desk with two phones. A computer sat on a table to the left of the desk. A light-skinned black man lounged in a big leather chair behind the desk. He stood up and came around it. With one look from him, the two men got up and left the room.

Pookie stared at LaMar for a time. "Been a long time."

"Long enough," LaMar said. "Uncle Clarence is doing okay. You oughta call him once in awhile."

"What for? He says he's only got two sons. Since I don't exist, I can't call him." Pookie wore an angry, resentful look.

"He's hurt at the life you chose. You can't buy his approval, Pookie. All this, it ain't no good." LaMar swept a hand around.

"You're my cousin, not my mama," Pookie snapped. "Like he's so righteous."

"He's not perfect . . ."

"That don't begin to cover it," Pookie said with a grunt. "But you didn't come here for no family discussion." He went back around the desk and sat down again. "Well?"

"There was a fire in Belle Rose, a dance hall." LaMar sat down in a chair facing the desk.

"What's that got to do with me?" Pookie picked up a can of beer with one hand and tossed peanuts in his mouth with the other.

"Nothing. Except maybe a couple of your freelancers might know something about it." LaMar looked up to find the blond at his shoulder. He accepted a can of beer from her before she wiggled out again.

"Nah, I doubt it." Pookie wore a guarded look. "You working for the cops on this one?"

LaMar shook his head slowly. "I only work for private citizens, you know that. Lady that owns it is under suspicion."

"Explain to me why I should care." Pookie munched on another handful of nuts.

"These freelancers, a couple of not too bright guys, could be planning something that will harm your business interests." LaMar saw the slight change in him. So slight those less observant and cautious would miss it. A light flickered on in Pookie's amber eyes, though he continued to seem at ease.

"One thing, you ain't never dumped crap on me. A lame lecture now and then, but you all right. Tell me about it."

Eighteen

Simon sat in his Ford Explorer feeling impatient. What was taking Marius so long? He drummed his fingertips along the rim of the steering wheel. A glance at the LED clock on his dashboard told him he'd been waiting over an hour. *Maybe he's settled in for the night. I'll wait another thirty minutes or so.* Simon relaxed against the seat and stretched his legs. In the darkness surrounding him, the rest of the apartment complex was relatively quiet. He was grateful for the occasional breeze that brushed his cheek through the lowered window. Bird song trilled from the trees to his right. It conjured up the image of lying next to Rae in her bed listening to night sounds through her window. Heat spread through him, a heat not caused by the seventy-five degree summer air.

Yet the sweet memory was tinged with guilt. Despite all his high-sounding words about not being a snob, he'd let years of upbringing influence him. It was painful to admit that he had been raised to set himself and his family apart. The St. Cyrs and Joves were among a group of old families, descendants of the Creoles of color with roots in Africa, Spain, and France. They considered themselves a culture apart. He'd grown up in a world where last names and bloodlines were important. His friends in school had all been from those families. Still worse, the elitist mind-set was more ingrained than he'd suspected. Shameful but true, his first thoughts had been how his grandfather and Mr. Henry were right all along about "those people." Then he remembered an unconscious slip of the tongue Toya made. She'd said something about Marius that implied he had knowledge of the fire. This caused Simon to wonder. He knew all too well that Marius had a dark side. Simon had seen Marius bailed out of the kind of trouble that led other young black men into the justice system. But he was a Jove. Prominent black judges and even the local assistant district attorneys were Creoles. Mr. Henry always dismissed his grandson's troubles as lack of judgment. Simon shook his head. What an understatement. His thoughts drifted back to Rae.

Maybe their breakup was inevitable. She might be better off without him. Who could tell when his prejudice would pop out like an unwelcome genie from a bottle? But he would never be able to forget how good she felt. Simon could smell the lush fragrance of her body, wet with perspiration from making love. The burning inside his stomach became a sharp ache. That intoxicating scent was now lost to him.

A movement to his right made Simon snap to attention. "At last," Simon muttered to himself.

Marius bounded down the steps from his second-floor town house. He was dressed in dark jeans and a dark blue short-sleeved shirt. A beeping sound signaled the disarming of his car alarm. Simon waited until the black Maxima turned onto the street before starting his engine. Marius led him down the highway toward the dance hall. Simon wondered if Rae was there alone. He'd wring the little punk's neck if he . . . But no, they kept going on for another fifteen miles until they reached the small community of LaLonde. Fortunately, there were plenty of other cars on the highway, even a couple of trucks similar to the one Simon owned. Marius did not appear to be the least bit concerned that he was being followed. The sporty car turned down a bumpy road leading to a poor neighborhood. Shotgun houses with sagging porches that all looked alike lined both sides of the streets. Men and women sat outside trying to beat the heat that held on even at ten o'clock. Loud music blared. Simon followed Marius to a rundown garage in a seedy, pitiful-looking ghetto business district of sorts. The garage was at the end of a street that also had a tiny grocery store and a few other storefronts.

Parking along the street about three blocks away, Simon

walked down a broken sidewalk. He slipped into an alley on one side of the garage. Light spilled onto the littered ground from a dirty window. Music thumped through the wall. Careful to crouch down, Simon risked a quick peek in. Marius sat on the hood of an old car in one corner while two guys in grimy overalls took apart a white Cadillac several feet away. Two other cars were lined up. *Who are those characters? Marius involved with stolen cars? This is no good. I've got to get closer.* Simon went down the alley and froze when his foot banged against an old aluminum garbage can. When no one came out to investigate, he continued around the back of the garage. The rear entrance was closed, lucky for him. He crept along the wall hoping to get near a window to hear the conversation between Marius and the two men. Soon he could hear a voice.

"Look, man, I told you we gonna take care of it." Sly-Man sucked in smoke from a cigarette. He let out a long stream in the air above his head.

"How? I don't want another screw up." Marius looked at them both with skepticism.

"You don't need to know, all right? Let's just say new evidence gonna show up." Tyrone grinned foolishly.

"No good. The cops went over her place with tweezers. You two are pathetic." Marius glared at them. "You won't stop until we're all in jail."

"What you think, I'm a fool?" Tyrone hunched his shoulders.

"No comment," Marius retorted.

Sly-Man stepped between them to block his offended partner. "Hey, cut it out. Look, we gonna put it on her property and have some pals of ours find it. Being good citizens, they gonna make sure the sheriff gets it."

"That's your plan? Like I said, pathetic." Marius gave a snort of contempt.

Sly-Man did not seem the least bit upset. "Well, this stuff belonged to her, we borrowed it to do the job. They'll be able to trace it back to where she bought the wires, turpentine, and stuff."

"I don't get it." Marius looked interested for the first time.

"She did a few things around the place herself. I'm sure the dude down at the hardware store will remember her. She's a fine woman." Sly-Man chuckled.

"Wish I coulda caught her out there one night by herself. Maybe later . . ." Tyrone gave a coarse laugh.

Sly-Man joined in. "Yeah, get me some of that."

Simon saw red. It took all his self-control not to shout a string of curses. He wanted to pound them into the dirt. Instead he let out a long, slow breath. With a great struggle, he pushed down the urge to lash out.

"Yes, she'll have a tough time talking her way out of that," Marius said. "Maybe I was wrong about you guys after all. Yeah, sounds like a winner to me. So you think a little booty action with the lady would be nice, eh?" He joined the two men in raucous laughter.

Simon inched closer to look inside when he heard a thump. A dark shadow took shape as it advanced straight toward him. Simon backed up and hid behind a rusty oil barrel. The bulky figure stepped over debris without making noise. The man held a gun.

Simon looked around for some way to escape. An old mattress leaned against the wall. He might be able to cause a diversion by shoving it forward while running in the opposite direction. Or should he just try a dash down the alley in hopes the man was a bad shot? As the man crept closer, Simon had to make a quick decision. He braced himself against the wall and waited until he could hear breathing. Simon shot up putting all his weight behind a shove.

"What the hell!" a heavy voice shouted.

His beefy arm struck out at his phantom attacker. Old hubcaps and other trash made a tremendous clatter as he stumbled about. Simon took a hard blow to the side of his head that made him dizzy. The huge man pushed forward. Simon scrambled back to avoid being pinned down. He leaped over a pile of garbage and sprinted down the alley.

"I got him. Ooff!" Tyrone landed on his back when Simon hit him at full speed. But he held onto his gun and fired.

Simon felt a hard slap to his left arm then a spreading

warmth. He ran only a few steps before another punch came down across his neck. Simon dropped to his knees.

"Drag his ass in here. Let's see what we got," Sly-Man barked.

"Whoever you is, you in a lotta trouble," the big man rumbled as he pointed a meaty finger at Simon's nose.

When the large man dumped Simon on the floor, Tyrone kicked him hard on the shoulder. "That ain't all I got for you, mother-" He lifted his foot again.

Marius pushed Tyrone away, causing him to lose his balance and fall against a stack of mufflers. "Cut it out, fool! We need to talk to him first," he yelled. Tyrone shot him a mean look before going out through the back door.

"How did you find this place?" Marius said in a deadly calm voice.

"You know him?" Sly-Man looked frowned. "You better tell me something, Marius."

"That's the Dalcour woman's boyfriend. He used to be married to my cousin." Marius rubbed his jaw with a worried expression. "Wonder if Toya has been talking too much." He squatted down to peer in Simon's face. "Is that what happened? You might as well tell me because you won't leave this place breathing."

The other man in overalls who had been chopping up cars held up both hands. "Hey, I ain't in this, man. I didn't sign up for no killing. I'm out." He darted through the front of the garage and away into the dark before the other men could react.

"Aw, damn! What else gonna happen!" Sly-Man paced. "You told us wasn't nobody else in on this, man! Now we find out your big mouth cousin been talking."

"Toya's crazy about this guy. She wouldn't tell anybody else." Marius jerked Simon's head back. "Are you alone?"

"Yes," Simon said in a voice hoarse with pain. His throat felt parched.

"Who else have you told about me?" Marius stared at him. He punched Simon hard in the jaw when he didn't respond after a few seconds. "Talk!"

"No one. I followed you only because . . ." Simon coughed

hard. "Toya didn't say anything except you were sure the fire wasn't an accident."

"So you kind of added things up. Smart man." Marius pressed his lips together.

"A little thing like the law never stopped you." Simon did not flinch from the evil look Marius gave him.

Tryone came back inside. "I didn't see nobody."

"You messed up bad, slick." Sly-Man bared his teeth in an ugly semblance of a smile. "Real bad."

"What we gone do?" Tyrone rubbed his hands together nervously.

Sly-Man looked to Marius. Minutes ticked by as Marius paced. Simon lay very still on the dirty floor, sweat pouring down his sides.

"Well?" Sly-Man lifted both hands.

The big man in overalls stepped up to Sly-Man. "Just say the word."

"I've got too much to lose." Marius slapped his right fist into his left palm.

"That guy got hurt in the fire took a turn for the worse last night." Sly-Man looked at them all.

"You mean—" Tyrone's mouth hung open with fear.

"A murder rap if he dies. Hell, it could be attempted murder if he lives," Sly-Man said.

Marius stood with his back to them. "Do what you have to." He strode out of the garage without looking back. Seconds later, they heard his car engine gun as he drove away.

The large man in overalls hefted Simon up onto his feet. Simon swayed, his vision became cloudy. He took deep breaths trying to clear his head. The shoes on his feet felt like blocks of concrete weighing him down so that each step was a trial. After the first few attempts to walk, Simon was dragged to a late model car parked on a dark side street east of the garage.

"Say, man, which way is it to the Black Cat Cafe?" A loud, slurred voice shouted to them.

"The opposite direction from where you at now, man. I'd get going thataway if I was you," the big man rumbled. He turned to block the newcomer's view of Tyrone and Sly-Man struggling to heave Simon into the car.

LaMar wobbled in front of the man wearing a senseless grin. "I'm ready to pa-artee." He shuffled his feet.

"You gone be ready for the emergency room if you don't—"

The big man reached for LaMar. LaMar did not back away. "Aw, man," he said. "Can't we all get along?" His foot came up fast twice, the tip of his heavy boot smashing into the big man's crotch.

"Ye-oow, oo-wee!" The big man bent double forward. His wide face contorted in agony. Knees together, he hobbled in a circle with tears streaming from his eyes. He crumpled to the ground when LaMar punched him in the face.

With Tyrone momentarily distracted, Simon put his head down and rammed into his midsection as hard as he could. Tyrone flipped over into a ditch beside the street. He rolled into a ball clutching his stomach. The force of the effort brought Simon down beside him. He lay still pretending to be unconscious.

Sly-Man stood in the open driver's side door holding a gun with both hands. It was pointed at LaMar. "You gonna die, slick!"

"You don't wanna do that." LaMar held up both hands palm out. "I got backup. No undercover operation happens without it."

"Bull. They'd a been here by now. You ain't no cop." Sly-Man wore a wolflike expression as he took one step closer.

While they talked, Simon crawled back up to crouch a few feet behind Sly-Man. He steeled himself against the pain and ran into his back with a loud growl. In the split second that Sly-Man looked away, LaMar dove down to flatten himself to the ground. Simon gained strength at the thought that this man wanted to harm Rae. He and the thug grappled with the gun. Their grunts and panting were the only sound for several seconds. Then a deep voice called out.

"Say, Sly. Whassup?" Pookie stepped from the shadows with four other men behind him. They stood several yards away. Both men froze and stared at the newcomers.

Sly-Man looked baffled. "Pookie, man, what you doin'

here?" He let go of Simon, looking at him as though he'd been holding a poisonous snake. "You with Pookie?"

"We ain't stupid," Simon said in his best imitation of gang members he'd seen in the movie *Boyz N The Hood*. But he could feel what little energy he had left draining away.

"Aw, damn!" Sly-Man had the look of a deer caught in the headlights of an eighteen wheeler.

"Here to get my merchandise, Sly. You know what I'm talking about."

"I just had me some delays. I got the money, man. And the shipment." Sly-Man's eyes were wide. "First I got to—"

"Nah, we gonna do our deal now. No more waiting." Pookie spoke in a calm tone that was loaded with danger.

LaMar stood up slowly. "He doesn't know . . . yet. Give it up, and you live," he whispered.

"What you sayin'?" Sly-Man mumbled. He darted a fearful glance over his shoulder.

LaMar made sure Pookie and his boys had not moved closer. "I haven't told *my cousin* how you've been skimming extra profit for yourself," he said in a low voice.

Sly-Man gaped at him, large drops of sweat dripped down his face.

"We ain't gonna hang out here all night." Pookie started toward Sly-Man.

"He just got a little sidetracked," LaMar called out. "But he's straight now. Ain't that right?" He looked at Sly-Man.

"Pookie, man, you know me." Sly-Man's voice was strained.

"I'll do what I have to." LaMar had a look of cold, hard steel. "Me and my pal are leaving. Handle your business." Sly-Man opened his mouth to protest.

"Naw, cuz, Sly-Man ain't got time to fight you. He's gotta take me to my merchandise and my money. Right?" Pookie stopped four feet from Sly-Man.

"I, uh . . ." Sly-Man looked around as though seeking some means of escape.

"Don't be no fool," LaMar said. "You ain't gonna win an argument with him."

Sly-Man lowered the gun. "Sure, Pookie. We cool."

LaMar crossed quickly to Simon who was leaning against the car fender. "You gonna be okay, bro. Take it easy.

"I haven't talked to LaMar for two days. We won't ever find out what really happened to Pawpaw Vincent. I've gone about everything all wrong, Mama." Rae's mood was in contrast to the bright morning sunshine. "And I'm telling you, the dance hall won't make it."

"Rae, this is my money. I know what I'm doin'." Aletha put both hands on her hips. "Now me, Neville, and Andy want to see this dance hall open again."

Aletha had come over for dinner while George attended a Masons meeting in the town. They were in Rae's kitchen cleaning up. The argument that began during dessert continued.

Rae felt defeated. Tony Baranco was still delaying payment on the policy. The bills were piling up fast. Her savings were dwindling.

"We're gonna make it, baby. Long as we stick together. Now I paid your electric, gas, and water bills for this month." Aletha took the dish cloth from Rae's hand and dried the rest of his dishes, then she started wiping the kitchen cabinet top. "We'll take it one day at a time."

"Mama, you shouldn't have done that. I'm a grown woman. I can take care of myself." Rae knew her voice sounded weak. She did not have the energy to be angry.

"You're going to pay us back. I know you will. Nothing wrong with accepting help."

"I just don't know anymore." Rae sagged down onto a chair at the table. "By the time I'm through, we'll all be broke."

"What's really eating at you is Simon St. Cyr." Aletha sat down beside her. "Call him."

"No," Rae blurted out.

"Pride won't comfort you in the midnight hour, sugar." Aletha's dark brown eyebrows arched. "You love that man—don't bother to deny it," she cut off a protest.

"Yes, but it's not enough. You ought to know that."

Aletha sighed. She glanced around at what used to be her

kitchen. "Sometimes I wonder if I made the right decision. Not that I don't love George. He's been mighty good to me," she added quickly. "A part of me never stopped loving Lucien. Maybe he wouldn't have let his health get so run down if I had stayed. Took me being gone for almost ten years to realize Lucien loved me. He woulda never left me for another woman."

"But you couldn't put up with his rages or the times he did more than flirt." Rae took her mother's hand. "There are things that just can't be fixed between two people." She thought of Simon talking to Toya, their heads close together.

"Maybe, maybe not."

Rae shook her head to clear away painful thoughts of Simon. "Anyway, looks like losing the dance hall won't be my only failure. LaMar has just about given up on finding out what happened to Pawpaw Vincent."

"I'm gonna tell you something I ain't never told nobody, not even George." Aletha's voice dropped so that Rae leaned forward as a reflex action.

"Mama, what is it?" Rae had never seen such an expression in her mother's light brown eyes.

"Lucien and me wasn't getting along good at all by the time you was a teenager. One night his monmon was at the house. Humph, she was always at the house, seemed like."

"Yeah, I remember."

"Monmon Marie didn't help none. I think she wanted Lucien all to herself. One night Lucien came in with liquor on his breath. I was fussing and he just went on to bed without paying me no mind."

"I remember how he could be once he'd been drinking." Rae did not need to be told that Lucien thought of little but himself at those times.

"Me, I started talking about how he was no-good. His monmon got furious at that. Monmon Marie flung it in my face that Lucien coulda done better than me. Said I was lucky to have him, so I should shut my mouth." Aletha twisted the towel in her hands. "Then she said 'I took care of one that tried to hurt my children, I'll do it again if need be.'"

"I don't understand."

"I thought about how Mr. Vincent just disappeared with not a bit of him left. Rae, if you coulda seen the look in her eyes when she said it. Right in this room," Aletha said in a shaky voice. She looked around as though afraid the old woman would appeared, conjured up from the dead.

"My, God!" Rae gasped, unable to believe what she'd just heard. "You can't be serious."

"More than once they say she threatened to kill Mr. Vincent and any woman she ever caught him with." Aletha looked at her hands. "I couldn't never work up the nerve to breathe this to a living soul."

"But that's incredible. Monmon Marie was so quiet." Rae felt her already upside down world tilt even more.

"You went off to college and the next year I left." Aletha smoothed out the dish cloth and began to fold it carefully on the table. "I knew Lucien would just go down, but I left anyway. Between his wild ways and Monmon Marie, I got so I hated being in this house."

"You can't blame yourself for Daddy's drinking. He was all ready out of control. We both know it. Even he knew it." Rae put an arm around her mother's shoulders.

"Monmon Marie fed that bitterness in him from the time he was a little boy, Rae. She poisoned him. But I was weak. By the time I met George, it was too late. We both had our own lives."

"But if Monmon Marie killed them both . . . No, they were seen in New Orleans." Rae felt a kind of giddy relief. "Mama, listen to me. They were seen after that night they disappeared. Monmon Marie had slapped Estelle once for running around with Pawpaw Vincent. That had to be all she meant."

Aletha did not look satisfied with her explanation. "If you think so. But the way she said it . . ." She shivered as though a winter breeze had blown across her.

"LaMar investigated. We've gone over old newspaper articles and papers at least ten times." Rae kissed Aletha on the cheek. "You've been worrying all these years for no reason."

"But—"

"And blaming yourself for what Daddy became is just plain wrong. Daddy said he had only himself to blame for not living his life right." Rae rested her head on Aletha's shoulder. "He even said he was glad you were happy."

"Oh, Lucien, even with your faults, you were one of a kind." Aletha spoke in a soft voice. "A good man. And you got a good man in Simon."

"Now let's not go back to that." Rae jumped up and started to put away dishes.

"Listen to me, Rae. Simon has a fine character. Everybody knows that." Aletha snatched a plastic tumbler from her hands. "So do you."

"Oh, sure. Fine character, moonlight and roses, soft music, great s—" Rae bit off her words and looked at her mother.

"Un-huh. Good loving is something every woman wants." Aletha wore a knowing half smile that made Rae squirm in embarrassment.

Rae got busy wiping the counter even though it was spotless. "It's not enough, Mama. We're from two different worlds. Besides, I wouldn't want to spend years apologizing for who I am."

"Didn't seem like he was expecting you to. I saw that look in his eyes. He loves every bit of who you are, cher." Aletha brushed back Rae's hair.

"You didn't hear him talking that last time we saw each other." Rae took a long time to hang first the dish cloth then dish towel on the wire arm over the kitchen sink. "He's listening to his family and the Joves these days."

"You mean Toya, don't ya? He didn't look to be that kind when I met him."

Rae turned around with an angry look. "Trust me, he is. You know how those uppity Creoles act." She was working up a head of steam to stave off the return of aching loss.

"You're trying too hard to hate him, cher. But I'm not saying anything else about it." Aletha held up one hand.

"Good."

"Not another word. No, ma'am." Aletha smoothed down the skirt of her sun dress.

"Perfect."

"If you wanna live out here all alone, in pain for that hand-

some man—long empty nights without his arms to hold you—
well, that's your business." Aletha shrugged.

"Mama, let it go," Rae said through clenched teeth. In truth,
Aletha's words exactly described how she'd been feeling. Which
made Rae even more aggravated with her mother.

"I'm not saying another word about it." Aletha's expression
said the subject was far from closed.

Tante Ina came by and the women spent the evening listening
to music and chatting away. Rae let them do most of the talking
while she turned over all her mother had said. She pushed
thoughts of Simon out of her mind. Or at least to a deeper part.
I'll be up all night if I get to remembering . . . No, she must
think about her future. How would she pay back her family?
The thought of letting them down filled her with dread. All her
energy had to center on making a go of the business now. No
more chasing old ghosts or impossible relationships. Once
again, she swore not to think of Simon or what might have been.
It would never happen and she had to let it go. Rae gazed out
into the night. *Now if I can just shut off these memories.*

"No, don't tell her." Simon's jaw jutted out in a stubborn
frown. He grimaced at the sharp pain moving his arm caused.

"Be still," the chief nurse cautioned. She lifted the bandage
with care. A plastic tag on her blouse pocket said CONNIE
RIDEAU, RN. "Looks good."

"Oh, yeah, I love having a hole in my body," Simon grumbled.

LaMar leaned against the white-painted wall of the hospital
room. They were in the small Lafayette General Hospital. It was
where he'd brought Simon once they left Pookie to deal with
Sly-Man and the others.

"You'll be just fine. No permanent damage the doctor said.
Though it'll be stiff for some months even after the bandage
comes off." Nurse Connie gave him a crisp, professional smile.
"Now I'll be back to check on you later."

"Look, Rae is going to find out sooner or later. And what
about your family? And your employees? You've got to explain

being gone somehow." LaMar picked up a piece of bacon still on Simon's breakfast tray. "You gonna eat this?"

"No. And it won't be a problem if I don't have to stay in here another night. I've already called Nola."

"I suppose nobody is going to wonder why you're all banged up and bandaged? You could have gotten yourself killed, you know." LaMar sat down to munch off Simon's plate. He sipped the coffee and frowned.

"Getting kicked around wasn't in the plan," Simon said with irritation, more for himself than anyone. "After Toya made that little slip of the tongue, I started thinking. I figured I'd follow Marius and then let Sheriff Thibodeaux know what I found out."

"Yeah, well next time leave it to the professionals. Mmm, these eggs are not bad." LaMar dabbed his mouth with a napkin.

"Point taken." Simon moved his arm gingerly.

"But that was great work for an amateur. Not bad with your hands either." LaMar winked at him.

"Sure, I had them shaking with terror." Simon grinned at him.

"You left your mark on them, sport. You done good. Thanks for saving my rear end, too."

"Same to you. Lucky for me you're such a good private eye." Simon held out his hand. LaMar clasped it.

"I do my best." LaMar went back to eating Simon's breakfast. "Rae is going to be happy when she hears how you helped save the day."

Simon's smile vanished and the stubborn look came back. "I don't want you to mention anything about me. Just tell her you followed Marius and got the goods on him. You would have without me anyway."

"You're wrong to hide this from Rae. She cares about you a whole lot."

"Really?" Simon glanced at him with a gleam in his eyes that quickly died. "I don't want her back because she feels obligated. Besides, we said some pretty nasty things and . . . Look, just forget it."

"You're making a mistake, man. But it's not my business to

interfere. It's forgotten." LaMar waved a hand as if to make the subject vanish.

Simon settled back against the pillow. "What happens now? I mean about the arson."

"I've taken care of it. Sheriff Thibodeaux has the info he needs to arrest those two clowns. I told him where to find the evidence they planned to plant on Rae's property." LaMar grinned. "They are in deep doo-doo, to say the least."

"And eager to spread it on Marius I'll bet."

"You know it. Things are about to heat up in Belle Rose." LaMar took a swig of orange juice.

"That's the truth." Simon looked thoughtful. "A lot of people were willing to believe the worst about Rae. Now they'll have to eat their words." He took a deep breath.

He wanted to tell Rae how sorry he was for being such a judgmental snob. Maybe they would not be able to make a relationship work, but he at least owed her respect.

LaMar studied him in silence for several moments. "Well, I think Rae will understand. We all make mistakes. She said even she is a quick to fly off the handle and . . . What am I doing? I'm dipping in your business again." The corner of his mouth lifted when he saw Simon's far away expression.

"People should at least tell her they're sorry," Simon murmured to himself.

"Uh-huh." LaMar smiled. "Things are going to pop in the old town more than you know."

"What does that mean?" Simon blinked at him.

"The skeleton they found is from a very prominent person's closet." LaMar's eyes shone bright at the prospect of being at the center of action again.

"Say what?" Simon leaned forward without feeling a sharp jab the movement caused.

"Those bones are fifty years old. I think we've found Vincent Dalcour. At least that's what I told the sheriff."

Simon let out a long, low whistle. "Damn! Does Rae know?"

"Not yet. But I need to tell her soon. You know how fast news travels around that parish, much less the town."

"Now I know I've got to get out of here. She'll need me."

Simon pressed the button to call a nurse. "That doctor has got to release me." He pushed back the sheets and swung his legs down.

"Say, man, Doc Vidrine should be here any minute. He'll probably let you go. Just take it easy." LaMar moved to the closet to get his clothes at Simon's gestures.

A pretty nurse with café au lait skin came in. "What you need now, cher?"

Simon wrestled with his pants. "To go home."

Nineteen

Rae stood inside the dance hall. Work was going well. She was getting encouragement from her suppliers and even cards from customers expressing hope that Rockin' Good Times would reopen soon. It was a gorgeous day. She and Andy were making plans to open in just a couple of weeks. Tony, her insurance agent, had even called to say her claim would go forward. Still, Rae did not feel the soaring joy she should. It seemed a hollow victory in spite of all the good news. With a sigh, Rae went out to sit on the porch.

"Looks like we're right on schedule, darling. Things are moving along real fine." Andrew gave a satisfied sigh as he sat in the rocking chair next to her.

"Yeah." Rae stared out at the bright green leaves waving in the warm air. She hardly noticed the rainbow of colors from wildflowers that normally brought her pleasure.

"And Jamal and Wes are going to be here to kick it off. That compact disc y'all put out is doing well. We can sell some of those."

"Uh-huh, you're right," Rae said in a listless voice.

"Lord, you look like you lost your best friend. Cheer up," Andrew said then grimaced. "Sorry. My mouth works faster than my brain sometimes."

"Forget it. I'm just tired, that's all. A lot has happened in the last couple of weeks." Rae gave a brief smile that faded quickly.

"You could call him." Andrew stopped writing and put down his clipboard on a small table between them.

"Not after the things I said. The worst part is he was right. I did plan to use him to get back at Toya." Rae pressed her lips together. "It's my fault."

What she had not foreseen was the strong love that grew with every hour that she spent with Simon. This was her punishment then. To know the ecstasy of a love so true and potent only to lose it because she would not let go of bitterness. A harsh sentence indeed. Yet one she deserved. She was following in Lucien's footsteps when it came to destroying relationships.

"I think you're beating yourself up too hard, cher." Andrew rubbed the stubble on his chin.

"I've done a lot of stupid things in my life, Andy. This was just one more." Rae's voice trembled. "But you're right. I shouldn't sit around feeling sorry for myself. Come on, let's get the bar set up." She went back inside with a grim look.

"Nah, that can wait until later," Andrew called to her. He grinned widely. "Much later."

"What? Get your butt in here Andrew Vincent Dalcour. We've got a million things to do." Rae stomped out to the porch again with both hands on her hips. "If you think you're going fishing today—" She came to a sudden halt at the sight of Simon standing in the sunshine.

"Hello." Simon gazed at her with a mixture of caution and desire.

"Hello." Rae could feel her heart speeding up. "How've you been?"

"Good."

LaMar strolled up. "Except for that flesh wound from a gunshot. Oops, I wasn't supposed to mention that." He did not look the least bit sorry.

Rae noticed the white bandage wrapped around Simon's upper left arm. "My God! You were shot? How? When?" She rushed to him and gently put her arms around him.

"Just solving the crime that someone tried to pin on you by tracking down the real arsonist. Right?" LaMar smiled in spite of the dark look Simon gave him.

"He's the one who really did the hard work. I just sort of bumbled into things." Simon shrugged then grimaced at the movement.

"Sit down. Let me get you something. Jackson! Bring us three creme sodas," Rae yelled over her shoulder at the same time she was leading Simon to a chair. "What happened? No wonder Tony called this morning saying the claim would not be a problem after all."

"Really, Rae. I wasn't hurt that bad." Simon clearly enjoyed the fuss she was making despite his protest.

"Yeah, these two knot-heads were hired by Marius Jove to torch the place and frame you for it." LaMar took the tray from Jackson. "Thanks, my man." He passed the frosty mugs around. "Simon here followed Marius to their hangout."

"Simon, you could have been killed? What were you thinking?" Rae felt a shiver of fear at the thought of him lying dead in the street. "Should you be up and around? Maybe I should take you home now. You look so tired. Oh, Simon." She touched his face.

LaMar grinned at the wink Andrew gave him. "Ahem, anyway. Tyrone started talking then shut up fast. My guess is either old man Jove has made him an offer or Sly-Man has threatened him. Either way, Marius is sweating heavy these days."

"He wanted to put you out of business so you'd be desperate for money and sell your land." Simon frowned. "The sleaze bag better hope they send him to jail."

"If I know Henry Jove, he'll have a smooth talking lawyer already working to make sure he doesn't," Rae said. She felt anger flash up like a lit match, not for herself but for Simon. She'd like to get her hands on Marius right now.

"Jail or not, he's scared spitless right now from what I hear." LaMar. chuckled. "Don't know if Granddaddy can save his rump. Under the law, he's as responsible as the guys who set the fire."

"And Mr. Calvin got hurt," Simon added.

"Right. All in all, the Joves have a lot more on their mind now than snatching your property." LaMar looked at Simon. "Uh, you want to tell her?"

"You found out. I think you should." Simon nodded at him.

"Tell me what?" Rae sat still.

"If you think so," LaMar said. He did not say anything more.

"Go on. I don't think—" Simon lifted his right shoulder.

"Somebody better start talking now." Rae glanced at Simon then LaMar and waited.

"Looks like that skeleton they found on Jove land is the remains of your grandfather." LaMar squinted. "It was buried at least fifty years ago and he didn't die of natural causes."

"Rae, I'm so sorry." Simon spoke to her in a soothing tone. "I know what a shock this must be."

The two men watched her. LaMar with interest, Simon with concern. Rae rocked back and forth in the chair a few times staring out over the bayou.

"I'm not real surprised," she said after a while.

"What?" Simon's mouth hung open.

"Uh-huh." LaMar nodded slowly.

"He vanished without a trace. It was like they jumped on the mother ship and flew off to another planet. Nobody disappears so completely unless . . ." Rae lifted both hands. "And then there's Monmon Marie's diaries."

"Yeah, I've been thinking about that myself." LaMar gazed at her with an odd look on his face.

"Have you? My mama brought this up to me a few days ago, but I didn't want to believe it. But the truth is, I started to suspect Monmon Marie knew more than she ever told." Rae shook her head.

Simon shook his head in amazement. "You think Miss Marie killed them? That little old lady?"

"She wasn't always old. And she had a temper," Rae said. "LaMar, did they determine the cause of death?"

"Repeated blows to the head. The skull was cracked in at two places at least from what I gather." LaMar took a sip from his mug. "Somebody hit him hard more than once."

Rae gripped the arms of her chair. "Someone in a rage maybe. Like a betrayed wife."

"This just keeps getting worse for you." Simon put a hand on her arm and squeezed it gently.

"I'll be okay, Simon. At least we can give him a decent burial," Rae said softly. "Right beside Daddy."

"But it's not definite that the bones are your grandfather's remains. Maybe it's not him." Simon tried to put a hopeful note in his voice. "He could still be on some tropical island surrounded by a dozen grandchildren."

"It's Pawpaw Vincent. I can feel it." Rae smiled at him. "But thanks for trying." The compassionate light in his handsome face touched her heart.

"Well I gotta go." LaMar stood up and bounced down to the ground from the porch in one smooth movement.

Rae forced her gaze from Simon with some effort. "Don't rush off. It's almost lunchtime. Jackson's got a fresh shrimp po'boy with your name on it."

"Yeah, and you haven't told me all the details on how you got onto Marius," Simon added. His hand was still on Rae's arm.

"Hey, I'm still on the case. I've got four days left to find out all the facts on Vincent and Estelle." LaMar put on his Perry Ellis designer sunglasses. He grinned at the baffled looks his words caused.

"But they've found Pawpaw," Rae blurted.

"And I hate to say it, but Estelle was probably buried in those same woods somewhere," Simon said.

"Or dumped in the bayou more likely. Which is why they won't find her body." Rae shook her head. "Of course, we will never know for sure if Monmon Marie killed them both."

"Exactly. We still have unanswered questions." LaMar took a deep breath. "I hate unanswered questions."

"Everybody who could tell us the whole story is dead. You're not going to get all the answers on this one." Simon shrugged.

"You don't mind if I keep looking? We might find out a few more details." LaMar said.

Rae struggled with a vague stirring at LaMar's comments. There was something, but what? "Sure," she murmured with her brows together. "Keep looking."

"Great. Now you two proceed with the kiss-and-make-up process," LaMar said.

"I, uh . . ." Rae felt the heat from Simon's touch heighten at his words.

"You'll see he gets a ride home, right? Sure you will." LaMar winked at them and strode off whistling.

Rae and Simon exchanged an embarrassed glance at his words. The engine of LaMar's Grand Jeep Cherokee roared to life and he drove away. Rae felt a return of that hollow feeling when Simon took his hand away.

"I just came by to make sure you would be okay once you found out about your grandfather." Simon did not look at her.

"That was nice of you. But you didn't have to come way over here." Rae pressed her lips together.

All the words she wanted to say so crowded her mind and heart that she was speechless. She had no right to expect more than kindness from this man. He was decent and caring. Yet she had taken it for granted. Her bad temper and need for petty revenge had damaged their love before it had a chance to really bloom, to become deep rooted and enduring.

"I wanted to," Simon said. "For my sake as much as yours. I'm selfish that way." He wore a shy smile.

"No, you're not the selfish one," Rae blurted out. "I don't blame you for being disgusted with me."

"Rae, I'm not disgusted—"

"I am. You were right. I flaunted our relationship to make Toya miserable. I wanted her to suffer the way I'd suffered."

"Well, that's kind of natural. I mean we're all human and have—"

"And then, when the dance hall was successful, I was able to show up everybody who had ever trashed the Dalcours." Rae looked out over the grassy fields to the woods. "Guess you should have listened to what folks said. But I never pretended to care about you."

"Will you shut up for one minute." Simon stood up and pulled her from her chair, too. He wrapped his right arm around her. "I love you, Rae. I shouldn't have gone off on you that way. I should never had doubted you." He punctuated this last sentence with a lingering kiss. When they finally stopped, she pressed her cheek to his chest.

"The feeling for you was so strong, I panicked. Deep down I decided to leave you and keep some dignity rather than see you walk away." Rae held onto him with a fervent wish to never let go. "Even though we grew up within forty miles of each other, we're from different worlds."

"No we're not. Your father wanted you to have a good life. Maybe he didn't go about it the best way all the time, but he did try." Simon stroked her back.

"You really want to get hooked up with wild Rae Dalcour? The one all those folks have told you about?" Rae gazed up into his face, her eyes bright with tears. She needed so much to hear a true answer to the question. The whole world seemed to stand still for a split second.

"Baby, I was hooked that first day I set eyes on you. Standing outside with the sun on your pretty face, your hair soft and shiny like black cotton." As he spoke, Simon ran his fingers through her hair. "I don't need anybody to tell me who your are, Rae. I love everything about you."

"I love you, too, honey. I love you so much." Pressing her body to his, Rae kissed him with such passion they were left breathless and dazed.

"My, oh, my. I wish I could get rid of all these bandages. Of course, there are ways . . ." Simon brushed his lips against her neck.

"No way. I'm sure the doctor told you no strenuous activity." Rae stepped back. Concern for his health overrode her rising desire.

"He was talking about work," Simon protested.

"I've been missing you something awful these last few weeks, Simon St. Cyr. Trust me, you'll need all your strength." Rae gave him a naughty smile.

"Have mercy! My doctor is going to have to come up with some space age, light speed healing techniques," Simon said in a raspy voice. "Or else, I'm just going to have to be in pain." He reached for her but Rae slipped away.

"Oh, no. You've had a serious shock to your body. Sit down here. The more you rest, the faster you'll heal." Rae made him sit down again. "I'm going to bring you lunch and we're going to have a calm, sedate afternoon together."

Simon let out a dramatic sigh of resignation. "Yes, nurse."

Rae served them both roast beef sandwiches and salads. She enjoyed making a fuss over Simon. His rich deep laughter was the most beautiful sound she'd ever heard. Nature seemed to join in their celebration as bird song trilled from all directions. They waved happily to several friends passing in boats on the bayou.

"Do you want anything else?" Rae poured him another glass of creme soda.

"Yes, but you already ruled that out." Simon chuckled.

"Glad to see you both smiling," Marcelle called out as she and Freddie approached. Baby Felicia was perched against her shoulder happily sucking on a tiny fist.

"Hi." Rae got up to.meet her. She gathered up Felicia in her arms. "How's my sweet *bébé,* huh?"

"I plan to make sure this lady smiles a lot for years to come." Simon gazed at Rae with deep affection.

"Now that's what I like to hear!" Marcelle beamed at them. "But be careful, that's how I got this little one and four other rug rats." She let out a robust laugh.

"Sounds good to me," Simon said. He gazed at Rae holding Felicia. "More love to share," he murmured.

Rae blushed with pleasure. She cuddled the baby close enjoying the feel of her tight curly hair brushing her chin. "You better concentrate on getting well."

"Yeah, I heard about it." Marcelle's eyes grew round. "You okay, cher?" She grew serious.

"Couldn't be better." Simon looked at Rae when he spoke.

"The whole town is buzzing like a beehive. They say Miz Cecile had to stop Mr. Henry from beating Marius with his cane when he found out. Course he's defending him out in the public eye, so to speak. But the housekeeper is my friend Suzette's second cousin's sister-in-law. Child, she saw it all." Marcelle rattled off the gossip without taking a breath.

"Have you heard the latest about the bones they found?" Rae

settled between Simon and Marcelle in a rocker still holding Felicia. "It's my grandfather."

"I heard whispers. Girl, this is too much. You think maybe Mr. Henry did 'em in?" Marcelle took a sip of Rae's soft drink.

"Rae thinks Monmon Marie murdered them," Simon said.

Marcelle choked on the soft drink then coughed loudly. *"Mon Dieu!* You gotta be joking!" she spluttered.

"I'm telling you, Marcelle, it makes sense. In the diary she talks about vengeance for the way Pawpaw treated her. She even wrote about that night like she saw him for one last time." Rae pursed her lips.

"But why haven't they found Estelle?" Marcelle said.

"Around these woods and bayous? Pooh-ya, a body could be buried and never be found." Freddie swept a hand around to the dense vegetation to make a point.

"That's the truth. Could be they weren't killed together. Who knows? After all these years, we'll probably never know." Simon made cooing noises at the baby that made Felicia's big dark eyes light up with a smile.

"Monmon wrote about Estelle with bitterness, said she was used to having everything come to her." Rae frowned in deep concentration. A picture formed in her mind.

"Uh-uh, something's missing. His body is buried right there, still there after fifty years. Seems like . . ." Marcelle paused to munch a potato chip from Rae's plate.

Rae stopped rocking and sat up straight. The baby blinked at her. "Shoot! I can't believe it!"

"What's wrong? Did Felicia's diaper spring a leak? Come here Mama's little sweet potato." Marcelle took the baby from Rae.

"Simon, no . . . It's crazy." Rae paced in front of them as Marcelle and Simon exchanged puzzled glances.

"What's this about?" Simon stood up.

"She's up to something. I know that look. Best stand back." Marcelle's eyes shone with excitement.

"Thank you, thank you." Rae hugged Simon hard and planted a big kiss on Marcelle's forehead. "I've got to get hold of La-

Mar. His cell phone number is in my office. He's going back and he's going to take me with him this time."

"Where? Take you where?" Simon stared at her in astonishment. He turned to Marcelle when Rae did not answer.

"I want to be right there, yes indeed. Andrew can take care of things while I'm gone," she yelled as she raced inside.

Marcelle shrugged. "How should I know? I'll say one thing for sure, nothing is gonna surprise me after all this."

Simon rubbed his jaw. "Don't count on that, Marcelle. I've got a feeling there is a lot more to come."

Rae stood in Sheriff Thibodeaux's office waiting. The female deputy seemed to have been gone an hour, though it had only been five or ten minutes. She tried to concentrate on what she would say, how she would act. What was going through the others' minds?

"This way ma'am." The deputy, a blond with a slight Cajun accent, led her down a hall to a large conference room that doubled as a classroom.

"What the hell is going on?" Henry Jove scowled at Rae when she came in. "I don't know why you've got this dramatic scene set up, sheriff. But you'd better have a damn good reason."

"Yes, sir. Like I said, we got some new information on the skeleton found and we—"

"Which should have nothing to do with the Jove family," Darcy shot back.

"My husband has been very sick. If he becomes ill here with all this nonsense, I'll hold you responsible." Cecile held her head high like a queen ready to pass sentence. Her silver gray hair was fluffed out in short soft curls making her look ten years younger than her seventy years.

"Legally responsible. Our lawyers will sue." Toya seemed to relish the prospect. "And what does our family have to do with that one?" She jabbed a forefinger at Rae.

Rae bit back a tart reply. "Sheriff Thibodeaux suggested I be here. This does concern my family, too."

"I got here as soon as I could." Simon came in. He stood

close to Rae and held her hand in a firm grip, fingers laced together. "Morning, everybody."

Toya's face went pasty. "Simon, what does this mean?" It was clear that she was not referring to the meeting. She stared down at his hand holding onto Rae's so tightly.

"I think that's obvious, Toya," Darcy said in a dry voice. He glanced at Rae then turned to the sheriff. "Ten more minutes and I'm leaving. So is my grandfather." He glanced at his watch.

Sheriff Thibodeaux did not appear the least bit disturbed by his attitude. "Mr. Henry, the skeleton we found on your property—"

"This is harassment," Toya burst out. "Grandfather, we should call our lawyer right now."

"I won't stand for this any longer." Cecile stood up. "Come on, Henry. We're leaving." The female deputy was standing at the door when she opened it.

"How dare you keep us here like common criminals!" Toya threw a look of pure venom at Rae. "This is your doing. All your life you been nothing but trouble. You no good—" She started toward Rae.

Simon pulled Rae behind him in a protective move. "Back up, Toya."

Henry pointed a forefinger at the sheriff. "You'd better have a damn good reason for this or I'll see you in court," he thundered.

"Thibodeaux, you've stepped way over the line," Darcy said in a low, threatening voice. "I don't think you realize who you're dealing with here."

"Simon, how could you?" Toya wailed. "She's nothing. A nobody living in a swamp shack."

"Everybody settle down," Sheriff Thibodeaux called out over the commotion in a loud voice. He no longer wore an expression of appeasement. "Close the door, Deputy Zeringue."

"Yes, sir," Deputy Zeringue said. The door shut with a solid thud.

"One thing you folks better understand, this is a murder investigation." Sheriff Thibodeaux looked around the room at them solemnly. "Fifty years ago don't matter. Ain't no statute of limitation on murder. Now it's almost sure that skeleton is Vincent Dalcour. There's a healed break in the left leg that matches. Plus old Doc Pinson's son still got his dad's dental records. It all matches up."

"Sad for the Dalcour family, but hardly a reason to imply that we have anything to do with it." Darcy had lost none of his poise.

"Vincent made many enemies, sheriff." Henry looked not the least bit sympathetic. "He had a habit of putting his hands on what belonged to other men."

"Not very nice, but no excuse for murder." Simon surprised them all by speaking.

Silence fell on the room. Rae glanced at the Joves. Gone was the aura of power, the glittering film that made them appear so different and better than others. Now Henry Jove looked like an anxious old man worried that the past had finally come back to haunt him. Toya sat twisting her hands, her face drawn with sorrow and resentment. An insecure woman craving attention from a man whose love she had never understood how to keep. Darcy, handsome and polished, was like one of those collector dolls with not a hint of warmth or regard for anyone else but himself. Cecile sat back down in the imitation leather chair, looking like a wilted flower. Even when she'd despised them most, Rae realized that she had viewed them as a kind of minor royalty just as everyone else did. With that veil stripped away, Rae now understood that nursing those old grievances had only given them more power. Lucien had never learned this lesson.

"They're here, sheriff." Deputy Zeringue spoke in a voice of awe.

Several other deputies hovered outside in the hall speaking in undertones. There was the hum of voices as it became clear that others in the station were just as excited.

"Unless you plan to charge me or a member of my family with this alleged murder, we're leaving." Henry stood up to his full height. "Come, Cecile." He held out his hand to his wife who took it with a look of relief.

"Yes, Henry. And sheriff, don't think you won't be hearing from— Ahh!" Cecile screamed. She turned pale, her mouth worked as a keening sound came out.

"What's wrong with you, woman?" Henry followed her gaze. He let go of Cecile's hand and walked across the room like a man hypnotized. *"Mon Dieu!"* he said in a quavering voice.

"Bonjour, Henri. Comment ça va?" A woman, her dark hair streaked with iron gray, walked into the room. Her smile was sad. "It's been a lifetime, eh?"

"Estelle!" Henry stopped within a foot of her. He gazed at her as though he could not get enough of looking. "My Estelle." He reached out and placed a fingertip on her right cheek.

"Not the same girl who hurt you so. No, not the same." Estelle gazed back at him with a look of hard-gained wisdom.

A hush descended over the entire station it seemed. The only sound was the soft mewling that came from Cecile. She collapsed into the chair and sat rocking, both arms wrapped around her body.

"She told me you were dead," Henry whispered.

Estelle looked at Cecile. "So that's how you finally got what you wanted. Not that I can pass judgment on you. I was a faithless wife, a thief, and . . . a murderess. I am old now. God has already punished me more any human could."

LaMar appeared behind her. "But you didn't kill Vincent, Mrs. Jordan."

"Jordan?" Henry asked.

"My third husband. None of them worth spit," Estelle said with bitterness.

"Wait a minute," Sheriff Thibodeaux broke in with a frown. "This is too bizarre and confused."

"An understatement," Simon mumbled close to Rae's ear.

"I thought my grandmother killed Pawpaw Vincent and Estelle," Rae said. "That theory was way off the mark, obviously."

"I am old with arthritis in both knees. I must sit now." Estelle eased down into a chair. Everyone else sat down mechanically and watched her with an air of expectation.

"Mrs. Jordan is very tired." LaMar treated Estelle like his elderly aunt.

"I'll start, if you like," Rae said.

"Thank you, baby." Estelle cocked her head to one side as

she looked at Rae. "You got his eyes. Yeah, I could see Vincent the moment I saw them pretty eyes."

"I really need a statement." Sheriff Thibodeaux

"Oui, you begin." Estelle nodded to Rae. She closed her eyes. "I'm so weary." Her russet face was etched with lines. Her tone said that her spirit was as worn down as her body.

Rae cleared her throat and glanced at Henry. "Vincent had been having an affair with Mrs. Jordan—"

"Estelle. Call me that, cher. Make me feel like I'm that young again, *mais oui?"*

"With Estelle. Estelle wanted to get away. She stole the money. Vincent didn't know until she told him. Then she played on his love for high living and convinced him that he deserved it." Rae had warmed to the tale. Everyone but Henry was looking at her. Henry could not stop staring at Estelle.

"But how did she manage it?" Toya spoke in a soft voice.

"Mr. Henry had the cash in a safe. He kept it there in his office. Vincent had been alone in the office several times that week so everyone assumed it was him," LaMar said.

"But no one noticed flighty Estelle left alone in the office. Henry was so preoccupied with his new business, he thought nothing of it." Estelle brushed back a stray tendril of hair. A small gesture that made Henry sigh.

"Anyway, Estelle asked Vincent to go away with her." Rae started to go on but Henry's hoarse voice cut her off.

"Why, Estelle? I gave you everything. I wanted nothing but to please you." Henry pleaded for an answer to the question that had eaten into him for fifty years.

"You treated me like a possession. That I was a prized possession did not make it better. Watching me, always watching with hungry eyes. I felt like I'd been swallowed whole. Like I was suffocating."

"So Dalcour played on this," Henry snarled, angry at a dead man.

Estelle opened her eyes to look back over the decades. "Vincent was so dashing. Always with that wonderful laugh. And such a voice. He sang to me so sweetly."

"Vincent met Estelle in the woods as they'd arranged. But

he got cold feet. He didn't want to leave his family or be called a thief. So he refused to leave." Rae felt a lump in her throat at the mere thought of what came next.

Estelle did not look at anyone but spoke as though she knew what Rae was thinking. "I loved him and here he was telling me it was all a game. He said, 'We just having a little fun, cher. You oughta know that.' He laughed when I threatened him. When he turned his back, I picked up a big rock and hit him hard. I was sure I'd killed him. But I hadn't, had I?" She stared past Vincent.

Henry blinked back tears. "I followed you that night."

"Grandfather, don't say anymore," Darcy said sharply.

"He's ill. The stroke has left him disoriented," Toya put in with fervor.

"Hush you two," Sheriff Thibodeaux commanded. "Go ahead, Mr. Henry."

"I was glad to see him there on the ground. How dare he touch my wife. Estelle wouldn't listen. She just kept crying and calling for him." Henry passed a shaky hand over his eyes.

"C'est pas de ta faute, cher," Estelle said in low voice. (I don't blame you, dear.) "I drove you to it."

"I choked her until she stopped breathing." Henry looked at his hands as though they were not his. "How could I kill the thing I love so?"

"But you didn't, cher. No, I just fainted." Estelle looked past him again. "Shall I go on, Cecile?"

"Why did you come back? The only reason I let you live, whore, is that you promised never to come back!" Cecile was transformed into a vengeful woman, face twisted with hatred. "Henry is mine!" The two women glared at each other for several seconds.

"Miss Cecile killed Vincent?" Simon shook his head to clear it. "This has more turns than a maze."

LaMar stood up causing all heads to turn his way again. "Cecile had followed Mr. Henry into the woods. She watched him choke Estelle then convinced him that he'd murdered her. He was so shook-up, he agreed to let her handle things from there."

"I couldn't bear to look at her. Not after . . ." Henry's strangled voice trailed away.

"Estelle came to after a few minutes. Cecile must have been startled but she acted quickly. She convinced Estelle that she'd go to the electric chair for killing Vincent if she stayed. Cecile would never tell, but only if she left and never returned." LaMar glanced at Cecile. "Real cool customer. What she didn't tell Estelle was that Vincent wasn't dead either. At least not yet." Everyone looked at Cecile with expressions of shock and horror.

"He started stirring around. Estelle was so dizzy she didn't notice, the fool. I scared her silly about the death house at Angola." Cecile cackled at her own cleverness. "Marie came out of nowhere. Said she'd see to Vincent while I hustled Estelle to the car and got her to drive off. *Oui*, she took care of him all right."

"Ain't that something," Sheriff Thibodeaux scratched his head.

"Marie had followed Vincent. She'd seen him laughing about how much fun he'd been having. He cut a hole into her heart and didn't even think twice. I knew exactly how she felt," Cecile said harshly. "He got what he deserved."

Rae recoiled at the toll a lifetime of hatred had taken on so many lives. She leaned against Simon who cradled her.

"It's okay, baby," he whispered. "I'm here."

"So Marie murdered Vincent while he was still lying on the ground semiconscious. Poor guy never knew what hit him. Estelle ran off convinced she was murderer." LaMar took a deep breath. "Estelle eventually settled in Trinidad after traveling through South America and the Caribbean for several years."

"Too scared to settle in one place," Estelle added by way of explanation.

Rae looked at Estelle. "But you were seen with a man in New Orleans," she said.

"Yes, I met him on the dock. My first husband. A drunkard and liar," Estelle replied. "I thought he would protect me. Always I chose the wrong man."

"How did you stay hidden all these years?" Simon asked.

"I never stayed in one place for long at first. But after fifteen years, I settled in Trinidad. I figured I was safe enough. Truthfully, I didn't care by then."

A stunned silence hung in the air until Sheriff Thibodeaux gave a grunt and stood up. "Well that's that. Miz Estelle, I'm gonna need a formal statement. Need one from Mr. and Mrs. Jove as well."

Darcy went to stand next to Henry. "My grandfather can't take much more today, Sheriff. Can't it wait until tomorrow at least?" There was no haughty demand in his voice now.

Sheriff Thibodeaux hesitated then nodded. "Guess you're right. He's not a suspect now. I don't want to put anymore strain on Mr. Henry."

"Have you come back for good, Estelle?" Henry resisted attempts by Toya and Darcy to lead him from the room.

"Mais, non."

"There is no need to hide now." Henry leaned toward her. "Even after everything, I can forgive you."

"My life is not here. Enough that I saw my grandchildren. Fine young people. You've done well by them, Henry." Estelle smiled at Toya and Darcy who could only stare back with empty expressions.

"Incredible," Deputy Zeringue said out loud. She echoed what everyone must have been feeling.

Estelle opened her purse. "Look, the one good thing that came from my marriages. See my fine sons, my other grandchildren? *Je m'en va a la maison."* (I'm going home.)

"Simon, that was the most terrible story I've ever heard," Rae said.

"Beats any Greek tragedy, that's for sure."

They sat outside in her backyard on a new cypress swing she'd bought. Late afternoon sunlight played across them, dappled by the leaves on branches of the large maple over their heads.

"How did you figure out Estelle was alive and where to find her?" Simon said.

"No bones. If they were caught out in the woods and murdered, why weren't there *two* skeletons? Why would the murderer risk discovery by moving one body from such a perfect burying spot? If one skeleton was so well preserved, then another nearby shouldn't have been missing. The answer had to be that Estelle escaped somehow."

"Good point. But how did LaMar trace her? He'd tried and couldn't find one good clue."

"He concentrated on looking for Pawpaw Vincent thinking he could find him easier by trying to find out where he'd worked. I remembered that Estelle and a man had been spotted in New Orleans. Estelle's reputation for collecting men made me think. I told LaMar to find out about the male passengers on that ship and track them down. One led us back to Trinidad eventually. Old marriage and birth records helped us narrow the search down to that island."

"Good detective work, babe." Simon nuzzled her neck.

Rae shivered, still feeling the chill of a deadly past that reached into the present with icy fingers. Simon pulled her close to him.

"Fifty years of treachery and lies to cover murder. All in the name of love." Rae sighed.

"Yes, but it's over. It's long past time for us to move on," Simon answered. He brushed her hair with his long fingers.

"Can we put it behind us? All that malice was like a poison plant with deep roots." Rae pressed against him seeking the comfort of his solid body.

"We will. Together we can do it." Simon kissed her, his tongue gently stroking the inside of her mouth. "Yes?" he whispered. His hands caressed her face.

Rae felt the warmth of his touch melt away the cold as desire spiked through her. There was a soft light of love in his eyes. A love for her alone. "Yes. Together."

Without speaking, Simon led her inside the house and into the beginning of a new life.

Lynn Emery is a native of the "Bayou State," Louisiana. She is a social worker by profession. Her first novel, *Night Magic,* was recognized by Romantic Times Magazine for Excellence in Romance Fiction-1995. Her other works include *After All* (11/96), a novella, *Happy New Year, Baby,* part of the holiday anthology *Silver Bells* (12/96), and *Tender Touch* (12/97).

Dear Readers,

I enjoy sharing my stories with you. I hope you enjoyed reading them. Thanks to all who took time to write me in the past. Your words of praise and support really mean a lot! If you would like to receive a signed bookmark, send a SASE to:

Lynn Emery
P.O. Box 74095
Baton Rouge, LA 70874

Best wishes,

Lynn Emery

COMING IN NOVEMBER

THE ESSENCE OF LOVE, (0-7860-0567-X, $4.99/$6.50)
by Candice Poarch

Once falsely accused of fraud, Cleopatra Sharp managed to flourish in her new aromatherapy shop outside of Washington, D.C. But suspicion falls on her again. Postal inspector Taylor Bradford goes undercover as a repairman at her shop, determined to keep dangerous drugs and fraudulent miracle cures out of his community. When he realizes Cleopatra is nothing but a tender, giving woman, he must choose between his head and his heart.

LOVE'S PROMISE, (0-7860-0568-8, $4.99/$6.50)
by Adrienne Ellis Reeves

Beth Jordan refused a marriage proposal from her long-time boyfriend, only to find that he was quickly engaged to another. Determined to show everyone in Jamison, South Carolina that she wasn't too flighty to accomplish anything, she took part in a community service contest. Cy Brewster, her contest partner, tested her good intentions, for now she was in it for love. And a secret from Cy's past tests whether theirs is a love that promises forever.

EDEN'S DREAM, (0-7860-0572-6, $4.99/$6.50)
by Marcia King-Gamble

Eden Sommers fled to Mercer Island, in the Pacific Northwest, after a tragic plane crash claimed her husband and left her devastated. As she searches for answers, the mysterious man who moves in next door and bears a striking resemblance to her husband, manages to distract her. Is it mere coincidence that has brought Noel Robinson to Mercer Island? Eden will discover his secrets before she submits to the love welling up between them.

ISLAND PROMISE, (0-7860-0574-2, $4.99/$6.5O)
by Angela Winters

Dallas schoolteacher Morgan Breck's reckless spirit led her to make an impulsive purchase at an estate sale, that plunged her into the arms of sexy investor Jake Turner. Jake is only interested in finding his missing sister, and when Morgan stumbles onto a clue that might locate his sister, he is thrilled to be with her. But when they are on the island where his sister may be, intense passion will force Jake to surrender to love.